Thomas Miller
Oct. 9, 2012

The Letter

Thomas Miller

The Letter

Thomas Miller

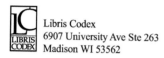

Libris Codex
6907 University Ave Ste 263
Madison WI 53562

This book is a work of fiction that uses historic and legendary data and locations. Individual names, characters, places, and incidents are products of the author's imagination and are used fictitiously. Any resemblences to persons, living or dead, are entirely coincidental.

First Libris Codex edition printed 2012

Libris Codex and colophon are trademarks of Libris Codex, LLC.

Book design by The Gunter Agency
www.GunterAgency.com

Cover photo by Simon Brown
www.simonjbrownphotography.co.uk

Author photo by Trevor Gunter

10 9 8 7 6 5 4 3 2

ISBN 978-0985751517

To Patrick "Pat" Boyle
A Friend for Life

Jerusalem

And did those feet in ancient time,
Walk upon England's mountains green:
And was the Holy Lamb of God,
In England's pleasant pastures seen!
And did the Countenance Divine,
Shine forth upon our clouded hills?
And was Jerusalem builded here,
Among those dark Satanic Mills?
Bring me my Bow of burning gold:
Bring me my Arrows of desire:
Bring me my Spear! O clouds unfold:
Bring me my Chariots of fire:
I will not cease from Mental Fight,
Nor shall my Sword sleep in my hand:
Till we have built Jerusalem,
In England's green and pleasant Land.

— *William Blake, 1804*

~Table of Contents~

Acknowledgements

The Letter lived in my brain for more than 30 years while family and work took top priority. When life changes allowed me to start writing, I found it far more difficult than I had expected, and for several months, I made precious little progress. Maybe it was just good fortune or maybe something larger, but a friend from my high school days (now 50 years past) somehow got involved. I really don't remember how or why Carol Mertins became my taskmaster and relentless pusher, but bless her for she was the push I needed and with her urging, the chapters began to roll out.

Carol involved another good friend from those high school days. Pat Boyle knew more about computers and technology than I could ever hope to know. It was the beginning of summer, 2010 and we were humming along, loving every minute. Three old friends working together, sharing stories, jokes and laughter. As is all too often true of life and love, laughter turned to sorrow. In August 2010, Pat Boyle suffered a massive heart attack and died. This book is dedicated to Pat, a friend for life.

Helen Tickanen, an incredibly resourceful and dedicated friend joined the team to help us recover from the loss of Pat. Helen recruited another friend, Bill Lauritch to help her manage a book sale mail order campaign. However, we still needed someone with Pat Boyle's technical expertise. I turned to Randy Gunter, a marketing genius who owns and operates The Gunter Agency, a marketing company headquartered in the beautiful rolling Wisconsin landscape near the small quaint town of New Glarus. Randy along with his son Trevor, who is a computer wizard, and the rest of the Gunter Agency opened my eyes to the new world of e-publishing. Cindy Gunter is the best editor one could ever hope to find. She didn't limit her input to just grammar, punctuation and sentence structure, but rather offered several significant content improvements.

My continued good fortune produced five reviewers who not only gave their honest reactions, but also supplied several storyline improvements. Tina Lang, an accomplished French horn musician and Methodist minister shared her knowledge of religious history helping to keep my work of fiction grounded in fact. Carolyn Mitchell, a retired teacher and Charles Mitchell, a retired engineer, both world travelers, offered their individual perspectives gained through an appreciation of diverse cultures. Julie Peterson, a master gardener and artist whose paintings, I contend, are on par with the Masters, helped transform my two-dimensional story into a three-dimensional life. Finally, Ann Blaisdell Tracy, a distinguished teaching professor at SUNY-Plattsburgh, where she teaches writing and Honors Latin, offered her review.

I sweated out her critique, thinking she might blow the whole project out of the water telling me not to quit my day job. But Ann loved it and her critique further spurred me on.

I could never have produced *The Letter* without each reviewer and technical expert. Their critiques were honest—sometimes painfully honest. Over 90% of what they suggested is incorporated into the final.

I will never find the words to properly thank all who helped produce *The Letter*. Everyone, especially my wife Nicki, sons Aaron and Matthew and daughter Margo, along with many friends, are all characters in *The Letter.* I appropriated and altered their names to protect the innocent. The owners of the names I borrowed will know. Some, who are yet too young to read, will know in time.

While my name may be on the title page, I did not do it alone. God bless each and everyone who helped along the way. I am an incredibly lucky man.

Thomas Miller

Author's Note

"and you will know the truth and the truth will make you free."
—John 8:32

Dear Reader,

Be forewarned. Although *The Letter* is firmly grounded in fact, it is a work of fiction. Some of the stories in *The Letter* may challenge things you believe are true. That is precisely its purpose.

Much of what is known about Jesus Christ is shrouded in mystery. Would you like an example? According to the Gospel of Luke, Jesus was twelve years old when he was "left behind" by Mary and Joseph. After a frantic three-day search, they found Him in the temple talking with the teachers. But then we hear nothing more about Jesus until He is thirty-one years old and starting His public life. Where was He for those nineteen years between twelve and thirty-one? What was He doing? Who was He with? Why did He come when He did? Will He come again? Did He laugh? Did He cry? Did He love? Did He really die?

Would you like another example? It is generally believed that the Gospels of Matthew, Mark, Luke and John were not written until roughly 70 to 90 CE, which is 40 to 60 years after the Crucifixion. Jesus' Apostles were rough-hewn men, laborers and fishermen. They were not scholars and most likely not even literate. This calls into question whether the Gospel writers were also the Apostles with the same names. If the Gospel writers were not the Apostles, did they know Jesus personally or did they simply record the legends about Him that they learned from song and story?

Here is one more. Saint Paul is regarded by many in the Catholic Church as the thirteenth apostle and as one of the most significant evangelists in all of Christianity. Paul writes that the resurrected Jesus came to him. Or did Paul make this up to enlarge his standing in the community and lay claim to being the thirteenth apostle? The fact is, Matthias, not Paul, was elected to be the thirteenth apostle, replacing the disgraced Judas Iscariot who betrayed Jesus to the Roman guards and later hanged himself.

Much has been learned from the discovery of the *Dead Sea Scrolls* and the *Nag Hammadi Codices*. The *Dead Sea Scrolls* consist of nearly 1,000 documents, some just fragments, discovered between 1946 and 1956 in eleven caves in the Qumran desert on the northwest shore of the Dead Sea. While the Scrolls are fantastic in their own right, some religious scholars are disappointed there is no mention of Jesus in any of the documents. Many wonder if there are more documents yet to be found.

In December 1945 near Nag Hammadi in upper Egypt, a collection of 13 ancient books dating from around 390 CE was discovered. Known as the *Nag Hammadi Codices*, they contain what are called Gnostic Gospels. These writings were thought destroyed by opposing sides in the struggle to define Christian orthodoxy. Among the documents is the famous Gospel of Thomas, which purports to be a record of sayings from Jesus Christ. The *Dead Sea Scrolls* and the *Nag Hammadi Codices* were discovered long after the Biblical Canon was closed. Since the canon is closed and will remain closed, the *Dead Sea Scrolls* and the *Nag Hammadi Codices* will forever remain Apocrypha (i.e., hidden or esoteric). But what if a new discovery, so compelling and so essential to the truth, were found? Would the canon be reopened? Would the Bible need to be rewritten?

The Letter is a story about a discovery that, if true, would be the most important discovery of all time. When the discovery is revealed to the public, the religious establishment is forced to challenge its legitimacy. They have little choice but to put forth the challenge, for if what is discovered is allowed to stand, all that they have built might come crashing down. The three seekers who made the discovery are called upon to defend its authenticity. I have included their defense in an Appendix to give readers a chance to analyze the discovery on their own.

In her classic novel, *O Pioneers!*, Willa Cather writes, "There are only two or three human stories, and they go on repeating themselves as fiercely as if they had never happened before." Stories about love lost and maybe, hopefully, found again. Stories about the triumph of the human spirit over forces that hold that spirit in bondage. Stories about renewal and the chance to start over. Then again, maybe these stories are really all the same. Maybe they are in some form just the search for the Truth—a search that believes in the promise that "the Truth will set you free."

The world of discovery is far from over. More catacombs may be unearthed. More scrolls may be discovered. And maybe a new codex will be found. *The Letter* asks many questions and provides only a few answers. Much more is yet to be learned. I invite you to join the search. All that is required is a burning desire to discover the Truth.

Chapter I

Trust not the man with only one book

SUNDAY EVENING, DECEMBER 19 – GEORGETOWN

It was late when he arrived at his darkened brownstone apartment in historic Georgetown. Thomas removed his coat and Roman collar and laid both across a table next to the door and turned on the Tiffany lamp, which gave just enough light to guide his way. The cold and rainy evening matched his dark mood. He poured a stiff glass of Jameson Irish Whiskey, added a splash of water and clicked on his CD player already queued to a disc of Vivaldi's violin concerto in A minor. The soft, warm leather of his favorite chair surrounded him and for the first time in four long days he was not a caregiver. He closed his eyes, relaxed his tense muscles and exhaled—*a sigh too deep for words,* his mind flashed to St. Paul's letter to the Romans. Thomas thought it strange to think of that passage, *I never cared much for Paul.*

Thomas enjoyed most music—from Beethoven to the Beatles, but on evenings like this he preferred the baroque style of Vivaldi. Someone once told him baroque music expresses the fundamental order of the universe. On this evening, "fundamental order" was something he badly needed. Thomas's affinity with the Italian composer went beyond music. Vivaldi was also a priest and virtuoso violinist. Thomas studied the violin as a youth, but never really got very good. However, he did excel as a scientist and priest.

Within the broad community of scientists and archeologists, Father Thomas Ryan was a bit of a celebrity, partly a result of his reputation as the world's foremost expert in the translation of Aramaic, the language of Jesus. But he also was a special kind of intellectual—the kind who appreciates and follows the rigors of the scientific method while possessing a rare intuitive ability to leap over obstacles and skip steps. He was a maverick, a trait that did not endear him with many Church leaders, leaving him more tolerated than admired.

Thomas's free-spirited style earned him a reprimand from his bishop on an earlier occasion, and now Thomas was at it again. He had begun to conduct research into the early life of Jesus Christ intent on answering the question of where was Jesus during His formative years—those nineteen years from age twelve to thirty-one. The Gospel of Luke tells the story of a twelve-year-old Jesus sitting in the temple among the teachers asking questions while His parents, Mary and Joseph, frantically search for Him. Then that's it—that's the last story in the Bible about the boy Jesus until He is thirty-one and about to be baptized by John the Baptist. Thomas had questions. Where was Jesus for those nineteen years? What did He do? Who were His teachers? Why did the gospel writers even bother with the Nativity and temple stories when it is the public life of Jesus that changed the world? Why not just start with Jesus as an adult? We know so little about him. Did He laugh? Did He cry? Did He love? Did He really die? Many questions needed answers.

When Thomas first made it known he was about to embark on a study of the "lost years of Jesus," the Vatican initially appeared supportive and offered their assistance. However, something in their offer didn't ring true. What the Vatican proposed was a process wherein they would edit Thomas's work, and when satisfied they would endorse and then publish the findings. "Publish it when the time is right," was the way they put it. Thomas felt their proposal was less of an offer to assist and more of a means to control. The Church had a vested interest in what was published about the Christ. They didn't want to be blindsided by a public release of information, which did not conform to their standard protocol. Right or wrong, the Vatican postured itself as the owner of the copyright on Jesus Christ.

Thomas flatly rejected the Vatican's offer, letting them know his investigation would take him wherever it needed to go. His refusal to bend to the requests from Church superiors touched a nerve. Their heightened angst suggested they had something to hide rather than something to share.

Science like nature abhors a vacuum. Empty spaces are unnatural as they go against the laws of nature and physics. Thomas was determined to discover what happened during those nineteen years and fill that empty space. A year later, in hindsight, Thomas's search for answers would prove to be more dangerous and controversial than he or anyone could have envisioned. He put himself on a collision course with the status quo and it had all the makings of a nasty train wreck.

The Vatican dealt not only with doctrine, but also with disciplinary matters, a point reiterated to Thomas after he rejected their request for editorial control. His bishop reminded him the 1960 Vatican Council not only defined the Pope's primacy in Catholic Church governance, it also clearly stated "the interpretation of scripture is a right of the Church, not a right of individual priests pursuing their own interests whether those interests be noble or not."

Thomas responded explaining his refusal to honor the Church's request for editorial control ran counter to the time-honored tradition of academic freedom. He explained, "Scientific inquiry is the search for truth," and reiterated St. John's famous wisdom aphorism, *"the truth will set you free."* Thomas then closed his letter with the words of St. Thomas Aquinas, *"Trust not the man with only one book."* This earned him a scolding from his bishop, as it appeared to Church leadership Thomas was attempting to lecture them. Although Thomas enjoyed tenure as a faculty member at Georgetown, he was well aware this was a hot-button issue and he needed to be careful. The bishop's reprimand was private. Nonetheless, Thomas realized he was now on a short leash.

This was Thomas's second warning and he knew he was getting close to "three strikes and you're out." He received his first warning two years earlier after he wrote an Easter essay for The Christian Scholar about a mythical second coming of Christ. The journal editors asked Thomas to write a fictional essay on what Jesus Christ might do, and how He might be received in today's world. Thomas produced a fictional account of Jesus descending to earth in a golden sphere and landing in New York's Central Park. The story was intended to draw a parallel to Jesus' last week on earth some 2,000 years before. During that last week Jesus rode into Jerusalem on a donkey while His followers spread palm branches in His path. By the end of the week, Jesus was crucified on a cross.

In Thomas's story, Jesus' appearance in Central Park was immediately heralded throughout the world as the promised second coming. However, within 24 hours, international political leaders began to realize Jesus could be much more than just a temporary annoyance. They understood His ability to awaken the masses could pose great danger to the status quo. Aware of His perilous position, Jesus decided to leave New York City before He could be forced to suffer a twenty-first century high-tech crucifixion.

Thomas's essay portrayed political leaders as arrogant, materialistic, and out of touch with the people they were supposed to serve. It implied the religious community was either complicit or feckless in its response to institutional injustice and crimes against humanity. The article angered many in the Church bureaucracy for it suggested little had really changed for the oppressed and the message coming from today's Jesus would be much the same as it had been 2,000 years before.

With strains of Vivaldi helping to add order to his universe, Thomas was able to reflect on the events of the last few days. It was Sunday evening and he just returned from counseling family members of a fellow priest who died on Wednesday. Thomas officiated at several funerals, but this one was different. This was the funeral of a dear friend—a young man struck down in his prime. He raised his glass to offer a toast. "Here's to you Michael. May you be in heaven one hour before the Devil knows you're dead."

Suddenly angry, Thomas let go of his glass not caring what spilled and scolded himself out loud, "That's not funny, Thomas." Father Michael Moriarity was a good friend—a mountain of a man with a barrel chest and a booming voice, a hearty laugh and an infectious smile. That laugh was now forever silent. In less than five months, cancer stripped away Michael's 250-pound muscled physique and left but the shell of a man.

Thomas sat there in the soft glow of the singly lit lamp surveying the clutter of his possessions. The soothing ticking of his collection of pendulum clocks kept cadence with the quiet strains of Vivaldi's violin concerto. Thomas's one-bedroom apartment was well appointed and quite comfortable. His bookcase was filled with handsomely bound books about history, religion, the end-of-days and the Armageddon. He was a Sherlock Holmes fan, and collected several of Sir Arthur Conan Doyle's novels. Inexpensive prints of Flemish painters Rubens and Van Dyck along with religious art of Rembrandt and Michelangelo adorned his walls.

Every inch of tabletop space competed with antiques and mementos, some given to him by his grandparents, others acquired on his travels to his treasured Ireland. Thomas Ryan was proud of his heritage. He learned much about Ireland as a young boy from his grandfather and from his several visits to the Emerald Isle. His apartment had the look and feel of an Irish cottage.

Then there were the clocks—twelve of them to be exact. Wall clocks competed for space with the framed prints and tabletop clocks competed with the mementos. And one stately seven-foot mahogany grandfather clock stood proudly in Thomas's living room.

Thomas's fascination with clocks began when he was a boy having spent as much time with his grandparents as was allowed. They were emigrants from the poor fishing village of Kinsale on Ireland's southern coast. Like the nearly one million Irish who immigrated to the United States during the potato famine, Thomas's grandparents gathered what few belongings they could carry to start life over in the New World. His grandparents were simple people, not stupid—just uncomplicated, open, and honest.

Thomas's grandfather was a clockmaker in Ireland, and he found work in America as a clock and watch repairman. He made enough money so he and Thomas's grandmother could buy a small house, raise three boys and see to it each became a productive member of society. Grandma Rose stayed at home to raise the boys and made sure each received a good Catholic education.

Grandfather's name was also Thomas, and the young Thomas was his namesake. His grandparents lived only a few blocks from his boyhood home, and he visited often on his way home from school. He had vivid memories of sitting on his grandfather's lap as the elder Thomas read to him. The old man didn't read children's stories; rather he read Shakespeare and history. Thomas didn't always understand what was read to him, but he loved listening. As Grandfather read, Thomas would daydream, eyes closed, safe and secure in the strong and soothing sound of the old man's voice.

The musical chime signaling the hour on his grandfather's pocket watch interrupted his daydream. Everything Thomas knew about clocks he learned from his grandfather, and his interest proved to be a bond between them. There were several grandchildren, but only Thomas was allowed to pull the chains winding the grandfather clock that stood in the parlor. It became a ritual they performed every Sunday after Mass. Thomas would gently pull the chains raising the heavy brass weights to the top of the clockworks.

When the old man died he willed Thomas both his pocket watch and the grandfather clock. Over the years Thomas acquired other clocks. While all kept regular time, only his pocket watch and the grandfather clock were allowed to chime. He either disconnected the chimes or simply didn't wind their chiming mechanisms. Had he not done so, each noon and midnight hour would result in an endless parade of chimes and gongs.

In the faint light of his apartment, Thomas studied the heirloom watch and thought back to the events of the week. He looked at the face of the pocket watch and remembered what his grandfather taught him. *You can learn a great deal just by looking at the face of an old watch. You can tell what time it is. You can look ahead for time yet to come and you can look back to see the time which was finished and would never come again.*

Thomas carried only that pocket watch. He was never interested in a digital watch, because it could only tell the current time—and as soon as you recognized the moment, it was gone, replaced by a new one. *No,* he thought, *that's not for me. I need to know what came before so I can appreciate the present and time yet to come.*

Thomas was with Michael Moriarity and his family on the night he died. Despite his weakened condition, Michael summoned enough energy to smile as he beckoned his friend to come closer. He whispered, "It's okay; I'll put in a good word for you when I get there, and Lord knows you need it." It seemed to take forever for Michael to utter those few words. Thomas, his eyes glistening, whispered: "Godspeed friend, I won't let the Devil know you're gone." Thomas administered the Last Rites and that was it. Father Michael Moriarity was dead.

Michael was just 43, four years younger than Thomas. They graduated together from the seminary. Thomas remembered Michael moonlighting as a boxer under the pseudonym, "The Preacher." His professional boxing career ended in their last year in the seminary when one of their classmates, a brown-nosing little snitch named Frederick Fulgrum, blew the whistle on their outside venture and Dean Jacobs closed down their business. Michael was proud he retired from boxing with a 9-0 record.

After graduation, Michael became a parish priest in inner city Washington, DC. He took scores of boys off the streets under the guise of teaching them how to box, and taught them how to be men. He taught them more than how to hit—he taught them why and when not to hit. Many of those men were in attendance at the funeral to pay their respects and to say, “Thank you” one last time to Father Mike.

Thomas smiled as he remembered how Michael conned him into being his sparring partner and then trainer, ring manager and cut man. *One dumb Mick conning another.* Thomas learned much more about boxing than just the fundamentals. Whenever they sparred he was aware Michael could take him out with one punch, but never did. Thomas reflected back on his one shining moment when he landed a left hook causing Michael to buckle at the knees. He didn’t fall, but the look on Michael’s face revealed a newfound respect for his sparring partner.

Michael was a man who knew his limitations and always seemed to stay within them. Thomas was the polar opposite, always questioning and always challenging. He remembered something Michael told him, partly as a compliment, partly as a warning. Michael said, “Thomas, you are the smartest man I know, but I know something you don’t. No one, not even you, can understand all things. There are mysteries in life put there, I believe, by the Almighty—put there to challenge your faith, not your intellect. Someday you will face a moment that will challenge both your intellect and your faith, which you will not fully comprehend. My advice friend, listen to your heart for that is where the soul resides.”

Listen to your heart, Thomas said to himself as he tried to make sense of a life cut way too short. *What part of God’s master plan required taking a man who was doing so much good?* Thomas felt his darker side demons beginning to rule his thoughts—a recurring problem as he battled depression for years. He considered his dark moods an occupational hazard—the result of too much time spent studying the occult, death, and the end-of-days.

The disease that killed Michael Moriarity came quickly and without warning. Thomas pulled out an album with photos he took just five months earlier. He had been invited to join a special group of Catholic clerics to view paintings recently made available for viewing; the oldest known images of Apostles Andrew and John, discovered under layers of white calcium deposits in the catacombs of St. Tecla in Rome.

As he reviewed the photos, he remembered how hard he lobbied and the many favors he called-in to bring his friend Father Moriarity with him. It was his way of saying how much he valued his friendship. Father Moriarity was the priest at St. Stanislaus Catholic Church, a poor parish where he served in relative obscurity, not the kind of position that would get one on the "special list" of invited clerics. But to Michael, St. Stanislaus was a place where he felt he was, in his words, "fighting the good fight." It was a dream of his to someday go to Rome, to see the Vatican and the catacombs. His friend Thomas made it happen.

Truth be told, Thomas also wanted to visit the St. Tecla catacomb. Visiting dead Christians in the catacombs of Rome fit with his tendency to gravitate to the darker side. Even though the paintings on the walls were discovered in the 1950s, the public still had not seen them. Curiously, the access to the St. Tecla catacomb went through an unmarked basement door in a rather ordinary looking Rome office building. Getting to the paintings required winding one's way through dimly lit corridors of damp tufa stone which served as the entrance to the final resting place for second and third century Christians.

When they arrived at the large open chamber, Thomas and Michael witnessed a veritable treasure trove of ancient renderings from the fourth century. In addition to the painting of Christ as the Good Shepherd, there were scenes including Jesus raising Lazarus from the dead, Peter drawing water from the well, Abraham preparing to sacrifice his son Isaac, and more. The several scenes with Peter, James, Andrew and John seemed to imply these four were the most important apostles in early Christianity.

Thomas recalled a strange event that he and Michael witnessed and attempted to record on camera. It was the first time he saw the notorious Cardinal Felipe Alvarez, the man in charge of security for Vatican antiquities, which included the recently opened St. Tecla catacomb. Raised on the streets of Madrid, Alvarez had a reputation of being able to handle himself in rough and tough situations. A man disguised as a monk slipped by security and made it into the main chamber carrying several vials of red paint, which he intended to throw at the walls and ceiling. As the impostor readied himself to launch his paint bombs, the cardinal produced a gun and pointed it at the man's head. The man, a somewhat deranged individual, was sane enough to recognize he needed to stop.

Within moments the Polizia Municipale was on the scene removing the intruder, and Alvarez' gun disappeared into his cardinal's attire as quickly as it appeared. Two members of the Swiss Guard in business suits confiscated Thomas's camera and took it to Cardinal Alvarez who removed the photos with the gun. The cardinal approached Thomas and Michael.

"Father Ryan, I believe you understand why I deleted a few of your photos. You are here, after all, to view the paintings. Let's just say this episode doesn't need to be discussed and certainly not described in detail."

"You know who I am?"

"Father Ryan, it's my business to know." Alvarez handed Thomas his camera. "I trust you and Father Moriarity can now renew your travel." Alvarez turned and exited the catacomb, leaving the two priests standing by themselves.

They returned to the States sharing the excitement of a story they could tell to only a select few. The trip was the "high point of my life. I feel complete." Michael's words. Little did he know how prophetic those words would be. Shortly after returning from Rome, Michael began to lose weight as well as his otherwise voracious appetite. He experienced constant stomach pain and fatigue, which at first he attributed to Italy—the time change and different foods had to be the cause. In August he was diagnosed with stage-four pancreatic cancer, and less than five months later he was dead.

To many people, Thomas was the man with the answers; but now as he sat alone in the dim light, he had only questions. He formed a fist with his right hand and banged it on the table causing his glass to jump. A split second later his phone rang as though the banging of his fist caused the phone to ring. It was nearing midnight and he didn't want to talk with anyone; Thomas wanted to be alone with his thoughts. But when he looked at his Caller ID, he saw "J. Christ." *What irony*, he thought. Here he sat with nothing but questions, and now calling him was the man with all the answers.

Thomas lifted the receiver, "Hello Jimmy. Your timing is perfect." It was one of Thomas's closest friends—James "Jimmy the Greek" Christopoulos. His name was too long to fit on most Caller ID screens, so it was shortened to J. Christ.

"How'd it go today, Tommie? Are you holding up all right?"

"To be honest Jimmy, it's been a rough couple of days. Michael was a good friend. In fact, I think his dying was even tougher because he tried his best to make it easy on all of us."

"I am truly sorry for your loss. I know you're hurting and I wish I could help."

"Thank you, Jimmy. I'm going to miss him. Your call really helps. I needed to come back to reality." Thomas paused and then said, "Where are you calling from?"

"I'm in London and I have something important to tell you, but I don't want to say too much on the phone. You never know who might be listening. Just know it concerns my life's quest. And Tommie, listen to this. I believe I know where my search will finally end. But I won't say anything more and must ask you to keep this call in strict confidence."

"Okay, what do you want me to do?"

"I want you and Matthew to join me here in England and just as soon as you can. Just tell me when you can come and I'll make the arrangements."

"What? Say that again. You want us to come to London? What's going on?" asked Thomas.

James answered, "No, not on the phone. You'll receive a FedEx Priority package tomorrow. Please sign for it yourself and don't open it in the presence of anyone else. Inside will be two identical letters—one for you and one for Matthew. I put both letters in the same package just to be safe. I didn't want to take the chance that someone else would receive and reveal what's inside."

"Jimmy, my favorite paranoid."

"Tommie, this is my life's work. I can't risk having the information made public before I'm ready to do it myself."

"All right, what do you want me to do?"

"The letter will explain all. Please get together with Matthew as soon as you can. Together, review what I've sent and then email me with the date when both of you can come here."

"You said when, not if."

"Believe me, when you read what I sent you, you and Matthew will want to come. I really can't say anymore. Please, when you email me, be careful what you write and do not mention the contents in my letter," cautioned James.

"Goodnight, Tommie. It must be getting late for you in DC. I'll let you go. Again, I'm sorry."

"Goodnight Jimmy, and thank you for the call."

As Thomas prepared for bed, he thought about the odd timing of Michael's death and Jimmy's call remembering how Michael was fond of saying, "A door closes and a window opens." It was just his way of saying life goes on.

Monday Morning, December 20 – Georgetown University

Despite a fitful night's sleep, Thomas arrived around the normal time at his office in Georgetown University's Healy Hall. *Life goes on, a window opens* lingered on his mind.

Father Thomas Ryan was on the faculty at Georgetown and was the resident expert on all things eschatological—that is, all things concerning the end-of-days. He was one of a handful of priests schooled in the nearly lost art of exorcism. Thomas had that special sparkle, the naughty-boy-turned-good persona, which seemed to captivate most people with whom he came in contact.

Father Ryan was more than just a media darling. His handsome Irish features and his flair for the dramatic sometimes overshadowed his academic credentials. However, Father Thomas Ryan earned Ph.D.'s from both

Marquette and Georgetown and his scholarship in early Aramaic writings placed him at the top of his profession. No one anywhere in the world knew Aramaic better than he.

Thomas served as a technical advisor for several movies with religious themes, including a movie where his assignment was to teach the actors to speak Aramaic—no small task, especially since Aramaic is virtually a dead language. Not only did he need to teach the actors to properly pronounce Aramaic, he had to help them understand which words required what kind of emphasis and which words were designed to evoke what kind of emotion. To the best of his knowledge, Aramaic is spoken today only in the tiny village of Ma'Aloula, Syria. The movie's producers took Thomas's advice and had the actors and directors spend a couple of weeks in Ma'Aloula just to listen to how Aramaic sounds.

For the Catholic bureaucracy, Thomas was an enigma. Yes, he was high profile and mostly in a positive way. When the Church handled the problem of pedophile priests so poorly, he helped deflect much of the negative press. However for many in the Church hierarchy, Thomas was too worldly, too modern, too handsome, and too charismatic. The Church was trying to move away from the pedophile issue, but many in the leadership simply did not fully understand or appreciate how Father Ryan's star power could promote a more modern image for the Church.

Some also easily bought into the rumor Thomas did not adhere to his vow of celibacy. There never was any proof, but the speculation of his active other life was enough for the closed-minded, cloistered Church bureaucrats who didn't like Thomas. Father Ryan came to the priesthood later in life than most other priests. He had more than a few romances before being ordained; that was never a secret. But when Thomas took the vow of celibacy, he remained true. Many young female students felt his heterosexual sobriety was a waste of a good man. Thomas was never shy about discussing sexuality, having once responded to a reporter that romance, passion and intercourse were beautiful, but also noted they were not without complication. "Giving up sexual intimacy and replacing it with a life of celibacy was merely trading one set of complications for another."

Another reporter asked Thomas, "Were you ever tempted to stray from your vow of celibacy?" He responded, "Yes of course. But by not giving in to temptation, I become even stronger in my faith and even more dedicated to Jesus." He paraphrased the Epistle of James, "When we are tempted, we must remember God is not tempting us. God cannot be tempted by evil, nor does God tempt anyone. Each of us is tempted when we give in to our own desires."

Ironically, Thomas shared a kind of kinship with Jesus over the issue of celibacy. There were the persistent questions about Jesus Christ and Mary Magdalene. Did Jesus have a sexual relationship with Mary? Did He father a child by her, as the controversial suggestion in *The DaVinci Code* would have readers believe? Thomas knew the power of sex, the joy, the thrill, the disappointment and the heartache. However, he was devoted to his calling precisely because he came to understand Jesus was also a man and regardless of how simply Jesus tried to live, His life was one long, painful complication.

At 10:30 a.m. the FedEx package arrived. Thomas signed for it, told Tracy, his secretary, he didn't want to be disturbed and closed his office door. The contents of the package were as James described the night before, two letters—one to Father Thomas Ryan and one to Rabbi Matthew Halprin. A note was affixed to one of the letters with the notation, "The two letters are identical. I'm just being cautious by enclosing them in one packet." Across the seal of each envelope was written: "James Christopoulos" presumably to help detect if the letter had been opened by some unauthorized person and then resealed.

Thomas poured a cup of coffee, sat down in an easy chair, and inspected the envelope. Thomas smiled as he saw James's signature written across the seal. *James Christopoulos, my favorite paranoid.*

James Christopoulos, Ph.D., was the Honors Professor in the Department of History and Archeology at the University of Athens, one of the oldest universities in southeastern Europe. To those in the archeology profession, he was Dr. James Christopoulos. Only Thomas and Matthew could call him "Jimmy the Greek." James spent most of his life in the field, returning only occasionally to guest lecture at the one class he was supposed to be teaching on a regular basis.

It was 2:30 p.m. in London, and James was anxiously awaiting word his top-secret package arrived. He sat nervously at his computer clicking the "check mail" icon much like someone who keeps pressing the elevator button hoping to speed up the process. Finally, the bell rang and a British female voice said: "mail has arrived." It was from Thomas and it simply read, "Package arrived. All is well. Seals are intact. More to follow. Thomas."

It wasn't his salary at the University of Athens that made it possible for James to spend so much time in the field; rather it was the fairly sizable trust established from the sale of his great-grandfather's business, Christopoulos Shippers. Nicolas Christopoulos started his shipping business on the island of Andros in the mid-1800s and over time it became a billion dollar business. In 2004 Christopoulos Shippers was sold to Kronos Freight Shippers and an endowment was established for each member of the Christopoulos extended family. James's share was $5.5 million. He rarely touched the account and only occasionally took interest payments. Over the years his portfolio grew to approximately $7 million dollars.

James never met his great-grandfather and was surprised to become a beneficiary along with everyone else in the Christopoulos family. The inheritance made it possible for him to devote his life to archeology. Having worked his whole life, even as a boy, it never occurred to him he could have a life of leisure. He wasn't in pursuit of his life quest because of money and fame. He loved archeology and didn't give a damn about money.

When James was a boy, he fell in love with King Arthur and the Arthurian legends. He led his two friends, Tommie and Matt, on make-believe hunts, scouring the countryside in search of the Holy Grail. His childhood passion became his life's vocation. His devotion and dogged pursuit of the Holy Grail, along with his paranoid nature, often made him seem like the least stable of the three friends. As an adult, falling in love proved to be easy, staying in love, much more difficult. Divorced twice, James decided to set marriage aside and place all of his energy on his quest.

The third member of this trinity of friends, Rabbi Matthew Halprin, was a byproduct of the ecumenical movement. His father was a Jewish rabbi and his mother was a Methodist who converted to Judaism. Halprin's mother won the naming choice when he was born and named him Matthew. For her, he was her "salt of the earth" (Matthew: 5:13). However, it was his father's influence more than anything that guided his career path, and like his father, Matthew became a rabbi.

Thomas, Matthew and James grew up together near Laurel, Maryland, when beyond the Washington, DC beltway was still rural. While each went to different religious schools, they got together after school and on weekends to play baseball and football or just go exploring. They roamed the countryside looking for Indian arrowheads or any artifact around which they could invent a mystery.

Their first meaningful discovery happened when the three boys were ten years old and their fathers took them on a weekend camping trip to Harper's Ferry, West Virginia. James once again led his two friends on a mystery search. As they ran across a field not far from their campsite, Matthew's feet came in contact with some wooden planks embedded in the dirt. He slipped, fell to the ground and landed spread eagle. He lay there unhurt as James and Thomas came to his aid. Under James's leadership, they inspected the moss-covered deteriorating wood that caused Matthew's fall. It appeared to be an oblong box hidden beneath a covering of grass and soil.

The three boys dug away with sticks and their bare hands revealing a crate about four feet long and one foot wide. The wet, moss-covered wood crumbled at their touch. If there ever was a latch or lock, it was long gone. They cleared away the wet soil and tangled roots and pulled the box from its earthen grave. With the lid removed, they revealed an object tightly wrapped in several layers of animal hide. The animal hair was very coarse causing the boys to speculate that it might have been buffalo or bear hide. Under the outer wrap was more animal hide further protecting the contents. They began to unwrap it freeing all kinds of creepy, crawling bugs which would cause most girls their age to run away screaming.

When they finished unwrapping the hide, they discovered an old rifle. Immediately they invented a story, as ten-year-old boys do, about the rifle having been used by a mass murderer. Excited, they rewrapped the rifle in the hide and took it to their fathers. Mr. Ryan was a policeman in Laurel and the boys figured he would appreciate finding a rifle from a mass murderer. But Mr. Ryan was also a Civil War enthusiast and he recognized the weapon as an old Enfield rifle. He explained to the boys the Enfield was the rifle used mostly by the South during the Civil War. While no longer able to fire, the gun was in remarkably good condition. The oiled animal hide helped protect the rifle from decay. Mr. Ryan showed the boys the brass plate on the rifle's stock. Some gentle on-the-spot cleaning revealed the initials "CSA" which Mr. Ryan explained stood for the Confederate States of America.

The boys' discovery was not earth shaking, but was still valuable. It made for a great discussion around that night's campfire as the three dads, but mostly Mr. Ryan, explained the causes and effects of the Civil War. Finally Mr. Ryan asked the boys what they were going to do with the rifle. He carefully couched the question in such a way the boys were essentially left with a Hobson's choice—selecting the least onerous outcome from a list of unhappy choices. When he said, "You know your mothers won't let you keep it," the boys nodded in agreement. Mr. Ryan continued, "I supposed you could put it back where you found it." That was an option none of the boys liked. Then he offered, "Or, maybe you could donate the rifle to the City of Laurel Historical Society for their Civil War exhibit."

"Why don't you boys talk about it and let us know what you decide to do," said Mr. Christopoulos. The boys huddled in their tent discussing their options into the night. When they got up the following morning, Mr. Halprin posed the question, "What have you decided to do with the rifle?" James responded on behalf of all three: "If we donate the rifle to the Laurel Historical Society, would you help us?"

Mr. Ryan answered, "You've made a good decision. We're proud of you and we'll help you make the donation." Mr. Ryan set up the donation process with the Historical Society. When the boys brought the rifle in, they were told the rifle would be cleaned up and put in one of the museum's Civil War dioramas. They were welcomed to come back when the rifle was ready. Unknown to the boys, the three dads arranged for a small ceremony when the boys returned to see their rifle.

Three weeks later when the boys went to the historical society building with their dads, they hardly recognized the old Enfield for it was cleaned and shining. Underneath the rifle was a plaque with their names and a statement of appreciation. The boys were given certificates of appreciation and had their picture taken. The following week, the picture was in the local paper with a story about what they had done.

The boys were happy and proud to get recognition in person and in the paper. They learned a valuable lesson about giving without expectation of a reward, and it was an experience that would stick with them for a long time. No one back then, including their parents, could have known these three boys would be reunited as adults in the pursuit of another discovery unlike any ever before.

Thirty plus years passed since their play days, and James was now a university professor and renowned archeologist, Matthew was a Jewish rabbi and *Dead Sea Scroll* expert, and Thomas was a Roman Catholic Jesuit priest and the foremost authority on the Aramaic language.

Matthew married Sara Anne Gold, daughter of the highly respected cardiovascular surgeon, David Gold, and granddaughter of Simon Gold, one of Baltimore's most famous attorneys. Simon's law partner was Julius Ruhle. Their firm, Gold and Ruhle grew to be one of the most prestigious law firms in Baltimore. Matthew and Sara and their three children lived in Reston Virginia, suburban Washington, DC.

The Gold family members were traditionalists. They subscribed to the belief that the pathway to success required every boy and girl to pursue a valued profession in medicine, law or finance. Sara chose Matthew as her husband and although the Gold family welcomed him warmly, he often didn't feel like he fit in. Frequently at Gold family gatherings, the doctors, lawyers and the Wall Street financiers would adjourn to the parlor for Courvoisier and conversation. While Matthew was never excluded, he never felt included in the discussions. Religion did not always mix well with medicine, law and finance.

Sara's life with Matthew was good and by most standards they lived quite well. Matthew was a valued member of the faculty at the Baltimore Hebrew University at Towson University and Director of the Ph.D. Program in Jewish Studies. Sara enjoyed her life and friends among the faculty wives.

Matthew Halprin was much more than just a rabbi; he was a recognized Biblical scholar who published several scholarly works. His research on the Hebrew Bible made him one of the world's preeminent Hebrew Bible experts and he was often sought out for help in translating ancient Hebrew writings. His Ph.D. studies at Yeshiva focused on interpretations of the *Dead Sea Scrolls* and the *Nag Hammadi Codices.*

The discovery of those ancient writings rocked the archeological world. The *Dead Sea Scrolls* consist of a large number of scrolls, many of which are poorly preserved while others have survived only as fragments or as tiny scraps. The discovery of the *Dead Sea Scrolls* was a pure accident. In 1947, a Bedouin shepherd, looking for his lost sheep, found a cave in Khirbet Qumran, near the north end of the Dead Sea. Instead of sheep, the Bedouin found several sealed jars, which contained a collection of the ancient scrolls. Once the find was taken seriously, a more coordinated effort led to the discovery of nearly 900 separate texts in eleven caves near Qumran.

The scrolls date from about 250 BCE to 100 CE. Among the first of the discovered scrolls is a fairly well preserved copy of the book of Isaiah, the oldest complete manuscript of a Hebrew scripture, dating to circa 100 BCE. However, for many, but especially for Christians, the greatest disappointment is that nowhere in any of the scrolls is the name Jesus Christ.

The Nag Hammadi Codices were discovered in Egypt in 1945 and are comprised of 13 ancient leather-bound books. These ancient codices consist of writings by different authors on separate pages or leafs, instead of on scrolls. Around 390 CE, these texts were hidden in a large sealed jar buried in the Egyptian desert. They survived over 1,500 years and are in remarkably good condition.

The codices contain previously lost or unknown sacred Christian writings. The most notable text is the non-canonical Gospel of Thomas. This controversial gospel is quite likely older than the four known canonical Gospels of Matthew, Mark, Luke and John. The richness of these texts and the wealth of knowledge they hold has caused the religious world to look again for clues as to who Jesus was and the meaning of His message.

James's writing style was always formal as if virtually everything he wrote was for publication. Thomas took a sip of coffee and began.

Dear Thomas and Matthew:

I need your help to complete a journey that has been both my work and my passion for my entire professional life. I am without a doubt a most fortunate man, for the two men I trust the most are not only experts in those areas where I am weak, but they also share my passion in the search for the truth. Together, we have the knowledge to unlock the door on a 2,000-year-old mystery. Please join me as quickly as possible for there are events, beyond my control, which may soon occur closing the window of opportunity.

Thomas reread the last two sentences focusing on "unlock the door" and "closing the window of opportunity." He paused reminded of his friend Michael who would often say, *a door closes and a window opens*. Thomas continued to read.

Just look at what we three bring to this adventure. Thomas, you are an expert in Aramaic. No one knows that ancient language better than you. In addition, your eschatological scholarship adds not only perspective, but also reason to the frenzy and fear surrounding modern end-of-days predictions.

Matthew, your ability to read and translate ancient Hebrew and Coptic has unlocked many of the mysteries of the Dead Sea Scrolls and the Nag Hammadi Codices. You also bring the scientific objectivity of a non-Christian.

My expertise in Koine Greek and work on lost scriptures, e.g., the Gospel of Thomas, as well as my lifelong pursuit of the mysterious Holy Grail, places us on the verge of a great discovery. We are precisely at the right place at the right moment.

To recover the Holy Grail would rank as one of the most significant discoveries of all time. To have documented proof Jesus Christ lived and is not just legend is important for all people, not just Christians. I believe the key to the Grail is through the last man who had it in his possession, Joseph of Arimathea. Know the man and you will find the Grail. I have studied the man and I am convinced Joseph of Arimathea will lead us to it. But there is much more.

I have reduced my research on Joseph of Arimathea into a brief paper, which is enclosed. I know both of you are familiar with Joseph, but let me share with you what I have discovered as it might add some perspective to a very important yet little known man.

It surely must be surprising such an important participant in the early Christian movement remains so obscure to most Christians. Joseph of Arimathea is mentioned in all four canonical Gospels, but only in the context of the Crucifixion. Nowhere before or after do we find any reference to him. According to Moody, throughout the Bible, the four evangelists seldom report the same story or account. If Matthew and Mark mention something, it is often omitted by Luke or John. However, Joseph of Arimathea and his actions are mentioned by all four gospel writers: Matthew 27:57-60, Mark 15:43-46, Luke 23:50-55 and John 19:38-42.

Even though Joseph of Arimathea appears in all four Gospels, we still know little about him. To learn more, I needed to search outside the canon. Two fairly obscure yet invaluable sources were the Gospel of Nicodemus and Acts of Pilate, which added illumination to the events surrounding the crucifixion and burial of Jesus. In a search of non-religious historical works, I discovered more about Joseph; the fact he was a wealthy merchant and trusted agent to the Romans is only the beginning. I sense I have discovered the essence of the man. Attached is a brief synopsis of some of what I have learned.

Thomas's interest had been piqued. James's enthusiasm was apparent. Thomas picked up the report and began to read.

Joseph of Arimathea, the Key to the Holy Grail

Finding the vessel popularly known as the Holy Grail will require the art and science of forensic archeology along with the ability to translate ancient Greek, Hebrew and Aramaic languages. A map leading one to the Grail does not exist. Selecting the starting point on our path to discovery is the first step. The most logical place to begin is with the last person known to have possessed the Holy Grail.

However, since there are several cups or containers mentioned in ancient writings, our first task is to decide which vessel is the Holy Grail. Ask yourself the following. Is the Holy Grail the chalice our Lord used at the Last Supper? Or is it the cup that was used to catch the blood of Jesus Christ as He died upon the cross? Or could it be a lesser-known vessel—one personally entrusted to Joseph of Arimathea by Jesus Christ himself?

Regardless of which vessel it is, the key to finding it begins with an understanding of the mysterious Joseph of Arimathea. I am convinced that by knowing the man we will know the whereabouts of the Grail.

Joseph of Arimathea is believed to have been an uncle of Mary, the mother of Jesus, which would make him Jesus' great uncle. Little is really known about Jesus' earthly father and Mary's husband, who was also named Joseph.

Mary's husband, Joseph, was much older than Mary and even older than Joseph of Arimathea. He answered God's call to serve as Mary's husband and Jesus' earthly father. There is no mention of him after he and Mary found Jesus in the temple talking with the wise men; so it may be fair to assume Joseph died when Jesus was twelve or thirteen. According to the Talmud, it was the Jewish custom, if a boy's father died, for an uncle to take on the role of guardian. I believe Joseph of Arimathea accepted and fulfilled that role.

Joseph of Arimathea's wealth came from his merchant business. He controlled the mining and refinement of tin in Britain and its transport to Rome. In Roman records, particularly from Jerusalem, Joseph of Arimathea was referred to as "Nobilis decurio" signifying his power and influence as "Minister of the Mines." The Latin Vulgate Gospels call him simply "decurio," while the fuller title "Nobilis decurio" inferred he also earned a place of nobility in Roman culture, usually considered impossible for a non-Roman.

Tin was vital to the Romans because it is needed to make bronze, an alloy made from copper and tin. Copper tools and weapons by themselves were too soft and did not remain sharp for very long. Tin made the copper harder and made the molten metal fill the mold more completely when it was cast into objects like axe heads, hammers and jewelry. So many articles were made of bronze in ancient times, no civilization could thrive long without a supply of it, or the copper and tin needed to make it.

The Phoenicians first discovered tin in the British Isles. They kept the knowledge of the Cornish tin mines a closely guarded secret so they could control trade and charge a higher price. After the Punic wars, the Phoenicians became less of an important economic power. The

Romans, under Julius Caesar, knew of the importance of British tin when they invaded the island nation in 55 BCE. After the conquest of Britain during the reign of Claudius, the Romans were in control of most of the world's supply of tin.

James had highlighted a portion of his report and in bold wrote: **"Thomas, the next section should be of particular interest to you."** Thomas set the report down, got up and poured another cup of coffee. The report was comprehensive and contained information Thomas was not familiar with. Joseph of Arimathea, like so many characters in the Bible, remains an enigma. Thomas sat down and continued to read.

Scholars have conjectured about the so-called lost or missing years of Jesus Christ. There is a gap in time from when Jesus was 12 until He reappears at age 31 to begin His public life. We know from the Gospel of Luke, Jesus, when He was 12, was sitting in the temple talking with the wise men. But then the next we hear of Jesus, He is 31 years old and about to be baptized by John the Baptist.

What is most strange is that John the Baptist did not recognize Jesus when he saw Him coming forth to be baptized. In the Gospel of John, John the Baptist is reported to have said, *"I saw the Spirit descending from heaven like a dove, and it abode upon Him. And I knew Him not."* I consider this to be quite strange because John the Baptist and Jesus were cousins, less than a year apart in age and most likely played together as children.

In addition, Jewish law stated all men, as well as all male children, were required, or at least expected, to go to Jerusalem for three feasts each year: the Feast of Unleavened Bread, the Feast of Weeks, and the Feast of Tabernacles. The families of Jesus and John the Baptist had to bring the boys to Jerusalem these three times each year, and because of the close family bonds, they most likely traveled together for safety's sake. If John saw his cousin three times each year, he certainly would have recognized Jesus, and if Jesus was in Palestine during those 19 years, John would surely have seen Him. Even if Jesus lived with the Essenes, John would have known. The fact John the Baptist appears not to recognize Jesus supports the premise Jesus may have been absent from Palestine for those 19 years.

The information extracted from both canonical and non-canonical sources demonstrates Jesus was considered a stranger in Palestine. Another example describes an episode when Jesus, at age 31, visited Capernaum, His home district of Galilee. When He arrived in Capernaum, He was required to pay a "strangers tax," or didrachma, which was a head tax levied by the Romans on all strangers. In the following passage from Matthew, chapter 17, we can see Jesus is aware they do not recognize Him and He consents to be viewed as a stranger.

"But, when they came into Capernaum, those who took up the didrachma came toward Peter and said: 'Does your teacher not pay the didrachma tax (the stranger's tax)?' Jesus then asks Peter (Simon), 'How does it seem to you, Simon? From whom do the kings of the earth take up custom-tax or poll tax? From their sons or from strangers?' And when he (Simon-Peter) said: 'From strangers,' Jesus said to him: 'Then the sons are free. But, so we do not scandalize them, journey to the sea and cast a hook and catch the first fish which rises up, and when you have opened its mouth you will find a silver stater; take and give it to them for you and me.'"

Several scholars agree if Jesus was not recognized by His cousin or by the people where He was raised from infancy to age 12, He must have lived elsewhere for those 19 missing years.

My hypothesis is Jesus Christ served as a merchant's assistant and apprentice for nearly 20 years with his great uncle, Joseph of Arimathea, and traveled with him to the tin mines in southwest England. As Jesus approached manhood, He ceased His travels and began His public ministry. Uncle Joseph also no longer followed the trade route. Rather, he settled in as a wealthy man and respected member of the Sanhedrin. It would have been 20 years since Jesus' father died and most people would have no longer remembered that Joseph of Arimathea had taken parental responsibility for the young Jesus.

Thomas was familiar with the "Jesus in England theory," but Jimmy's report put much more emphasis on the important role Joseph of Arimathea played. He read on.

Joseph of Arimathea was also a secret follower of his nephew. He was there at the cross as Jesus breathed His last breath, and he caught those precious drops of blood in a cup. Then using his position as a member of the Sanhedrin, along with his legal right as a relative, he petitioned for the body of Jesus knowing it would cost him dearly. Joseph and fellow secret believer and Sanhedrin member, Nicodemus, washed Jesus' body and anointed Him with expensive oils, wrapped Him in fine linen and laid Him in the tomb Joseph previously prepared for himself. Joseph and Nicodemus had to hurry to complete their task before night fell and the Sabbath began.

What happened next to Joseph of Arimathea? According to the non-canonical Gospel of Nicodemus, the Jewish elders expressed anger at Joseph for burying the body of Christ. Note the following exchange from the Gospel of Nicodemus: *"Joseph stepped out and said to them: 'Why are you angry against me because I begged the body of Jesus? Behold, I have put Him in my new tomb, wrapping in clean linen; and I have rolled a stone to the door of the tomb. And you have acted not well against this just man, because you have not repented of crucifying Him, but also have pierced Him with a spear.'"*

The Jewish elders captured Joseph and imprisoned him, placing a seal on the door to his cell after first posting a guard. Joseph warned the elders: *"The Son of God whom you hanged upon the cross is able to deliver me out of your hands. All your wickedness will return upon you."*

Later the elders returned to the cell to talk further with Joseph. The seal was still in place and the guard stood watch, but when they opened the cell, Joseph was gone. The elders later discovered Joseph returned to Arimathea; they knew not how. Having a change of heart, the elders wanted to have another conversation with Joseph about his actions. So they sent a letter of apology by way of seven of his friends. Joseph traveled back to Jerusalem to meet with the elders, where they questioned him about his escape.

He told them this story: *"On the Day of the Preparation,* (Preparation Day is a reference to the day before the weekly Sabbath, i.e., Friday) *about the tenth hour, you shut me in, and I remained there the whole Sabbath. And when midnight came, as I was standing and praying, there was a flashing of light in mine eyes. And I fell to the ground trembling. Then someone lifted me up from the place where I had fallen, and poured over me an abundance of water from the head even to the feet, and put round my nostrils the odor of a wonderful ointment, and rubbed my face with the water itself, as if washing me, and kissed me, and said to me, 'Joseph, fear not; but open thine eyes, and see who it is who speaks to thee.'*

"And looking, I saw Jesus; and being terrified, I thought it was a phantom. And with prayer and the commandments I spoke to Him, and He spoke with me. And I said to Him: 'Art thou Rabbi Elijah?' And He said to me: 'I am not Elijah.' And I said: 'who art thou, my Lord?' And He said to me: 'I am Jesus, whose body thou didst beg from Pilate, and wrap in clean linen; and thou didst lay a napkin on my face, and didst lay me in thy new tomb, and roll a stone to the door of the tomb.'

"Then I said to Him that was speaking to me: 'Show me, Lord, where I laid thee.' And He took me from my cell and showed me the place where I laid Him, and the linen which I had put on Him, and the napkin which I had wrapped upon His face; and I knew it was Jesus. And He took hold of me with His hand, and put me in the midst of my house though the gates were shut, and put me in my bed, and said to me: 'Peace to thee!' And He kissed me, and said to me: 'For forty days go not out of thy house; for, lo, I go to my brethren into Galilee.'"

Then we hear nothing more about Joseph of Arimathea until an obscure text by twelfth century British historian William of Malmesbury entitled, *Antiquities of Glastonbury*. In that text, William states Philip the Apostle (one of the twelve) sent twelve Christians to Britain, one of whom was his dearest friend, Joseph of Arimathea, who then founded Glastonbury Abbey. Legend has it Joseph brought with him a gift, which was personally entrusted to him by Christ.

Thomas finished reading James's report and again returned to his letter.

The evidence I have collected will show Jesus entrusted something to Joseph of Arimathea of even greater importance than a chalice. However, I will reveal the evidence to you only in person. If the existence of this other artifact were made known before it can be found and verified, unscrupulous forgers would flood the antiquities market with fakes.

Thomas/Matthew, there is so much more I will share with you in person. I have a source here who is senior and he has intimated to me he feels his remaining time is limited. He knows so much, when I sit and talk with him, I feel like a schoolboy. I have reviewed several of his books; he has an impressive collection of ancient literature. When I first met him, it was almost as though he were waiting for me. He is a fragile treasure and I need both of you to meet him.

Guys, this is just like old times. I promise this will be the adventure of a lifetime. I know together we will solve a 2,000-year-old mystery that has confounded all who have embraced the challenge. Please come as quickly as you can.

Sincerely,
James

When you can come, not if, thought Thomas. James was right, that notation about the lost years of Jesus piqued his interest. Thomas was certain Matthew would be interested enough to beg leave of Sara and his position at Towson to join Thomas on the trip to England.

Thomas called Rabbi Halprin at his office at Towson: "Matt, do you have a couple of minutes?"

"For you, any time. How are you doing? I know how much Father Moriarity meant to you."

"Matt, I've been on the go so much this week, I frankly don't know what I feel. Michael was a good friend and I'm going to miss him. In an interesting way this week has almost been a tribute to him. You know he was all about living in the now. His mantra was: 'a door closes and a window opens.' Ironically as the door closed on Michael Moriarity, Jimmy opened a window."

"Jimmy? What's up with Jimmy?" asked Matthew.

"I got a call last night from him. I really need to bring you up to speed on what he's doing and what he needs from us."

"What did Jimmy have to say? Did you say he needs something from us?"

"He was his typical secretive self. He didn't want to say much on the phone, but told me I would be getting a FedEx package today. I got it this morning."

"What was in it?" asked Matthew.

"A letter to each of us. He said they were identical, so I read mine. Yours is still sealed with his name written across the flap, to make sure it wasn't tampered with."

"What did he say in the letter?"

"At the risk of sounding like Jimmy, I don't think it wise to discuss over the phone. We have to get together and soon. Any chance you can meet me at Rosy's after work today?" asked Thomas.

"For you to move so quickly, it must be pretty important. I've got some commitments with Sara later this evening, but could meet for about an hour around 5:30. I need to be home by 7:30. You know we need to get together anyway to discuss the lecture we're giving on January third."

"You're right Matt; let's get together at Rosy's at 5:30."

Rosy O'Grady's Irish Pub

Matthew was just getting out of his car when Thomas pulled into O'Grady's parking lot. Both were dressed casually, not hiding their religious identities, but not advertising them either. Thomas was wearing a Georgetown University sweater and Matthew was wearing a light blue oxford shirt.

As they entered O'Grady's, the ubiquitous hostess, Rosy, met them at the door. "Welcome boys. Looks like you're off duty. I sure hope no one has to go to confession or needs a quick circumcision."

"Thanks for keeping our cover, Rosy," said Matthew.

Thomas and Matthew moved toward a booth by the window.

"I love that woman," said Matthew. "She knows how to keep us grounded."

Rosy was a woman whose age was next to impossible to guess. She was short and stout with auburn hair and the map of Ireland all over her round reddish face. She could be as rough as a longshoreman or as gentle as a mother singing Irish lullabies to her baby. Rosy liked Thomas and Matthew, and they held her in the same high regard.

She owned Rosy O'Grady's and loved working out front with the customers. She seemed to know when she could tease and when she needed to back off. Rosy was born in Galway, Ireland, and was brought to the United States as a baby by her parents who opened the original O'Grady's. Rosy O'Grady's is an authentic Irish pub and most of the décor and furnishings were imported from Ireland. The regular clientele was heavily the Georgetown University crowd, but O'Grady's attracted Irish men and women from all around DC.

Rosy made it clear she came from the Republic of Ireland, not Northern Ireland. That was part of the authentic charm of the place. There's a legend

Rosy tossed a couple of customers out because they insisted they wanted Old Bushmills Irish Whiskey. For Rosy, real Irish meant Catholic Irish; and Catholic Irish drink Jameson, which is distilled in the South. Old Bushmills is distilled in the Protestant Northern Ireland. Her rough handling was probably more fiction than reality, but Rosy enjoyed being thought of as someone tough enough to refuse customers until they came to their senses.

Matthew and Thomas slid into a booth and Rosy was immediately at their side. "Rosy, you're one of a kind and we love you," said Matthew.

"I love you too. What'll it be; wine for the rabbi and Jameson for the good father?" Rosy put her hand on the back of Thomas's neck. "Father, I know you're hurting. Father Moriarity was a fine man and he's going to be missed."

Thomas smiled weakly and nodded. Rosy took the cue; the boys did not want to be disturbed.

"Matt, I know we need to talk about the lecture we're giving in a couple of weeks, but first let me bring you up to speed about Jimmy."

Thomas pulled the letter from his bag and slid it across the table to Matthew. Matthew held it up to the light, turned it over, then sideways and then turned it over again, pretending to carefully inspect it.

"What are you doing?"

"Just making sure my letter hasn't been tampered with. You know Thomas you can't be too sure who to trust these days."

"Very funny Matt; just open your letter."

"Here you go boys," said Rosy. She set the drinks down and went back to the hostess station.

Matthew slit open the flap on the envelope.

"Take your time Matthew. I'm going to lean back and get a little rest. It's been a long week for me and it's only Monday."

Matthew studied his letter as Thomas sat gazing nowhere as he replayed in his mind the events of the past five days. He said goodbye to a good friend, counseled family and friends, only to be jolted back to reality by another friend who needed his help to find King Arthur and the Roundtable. So much happened in such a short time. It was almost as though the commissar of the clocks slowed time to allow all the events to take place at their own pace. Thomas's mind was still deep in thought as Matthew finished his letter.

"Earth to Father Ryan. Earth to Father Ryan," said Matthew.

Thomas shook his head as though he were coming out of a trance, which in fact he was.

"What do you think, Matt?"

"Quite a story. It sounds as though Jimmy may be on to something, and don't get me wrong, I'd love to be there, but I'm not sure what I bring to the game. I can see how Jimmy needs you, especially with your expertise in Aramaic, but why does he want me?"

"Matt, Jimmy trusts you and has high regard for your intellect and honesty. Maybe what he needs from you is objectivity. You've always been the steadiest of the three of us and when Jimmy and I go off on a wild goose chase, you bring us back to reality. Besides, two witnesses are always better than one. I may be as biased as Jimmy and you can keep us both grounded."

"It all sounds very interesting, but you have to understand, I lead a much more structured life than you two bachelors, or is Jimmy still married? I'm not saying you two don't have commitments, but I have a wife and three kids. That means lots of clothes, college funds, braces; expenses you don't have."

"Actually Jimmy says wife number two is another ex-Mrs. Christopoulos and, I believe, he's sworn off adding a third."

Matthew paused, "Well what do I tell Sara and my dean about how long I'd be gone?"

"Tell them ten days. If we need more time, we can bring it up later," answered Thomas.

Matthew took a deep breath and exhaled, his lips pursed as if he were about to whistle. "My life is more complicated. With commitments to my wife, my family, and my job, for me to just take off and go to London is all the more difficult. Gone are the days when my actions only affected me. Tommie, in many ways I envy your freedom, your ability to pick up and go as you please."

"Matt, the grass only looks greener. I have fewer personal commitments than you, but I don't have anyone waiting for me to return either. I can't decide for you, but let me add this. If Jimmy is right, he might be on the verge of a discovery that could require the rewriting of history books, including the Bible. It would be a discovery that could validate the hope of billions of believers worldwide. For me, it could hold answers to questions that burden my soul."

Thomas continued, "Maybe Jimmy wants to share it with the two people he trusts most. If he's alone when he finds the Grail, how will he react? Will he whoop and holler or will he just quietly put it in his rucksack and move on? While you lament commitment, Jimmy laments aloneness. If the only reason to go is to be there to share a moment with a friend, well, that's not such a bad reason. And don't worry about Sara and the kids; they'll be fine. If Sara came to you and said a friend needed her, you would say, 'go.' You know Matt they might just need a break from you anyway."

"Father Ryan, you would be an excellent marriage counselor. I'll find a way to explain it to Sara. Tell Jimmy I'm in and will be ready to help any way I can. When do you suggest we go?"

"Jimmy wants us there as soon as we can. As he mentioned in his letter, his main source is an elderly gentleman he doesn't feel will be around much longer. We could leave the day after our lecture on January third? I don't see how we can go any sooner. As far as when we return, it might be a week; it might be little longer. I'll see what Jimmy suggests when I email him."

Thomas continued, "Matt, we need to switch gears and talk about the seminar. Ours is the first in Georgetown's new lecture series and Dean Carroll's pretty nervous. You're scheduled to present on Bible codes. I'll precede you and speak on doomsday prophecies. We'll each also address the end-of-days. You know, that choice of topics is really pretty smart. If we bomb, it'll be easy for Georgetown to cancel the lecture series and call it the end-of-seminars."

"Cute. I've been working on my presentation for a couple of weeks. I think it's solid—all new information I haven't presented before, like ELS, Equidistant Letter Sequencing, and some other Bible oddities. I didn't want to simply recycle some old lectures."

"You're way ahead of me. I've gathered some data on doomsayers and I think I may have found something to make my presentation a little edgy," said Thomas.

"Why am I not surprised? Remember, the Diocese already has given you a private scolding. I don't want you hauled off in chains during the middle of the lecture. But, I guess if you didn't add some controversy, your students and followers would start to wonder what's wrong with Father Ryan; has he gone over to the other side?"

"Matthew, the truth does not take sides. The truth is the answer, not the question."

"Oh boy, this is going to be good. What did you find to give it an edge?" asked Matthew.

"You've heard of The Doorway, the cult selling people the chance to escape when the world comes to an end?"

"Yes, but I really haven't looked closely at what they're all about," answered Matthew.

"The Doorway is different from other apocalyptic schemes. Those who believe the predictions in the Mayan calendar are accurate believe the world is going to end and there's nothing anyone can do about it. The Doorway people are different—they offer an alternative. They're predicting the end, but they're also offering, that is, selling, a way out."

Thomas paused to collect his thoughts. "But there's something more about them—something sinister I can't quite get a hold of. There is a dark side to them."

"What do you mean?"

"Matt, I'm not sure I can give you a good answer. I've reviewed what The Doorway has online, but right now all I have is a feeling, something foreboding, maybe something evil. I need to do more research before I can talk intelligently about them. Right now, it's just a hunch, a feeling—a very dark feeling."

"Tommie, sometimes you scare me. I know you know what you are talking about, but when your dark side takes over, you can be scary. Just know if you want to talk about it, I'm here."

"I know," sighed Thomas. "Thanks. I just might take you up on it when I know a little more."

Thomas checked his pocket watch, "We better get going. Sara will be waiting for you. I'll email Jimmy and tell him we'll meet him in London on January fifth. He'll make the arrangements and email our travel documents. Our lecture is on Monday the third. That'll give us most of Tuesday to pack and get ready. I'm guessing we'll be leaving in the late afternoon out of Dulles."

Thomas signaled Rosy. Using his best Bogart imitation, Thomas said: "Rosy-girl, we have to go, but don't worry; we'll be back."

Matthew looked at Thomas. "Great Schwarzenegger."

"Schwarzenegger? That was Bogart."

"Okay, Arnold Bogart, we have to go."

When Matthew got home he told Sara about the letter from Jimmy and of the trip to London. He asked if she was all right with him leaving for a week or more, and Sara responded by saying: "Matthew, go. Your friend needs you. You know if I came to you and said I have a friend who needs me, you would say go. Besides, it will be good for both of us; a little break from each other is good every now and then."

Wow, Matthew thought, *Father Ryan is really good. He may be a single man, but somehow he does seem to understand women.*

Thomas went back to his office to send an email to Jimmy and another to his boss, Monsignor Jude Carroll, Dean of the Department of Religious Studies requesting a brief leave from his teaching responsibilities at Georgetown.

Dean Carroll was very much a traditionalist who was averse to rocking the boat. He was unsure of how he felt about Thomas. Carroll and Ryan were separated by more than just a generation. Father Ryan was an anti-bureaucratic free spirit and Dean Carroll was comfortable having his identity defined by the Georgetown staff organizational chart. Carroll felt Father Ryan's popularity with the press was a double-edged sword. Thomas did bring mostly positive publicity to Georgetown. However Dean Carroll did not fully appreciate Thomas's renegade style and resultant popularity among the students and the young priests who were just finding their way. They coexisted by agreeing to accept each other as they are.

Email to: James Christopoulos, cc to: Matthew Halprin
From: Thomas Ryan
Date: December 20
Subj: FedEx Pack

Jimmy, your package arrived safe and secure. The contents were tamper free. Matthew and I got together and agree to join you. We're giving a lecture together on Monday evening, January 3 at Georgetown. We'll be able to leave the following afternoon, January 4 and arrive in London on Wednesday morning, January 5. I know you want us there as soon as possible and this is really the best we can do. I am looking forward to seeing you my friend, and I sure can use the break. Send travel details and anything else you can share when you can.

Tommie

Email to: The Reverend Monsignor Jude Carroll, S.J.
From: Father Thomas Ryan, S.J.
Date: December 20
Subj: Request for Leave of Absence

Dear Monsignor Carroll:

I would like to request a brief leave of absence beginning January 4. I apologize for such short notice, but I have just been offered an opportunity to assist in an archeological exploration in England that is nearing its completion. I wish I could be more specific about the end date, but I anticipate my absence to be no more than two weeks. I would be most willing to arrange for a series of guest lecturers to cover my classes while I am away. Realizing how important the new lecture series is to you and the school, I can assure you the leave will have no effect on the lecture I am scheduled to give the evening of January 3.

Again, I apologize for such short notice.

I remain yours in Christ.
Thomas Ryan, S.J., Ph.D

Chapter II

Attempt to strike a balance between good and evil and you will have sided with evil

MONDAY, JANUARY 3 - GEORGETOWN UNIVERSITY

Lightning crackled in the distance as Father Ryan hurried up the marble steps of Healy Hall. It was one of those rare warm January evening thunderstorms out of sync with the season. Even though he was running late, Thomas paused when he reached the top of the steps and looked out over the city lights. Washington, DC after a rain was all the more electric. The wet sidewalks glistened with energy emblematic of the power that is Washington, DC. On nights like this, the city engaged all senses. The fragrance of last year's cherry blossoms seemed to linger while in the background sirens blared and lights flashed, signaling either the passing of a VIP motorcade or police in hot pursuit.

Father Ryan believed Healy Hall was the most impressive building on the Georgetown campus. Eerily gray with gothic spires and granite gargoyles, the edifice served as the perfect venue to host that evening's new lecture series: "Ancient Beliefs in Modern Times." Instituted by the Committee on Jesuit Identity, the interfaith lecture series was open to all. If the series were to be a success, the inaugural lecture would need to be a blockbuster. Because no one could be certain what Father Thomas Ryan might say, several in the administration were hesitant to have him keynote the first lecture. Yet, Father Ryan was their proven star and Dean Carroll decided to take a chance. The placard outside Healy Hall's Gaston Auditorium read, "The End-of-Days: Doomsday Prophets, Bible Codes and the Apocalypse." Presenters: Father Thomas Ryan, S.J., Ph.D., and Rabbi Matthew Halprin, Ph.D.

It was just after 6 p.m. and people were beginning to arrive for the 7:30 lecture. Brother Roman was waiting for Thomas and quickly ushered him into the pre-lecture social hour. Dean Carroll invited several members of Georgetown's administration along with several clerics of different faiths to meet with members of the media. Thomas caught Matthew's eye as he entered the room and went immediately to his rescue. Some Georgetown senior administration types, who were good at huff and puff, but short on real life conversation, surrounded Matthew. When Thomas punctured the circle, several of the huffers and puffers beat a speedy retreat to join another huddle of comfortable banalities.

About fifteen minutes before the start of the lecture, Brother Roman led Thomas and Matthew to their positions on stage. This was also the signal for the social hour to end and for the invited guests to proceed to their reserved seats. The Georgetown administration politely rejected requests by the media to set up television cameras, but agreed to videotape the lecture and make edited copies available. With the always-unpredictable Father Ryan on the program, the administration viewed this as the best way to control any potentially embarrassing spontaneity.

The lecture was sold out—all 750 seats, including the balcony, in the renovated Gaston Auditorium. While predictions about the end-of-days had been around since the dawn of man, recent events were causing interest levels to rise. The Rapture prediction prophesied by the founder of the Family Radio Ministry did not occur on the date he selected or even the revised date. Hundreds of thousands, possibly millions of people, believed so strongly in the Family Radio prophesy they altered their lifestyles, divested themselves of their financial assets or redirected them to the Family Radio Ministry. With faith in their founder severely damaged, many of the believers searched for a new leader—a new prophecy. While hardly considered new, the Mayan calendar was next in line in the litany of end-of-days' forecasts and it began to take on added significance. Sometimes ridiculed, but now no longer ignored, interest in the Mayan calendar and its forecast reached its zenith.

Brother Roman made sure both presenters' lavalier microphones were working and properly attached to their lapels. They were seated at a draped table with the Georgetown seal prominently on display. A third seat at the table was reserved for Monsignor Carroll who was the moderator. Carroll was talking with Rabbi Halprin allowing Thomas a few moments to reflect on how he came to be on the dais.

Thomas looked around the auditorium. Even though he was there nearly every day, he still found Healy Hall to be a mysterious place. Rumors about catacombs and undiscovered underground passageways continued to interest his ever-curious mind. As a boy, he was always intrigued with ghosts and spirits and things that go bump in the night. His boyhood fascination with devils, demons and good angels graduated into a serious professional pursuit. While some of his friends joked he was a "ghost buster," he was really a preeminent scholar who tried to make sense out of those things that don't make sense.

His fascination with things otherworldly began when he was eleven. *The Exorcist* was being filmed around the Georgetown campus and Thomas hung out on the set so often he became a volunteer gofer. Controversial at the time of its release, *The Exorcist* kicked off intense debate about demonic possession and the role of the Catholic Church in the seldom-used ritual of exorcism.

The clarity of good versus evil motivated the young Thomas to set his goal on becoming a Jesuit priest. He wanted to do battle with the Devil and it seemed the Jesuits were the ones most involved in the fight. He remembered the lesson taught him by his grandfather: *Thomas, always be on guard, and remember, if you attempt to strike a balance between good and evil, you will have already sided with evil.* For Father Ryan, there was still plenty of black and white in an increasingly gray world.

Thomas lost count of how many times he saw *The Exorcist.* But now, years later, here he was in spirit-infested Healy Hall just a few hundred yards from where the movie's Father Karras was filmed throwing himself down a steep flight of steps. Father Karras forced the Devil to leave the little girl, Regan, and enter his body, freeing the girl of her demonic possession. The priest knew he couldn't kill the demon, but he could deny the demon a host. So he hurled himself to his death down the 75 steps, causing Catholics leaving movie theaters to wonder if the priest's action was a sinful suicide or the ultimate sacrifice.

Thomas related to the Father Karras character, not only in their shared dark, rugged good looks, but also in an emotional kinship. Father Karras was a Jesuit who suffered from a crisis of faith, as well as depression. Thomas believed, to effectively battle evil forces, one needed to know the enemy, which required spending time in the enemy's territory. Familiarity may breed contempt, but it also makes one more vulnerable to becoming compromised. Both Father Ryan and Father Karras were unlikely visitors to the nether reaches—pilgrims in an unholy land.

Thomas snapped back to reality as Monsignor Carroll rose and quietly said, "It's time to begin."

As Dean Carroll approached the podium, Thomas scanned the audience. He spotted a couple of priests he recognized sent by the diocese presumably to monitor whether he was going to be a good boy tonight. The two priests were canon law lawyers who Thomas knew from his seminary days. He discretely pointed them out to Matthew who noted with a smile they were there to monitor the end-of-days for Father Ryan. Thomas whispered back to Matthew he was afraid he would have to disappoint the inspectors. Thomas then noticed another familiar face.

"Oh crap, it's Freddy," whispered Thomas, elongating his words. He sighed and closed his eyes.

"Freddy? Who's Freddy?"

Thomas sighed again, "Freddy Fulgrum. What the hell is he doing here?"

"What are you talking about?" asked Matthew.

"Father Frederick Francis Fulgrum, a seminary classmate of mine—a real brown-nosing suck-up. He ratted on Michael and me and our boxing business just to curry favor with the administration. He's a perfect example of what's wrong with the Church."

"Don't sugar coat it Tommie, just tell me how you feel," whispered Matthew smiling.

Frederick Fulgrum was easy to spot in a crowd. He was tall and thin with sharp angular features, which made him resemble the cartoonish figure of Ichabod Crane. He stood in back, apparently in charge of the seated lawyer priests, his arms folded across his chest and a scowl across his face.

Thomas and Matthew brought their attention back to the podium. Monsignor Jude Carroll was a brilliant writer, but not a very good speaker. He often appeared stiff when addressing an audience and was only slightly more comfortable as a moderator. His task was to introduce the evening's presenters and moderate the Q & A session. Carroll managed to recognize "an honored guest presenter Rabbi Matthew Halprin, Director of the Ph.D. program in Jewish Studies at the Baltimore Hebrew University at Towson University." Then somewhat clumsily continued, "And our very own Father Thomas Ryan, the Church's point man on all things related to the end-of-days."

Strange introduction thought Thomas, *the Church's point man on all things related to the end-of-days? It's not as though Church leadership checks in with me whenever there's a debate about the end of the world.* Thomas looked toward the back row at Freddy, who stood arms folded purposefully avoiding his stare. He leaned towards Matthew and whispered, "Methinks something foul is afoot."

"Great Bogart," quipped Matthew.

It was becoming clearer to Thomas why his request for time off was responded to so quickly and with such an apparent show of generosity. Earlier in the day it was announced the Pope would be visiting the United States in March and April and would celebrate Easter Mass at Saint Patrick's Cathedral in New York City. Dean Carroll gave Thomas the entire spring semester off and told him to treat it as the sabbatical he earned but never took. Thomas was certain the diocese and the university were glad to be rid of him for a while. It would seem those who didn't like Thomas, and maybe even his friends, thought it best he be out of sight when the Pope paid a visit.

Dean Carroll was explaining to the audience that Father Ryan and Rabbi Halprin would each present for approximately 30 minutes and then open the lecture to questions.

"Now, would you please welcome Father Thomas Ryan."

There was a longer than usual applause and even a few whistles from some of his students. It was the kind of welcome reserved for someone whose message is worth waiting for.

"Thank you, Dean Carroll." Thomas redirected his attention to the audience. "And thank you for your kind welcome. My good friend, Rabbi Matthew

Halprin and I will do our best this evening to shed light on some very important issues which have caught the attention of people in all walks of life."

Thomas continued. "From the beginning of recorded time, humans have pondered when the end of times will arrive. Today, for far too many people, every new day may be their last. I speak of the millions of people who live under oppression on the verge of death by starvation or genocide. Or of the thousands of soldiers presently engaged in mortal combat. Or the countless souls who are alone without anyone to comfort them in their time of need. Their days are filled with the struggle to stay alive. Thinking about the global end-of-days is a luxury they simply cannot afford. Only philosophers are able to sit in relative comfort and engage in the age-old metaphysical question of how many angels can dance on the head of a pin.

"Tonight, I would like to share with you some examples of past and present beliefs about what is called the end-of-days—the end of life on our planet. Today's spike in interest regarding the end of time is to some degree the result of the belief the Mayan predictions may have some validity. According to the Mayans, the end of their long count calendar will arrive on December 21, 2012. No one from that Mayan society is alive today to claim ownership of those predictions, which makes the debate about their validity all the more abstract. The facts are what they are. The Mayan predictions are either correct or they are not and the answer will come fairly soon."

Thomas continued. "Since we tend to learn best when we use multiple senses, please sit back and view a brief video prepared by our good friends at the *National Geographic Network*."

Actually these were Thomas's good friends at *National Geographic*. He was well thought of by the media, as he was always available when they needed a religious perspective on virtually any story, and they were only too pleased to reciprocate.

The video was a montage of images using some footage from Mel Gibson's 2006 film, *Apocalypto*. Gibson, a prominent Catholic, produced several movies with the support and encouragement of the Church. However, a very public midlife meltdown and divorce became an embarrassment to the Church. In the darkened room, Thomas imagined one of Freddy's men in the back row placing Mel Gibson's name in his notebook.

The video began. "The Mayan civilization, known for its advanced writing, mathematics and astronomy, flourished in Mesoamerica from roughly 250 CE to 900 CE. Their study of the stars was as much a religion as it was a means for marking time. Dark nights, unaffected by artificial lights, brought the Milky Way galaxy into clear focus enabling these ancient astronomers to detect minute changes in the position of stars over time. Using the orientation of the stars to create detailed measurements, the Mayans were able to build the pyramid in Chichen Itza to be perfectly aligned with the setting sun such that on both the vernal and the autumnal equinox a shadow of a serpent would be cast onto its northern steps.

"Through extremely precise observations of the stars, the sun, the planets, and the Milky Way, the Mayans devised one of the most intricate calendars known to man. Their long count calendar covered a period of over 5,126 years beginning on August 11, 3114, BCE, and ending next year on December 21.

"Using hallucinogenic mushrooms such as teónanácatl to heighten their ability to observe the stars, the Mayans projected what will occur at the end of this calendar cycle. These ancient astronomers, having plotted the exact location of the center of the Milky Way, knew over a thousand years ago there would be an astronomical alignment of our sun with the center of the galaxy on next year's winter solstice.

"They even produced a pictograph representing a black hole in the center of our galaxy. Such knowledge baffles today's scientists. Only just recently did modern astronomers discover that a super-massive black hole exists at the center of the Milky Way Galaxy.

"The Mayan astrologers believed our world moves through cycles of birth, death and rebirth. Not very long from now, we will see the end of the cycle. Some modern-day prophets interpret this to mean our civilization will end in a ball of fire and then be reborn in a new, different and more evolved form. However, to most in the scientific community, December twenty-first simply means the Mayan long count calendar will end and a new cycle will begin, much like the odometer on a car when it reaches 100,000 miles."

The voice over on the video concluded. "We are in completely uncharted territory. What may occur on December twenty-first is an event never before recorded by human beings." The video's final image was of the sun on the horizon.

The auditorium lights were brought back up and those in attendance focused again on Thomas at the podium. For a moment, there was an eerie silence as the audience contemplated what they just viewed.

Father Ryan interrupted the silence. "Let me put at ease those of you who are wondering if the sun was rising or setting. My money is on the rising sun. But I must admit my position is a guess primarily because that society of Mayans vanished from earth's population without leaving any forwarding address. While there are some Mayans in Central America, there are no descendants of that ancient culture around to defend or explain what they believed will happen on December 21.

"Within the Catholic Church, the concept of the end-of-days is an article of faith found in the Nicene Creed of 325 CE. The Creed says of Jesus Christ,

'From thence He shall come again to judge both the quick and the dead.'"

Thomas continued. "Even though the Second Coming is stated in the Nicene Creed, the concept is not without controversy.

"Jesus spoke about the signs foretelling the coming of the end, including the destruction of the temple, earthquakes, war, famine and more. The early followers of Jesus believed the end-of-days would come in their lifetime because Jesus said it would. Mark 13:30-31 quotes Jesus, 'Truly I tell you; this generation will not pass away until all these things have taken place.'

"Followers of Jesus prepared for the end to come, but when it became apparent the end would not occur in their lifetime, they were confused. Was Jesus wrong? But how could He be wrong? He is God."

Jesus was wrong! Wrote one of Freddy's men, thinking he caught Thomas.

Jesus was wrong! Scribbled some in the media, thinking they had a headline.

Thomas continued: "But as the British religious scholar, C.S. Lewis, has astutely noted, this embarrassment in the scriptures is actually a testimony to its historical accuracy. I know it sounds like a contradiction, but stay with me. The logical question is, why would the scripture writers write something wrong—something they knew never happened? Why would later day scripture copyists continue to write something they knew was not accurate? Lewis noted, 'this is the strongest proof the New Testament is historically reliable. The evangelists have demonstrated the first great characteristic of honest witnesses, they mention facts which are, at first sight, damaging to their main contention.'

"Let me translate this to today's times. Whether we are members of the media, or of the religious community, or students, or people in business—we sometimes come upon information that may not be beneficial to our cause. We have choices. We can ignore what we have found. We can report what we have found. We can deny what we have found. Whatever suits our self-interest. Cigarette manufacturers surely knew smoking was harmful to one's health, but they chose to ignore and even deny the obvious."

Thomas surveyed his audience making sure they were still into the presentation. "The Scripture writers understood for Jesus to be wrong only proved his humanity. They believed Jesus, the God-Man, was omniscient as God and yet as vulnerable as man.

"Throughout human history there have been many who professed they knew when the end-of-days would occur. Let me offer a few examples—some sad, some tragic, some with evil intent and some who simply intend to make a profit."

Thomas continued. "One such sad individual was William Miller, an upstate New York farmer, Baptist layman and student of the Bible who was convinced Christ's second coming was revealed in the Old Testament. His followers were known as Millerites. Relying heavily on the prophecies of Daniel, Miller initially predicted the Second Coming to occur between March 21, 1843, and March 21, 1844. As those dates passed without Christ's return, Miller recast his dates and announced they were now in the 'tarrying time.'

"One of Miller's evangelists, Samuel Snow, then predicted the second coming would occur on October 22, 1844. October 22 ended just like the previous predictions to the disappointment of the Millerites. Some of Miller's followers continued to predict new dates, but most just drifted away, and Miller himself became reclusive. The movement, which attracted millions of followers in the U.S., Canada and England, became known as 'The Great Disappointment.'

"While the Millerite Movement is a somewhat benign example of a belief system which mainly caused disillusionment, there are other examples with a more tragic and deadly result. Quite possibly one of recent history's most bizarre and tragic events was the end-of-days for the Peoples Temple Agricultural Project, popularly known as Jonestown. This American cult became front-page news in 1978 when more than 900 Temple members committed suicide or were murdered under the direction of their founder and spiritual leader, Jim Jones. Most of the members drank arsenic-laced Kool-Aid; others were shot in the head, presumably by Jones, who then took his own life. This mass suicide proved to be the genesis of the modern phrase 'drinking the Kool-Aid' referring to people blindly following the direction of their leader.

"Another mass suicide occurred in 1997 when Marshall Applewhite and 40 of his Heaven's Gate cult members took their own lives in order to leave the earth and board a spaceship they believed was following the Hale-Bopp comet. The spaceship was to take them to another level of existence above human. They consumed applesauce and pudding laced with phenobarbital, washed it down with vodka and then placed plastic bags over their heads to ensure asphyxiation in case the drugs didn't kill them. Some of you may remember seeing photos of row upon row of beds containing bodies wearing blue jumpsuits and white tennis shoes in a large home in an exclusive San Diego neighborhood. Marshall Applewhite even videotaped a farewell message. It was an eerie video of a man looking completely at peace saying farewell to those left behind. These are but two examples of self-fulfilling prophecy cults who caused their own end-of-days scenarios.

"As is true of most populist movements, there will always be some individuals who pretend to believe in the cause just to take advantage of the opportunity to make money off the trust of the gullible. The Mayan end-of-the-world prediction has become a hot worldwide financial commodity. Dozens of books and movies based on impending doom are already on the market or will soon be released.

"A fairly new organization based in England known as The Doorway has come on the scene. I must admit my knowledge about them is limited, but what I do know causes me great concern. They are patterned somewhat after the Heaven's Gate cult as they purport to offer a way out when the world comes to an end. However, there is something beneath the obvious which is troubling and possibly sinister and dangerous about their message and their approach to salvation.

"You may have noticed their billboard-sized digital clock at Reagan National Airport. They've erected billboards in large cities around the world, counting down the exact day and time when The Doorway predicts the world will end. At the bottom of the clock's display are the numbers: 12/31/2016 - 24:00:00 GMT. The sign also carries the message: 'The Door opens but once and when it closes, it will be closed forever. Only those who are prepared may pass through.' This message is followed by The Doorway's website address, www.thedoorway.co, along with an invitation to join the organization.

"To arrive at the exact moment when the world will end, they revised the Mayan calendar. By accounting for changes between the Julian and Gregorian calendars, and considering the quadrennial leap year, they predict the end-of-days will arrive at midnight on December 31, 2016, Greenwich Mean Time.

"I would assume the addition of several extra years over the Mayan prediction allows The Doorway more time to help its members prepare for the end. It also gives them more time to sell salvation memberships at a substantial amount. Their marketing is most ingenious. They offer what they describe as a lifetime membership for $3,000, which can be paid in installments, but must be paid by the cutoff date of December 1, 2016. End-of-days lifetime membership, now that's an oxymoron if I ever heard one."

That comment was met with laughter from the audience. Fulgrum was not amused—he swallowed hard thinking, *the man is dangerous. He gets the audience on his side with sarcasm and then leads them where he wants them to go.* Freddy's dislike of Thomas was intense.

Thomas hadn't intended to say what came next, but he put himself in a box and needed to extricate himself. "Please don't misunderstand what I am saying. That was not a commercial endorsement of The Doorway when I gave you their website address. In fact, I would caution anyone to avoid any like-styled organization for the principle reason the whole idea is a sham. No one knows when the end-of-days will come. The Gospel of Mark cautions against any attempt to predict the end. He states, 'But about that day or hour no one knows, neither the angels in heaven, nor the Son, but only the Father. Be aware; keep alert; for you do not know when the time will come.'"

Thomas continued down the road he wished he hadn't started. "If the Millerites could attract millions of followers in the 1800s, it is not surprising The Doorway could attract tens of millions or possibly hundreds of millions of people looking for answers to the vexing questions of this ever increasingly complex world. Organizations like The Doorway succeed because many of the faithful lost their trust in organized religion. They lost trust in us because of our transgressions. I do not place the blame on the Catholic Church alone, but we cannot deny how badly damaged we are because of the actions of a relatively small number of pedophile priests. We are in Washington, DC where the axiom is, it's not the crime but the cover-up. And the attempt by the Church to cover-up the transgressions has led to greater and greater suspicion among the faithful."

Frederick Fulgrum was finally getting what he wanted. Thomas's criticism of the Church was on display in front of 750 witnesses and Fulgrum could twist that criticism and present it as an indictment of disloyalty.

Thomas continued. "How can we criticize organizations like The Doorway when we have acted in the same way? In the past, the Catholic Church was guilty of selling salvations and granting dispensations and annulments in return for money or favors. Ironically when King Henry VIII couldn't negotiate a deal with the Church in Rome to grant him a divorce from Catherine of Aragon, the Reformation was underway resulting in schism and the ultimate separation of the Church of England from the Roman Catholic Church.

"The Doorway's recruitment message reminds new members the cost is a small price to pay since money will be worthless after December 31, 2016. They claim they need the funds to insure all members will receive instructions on how and where to access the nearest Doorway Portal to the other side at the exact moment of the apocalypse. I must caution all of you, I am not at all sure what is on the other side."

More laughter followed Thomas's next comment about the members of The Doorway being most fortunate that some of the leaders volunteered to stay behind to complete the final banking transactions, even if it meant they would miss their opportunity to pass through the portal.

"Throughout time, men and women have sought comfort in the arms of religious organizations which claim to have the answer to why we are here and what will become of us after we are gone. Many religious organizations have established elaborate ceremonies to validate who they are to maintain a tight hold over their followers. There are many ceremonies religious practitioners, and I include myself, continue to perform without knowing why, other than that is what we do. The more elaborate the ceremony the better, for it adds an element of the mysterious. Few of the faithful challenge the ceremonies because they do not want to damage their chances of salvation. I admit I have been guilty of participating in many ceremonies without ever questioning what they mean."

Thomas could see Freddy was furious as he poked one of the lawyers in the back with a long boney finger. "I admit I'm guilty of going along, but with one exception. And that exception is the simple ceremony which Jesus conducted for His apostles at the Last Supper when he took bread, blessed it and gave it to his disciples and said, 'this is my body,' then took the chalice of wine and said to them 'this is my blood. As often as you do this, do it in memory of me.' You see people, not only was it a simple ceremony that had a purpose, but it was a ritual that was clearly explained for all."

The audience was silent, but fully into every word Thomas uttered, which surely added to Freddy's frustration. Thomas's unintended comments caused him to exceed his presentation time. "You have been a wonderful audience and I want to thank you for this opportunity to share these thoughts with you, but we are far from finished. I invite you to listen to the message from my friend, Rabbi Matthew Halprin, who will explain how some of the predictors of the world's demise have accomplished their calculations."

The applause for Thomas was smoothly transferred to Rabbi Halprin as the two men exchanged a visibly powerful handshake. Thomas took his seat next to Dean Carroll at the table. Carroll heard the warm applause and saw a look of calm on Thomas's face. He looked out over the audience and caught what appeared to be a mixture of anger and frustration on Father Fulgrum's. Carroll, who always sided with the administration, thought it somewhat odd he was harboring some feelings of animus toward Father Fulgrum and was feeling an unusual sense of kinship toward Father Ryan.

"Throughout history," Matthew began, "man has tried to predict what the future holds. Early prophets used stars, stones, bones, clouds, weather, birds—whatever was at hand. When humans became literate, they began to look for messages coded in the writings of the early prophets and teachers. The Bible has been a source for encoded messages for nearly two thousand years.

"Sir Isaac Newton searched for divinely encrypted messages within the Bible. The brilliant scientist was a devout Christian who studied the Bible daily and believed God created everything, including the Bible. Newton believed the universe was a cryptogram set by the Almighty, and the Bible was the source for the answer to all questions. He felt everything in the Bible was a code, even the structure of the Bible itself.

"Newton believed the Bible was just too intricate to be an accident or a coincidence and must be the inspired work of God. The following example is what Newton described as structural code in the Bible. The shortest chapter in the Bible is Psalm 117 in the Old Testament. The longest chapter in the Bible is Psalm 119 also in the Old Testament. The chapter at the center of the Bible is Psalm 118. There are 594 chapters before Psalm 118 and 594 chapters after Psalm 118. Adding 594 and 594 yields the number 1188. The center of the Bible is Psalm 118:8. And the message in the Psalm: 'It is better to take refuge in the Lord, than to put confidence in man.'"

Matthew continued. "While the search for encrypted messages in the Bible has been around for ages, it wasn't until 1994, when a small group of cryptologists using computers developed a method known as equidistant letter sequencing or ELS. The process works like this: one chooses a starting point, essentially any letter from a Bible text, and then selects letters in a sequence established by a predetermined skip number between letters.

"In 1997, Michael Drosnin wrote a bestselling book titled *The Bible Code*. Drosnin undertook the enormous task of arranging each of the 304,805 Hebrew letters of the Bible in a massive array. He then removed every space or punctuation mark causing all the words and letters to run together. The image on the screen captures a small sampling of Drosnin's work."

Matthew projected a portion of the enormous array of Hebrew characters on a huge screen to demonstrate the discipline required to establish the base document.

"Drosnin used only the Hebrew Bible and only the original characters which are said to have been given to Moses by God one character at a time. The Hebrew Bible, also known as the Pentateuch, consists of the first five books of the Old Testament—Genesis, Exodus, Leviticus, Numbers and Deuteronomy. The code is considered to exist only in the Hebrew Bible and not in translations or any other books.

"Skeptics contend the messages are just accidents; encrypted messages can be found in any text, from *Moby Dick* to the LL Bean catalog. Believers countered that no human could encode the Bible this way—it must be the work of God. Drosnin and his colleagues assert the odds of getting coded messages by accident are more than 3,000 to 1. Although, I must admit I am not sure where Drosnin gets his odds.

"Father Ryan introduced the Mayan calendar and its end-of-days prophecy. In Drosnin's work, encrypted messages touch on many subjects, but those that coincide with the Mayan calendar's prediction tell of a large stone-like comet due to approach earth. One tight Bible cluster, using the ELS approach, has the words 'comet, large, stone-like, stony object, tongue-like fire, earth annihilated, and smitten.' Compare this with what is written in the Book of Revelation 16:21 'From the sky huge hailstones of 100 pounds each fell upon man.'"

"Hopefully, what will occur according to the Mayans or The Doorway's predictions will be analogous to what happened on Y2K. As any of you who are at least 19 or 20 may remember, on the eve of the new millennium, January 1, 2000, there was enormous speculation that because of our dependence on computerization, the world would suffer wide-scale system shutdowns. It was feared banking systems, the electrical grid, municipal services such as power and water, and much more would all shut down on New Year's Day. People were encouraged to withdraw money from their bank accounts, stock up on canned foods, and buy power generators with a sufficient amount of fuel. Some even suggested filling bathtubs with water since they believed municipal water systems could fail.

"The Y2K New Year's Eve Armageddon party in Times Square took on added significance. A citywide call-in of police officers further demonstrated city officials were taking precautions just in case all hell broke loose."

Matthew followed with "no pun intended," which brought some mild laughter.

"But January 1, 2000, arrived with little to no interruption in the normal daily routine. Had there been system breakdowns on Y2K, they would have been rapidly fixed and people would have experienced only some mild inconvenience. The same cannot be said for December 21. On that day, the sun will be aligned with the center of the Milky Way. Whatever energy typically streams to Earth from the center of the galaxy will indeed be disrupted on December 21 at 11:11 Greenwich Mean Time.

"An unscientific survey of scientists, astronomers, and economists undertaken last year attempted to elicit opinions on what might occur on December 21 that could cause the end of the world. The experts surveyed were simply asked to use their imagination without requiring any proof. Some of the suggestions were startling. Let me share just a few.

"Among the first survey responses of what might destroy the planet were an asteroid, meteor or comet strike, including so-called dark comets which could strike with little or no warning. While international space agencies are tracking a large undisclosed number of asteroids, there is no way to track dark comets. One could hit us at any moment," Matthew paused, "which might be a dramatic way to end this lecture series.

"The next suggestion was an event called Coronal Mass Ejection or solar storm. Solar storms occur regularly and are really nothing new. However with our sun aligned with the center of the Milky Way, we might be impacted by an unprecedented solar storm of such magnitude, that our antiquated, overloaded power grid simply could not handle it, causing a worldwide power outage. We have seen the impact of temporary shutdowns to the grid in the past, which have caused significant inconvenience, but a complete shutdown could be a global catastrophe.

"Other suggestions from the scientific community were more colorful and graphic. Remember, those interviewed were not asked for scientific substantiation. The freedom from scientific proof produced a surprisingly popular suggestion that an explosion in the black hole at the center of our galaxy could produce a cosmic ray induced gravity wave much worse than the one which caused the 2011 tsunami. Such a gravity wave could set off earthquakes and tsunamis around the world. Large inland bodies of water such as the Great Lakes would not be immune, and even Chicago and Milwaukee could be placed under a tsunami alert.

"Several scientists suggested the alignment of the Milky Way galaxy would produce an enormous strain on the earth's fault lines, as though two giant hands were pulling and twisting on opposite ends of the world, causing an explosion of the super volcano in Yellowstone. If that were to occur, half of the United States could be wiped out in a matter of days and a major impact on global climate could last for hundreds of years. It might even cause the dreaded nuclear winter, ending life as we know it.

"Human beings were also cited as potential unintentional actors in the world's destruction. An international consortium has constructed the world's largest energy particle accelerator. It's the Large Hadron Collider, a circular track with an approximate 17-mile circumference buried almost 600 feet underground near the French-Swiss border. The Collider's purpose is to cause opposing particle beams of protons, with an energy level of 7 trillion electron volts, to collide into one another. Scientists hope the collision will address the most fundamental questions of physics, allowing progress in understanding the deepest laws of nature.

"I am not entirely sure I understand the intentions of these scientists. Future, more aggressive experiments in Switzerland have sparked fears a massive particle collision might produce a doomsday phenomenon involving the production of microscopic black holes. The production of miniature black holes is exciting to the scientists working on them; the fact they may not be around to appreciate their work doesn't seem to dampen their enthusiasm.

"I would like to suggest, just to play it safe, the scientists should not conduct experiments on December twenty-first. Take the day off, boys. There are enough potential catastrophes slated for that day and we don't need the boys at the Collider mucking things up.

The audience clearly enjoyed Matthew's dry wit. He was not poking fun at the serious scientific work being done; rather he was attempting to keep the doom saying in its proper perspective.

Matthew concluded: "Lastly, but certainly not out of the realm of possibility, could be nuclear detonations by rogue governments. We know both Iranian and North Korean leaders have stated their intent to do so, causing great concern for the civilized world. Iran's president has declared his intention to wipe Israel off the map. North Korea's current posture is an even more dangerous enigma, for no one knows who is really in control or what the collective leadership may do. They brandish their nuclear weapons on special state occasions, and someday may decide it is time to show the rest of the world just how powerful they are."

Rabbi Halprin apologized for such a gloomy presentation and admitted he was hard pressed to find a way to conclude his lecture in any uplifting or positive manner. "It would sound so insincere to simply say, have a nice day." Actually, he succeeded, for that comment drew laughter and applause.

Matthew joined Thomas at the table as Dean Carroll returned to the podium to moderate the question and answer session. "Dr. Halprin, Dr. Ryan, thank for your presentations, which I can only describe as thought-provoking as well as somewhat ominous. We did ask you to speak about the end-of-days and you certainly did do that. You have supplied us with so much information it's difficult to know where to start. However, let me offer up the first question before we open up to our audience."

Dean Carroll, straining to sound like one of the boys: "Father Ryan, Rabbi Halprin, this whole impending end-of-the-world business is getting to be quite the topic of conversation. Except for the true believers, most think it's much ado about nothing. But there are still many in the middle, not really believing, but still a little nervous. What do each of you think will happen on December 21, 2012, or on The Doorway's prediction of December 31, 2016?"

Thomas spoke first. "No one really knows what will happen on either of those dates. I suppose if the world does not end as the Mayans predicted, The Doorway will become even more emboldened. We saw that happen with the Millerites and their multiple predictions. Even the genius mathematician, Isaac Newton was convinced the book of Daniel professed the world would end in, I believe, 2060."

Thomas continued, "No one knows what will happen next year, in 2016, in 2060, or for that matter, what will happen tomorrow. I once heard Vin Scully, the Los Angeles Dodgers' sportscaster, talking about an injured player and when he might be able to return to the game. Scully noted the medical staff said the player was 'day to day.' Then Scully paused and said, 'Well, aren't we all?' Scully was simply saying, we need to live each day as if it's our last. Luke tells us not to worry, because life is more than food and clothing. Having said that, I'm concerned about what others may believe and how they may act out."

Matthew agreed. "My concern is people may become so fixated on these upcoming dates they stop doing what they must do every day. If the end comes when the Mayans or The Doorway predicts, it comes and nothing we can do will stop it. If it doesn't happen and we spend our days preparing for the last day, we'll have wasted the only life we have, the life we have now.

"I'm pretty sure most everyone will be talking about December 21 as that day draws near—much like what happened on Y2K, when a lot of people were holding their breath waiting for the moment to pass," Matthew added. "I'd like to suggest that people plan to spend that day and the day before with family and friends and treat those days as if they were their last. Maybe something good would come of it. Maybe it would become a tradition where people come together in quiet reflection as if it is their last day on earth."

Father Carroll responded, "Thank you, and now we will open the questioning to our audience. Please use the microphones in the middle of the aisle and the portable microphone in the balcony. State your name and affiliation."

"Hi, I'm Jennifer Gooding. I'm a student here at Georgetown. Rabbi Halprin, you and Father Ryan both believe in God but you differ on who Jesus was. Who do you think God is? How would each of you describe or define God?"

Matthew responded first, "Thank you Jennifer. I hope my response doesn't sound critical of your question, because it really is an excellent one. However, I don't believe we can describe or define God. And here's why. God is infinite. God cannot be and should not be personified. God is not an old white man as He is so often depicted. Describing God is an oxymoron. In order to describe or define God, you need to set limits and that's where the definition falls apart. You simply cannot limit those things which are infinite."

Thomas interjected. "I agree with Rabbi Halprin, but allow me to add something. I've always had a great respect for Native American spiritual belief systems. In many Native American religions, God is called the Great Spirit, and the Great Spirit is everywhere and is in everything. That belief is similar to the message found in the Coptic Gospel of Thomas, one of the writings found in the *Nag Hammadi Codices*. In his gospel, St. Thomas writes, the 'Kingdom of God is all around, it's inside of you, and it's outside of you.'"

Thomas was certain Freddy caught his reference to the Gospel of Thomas, a non-canonical gospel not well regarded by the Church establishment.

Thomas continued. "The belief the Great Spirit is everywhere is not just found among Native Americans. It has also been incorporated in twentieth century Hollywood mythology. I don't mean to introduce something some might think as silly or not serious. But based on the economics of the movie industry, public acceptance of what they present is critical to their economic viability.

"Follow me on this example: in the *Star Wars* movie trilogy, we find a mythical character named Yoda who has supernatural powers. Yoda describes his power as belonging to "the Force." Compare what Yoda says to what the Gospel of Thomas quotes Jesus as saying. Yoda says, 'The Force is all around you, it's between you, me, the tree, and the rock, everywhere.' In saying 77 of the Gospel of Thomas, Thomas writes Jesus as saying, 'Split a piece of wood, and I am there. Lift a stone, and you will find me there.'

"Jennifer, God cannot be personified, defined or limited in any way. God is everywhere and is a part of everything. God has also endowed human beings with free will, which means we can reject God if we so choose.

"Wesley Evans, *National Public Radio*. Rabbi Halprin, you stated the ELS method was done on the Pentateuch, the first five books of the Bible, and you said God gave Moses the books letter by letter. This may be a difficult question to answer, but how did God do that—how did He give the Pentateuch to Moses one letter at a time?"

"Ah, the question I didn't want to hear," replied Matthew. "The short answer is I just don't know. Actually, I didn't say God gave Moses the Pentateuch one letter at a time; Drosnin did. But that's just splitting hairs. Many believe God gave Moses each letter in the Pentateuch and Moses was His loyal scribe. However, the issue is made complicated by the story in Deuteronomy that tells of Moses' death and his burial in the valley in the land of Moab. I am at a loss to explain how Moses could write Deuteronomy, especially where it describes his death and subsequent burial? Moses' service to God as His voice on earth is more important than who wrote the books of the Old and New Testament."

"Ezra Silversteen, I'm also a student at Georgetown. Father Ryan, I don't want this to sound like an insult, but do you ever have a crisis of faith? Do you ever wonder if there really is a God?"

Thomas took a breath while thinking *Freddy is going to love this*. "Thank you Ezra. What a perfect segue from the previous question. Do I ever have a crisis of faith? The short answer is yes. Not every day, but probably more often than most lay people. Why? Because, Ezra, while I may be a priest, I'm also a man. God is not easy. Believing takes a lot of effort. Not believing is much easier.

"There is so much which must be taken on faith. There are so many questions. Were we created in God's mind and image or did we evolve? Was there a Big Bang? What was there before the Big Bang? Is there intelligent life elsewhere in the universe? If yes, do they have the same God, or a different God? Einstein posited the theory that space is curved. If that is correct, then the next logical question must be: what is on the other side of the curve? If space is like an enormous ball, are we on the inside of the ball or on the outside?

"Truly, the more we know about our world and other worlds, the more questions we have. I mentioned Einstein. While he considered himself first a scientist, Einstein believed the universe was simply too complex to be an accident—there had to be the hand of the sovereign at work in the beginning. Our job as religious scholars and scientists is to pursue the truth, to discover lost knowledge, such as in the *Dead Sea Scrolls* and the *Nag Hammadi Codices*.

"But we must also be guided by faith in our search for answers. I mentioned the *Dead Sea Scrolls*. Must we accept the scrolls as true just because the manuscripts are old? We stand in awe of that find. But what if the author of the scrolls was wrong; or worse yet, writing with an evil intent? I have faith the sun will rise tomorrow and yet I know the sunrise is an optical illusion. Ezra, I may not have fully answered your question; just know it is important for you to continue questioning and keep on challenging. Don't be afraid to accept some things on faith."

"Randy Cross, religion reporter for the *Washington Post*. To either or both of you, do you feel your respective faith establishments are meeting the needs of the faithful?"

Thomas and Matthew exchanged looks. Matthew responded, hoping to save Thomas from one more checkmark. Matthew's response, "Is this on or off the record?" was met by laughter from the audience. "Seriously, that's a very good question. I'm sure Father Ryan would agree we can and must do more to satisfy the needs of the faithful. Please remember, the Church leadership and membership are just human. We try to do right, but we often fall short.

"Mostly our intentions are honorable, but as humans our abilities are limited. We think of ourselves as God's disciples regardless of which faith we profess. Even though I am a rabbi, I am well acquainted with the New Testament. The Gospels claim Jesus selected twelve apostles to follow him and build his church, but yet they often failed him. Jesus called Peter his rock and upon that rock, he would build his church. Yet on the night before Jesus was crucified, Peter denied knowing Jesus three times. I'm not offering up excuses. Most of us do the best we can. As the Gospels say, the poor will be with you always. We'll keep doing our job even knowing our work will never be done."

Thomas could not let a question like that go without a comment. As Matthew finished, Thomas interjected. "Let me say something further on the role of the Church."

Matthew closed his eyes thinking, *I guess he can't help himself. He's just got to stir the pot.*

Thomas continued, "This will not sit well with traditionalists in the Church and I may disagree slightly with my friend Rabbi Halprin, but I believe Jesus did not come to build a church or to start a religion. He came to start a revolution. He came to change the order of things. He overturned the moneychanger's tables in the temple.

"How is the Church meeting the needs of the faithful? Not all that well, I'm afraid. Instead of building buildings, we need to build congregations. Jesus was not opposed to people gathering together to serve God by serving one another. We need to remind ourselves of why we are here. I believe for Jesus the church was not a building; rather it was a congregation of people. We can do better. And the only way we can do better is to invest more in people and less in bricks and mortar."

Matthew smiled to himself, *he can't help it.*

Freddy on the other hand was not smiling. He was furious. *There he goes again, always attacking, never supporting what we are trying to do. Sure the students love it, but he has no idea what it takes to support the Church, especially when people are always taking potshots at us.* Freddy jabbed a boney finger into the shoulder of one of his watchdog priests. "Make note of what the man just said and mark the time on the tape so I can play it back later." Freddy thought, *I've got you Thomas.*

As Thomas was finishing his answer, Matthew scratched out a short note and slid it to Thomas. It simply said: "Way to go, buddy."

Father Carroll, noting the hour was getting late, interjected "I believe we have time for one or two more questions."

"Cecil Peters, book review editor for the *Washington Post*. Father Ryan, have you read *The DaVinci Code* and if you did, what did you think about its premise?"

"Yes, I read *The DaVinci Code*. I found it to be an interesting read and not a half-bad movie. But the premise of Mary Magdalene as the Holy Grail is completely erroneous and nothing more than a work of fiction."

"Could you elaborate, Father?" questioned Peters.

"Well, the book's premise revolves around DaVinci's painting of *The Last Supper* and the portrayal of the person immediately to the right of Jesus. DaVinci is supposedly saying the person is not the apostle John, but, in fact, is Mary Magdalene. My point is simply this. DaVinci painted *The Last Supper* around 1500. He clearly was not at the Last Supper and he surely wasn't working off of the official photograph."

This comment was met with polite laughter from the audience.

"DaVinci depicted the scene which he believed must have occurred immediately after Jesus told His disciples one of them would betray Him. In the painting, all twelve are showing different degrees of horror, anger and shock. However, we know DaVinci was a rebel and he would often add his own touch to his paintings as a way to challenge those who commissioned his work. I'm halfway surprised that he didn't paint in a puppy dog at the end of the table. DaVinci had a naughty-boy way about him, always wanting to tweak the establishment. Most of the people who commissioned his work never caught on."

"Cynthia Jennings, *Baltimore Sun* religious editor. If I may follow up? Father, you have said Mary Magdalene is not the Holy Grail. Why do you take that position?"

"Thank you for the question Cynthia. We know very little about Mary Magdalene. Clearly she was very important to Jesus, but we may never know what their relationship was. Let me add a couple of important points to consider about *The DaVinci Code*. The author is telling a story and he wants to puncture some holes in the Church bureaucracy, which I admire for the artful way he does it." Thomas knew his statement would score him more black marks, but he couldn't resist.

Thomas continued, "First, regarding the painting, when you look closely at DaVinci's *Last Supper*, you do not see any chalices on the table. There are plates and some small cups, but no chalices. From that observation, the book leaps to the conclusion DaVinci is revealing Mary is herself the chalice. However, it's completely illogical to assume the Last Supper table was void of chalices. Jesus and the apostles could not have dined without something to drink and therefore, they needed some type of vessel to drink from.

"More importantly, it was there that Jesus initiated what we have come to call the First Communion, when He took bread, broke it and gave it to His disciples saying, 'This is my body.' Then, He picked up the chalice saying, 'This is my blood.' Without a chalice, the First Communion could not have taken place."

Thomas was not finished, "I'm not saying the chalice Jesus used at the Last Supper is the Holy Grail. I'm not even suggesting the chalice used at the Last Supper is the same one St. Joseph of Arimathea used to catch Jesus' blood as He hung upon the cross. I'm simply saying there had to be a chalice at the Last Supper and that chalice, or Joseph of Arimathea's chalice, could be the Holy Grail, not Mary Magdalene.

"Let me add another critical element here, and it is one that stirs up quite a bit of controversy." Thomas was about to go out on a ledge without a safety net. He knew it, Matthew knew it and Dean Carroll knew it. Freddy perked up, knowing he might catch Thomas in a misstep.

Thomas continued, "It is important for all of you to know, what was written about Jesus in the four Gospels was, at best, based on secondhand information. It may come as a surprise to some of you, but the gospel writers, Matthew, Mark, Luke, and John are not Jesus' apostles of the same names. Most scholars believe the Gospel of Mark was written first, around 70 CE. Matthew was written in the 80's, while Luke and John were written in the 90's. The four Gospels were written at least 40 to 60 years after the Crucifixion.

"Keep this in mind—the four writers were each excellent scholars. On the other hand, the apostles Jesus selected were roughhewn men—fishermen and laborers. They were most likely illiterate. They were not stupid men, but they were not men of letters when Jesus recruited them and it is most unlikely they became scholars later in life. The gospel writers, whatever their names, wrote their gospels based on song, story, legend, and what few written accounts may have existed at the time. Many scholars contend Mark was the source document for Matthew and Luke. While others contend the source for Mark was a mysterious, lost document known as the Quelle document or "Q" for short. Quelle is German, which means "source." I have some strong beliefs about who might have been the author of "Q", but that is another lecture for another time.

"Please stay with me on this point just a bit longer," said Thomas. "Matthew, Mark and Luke are known as the Synoptic Gospels, for they follow the same pattern or synopsis. John, while compatible with the Synoptic Gospels, delves more deeply into the person of Jesus and he writes less on the events in Jesus' life.

"With the possible exception of the Epistle of James, the minor New Testament Letters from Peter and Jude, and both the non-canonical Gospels of Peter and Thomas, there are few other first person written accounts of Jesus. Some of the earliest Christian writings are those of St. Paul, written around 45 or so CE.

"I mentioned some controversy a moment ago, and here it is. Despite what St. Paul claimed to be true in his letters, I fall into the camp that believes St. Paul never saw Jesus, and he never knew Jesus. St. Paul was not at the Last Supper or at the Crucifixion. His 'knowing' of the Christ came from his personal epiphany on the road to Damascus. However, Paul, in his first letter to the Corinthians, claimed Jesus appeared to several people after his resurrection, and then, at last, He appeared to Paul."

Thomas promised he was nearly done. "In the same letter to the Corinthians, Paul referred to himself as the 'least of the apostles.' I apologize for my anti-Paul stance, but I find Paul to be somewhat of a shameless self-promoter. He claimed to have seen Jesus, but I have my doubts. In my opinion, Paul is less than the 'least of the apostles.' While it would be fair to call Paul more than just a follower of Jesus, he was not one of the original twelve apostles. After Judas committed suicide, the eleven remaining apostles cast lots and chose Matthias over Barsabbas. Paul was not even considered as a possible replacement.

"I realize my personal opinion puts me outside the main body of Pauline Christians, and that I can accept."

Thomas could accept it, but Freddy couldn't. The Vatican just concluded its "Pauline Year," where several events celebrated the birth and ministry of St. Paul. Freddy found Thomas's criticism of St. Paul to be offensive since the Pope himself declared he was in concert with Pauline Christians. The Pope was the boss and Freddy was a loyalist. Freddy believed anyone lacking in fealty to the Pope or to the Pope's wishes was someone not be trusted and, in fact, someone who required careful monitoring.

Thomas continued. "When you think about it, this has got to be one of the greatest mysteries of all time. How a humble man of the people became, quite possibly, the most important human being to walk on earth. I'm not saying this as a Christian theologian. I'm sure Rabbi Halprin would agree that Jesus, whether you believe He is the Messiah or not, forever changed humanity." Halprin gently nodded agreement. "And because the story is so implausible, it has to have the element of the divine. How, 2,000 years ago, could a poor man of the people, without radio, television, newspapers, or even a slick P.R. firm, cause a movement that would change the world? And further, the philosophy behind the movement was passed down based on second, third or fourth-hand accounts.

"You might ask, why didn't Jesus appear later when his arrival could have been recorded? When we could have seen what He looked like or heard His voice? I agree it would have made believing easier; but then, what is the value of faith? We have no pictures, no paintings, and no writings of Jesus. We have to take what we know on faith. There is a classic conflict between St. Paul and St. James. Paul weighs in heavily on faith and James weighs in heavily on works. James says faith without works is dead. 'Show me your works and you will show me your faith.' Paul contends it is through faith we gain salvation. They are both right. Jesus must be believed based on faith. But Jesus expects us to do more than believe in Him, He expects us to act. We must each search to find the real Jesus and, let me suggest, we will not find Jesus on the easy path; rather he will be on the road less traveled.

"I'm sorry for rambling on, but it truly is a fantastic story." Thomas paused. "You have been a wonderful audience and I'm sure you've had quite enough, so if there are no further questions, this may be the right moment to end this discussion." Thomas looked out at the audience; no one stirred. They were not at all bored—rather they were drinking in his every word.

Jennings was still standing at the microphone. "So then, Father, is there a Holy Grail?"

"Okay, that is a perfect final question. Rabbi Halprin and I have a close friend, a preeminent archeologist, who believes there is a Holy Grail. He has devoted every available minute researching and seeking the Grail. His search is not a lark or hobby. Ask yourself, what would it prove if the Holy Grail were found? For me, I have no doubt. For if a discovery is made of an object proven to be from or of Jesus Christ, I believe it would be the most significant historical find of all time."

Dean Carroll was at the podium. "Thank you, Father Ryan and Rabbi Halprin." Turning to the audience, Carroll requested, "Please join with me in appreciation for tonight's presentation. This is going to be a difficult act to follow."

The audience rose to their feet serving up a long and generous applause. Thomas and Matthew waved to the crowd in appreciation. There were handshakes and well wishes around the stage as the audience slowly filed out. It was past 9:30 p.m.; the lecture lasted longer than anticipated, but no one seemed anxious for the evening to end. Freddy, however, was not pleased. He hoped to gather more direct evidence to verify his supposition Father Ryan lacked the requisite allegiance and loyalty to the Church leadership. Even Thomas's admission he was not a Pauline Christian was not enough. Freddy left the evening's lecture without the "smoking gun." Freddy's vendetta was personal. He did not like Thomas and he was envious of Thomas's status with the press and the students. However, he was mostly jealous of Thomas's credential within the Church as the foremost authority in the interpretation and translation of ancient Aramaic. He felt if he could bring Thomas down even a little, he would elevate himself.

Monsignor Carroll was pleased the lecture series, which was his idea, was off to a great start. However, he was also a bit confused. He saw the sincerity of Father Ryan up close and he came away with a somewhat changed impression of him. Maybe some believed Thomas lacked allegiance and obedience to the Church leadership, but Thomas did not lack loyalty to the One who counted above all others. *It may be only a few months, but I am going to miss him,* Carroll thought to himself.

Thomas turned to Matthew. "Well, professor, may I buy you a drink?"

As the two men left the auditorium, Thomas slipped into the men's room with a small gym bag. He removed his Roman collar and suit coat and donned a sweater. Matthew removed his tie and the two left Healy Hall and went to O'Grady's.

"Welcome," said Rosy. "A Guinness for the good father and a glass of red wine for the rabbi."

The two men settled into a corner booth.

"Matt, what do you really think about the Mayan calendar talk?"

"Honestly, I think it's just that, talk. Although, I wouldn't mind cornering the market on the end-of-the-world T-shirt business. I can imagine the Cataclysmic Eve party. It would put New Year's Eve to shame. Picture Dick Clark in Times Square with a big comet-shaped ball descending at 6:11 in the morning—11:11 Greenwich Mean Time. People will be partying like there's no tomorrow—pun intended. In fact, I think December twenty-first is on a Friday. It's either going to be the beginning of a wild three day weekend or a very short party. And if nothing happens, we can do it all again in 2016."

Thomas concurred, "I'm guessing not many people will go to sleep the night before and more than a few will be on their knees. And then nine months later the world's population will take a big jump. There are going to be a lot of nut cases like The Doorway claiming they have the inside track on the way out, fleecing people for whatever money they can make. One thing for sure Matt, our business is going to pick up. The Church may have to hire 'Rent-a-Priest' just to handle the late surge to the confessional."

Matthew's tone changed. "Seriously, I'm afraid this is going to be a dangerous time. A lot of people with no concern for tomorrow might act without fear of any consequences. If Iran has the bomb, what's to say they won't drop it on Tel Aviv? Iran has vowed to wipe Israel off the map. Who's to say Israel won't launch a preemptive strike? If violence breaks out, it'll be next to impossible to stop it. Rogue nations might seize the opportunity to test out their weapons. North Korea could fire their missiles at San Francisco. Al Qaeda might take their best shot at New York or DC. Hamas could breach the Gaza wall. It could be a hellish time adding fuel to the belief Armageddon has arrived."

Thomas added, "I'm afraid you might be right. On top of the major assaults, there will most likely be the run-of-the-mill thugs with their smash-and-grab robberies and muggings. Not to mention all the lunatics who hear voices telling them to kill as many people as possible. We might all be in for one hell of a night. Ironically, it'll look as though the prophecy came true when on the next day we take stock of what was done. It's not going to be pretty and I'm afraid a lot of people are going to get hurt."

"And there will be a big mess to clean up," added Matthew. "You're right, Tommie; it'll be the classic self-fulfilling prophecy. And what a waste. Nothing otherworldly will happen on either day, but man will wreak destruction that may take years to recover from. I guess our response to the question was appropriate, but obviously incomplete."

Matthew asked Thomas, "Where did the question about meeting the needs of the faithful come from and who was that guy?"

"Oh, that was Randy Cross from the Post. The guy used to be a priest, but left the priesthood and got married. I think he has a couple of kids.

Great name, eh? Father Cross? I knew him fairly well some years back. Bright guy, but always swimming against the current. He's got some issues with the Church and frankly he's not wrong. He's concerned the Church hierarchy has grown fat and greedy and the leadership doesn't recognize the needs of everyday people. He thinks the Church's main interest is preserving the status quo. He's not wrong, but I think he's a bit of a Don Quixote. You know though, you would like him and so would Jimmy."

"Ah! Jimmy," said Matthew. "I can hardly wait to see him. I envy you, you have six months off, but the most I could squeak out is two weeks."

"What does Sara think of you going to England? I apologize for not asking sooner, but how are she and the kids?"

"Sara's fine. She's a little jealous, but with school for the kids and her work, she wouldn't have been able to join us anyway. Plus, she knows how much this means to me. It's been some time since you and Jimmy and I have been together. I know I need this trip and I sense you do to. Have you heard any more from Jimmy?"

"He emailed me a couple of days ago, but as usual spoke in code," answered Thomas. "He thinks he's really on to something, but didn't want to say too much. You know the guy always has been a little excessively cautious. Must be an occupational hazard—a result of crawling around in caves with bats."

"Did he say anything about what we'll be doing? I really hope we aren't going to have to do much crawling. I'm kind of over those days."

"Matt, you're getting old. Relax, it doesn't sound like we're going to need to pack any caving clothes. In fact, Jimmy suggested we pack more professional attire, suits and ties. Everything we'll be doing will be above ground. He's going to pick us up on Wednesday morning at Heathrow. We'll spend Wednesday night in London getting used to the time change and after a good night's sleep, we should be ready to go Thursday morning. Jimmy, as usual, has arranged everything. The man is not only paranoid, but lucky for us, he's anal as well."

"Where are we going when we leave London?" asked Matthew.

"A small town, Glastonbury, about 100 miles west of London. I've been doing a little research on Glastonbury, it's an interesting city. And get this—the headquarters of The Doorway is located there."

"Fascinating, we'll have to pop in and see firsthand what they are up to. We can pose as interested pilgrims."

Rosy showed up at the table. "Another, gentlemen?"

"We can't Rosy, we have a busy day tomorrow. In fact, we're going to be out of town for some time. So don't think we don't love you anymore when we don't shine around here for a while."

"Well, you boys behave and be safe, and don't be away too long."

"We promise," said Thomas with a smile.

Rosy returned to the entrance station to welcome some new patrons.

"Sorry Matt, you asked me something a moment ago. What did you want?"

"I was just wondering what we'll be doing when we get there."

"I know Jimmy has said this before, but he really believes he's on to something which will put him close to his quest. He's being very hush-hush. If word got out he was seriously close to the Holy Grail, the man wouldn't be able to breathe. All he said was he has a source like none other before, but his source is senior and Jimmy is most anxious for us to meet him."

"Well, I'm looking forward to the change of pace. I sure can use the break," said Matthew.

"We better get going. You need to say goodnight to your children and spend one more night with Sara. I'll pick you up around 2 p.m. and we can drive up to Dulles together. We have a five o'clock departure so we should be there no later than three."

"Why don't you come to the house for lunch? The kids will all be in school, but Sara would love to see you. She talks about you often. You know, I think she has a crush on you."

"It must be my Bogart imitation. Tell Sara I'll be there around 12:30."

"Tommie, I need to tell you something. Tonight's presentation and the passion of your responses to the questions was the best I've ever seen you. But at the same time, there was something different I can't quite grasp. I sense something is going on inside you—like there is some voice or message struggling to be set free. I know I'm not making much sense, but I just wanted you to know I'm here for you, if you need a sounding board."

"Thank you, Matthew. I may take you up on your offer. Well, I think it's time to go."

"Goodnight boys," sang Rosy as they made their way to the door.

"Goodnight Rosy," the boys sang back in unison.

Glastonbury, England

Some 100 miles west of London, Dr. James Christopoulos prepared for the reunion with his two closest friends. More than just friends, Thomas Ryan and Matthew Halprin were two of very few people he felt he could trust. Maybe he was a little paranoid, he thought. But he knew he was on to something big and he needed help from people he knew he could count on. James felt fortunate. Here he was at precisely the right time and place and was able to count among his closest and trusted friends two of the world's preeminent Biblical scholars.

His was a quest to find the Holy Grail, and now he was certain just where to look, but more importantly what to look for. There were two cups or chalices mentioned prominently in the Bible. Certainly, throughout his short three-year public life, Jesus drank from many different cups, but only two played a significant part in the Passion. The Grail could be the cup Jesus used at the Last Supper to celebrate the first Communion—the cup the Gospels tell us Jesus raised and said, "This is my blood which will be shed for the new and everlasting covenant." Or it could be the cup Joseph of Arimathea used to catch the blood of Jesus as He hung on the cross after having His side pierced by the Roman centurion's sword.

James felt it was highly unlikely the Grail could be both of these cups. Joseph of Arimathea wasn't present at the Last Supper. Even if he was, being a wealthy man, it is unlikely he left with a cup. No, the cup at the Last Supper belonged to the proprietor of the upper room. The room was borrowed and it most likely came equipped with tableware. The cup Jesus used that evening was significant, but it contained wine, not blood.

On the other hand, Joseph of Arimathea was at Jesus' side as he hung upon the cross. There are documents describing Joseph with a cup catching the blood of the dying Christ. That cup—the cup that held Jesus' blood—could also be the Holy Grail.

However, there was yet another lesser-known vessel which his research uncovered. It was a secret hiding in plain sight. James had done the research and he now knew what to look for. To find the Grail, one needed to follow the person who had it last—Joseph of Arimathea.

James devoted much study to this mysterious man, Joseph of Arimathea. Jesus was a condemned man, an enemy of the state, a criminal. Why was Joseph one of the last people at the cross? Just who was he? Why did he petition Pontius Pilate for the body of Jesus? Why did Pilate give him the body? Was Joseph at all concerned about the retribution he would suffer for so openly associating himself with this criminal? Why did he place Christ in the tomb he built for himself? Why did he and Nicodemus anoint the fallen Christ with precious oils and wrap Him in fine linen?

James took one last look at his Joseph report. This version was considerably more detailed than the one he sent to Thomas and Matthew. In that report, he gave them just enough information to get them excited and willing to join him in his quest. He stuffed three copies in his briefcase. *Find the man and you find the Grail,* he said to himself and he was off to London.

Chapter III

Bring me my arrows of desire…Bring me my chariots of fire

TUESDAY MORNING, JANUARY 4 – GEORGETOWN UNIVERSITY

Thomas stopped at his office to pick up one more file to take on the flight to London. As he was about to leave, he found Dean Carroll standing at his door.

"Dean?" said Thomas respectfully, with a hint of surprise.

"I was hoping to see you before you left. I just wanted to tell you how much I appreciated your presentation last night. This lecture series is important for Georgetown and the community, and you and Rabbi Halprin provided an excellent beginning."

"Why, thank you sir." Thomas and the dean did not always hit it off, and this was most unexpected and even a bit awkward.

"I wish you a safe and successful trip," continued Dean Carroll.

Thomas nodded. Clearly the dean wanted to say more, so Thomas waited.

"Father Ryan, let me say one thing more." The dean paused again and then said, "Be careful."

"Always Father, I am the soul of caution," answered Thomas.

"Thomas, Rome is aware of Dr. Christopoulos and his research. Be aware and on your guard."

The dean's demeanor was fatherly and Thomas was taken by surprise. He had not seen this side of Dean Carroll before.

"I had a conversation with Father Fulgrum yesterday. He told me he was a friend of yours from back in your seminary days. He wanted to know where you were going on your sabbatical so he could keep in touch with you. I mentioned Dr. Christopoulos and he acted as though he knew precisely what you would be doing. Thomas, I know we have not always seen eye to eye, but I must tell you I found Father Fulgrum to be insincere and a bit menacing. I hope I was not out of line in mentioning Dr. Christopoulos. I have an uneasy feeling and I just wanted you to know so you would be on guard."

"Thank you, Dean, there's nothing to worry about. I appreciate your concern."

Carroll was not finished. "You and Fulgrum weren't friends in the seminary, were you?'

"Let's just say we didn't always view the world in the same way." Thomas was being cautious. He wasn't certain this new side of Dean Carroll was real or a ruse to draw out information Thomas did not want to share.

"Thomas, I know you need to get going, but allow me a few minutes. I feel a need to share more. To tell you the truth, I have no idea why I feel this way, but I know it's the right thing to do. The main reason I authorized your request for a leave of absence so quickly was to protect you. You're a valuable member of my staff. You question, you challenge, but never in a disrespectful or hostile manner. You cause us to think, and if your arguments do not cause us to change, they help clarify and make our positions stronger."

Carroll continued, "I find Father Fulgrum to be a dangerous man. He brandishes his authority about as though it were a weapon. I'm not sure if you know why he was here last night and what his role is within the Church?"

"I don't know, but I would like to know, if you feel comfortable telling me."

Carroll responded, "Father Fulgrum is a special assistant to the Vatican finance officer, Cardinal Pietro Castillo. I believe the cardinal heads the department at the Vatican that is responsible for all matters related to Church patents and copyrights. You do know the Church is deeply concerned about its image, and Father Fulgrum's job is to monitor how people in the Church portray Jesus. He's supposed to be a watchdog—to observe and report—but I think he's making it all about control. He was here last night to monitor you. The diocese was asked to provide two lawyers to be under his direction to observe your presentation."

"Well, if it involves money and control, they have the right man for the job. Fulgrum is not as much a watchdog as he is a pit bull. But why is he monitoring me?" asked Thomas.

"Thomas," answered Carroll, "it is no secret you are researching the lost years of Jesus. You could not have picked a topic that scares the Church leadership more. And you, Father, are just enough of a renegade to cause great concern. You are dealing with an issue where there are very few agreed upon facts. So much of what you will write will be opinion—your opinion. You better believe the Church will do all it can to review and edit your work before it goes to press. Be careful, the Church has power and connections in the media and they are not afraid of using them."

"Dean, I really do appreciate the warning, but may I ask why you are telling me this? You and I haven't been close and yet you're telling me things that could get you in trouble if your superiors found out. Why?"

"Because I do believe the right to question is what makes us free. Thomas, you have a reputation as an honest man. The story you are about to tell needs to be told and I believe you are the man to do it. However, there are others who don't share that opinion. I have said enough. Father Ryan, have a safe trip, be careful and keep in touch. I will contact you to let you know what's happening here."

"Yes, certainly. Again, thank you, sir, for the compliment and for your concern," Thomas replied awkwardly.

Dean Carroll departed leaving Thomas to wonder just what the hell was going on. *Could Freddy know more about what Jimmy is doing than Jimmy has shared with Matthew and I? Could Freddy be part of Jimmy's paranoia? Could he be the "wrong hands" Jimmy wrote about? Does Jimmy even know who Freddy is or that Freddy is watching him?*

Why is the Vatican so concerned about what I might write about the lost years of Jesus? What did the dean mean when he said, "You could not have picked a topic which scares the Church leadership more?" Why? Why does it scare them? What might I discover in my research? What does the Vatican know that they don't want me to find out? Do they know where Jesus was during the lost years and are withholding that information from the public? And if so, why?

Thomas continued to reflect. *Jimmy's search for the Holy Grail certainly isn't the first ever attempted. The search for the Grail has gone on for centuries. But Jimmy said he is getting close—maybe too close? Does his search for the Grail and my research on the lost years coincide? Maybe this isn't just Jimmy's adventure. Maybe it is mine also.*

Thomas stuck the last file into his much traveled leather briefcase, said goodbye to Tracy, and left to pick up Matthew.

Reston, Virginia

"It's so nice you were able to join us for lunch. The children are going to be disappointed they didn't get to see their favorite non-Jewish uncle," said Sara as she invited Thomas in.

"Thanks Sara. It's been way too long," he said as he gave her a hug. "Let them know I'll come back and tell them all about our adventures in England. How are they doing in school?"

"Thomas, please sit down. I'll be right back with sandwiches and coffee."

Sara returned and picked up the conversation where they left off. "All three are doing well academically, but each is different in their own way. Kyla has an eye for art, Hannah has a flare for music, and Jackson—well, Jack is the athlete. They get along as well as siblings can and really are a delight to have around—most of the time, that is. Matthew tells me you two wowed the audience last night," Sara said as Matthew joined them in the dining room.

"I haven't had the chance to tell you, Matt. Dean Carroll caught me this morning as I was leaving the office. He stopped by to say thank you to both of us for last night's presentations."

"It was certainly a fun and interesting evening," commented Matt.

"So, what are you going to do while Matt's gone?" Thomas asked Sara.

"I will be going alone," Sara looked sternly at Matthew, and then smiled, "to Hannah's concert and Jack's soccer game. But we'll have a good time. We'll spend the weekend with my parents and probably shop till we drop."

"Thank you for loaning us Matt for a week or so. I'm not sure exactly what Jimmy has in mind, but he swears he needs both of us."

"We will be just fine. Enjoy yourself. Just let us know where you are and what you're doing. We better get going. You never know about the traffic around Dulles," cautioned Sara.

"Sara thank you for lunch, and also for dropping us off and keeping my car while I'm gone. Feel free to use it if you wish," offered Thomas.

Sara smiled. "I think I can manage with the two we have, and no offense, but your car reminds people of Columbo's Peugeot," she said referring to the TV show starring Peter Falk as Columbo, the rumpled detective who had an unorthodox and humorous way of always getting his man. Columbo drove a beat-up looking gray Peugeot.

Thomas looked at his dingy-gray, pockmarked car as they went outside and thought, *I suppose it could use a wash and a wax, but it's a darn good-looking car, if you ask me.*

Sara drove Matthew and Thomas to Dulles, gave Matthew a kiss and Thomas a hug. "Have a good time. I'll be here when you get back."

Thomas and Matthew entered the airport and wormed their way through security.

"You're a lucky man, Matthew. Sara's a good woman."

Thomas continued, "Dean Carroll told me something else this morning, however I didn't want to say anything in front of Sara. He said to be careful. Apparently Freddy Fulgrum was nosing around trying to find out from Carroll what you and I are going to be doing in England. Apparently the Vatican is aware of Jimmy's research, and he implied Rome would be watching us."

"What does that mean?" asked Matthew.

"I'm not sure, but the Vatican has tentacles, many tentacles. If they sense anyone poses a threat to their ownership of Jesus, they'll descend like a velvet curtain. Sometimes I think the Vatican lives in constant fear of being found out."

"Found out. Found out about what?"

"The Catholic Church owes its continued existence to secrecy. In the early years, secrecy was necessary to stay alive. To have been recognized as a Christian in the early years under Roman rule almost surely resulted in martyrdom. Christians met and prayed in secret. Secret societies were formed and deception was the norm. Somewhere in the early history of the Church, the leadership made compromises with the truth. They passed on a legacy of deception to the next set of bureaucrats and invented elaborate ceremonies to house secrets."

"Secrets, what secrets?" Matthew questioned, as he turned to face Thomas.

"I don't know. Maybe they don't even know, but they're afraid someone may discover the secrets and reveal them. And then, poof, suddenly they're no longer needed."

"Thomas, I'm afraid you're losing me. Let me try to rephrase what it sounds like you're saying. You're saying the Church leadership is protecting secrets and they don't even know what the secrets are; but by being the guardians of the secrets, they have purpose."

"That is precisely what I'm saying," answered Thomas.

"Are you playing a game with me to demonstrate how convoluted this whole thing is? I hope you are, because it's working. I'm completely confused. You're going to have to give me an example of what this is all about."

Thomas began, "Okay, stay with me on this. The Church is paranoid and even somewhat schizophrenic on just about all things related to sexuality. Their problems are several and I don't just mean the pedophile problem—that's just the one that's currently most visible. The Church also has a serious problem with priests failing to remain true to their oath of celibacy since they regard normal sexual desires and sexual relations as sinful. Yet the Church has no problem with married Catholics having lots of children. In fact, the Church contends one of the holy purposes of marriage is to propagate. Therefore the sanctity of marital propagation forms some of their basis for regarding most forms of birth control as sinful.

"The position the Catholic Church takes regarding women is also a good example. Women are barred from the priesthood and are given menial roles to play; yet at the same time, the Virgin Mary is adored and venerated above all others except Jesus. The Church staunchly defends its belief in Mary's perpetual virginity denying she ever had other children or even intimate relations with Joseph. And then there's Mary Magdalene; they haven't a clue what to do with her and she was a person Jesus dearly loved."

"If I understand what you're saying, I would agree," responded Matthew. "A long time ago, Jews adopted rules and laws regarding women we now consider misogynistic. And since Jesus' disciples were all Jewish men, their prejudice toward women was evident. The social mores and norms of that society were in stark contradiction to the way Jesus lived. Jesus was not a misogynist; women were always part of His gatherings. Unfortunately when Jesus departed, the boys returned to their old ways."

"Let me give you another example of what I mean," said Thomas. "There is a story in Mark's gospel about Mary Magdalene. With her own money, she bought some expensive perfume to wash Jesus' feet—perfume which could have been sold for 300 denarii, equal to a year's wages. The disciples were indignant, claiming the money could have been given to the poor. Judas was the most offended, because he kept the group's purse. But Jesus scolded them telling them to leave Mary alone. The perfume was hers, and she could do with it as she saw fit."

"Thomas, I'm beginning to see why the Vatican thinks you are so dangerous and why you are watched so closely. Do you really believe the bureaucracy controls Jesus' message just so it fits their purpose and maintains order within the Church. Even for you, that's a bit sinister."

"I don't want to believe it Matt. I didn't join the priesthood for personal gain. Some of what is done in the name of the Lord is done more to satisfy human desire than spiritual good. The Church does much good work, but also much of what it does is self-serving. Most of all, when mistakes are made, I want the Church to be honest and come clean. I want the Church to be true, because I do believe it's the truth that sets one free."

"I think we ought to ask Jimmy if anyone representing the Church has shown more than normal interest in his work," suggested Matthew.

Matthew and Thomas headed to their gate to board the British Air nonstop flight to London. James arranged for Thomas and Matthew to fly first class and they were most appreciative. It was going to be a long flight and it felt good to be able to stretch out. Once the jet was airborne, they removed their shoes, elevated their leg rests and reclined their seats. Shortly after takeoff, a very attractive flight attendant handed each passenger a warm, moist towel. The moist heat felt soothing and was a nice touch to help travelers relax. Even before the attendant could retrieve the towels, Matthew was sound asleep. *Odd,* thought Thomas, *Matthew, the worrier-in-chief, has no trouble sleeping on a transoceanic flight.*

Thomas took out his grandfather's pocket watch just as it began to chime six o'clock. The flight attendant noticed the watch and its delicate sound and asked if she might see it. Thomas handed her the watch. Some of the filigree on the gold exterior was worn down from regular handling, but the harp, the Irish national symbol was still visible. The young woman asked Thomas if there was a story behind the watch, seemingly wanting to engage him in conversation.

She was a very attractive woman, with medium-length auburn hair and a lovely English accent. Instead of immediately answering her question, Thomas, distracted by the scent of her perfume, told her how beautiful he thought she was and how her perfume only enhanced her beauty.

She was not at all put off by the compliment, for it wasn't the first time, but Thomas's sincerity and gentleness was noticed and appreciated. Thomas proceeded to tell her about his grandfather and the watch. He then pointed to Matthew, still asleep, and told her how the two had just been discussing women moments before, in particular, Mary Magdalene and her perfume. She introduced herself as Robin and admitted she was a bit taken by his compliment and his quiet confidence and would enjoy talking with him some more.

"Robin," said Thomas, "I can afford to be honest and complimentary without it being a pass. I am a Catholic Priest; but I am also a man and I appreciate beauty."

This time his comment caused her to blush.

Matthew, feigning sleep, smiled and said, "Robin, he does have a way about him doesn't he? My wife has a crush on him. Its okay, he's quite harmless; he's married to the Church. But I would agree; he has excellent perception on all things beautiful, including you."

Robin was now in full blush. "Why thank you, both of you. You have truly made my day. If either of you gentlemen requires anything at all, please press the attendant button and I shall be here in a jiff. Now, if you'll excuse me, I better attend to the others."

Matthew smiled at Thomas and just shook his head. "You really can't help yourself, can you?"

Thomas, smiling, said, "Why don't you go back to sleep and leave Robin and me alone."

Both men laughed quietly. Matthew closed his eyes and Thomas turned to look out the window.

The flight was not full and both men had plenty of space to spread out. Thomas was seated next to a window on the left side of the plane; Matthew was in the aisle seat on the right across from Thomas. Thomas intended to use the trip to review the article he was writing, but as evening slowly engulfed the Eastern Seaboard, lights from cities and towns formed a long radiant ribbon of humanity and he was hooked. The route took the British aircraft up the East Coast, along the Maine shoreline, and finally over the Atlantic Provinces of Nova Scotia and Newfoundland. The lights, at first tightly packed, became isolated, then few and far between, and finally flickered into total darkness. For a while it seemed the flight would be over land all the way to Britain.

With the view of humanity finally gone, Thomas opened his briefcase and retrieved the draft copy of the article he was writing for the summer edition of *The Christian Scholar*. While he procrastinated getting the article written, James's letter about Joseph of Arimathea motivated him to get back to it.

The first draft was fairly well completed, but Thomas felt it was too choppy and planned to use the flight to review it. The Church requested the right to read and edit the piece, but Thomas refused any editing and there really was no way the Church could compel him.

Thomas had been a priest for close to twenty years and had given many sermons and lectures on Jesus and Christianity. However, it wasn't until he started to write about the life of Jesus that he realized how relatively little was known about the years between His adolescence and His public life. However, there was no shortage of books about Jesus' public ministry.

The California-based Westar Institute launched a study group known as "The Jesus Seminar" to discover and publish a scholarly consensus on the life, works and especially the sayings of Jesus Christ. The study group now numbers over 150 members, but it was a smaller group of scholars who met in 1985 that deserve the credit for reawakening interest in Jesus Christ. It was this initial group that reviewed the Gospels and other non-canonical works, such as the Gospel of Thomas, to produce a lexicon of the sayings attributed to Jesus.

Thomas wished he'd been able to participate, but the seminar convened before he became a priest. He attempted to make up for it by absorbing every bit of information he could. He had to settle for whatever the Westar Institute published and whatever he could glean from those involved.

Criticized by religious scholars for being unscientific, The Jesus Seminar had members vote on the authenticity of each of the supposed sayings of Jesus. The voting was accomplished by having each reviewer cast his or her vote by placing a colored ball in a ballot box. The color-coded balls ranged from red (likely authentic words of Jesus) and pink (somewhat likely) to gray (somewhat unlikely) and black (unlikely). The findings were published in 1993 in the book: *The Five Gospels: The Search for the Authentic Words of Jesus.*

The Jesus Seminar succeeded in causing renewed interest in the works and sayings of Jesus Christ. As a result, many books were produced including: *Jesus Christ, Magic and Myth; Jesus, Prophet of Social Change; Jesus Man of the Spirit; Christ the Savior; Jesus Wisdom Sage.* Thomas collaborated with a few other scholars to produce, *Jesus the Revolutionary.* However, there were no books about Jesus as a young man—no books about His adolescent years.

Thomas remembered a comment he made the previous evening at the Georgetown seminar: "All we know about Jesus is, at best, secondhand." There are no first-person written accounts of Jesus. Thomas was convinced Paul did not know Jesus, and that he never saw Jesus despite what he claimed in his letters. For that matter, the gospel writers, Matthew, Mark, Luke and John did not know Jesus either, and merely wrote what was passed on to them in song and story.

Thomas believed the followers of Paul hijacked Christianity. There have been several attempts to elevate Paul to a status that Thomas was convinced he'd not earned. Over the years religious revisionists attempted to cast Paul as the thirteenth apostle, being selected by God to replace the traitor Judas who hanged himself. But when the apostles cast lots to replace Judas, it was Matthias they selected over Barsabbas. Paul was not even nominated.

Thomas was suspicious of Paul, feeling he was an unabashed self-promoter. When asked by His disciples to whom they should go after He was gone, Jesus responded, “Go to James.” The letter from James, although brief, is clear and unequivocal—even poetic. Thomas believed James’s letter told more about Jesus’ philosophy than all of Paul’s letters combined.

Even though James was considered by many to be Jesus’ brother, his letter sparked much debate and was finally included in the canon, but over much derision and doubt. Even though James’s letter was included, it’s seldom used or even referenced by Protestant Christian denominations. Thomas wondered why James is held in such low regard. Could it be that the path he laid out to salvation, through works and not by faith alone, was just too difficult?

Thomas was one of the scholars who believed most of the New Testament entries were written from secondhand or hearsay accounts. The mysterious, lost “Q” gospel was thought to be the source document for the three synoptic Gospels of Matthew, Mark and Luke. “Q” might hold answers for many questions, but its whereabouts are unknown.

In the darkened cabin of an airplane 35,000 feet over the Atlantic, Thomas reviewed the inventory of what is known about Jesus. Thomas asked himself silently, *So Father Thomas Ryan, what do you really know about Jesus Christ?* He began to list the attributes agreed upon by most people. Jesus was a Jew. He was raised in a Jewish household in the Jewish hamlet of Nazareth in Jewish Palestine. He kept the Jewish traditions, was circumcised and probably ate Kosher. He was baptized, attracted followers, spoke in parables, performed miracles, was crucified, died and rose again from the dead. A short while later, He ascended into heaven and promised to come again to judge the quick and the dead.

He spoke Aramaic and probably Koine, early Greek. Some have conjectured Jesus was illiterate. The Catholic Church hierarchy did not dispel the rumor, leaving open the possibility. Thomas thought to consider Jesus illiterate to be absolutely absurd. While nothing written by the hand of Jesus was ever discovered, Thomas was satisfied there was ample documentation that Jesus was literate.

In the Gospel of John, he tells of Jesus writing in the dirt. He had been challenged by the Pharisees on what to do with a woman found guilty of prostitution. The Pharisees were attempting to lay a trap for Jesus so they could use His words and actions against Him. The Pharisees reminded Jesus the Law of Moses commanded them to stone the woman, and they asked Him what they should do. John's gospel contains the following: "And this they said tempting Him, that they might accuse Him. But Jesus bowing Himself down wrote with His finger on the ground. When therefore they continued asking Him, He lifted up Himself, and said to them, he that is without sin among you let him be first to cast a stone at her. And again stooping down, he wrote on the ground."

When Jesus next looked up, all the woman's accusers were gone. Jesus covered over what He had written on the ground and asked the woman, where are those who condemn you? She responded that they were gone and Jesus said, "Neither will I condemn you. Go and sin no more." Some have suggested what Jesus was writing on the ground was a list of the sins of the accusers.

Also, if Jesus is God, then He is omnipotent and anyone who is all knowing cannot be illiterate.

Thomas knew that the New Testament did not contain any information about the adolescent years of Jesus. The four Gospels are a source for much of what we know about Jesus. But only Luke tells the nativity story. Matthew does discuss Mary's virgin conception and Jesus' birth, but that's all he says about Jesus' childhood. Even the famed story about the 12-year-old Jesus talking with the elders in the temple is only found in Luke.

All four gospel writers tell the Jesus story in earnest beginning when Jesus began His public life. In fact the Gospels of Mark and John begin with the baptism of Jesus by John the Baptist. Neither Mark nor John has anything to say about Jesus' childhood. Thomas found that to be odd. Why didn't the gospel writers just start with Jesus' public life? Why even bother with the nativity and virgin birth stories if the essential Jesus began at age 30 or 31?

Thomas developed a litany of questions. Did Jesus leave Palestine? If yes, when did He leave and where did He go? Why did He leave? Where did He stay? What did He do? Why did He return when He did? If He left, did He have contact with his mother during His time away?

Thomas was beginning to understand why the Church was so concerned and wanted the right to edit his work. He remembered Father Carroll saying, "So much of what you will write will be opinion, your opinion." Thomas realized the absence of any scholarly work left a dangerous vacuum. Dangerous because, whoever filled the void first would be setting down a marker around which future investigators would have to contend. Thomas thought about the works of the first century Jewish historian Josephus. His writings have value because there is so very little written material of that era remaining. Josephus is accepted as valid because there are no others to refute what he has written. Such is the power of not only being first, but also being the only work of its kind.

Thomas had two reasons for wanting this article to be as complete and honest as is humanly possible. First, this would be a baseline document future writers would cite. It had to be more than accurate; it needed to be true. The second reason was personal. Thomas knew he was a renegade, an opinion held by most people, whether they were friendly or unfriendly to his perspective. He enjoyed the celebrity and notoriety, but he could only enjoy that status if his work commanded respect. You could love him or hate him, it didn't matter. What mattered most to Thomas was that people believed he was intellectually honest. He had an opportunity to fill a void and he was not about to be cavalier about the story he would tell. He would tell the truth as he found it to be.

He understood the Church leadership's angst about their request to review his work. Thomas finally agreed he would share his report with the appropriate people in the Church bureaucracy before it was published. He would review any comments they might make, but he would not give them editorial control. If the Church wanted to provide comments on his article, he would encourage the editors of *The Christian Scholar* to include the Church's reaction in the same issue.

Thomas's premise was uncomplicated, but nevertheless still fantastic. He was convinced Jesus served as a merchant's assistant to his great uncle, Joseph of Arimathea. The Torah is clear on where the responsibility lies for the education and supervision of a young boy whose father has died. That responsibility falls upon an uncle who then becomes head of the family. It was Thomas's assertion Uncle Joseph assumed responsibility for Jesus during His adolescent and young adult years. Thomas was comfortable with the evidence supporting the premise that Jesus accompanied Joseph of Arimathea to the tin mines in Southwest England and took up residence there. When Jesus was 31, He left His home in England and returned to Jerusalem to begin His public life. Uncle Joseph no longer followed the trade routes; rather he 'retired' as a wealthy man and respected member of the Sanhedrin.

Thomas opened the draft and began his review.

Article for: The Christian Scholar and National Geographic
Working Title: Amber Alert, boy age 12, answers to Yeshua or Jesus; Last seen in the Jewish Temple in Jerusalem in the company of several older men.
Author: Thomas Ryan, S.J., Ph.D.

Two thousand years ago, a very special baby boy was born. Born, as believers hold dear, to a virgin mother, named Mary, who herself was just a teenager. Young Mary, chosen by God, immaculately conceived the child. A good and saintly older man named Joseph was called upon to secure the virgin mother's reputation by agreeing to marry the young woman and raise the child as his own. In time, the baby was born and they named Him Yeshua (Jesus).

The story is told of an infant who was born and placed in a manger in a stable. Joseph and Mary just traveled a considerable distance to comply with a Roman decree. As described in the Gospel of Luke: "And it came to pass in those days that a decree went out from Caesar Augustus that all the world should be registered. So all went to be registered, everyone to his own city. Joseph also went up from Galilee, out of the city of Nazareth, into Judea, to the city of David, which is called Bethlehem...to be registered with Mary, his betrothed wife, who was with child. So it was then while they were there, the days were completed for her to be delivered. And she brought forth her firstborn son."

With the passage of time, the event became known as the first Christmas. Tradition has Christmas celebrated each year on December 25. But was this really the first Christmas? When was Jesus really born? This may come as a surprise, but Jesus wasn't born on December 25. Birthdays were not celebrated during the first three centuries of the new or Common Era (CE). Birthdays were not important. It was more common to commemorate the death of a truly remarkable person.

If Jesus wasn't born on December 25, when was he born? Since December was wintertime throughout the region, Roman and Judean rulers knew taking a census then would have been impractical and unpopular. Generally a census would take place after the harvest season, when the weather was still good and the roads were still dry enough to allow travel.

Jesus' birth story talks of shepherds keeping watch over their flocks by night. It was common practice to have sheep in the field from April to October and to shelter them during the cold and rainy months. It makes much more sense to surmise Jesus was born in September, rather than on December 25.

Let's follow the clues to see what they suggest. The Gospel of Luke tells us Elizabeth, wife of Zechariah and mother of John the Baptist, was six months pregnant with John when the angel Gabriel came to Mary to tell her she had received the Holy Seed and was with child. Jesus' soon-to-be second cousin, John the Baptist, would be born around Passover. Assuming Mary had a normal pregnancy of 285 days, Jesus would have been born on or around the fifteenth day of the Jewish month of Tishri. This would translate to approximately September 28-30.

Jesus was born when Herod the Great was still alive. Herod was afraid of the potential power of the Messiah and wanted Him dead. According to the Gospel of Matthew, "Herod realized he'd been outwitted by the wise men," who did not report back to him after visiting the baby Jesus. "Herod was furious and he gave orders to kill all the boys in Bethlehem and its vicinity who were two years old and under, in accordance with the time he learned from the wise men." According to the Jewish Historian, Josephus, Herod died in 4 BCE. Therefore Jesus' birth year would most likely be either 5 or 4 BCE.

We no longer use the designation B.C., which meant "Before Christ." We now use the politically correct designation, BCE, which means "Before Common Era." Likewise, CE, "Common Era," has replaced A.D., "Annum Domino" or the year of the Lord. For our purpose here, we are going to select September 29, 4 BCE as the day on which Jesus was born.

How and why is it we have come to celebrate Jesus' birthday on December 25? Before Rome's empire-wide conversion to Christianity, most Romans were pagans and had pagan gods. The Romans' most sacred and revered god was Mithras, the Persian sun god. Mithras' birth was celebrated on December 25. Pope Liberius, in 354 CE, found it convenient to institute the twenty-fifth of December as the feast of the birth of the Christ. It was a clever way of diverting the Romans from the pagan feast in honor of the invincible Sun God Mithras, the conqueror of darkness, to Jesus, the savior of humankind.

If we accept Jesus' birth date as September 29, 4 BCE, we then need to determine the date of the Crucifixion and the Resurrection. A considerable amount of scientific work has already been done to fix the exact date of both of these events. Scholars, including Sir Isaac Newton, J.K. Fotheringham, Colin Humphreys and W.G. Waddington, took into consideration the Jewish calendar, the presence of a full moon at Passover, and a lunar eclipse that made "the moon turn to blood."

We can accept the considerable scholarship that Friday, April 1, 33 CE was the date of the crucifixion and Sunday, April 3, 33 CE was the resurrection, the first Easter Sunday, because they do not materially affect the mission of this article. We are looking at a period of 19 years, so having the exact dates is not necessary for our purposes here.

According to this timeline, Jesus was born in 4 BCE and was crucified in 33 CE. That would make Jesus 35 years old when He was crucified. In counting the years, it must be remembered there is no year "0". The count goes from 1 BCE to 1 CE. Jesus died before His 36th birthday. According to the Gospel of John, three annual Passovers occurred during Jesus' ministry. From that we can assume John the Baptist baptized Jesus in 29 CE when Jesus was 31 years old.

With Jesus' birth, crucifixion and resurrection in place, we are able to develop a timeline of critical dates in the life of Jesus Christ. For our discussion here, we will assume the following:

Jesus' Birth	4 BCE	Age 0
Temple Meeting with Elders	9 CE	Age 12
Jesus' Earth Father's Death Est.	10 CE	Age 13
Jesus Baptized by John	29 CE	Age 31
Public Life Begins	29 CE	Age 31
Jesus' Crucifixion	33 CE	Age 35
Jesus' Resurrection	33 CE	Age 35

Very little has been written about Jesus' preteen years. There are a few early stories found in the non-canonical writings that reveal the young Jesus as quite a precocious child. This collection of stories was found in the late second century Infancy Gospel of Thomas, not to be confused with the more infamous Sayings Gospel of Thomas.

There is a fascinating story about Jesus at around age five. He was at play, forming sparrows in the clay when His earthly father, Joseph, criticized Him for "working" on the Sabbath. The boy Jesus merely clapped His hands and the clay birds flew away.

There is another story of Jesus, around age seven or eight, playing in His father's workshop. Joseph was a tecton, meaning he was a craftsman and as such often worked with wood, which led to him being referred to as a carpenter. Joseph made a critical measuring mistake and cut a piece of wood too short. It was an expensive mistake that he could not afford. The boy Jesus stopped playing and laid His hands upon the wood, stretching it to the precise length which Joseph intended.

The story of Jesus at age twelve, mistakenly left behind by His parents, is the last story in the Bible before His baptism by John the Baptist. When Mary and Joseph discovered Jesus was not with other family members, they returned to the temple only to find Him in the midst of several wise men, lecturing and answering questions.

Over the years, people have wondered how Joseph and Mary could leave their child behind and not worry about Him for days. How could you not know where your twelve-year-old boy was for three days and still be considered a good parent?

Thomas paused, removed his reading glasses and pressed his thumb and index finger hard against the bridge of his nose. He was about to reach for the call button, but before he could, Robin was already there.

"Is there anything I can get for you, Father?" asked Robin.

"When you say in a jiffy, you really mean it," responded Thomas.

"You looked like you were hard at work and ready for a break. You know, if you sleep, the flight will go much faster."

"I need to work just a short while longer," said Thomas as he reached for his pocket watch. It was five minutes to ten, DC time. "Robin, if you wait five minutes, you will hear the watch chime again."

"I would like that," said Robin. "Is there anything I can get you and be back in less than five minutes?"

"If you can find a glass of Jameson straight up and a glass of water on the side, that would be perfect."

"I will be back in three minutes."

When Robin returned, she set the glass of Jameson and the glass of water on Thomas's tray along with a freshly baked Macadamia nut cookie. "They are fresh out of the oven."

Thomas handed her the pocket watch.

"Father, are you going to be in London for a while?"

"Robin, I'm not sure. My friend, Matthew and I are joining another friend in London for one night and then we will all be heading to a small town about 100 miles west, Glastonbury."

Robin was looking at the watch as it began to chime ten times. "What a lovely chime, it reminds me of a harp." Robin handed the watch back to Thomas. "Father, have you been to Glastonbury before? It's quite the magical, mystical place."

"Please feel free to call me Thomas. No, it'll be a first for me. We're not yet sure how long we will be visiting. The friend we're meeting is a bit mysterious himself."

"Father…sorry, Thomas, I live in Bath, which is not far from Glastonbury. If you have time to spare, you might want to visit Bath. It's an old city, actually founded by the Romans over 2,000 years ago. If you wish, I can give you my number. I would be happy to show you and your friends around."

"Thank you Robin; that is most kind."

A call light went on a few rows ahead. "I'd better get back to work. I'll stop back later."

I better get back to work too, thought Thomas. He paused before he picked up his article. *What a lovely creature, God lives.*

Matthew was awake and, as though he could read Thomas's thoughts, said, "I think Sara is going to be jealous."

"Go to sleep, Matthew," Thomas said with a smile.

A good friend of Thomas's sent him an obscure 75-year-old publication by C.C. Dobson. Dobson, an Anglican Vicar in Hastings, England, closely studied the theory that Jesus spent much of His youthful years in England. Thomas was about to share the Dobson piece with Matthew, but Matthew followed Thomas's directive and was sound asleep. Thomas picked up his article and continued to edit.

> In 1936, C.C. Dobson published a fairly lengthy essay, "Did Our Lord Visit Britain?" Dobson's perspective not only put to rest any criticism of Jesus' earthly parents, but he also introduced the closeness of the

extended Jewish family and the possible role Joseph of Arimathea played in the life of Jesus. Dobson asked the question: "How came Joseph and Mary to start off for home without assuring themselves that He [Jesus] was with their party?" Dobson also wanted to know why Jesus' parents were not worried, where Jesus stayed for those three days, who fed the young boy, and who took care of Him.

Dobson noted that Joseph of Arimathea, Jesus' great uncle, was a wealthy man who had residencies in Jerusalem as well as in Arimathea, which today is Ramah or Ramallah. Joseph, Mary and Jesus would have stayed there on their way to Jerusalem and back. Ramallah (Arimathea) is about eight miles due north of Jerusalem on the Jerusalem-Nazareth road. It was the first stopping place for caravans traveling north from Jerusalem. Dobson added that Joseph of Arimathea "would welcome our Lord and take charge of Him and act as kind of a godparent."

The Feast of Unleavened Bread lasted seven days, but many attendees would stay for only the first three or four. Dobson conjectured that Joseph and Mary set out for home on the fourth day, stopping to rest at Joseph of Arimathea's home in Ramallah. When Jesus didn't arrive after two nights, Dobson suggests Joseph and Mary went into full-panic mode as they retraced their steps and found their son in the temple with the elders. Dobson and others have suggested Joseph of Arimathea was also in the temple when Mary and Joseph arrived.

Besides feeling Joseph and Mary were somewhat negligent, there is also the comment from Jesus that sounds disrespectful to His parents. Jesus, according to the Gospel of Luke, says: "Why were you searching for me? Did you not know I must be about my Father's house?"

Rather than view it as a disrespectful comment, think of it as Him expressing surprise, wherein Jesus assumed His parents knew He was safe with His uncle Joseph and His whereabouts would have been known to them. Read again Jesus' comment and interject the element of surprise and it will make more sense. It would sound much like, "Mom, Dad, I'm sorry. I thought you knew I was with Uncle Joseph."

Very little is known about Joseph, Jesus' earthly father. Even though Joseph was said to be of the house of David, Joseph and Mary were not wealthy. Some say the gospel writers identified Joseph as from the house of David in order for Jesus to also be of the house of David and to thereby satisfy scripture. Joseph needed to go where there was work to be had. Since he was a tecton, a craftsman and carpenter, it would be fair to assume Joseph would have found work in the new Roman city of Sepphoris, about four miles from Nazareth. Industrial accidents were common in those days and some have suggested Joseph may have died in an accident, leaving Jesus, a boy of 12 or 13, without a father.

Where could a boy of 12 or 13 go and what could he do? He was not old enough to go off to Sepphoris on His own. He was at the age where a young man would begin an apprenticeship working and learning alongside His father. However, there was no father around to serve as His mentor. Had his father lived, Jesus most likely would have remained at home learning the skills of a tecton. But that appears not to have been the case. Rather He seemed to be much more adroit around seafaring men. There are several stories about Jesus in boats, calming seas, even walking on water. If his uncle mentored Him, it would have been in learning the ways of the sea.

If He stayed with His mother, He could do chores, but that would not significantly change or improve His mother's life, nor would it prepare Him to become a man. He had relatives among the Essenes, but His mother and father had not lived an Essenes' life. There is no record or story about Jesus living with the Essenes.

All four Gospels are silent on the years between age 12 and 31. It would seem Jesus just "disappeared." Where was He? What did He do during those years? Did He leave home? Did He stay at home with His mother? Why do the four gospel writers simply ignore this important time in this young man's life?

Local English legends support the belief Jesus spent many years as a young man in quiet reflection in England. According to Dobson and several others, Jesus' mother, Mary, also spent a considerable amount of time in England.

Thomas incorporated the information from James's report about Jesus having to pay the "strangers tax." He also included the quote by John the

Baptist, *"I saw the Spirit descending from heaven like a dove, and it abode upon Him. And I knew Him not."*

Thomas asked himself two questions. If Jesus' cousin John did not recognize Him, and if the people in the town where He was raised did not recognize Him, what is the logical conclusion? To go from familiarity to stranger status could only mean He had to have been gone for a significant period of time. And during that time, He grew from a child into a man.

Thomas continued his review.

> If we accept the premise Jesus was not living in Nazareth, where could He have gone? In 1894, Nicolas Notovitch, a Russian explorer published "The Unknown Life of Christ" based on legends about the life of a Middle Eastern holy man known to the Tibetan priests as Saint Issa. Notovitch believed Jesus spent those formative years of his life traveling and studying mysticism in Tibet, Nepal, India and Kashmir. This theory suffers from the fact that in Jesus' later teachings, works and parables we do not find any connection to Eastern religions and traditions. No, Jesus was a Jew. While He upset Jewish leaders to the point of His execution, His teachings were rooted in Judaism, not Eastern mysticism.
>
> Clearly, Jesus was gone for those 19 years; but where did He go? He did not go to live with the Essenes. He did not stay home. He did not go off to study mysticism from priests in the Far East. Ockham's razor tells us, in a choice between multiple possibilities, the simplest answer is the one that requires the fewest assumptions and is often the correct one.
>
> *Note: Ockham's Razor states "entia non sunt multiplicanda praeter necessitate" (entities must not be multiplied beyond necessity) and the conclusion thereof, the simplest solution is usually the correct one, is the principle attributed to fourteenth century English logician, theologian and Franciscan friar, William of Ockham.*
>
> Joseph of Arimathea was a wealthy merchant with a lucrative business, supplying tin to the Romans. Joseph was said to have many ships for his use, therefore giving him the ability to travel anywhere within the known world. However, his position as Roman Minister of the Mines meant his hands were full with travel to and from Rome and Great Britain.

Thomas paused for a moment and tried to imagine living and working in those times. Here he sat in comfort flying to London, a trip of a few hours, whereas travel between Rome and Britain had to be both difficult and dangerous 2,000 years ago. He thought for a moment about his grandparents who also made a difficult and dangerous voyage from Ireland to the United States. *We have no idea today what those voyages must have been like,* Thomas thought.

Thomas looked down at his manuscript. If it's true Joseph of Arimathea took charge of his nephew, he would have been the one who taught Jesus about making His way in the world—a bigger world than He would have found in His father's workshop. Joseph would have exposed Jesus to more than just the sea. Jesus would have encountered different peoples—the Britons and the Druids, for example. He would have learned about smelting tin and, more so, learning how to manage people and negotiate with merchants and other sellers and buyers.

The stories about Joseph of Arimathea picture him as a good and honest manager and employer. He would have instilled in his workers the concept of quality craftsmanship and trust. His principle client was Rome, and Rome was not a client that would accept inferior merchandise. But was Joseph of Arimathea Jesus' mentor? Was Joseph Jesus' teacher? Thomas searched his mind to answer the question. *It's too easy, too neat to make Joseph the teacher,* thought Thomas. *Jesus learned much from Joseph about the ways of the business world, but in the end, Joseph was a follower of Jesus. No, Joseph was not "the teacher."* As Jesus grew into manhood and Joseph busily continued his trade, someone else must have helped the young Jesus learn and become the man He would later become. But who was it? Who was "the teacher?" It was a critically important question that needed an answer. Thomas returned to his manuscript.

> There is a local belief in the Somerset region of England that Joseph of Arimathea made several trips to the area, and Jesus, during the unrecorded years of His young manhood, came with Joseph. Archeology documents the fact that commerce in tin existed in Somerset for a very long time. Lead mines dotted the nearby Mendip Hills. The mines are now silent, but during that era, one could hear the miners call out "Just as Joseph did it!" when pouring the molten metal.
>
> 250 years ago, William Blake penned his famous poem "Jerusalem" in which he immortalized the legend that Jesus came as a boy to England accompanying His uncle, Joseph of Arimathea.

JERUSALEM

And did those feet in ancient time,
Walk upon England's mountains green:
And was the Holy Lamb of God,
In England's pleasant pastures seen!
And did the Countenance Divine,
Shine forth upon our clouded hills?
And was Jerusalem builded here,
Among those dark Satanic Mills?
Bring me my Bow of burning gold:
Bring me my Arrows of desire:
Bring me my Spear! O clouds unfold:
Bring me my Chariots of fire:
I will not cease from Mental Fight,
Nor shall my Sword sleep in my hand:
Till we have built Jerusalem,
In England's green and pleasant Land.

England's holy legend that Christ visited England has been believed for hundreds of years. Blake believed it and was not making it up or simply alluding to an event he heard about. "Jerusalem" was set to music and millions sing the words as part of England's alternative national anthem, possibly without giving any thought to the holy legend. When the popular hymn was chosen for the wedding of Prince William and Kate Middleton, Britons joined in song with the immortal words: "And did those feet in ancient time, Walk upon England's mountains green."

So where did this amazing legend come from?

Several historical documents indicate Joseph of Arimathea founded the first Christian Church in Glastonbury. These records also indicate Joseph took Jesus with him on his journeys to Glastonbury and to a place known as Avalon, the same Avalon of King Arthur's legend.

Dobson writes: "As a boy, Jesus was brought for a visit by Joseph of Arimathea on one of his voyages. Later as a young man He returned and settled at Glastonbury for quiet study, prayer, and meditation. Here, He erected for Himself a small house of mud and wattle."

Thomas paused again. It was fortunate they would be spending time in Glastonbury. While Thomas was familiar with Druid ways and philosophy, he also believed there is no better way to learn than being on the ground where the story took place. Thomas picked up the Dobson piece and read further.

> In a 595 CE letter to Pope Gregory, St. Augustine states there was a church in Glastonbury "constructed by no human art, but divinely constructed (or by the hands of Christ Himself), for the salvation of His people."

Thomas asked himself: *Is St. Augustine saying a young Jesus built a church with His own hands? Is it possible Jesus built such a church?* Throw out any consideration of "divine" participation or even where such a church may have been built and the answer must be yes, it is possible. Jesus' earthly father was a tecton. Although cut short by His father's death, Jesus nonetheless spent some time learning from his father; lessons learned at a young age, combined with the trustworthy help of the miners who were in the employ of His uncle. Yes, they were miners and smelters, but that could only mean they were skilled at working with their hands.

Yes, Jesus could have, with the help of others, built a church as St. Augustine states. That there is no church still standing is not the point. The point is St. Augustine believed Jesus Christ was in Britain and built such a church in Glastonbury. Taking the point to its next logical conclusion is to answer the question, "When did Jesus build this church?" The only answer can be, Jesus built it before He began His public life in Jerusalem. Thomas believed he uncovered one more piece of evidence to support the contention Jesus spent much of His formative years in England.

Thomas referred back to a short book, *The Traditions of Glastonbury,* written by E. Raymond Capt. Referencing Capt, Thomas added:

> Old Cornish mining maps show two interesting names. "Corpus Christi" (Body of Christ), and "Wheel of Jesus" (wheel is a Cornish name for mine). Capt tells a story about the Mendips' mining area. The Mendips are the high hills around Glastonbury. Capt states the "traditions among the hill folk of Somerset [Glastonbury] note that Joseph of Arimathea, after first seeking tin from the Scillies (islands) and Cornwall, came to the Mendips and was accompanied on several occasions by the boy Jesus. At the parish church in the small town of Priddy, on top of the Mendips, they have an old saying: "As sure as our Lord came to Priddy."

Cardinal Baronius, a Vatican church librarian and historian noted for his meticulous records, quotes a Vatican manuscript dated 35 CE which reports the Jews arrested Joseph of Arimathea, Lazarus, Jesus' mother Mary, Martha, and two other followers of Christ, put them into a boat and set them adrift in the Mediterranean. Without oars or sails, they drifted about until they finally reached France and made their way over land to Britain.

Several historians of those times, such as St. Gildas and William of Malmesbury record that King Arviragus granted a large area at Glastonbury to Joseph of Arimathea, to be held forever, free from all taxes, as a site for a church. This is not just legend. It is fact, based on one of the greatest official records of all British history.

In the year 1066 CE, William the Conqueror had a survey made of all the lands of the kingdom, including what taxes each paid. This record, called the "Domesday Booke," was completed in 1086 CE. It contains this record: "The great Monastery of Glastonbury, called The Secret of the Lord, is set on land which has never paid tax." This record names the early church "Domus Dei" or "The Home of God" and "The Secret of the Lord."

According to Capt, well-substantiated ancient records tell of the death and burial of Joseph of Arimathea at Glastonbury. The epitaph on his tombstone read, "I came to the Britons after I buried Christ. I taught. I rest."

Not only ancient legends and ancient historical records, but also the official acts and records of kings of the Middle Ages, have recognized the close connection of Joseph of Arimathea with Cornwall and Glastonbury. All of these lend strong support to the ancient legend Jesus Christ spent many of those 19 years of His life in and around Glastonbury.

Thomas finished his review. He was pleased with the first draft, but he also realized there were questions left unanswered. Thomas sensed the conclusion had not yet been played out and, therefore, could not yet be written. He decided to wait on writing the conclusion until he had a chance to visit Glastonbury and see some of the legendary sites firsthand. He also wanted to give Matthew and James an opportunity to add their scholarship to the essay. With Matthew and James sharing authorship, the credibility of the article would be significantly strengthened. Thomas felt he and his friends were living the story he was writing; the secrets would be revealed and the conclusion would be found on this journey.

It was quiet in the cabin. Almost all reading lights were out and Thomas was ready to grab some sleep. Robin arrived almost on cue for it was two minutes to midnight, DC time. She handed Thomas a card that included her address in Bath, both her landline and cell phone numbers, along with her email address. As she handed him the card, he handed her his watch. She stood and listened as the watch chimed twelve. Robin returned his watch and picked up the empty glasses. "Thomas, try to get some sleep."

"I think I will."

Robin left. Thomas looked out his window at the darkness and closed his eyes.

Chapter IV

Feed my lambs

Wednesday, January 5 – on board British Air to London

Thomas woke to the warm sun shining through his window. He blinked hard and rubbed his face insuring he was fully awake. Matthew was not in his seat. Presumably he had gone to the lavatory to freshen up. Thomas reached for the water bottle in the seat compartment to erase his dry mouth as Matthew returned to his seat across the aisle.

"Good morning Thomas. The lavatory is available if you need it."

"Thanks and good morning to you too. It looks like you got a fair amount of sleep last night," replied Thomas.

"I slept well, except for a few times when you and your girlfriend woke me with your talk. You better splash a little water on your face before she arrives."

"Cute, Matthew, very cute."

Thomas unbuckled his seat belt, rose and dusted himself off. He picked up the complimentary toiletry bag given to first class passengers and went to the forward lavatory. One of the advantages of flying first class is the relatively spacious restroom—a room where you can turn around without having to hold your arms close to your body. Thomas washed up, brushed his teeth and returned to his seat just as Robin arrived to take their breakfast orders.

"Good morning gentlemen. I hope you both got some rest," said Robin. She looked as fresh as she did several hours before, while Matthew and Thomas were feeling rather rumpled.

"I'm here to take your breakfast order. We have warm oatmeal, cold cereal or a bacon and egg omelet," offered Robin.

"I'll order for both of us," joked Thomas. "My friend Matthew is a rabbi so he will have the warm oatmeal and I'll have the bacon and egg omelet."

"I have the feeling you two know each other fairly well," said Robin. "We'll be landing in about an hour. I'll get your breakfast right away." This was a busy hour for Robin and she had little time to visit. She returned quickly with their orders and moved on to the other passengers.

Matthew and Thomas conversed lightly over breakfast and when they finished they began to gather up and pack away the papers and laptops they had taken out the evening before. Thomas had dozed off while reading and was surprised to see all his files neatly stacked on the seat next to him. "Matt, did you straighten away my files last night or this morning?"

"Not I sir. It must have been your girlfriend."

As the passengers began to prepare for landing, Robin returned to tell both men she enjoyed visiting with them and it was passengers like them that made her work enjoyable.

"Don't lose my address," she said to Thomas. "I hope I see you both again during your stay in my country. Do you two have business cards?"

Matthew and Thomas each handed a card to Robin.

She looked at the cards. "You're both professors. How long have you known each other?"

"Since childhood," responded Matthew. The fasten seatbelt light went on and the captain announced their approach into Heathrow.

"I must go," said Robin. "Please make sure your seat belts are buckled." And she was off to check on the other passengers.

"That is a beautiful woman," remarked Thomas.

"I wondered how long it would take until you said something like that," laughed Matthew.

They heard the landing gear locking into place, and moments later they were on the ground. The plane pulled up to the gate, they gathered their belongings and made their way to the door.

Robin was there saying goodbye to the passengers as they disembarked. "Goodbye Rabbi Halprin, it was nice to have met you." She looked at Thomas. "Goodbye Father, call me." It sounded almost like a plea.

"Yes. Yes I will," said Thomas.

HEATHROW AIRPORT

James was sitting in the lounge opposite the international arrivals area at Heathrow as the British Air jet taxied to the gate. Once Thomas and Matthew made it through customs, three old friends would be reunited. James was trying to recall when he had last seen his two best friends. *Time just keeps slipping away,* he thought, remembering the last time all three were together was a little more than two years ago at an archeological seminar in New York. That reunion was too brief—just a day and a half. Between professional demands and papers to present, there was hardly any opportunity to share war stories. This time would be different. There was much to do, but there would be time to reconnect.

He saw Thomas and Matthew emerge from customs. Matthew was alternately sneezing and coughing into his handkerchief and Thomas looked like he hadn't slept. *They're looking weary and older*, he thought. As they came together, they shared the ritual hugs and handshakes.

Thomas sized up James: “Jimmy, you’re looking a little weary and a little older.” Jimmy laughed. They were all a little older and hopefully wiser. Jimmy displayed signs of graying in his mustache and goatee and Matthew’s hair was beginning to thin on top. But the lines on Thomas’s face seemed to enhance his rugged good looks and he still had an impish twinkle that would elicit return smiles from others. Thomas could work a room better than most and he had a way about him which made strangers feel comfortable in his presence.

“You two must be tired. Let’s get you to the hotel so you can get cleaned up and catch a nap. Later we’ll have dinner and get caught up. We’re only going to be in London for one night, so if there’s anything you want to do or see, let me know,” suggested James.

“Tommie and I got some rest on the flight. Thank you for the upgrade. The older we get the more we appreciate comfort.” Matthew, still sneezing, answered a question that wasn’t asked. “Allergies; happens every time I travel. There’s really nothing in London I want to see, except to catch a glimpse of The Doorway’s Doomsday Clock.”

“Oh, you’ll see it all right. The damn thing is right next to our hotel. Tomorrow we’ll be in Glastonbury where The Doorway’s headquartered. I’ll tell you this, those Doorway people are good businessmen. They have a new toy on the market and it’s selling like crazy,” said James.

“What’s the new toy?” asked Thomas.

“It’s a miniature replica of the Doomsday Clock which is being marketed as an office desk accessory, but clearly their intent is to increase awareness in The Doorway. The mechanism that powers the replica is supposed to be synchronized with the big clock maintaining the exact same countdown. They even guarantee the battery powering the clock will last until the big moment and won’t need charging. You can buy one for £60 or about $100 and you don’t even need to join The Doorway. Of course, if you join The Doorway as a Life Member, you get the Rolex version. It does the same thing, but has more jewels and is guaranteed to be accurate. The Timex version is also supposed to be accurate, but over the next few years, it could be off by a second or two.”

Thomas joked, “Wouldn’t that be a shame to have the world end and you still have two seconds left on your clock? Does it come with a money back guarantee?”

“Good question. I have no idea what The Doorway bosses plan to do if the world doesn’t come to an end. I’m guessing some of them will slip through the Portal and get out of town while everyone’s watching the clock.”

“Why is The Doorway headquartered in Glastonbury? Wouldn’t London be more convenient?” Matthew questioned.

“You’re going to find out tomorrow,” answered James. “Glastonbury is full of myth and legend, and the New Agers have flocked there like sheep.

They feel the vibrations. Glastonbury may be the cradle of Christianity in England, but it was also the center of worship for the Druids three thousand years ago. The whole area is magical. Stonehenge is not far away, less than 50 miles. And, whether hoax or not, the area is crop circle headquarters. So, it's a comfortable fit for The Doorway."

James drove Thomas and Matthew to the Edwardian Heathrow Hotel just a few miles from the airport. It was a little before 11 a.m. London time.

"I've arranged for an early check-in for you two. This is actually a nice, quiet hotel, even though it's so close to Heathrow. Why don't you two get refreshed and take a nap? I have an errand to run, and I'll be back around four. We'll have dinner and I'll bring you up to speed on what we'll be doing," James dropped his friends off and excused himself.

As Thomas and Matthew checked into their rooms, James drove away to his appointment with Rowland Hawkes, one of the more knowledgeable, and more expensive, English solicitors specializing in property and estate law. They were meeting to finalize the purchase of the home and contents of Robert Christian Thompson of Glastonbury, England. The Thompson home was over 400 years old and had been in the Thompson family from the beginning, having been passed on from generation to generation. However, Robert was the last of the family line and he had grown increasingly concerned about what might happen to the home and its contents when he was to die. The sale was a somewhat tricky transaction. The English government had instituted new procedures and new taxes on the sale of property.

The purchase was made more complicated because the sale of the estate would be paid in cash by a foreigner, and was to also include all the home's contents. The English government established a goal to have all homes registered, and if a home was not yet registered, it was to be done and the fee paid whenever the ownership changed hands. Solicitor Hawkes managed to negotiate all the government requirements and forms.

Heather Bean, Robert's solicitor in Glastonbury, certified the value of the contents to be £1,275,000, which was more than the price of the home itself. Robert had several valuable paintings, antiques and a few first edition books. Solicitor Bean's certification included the wording, "...all contents identified in the official survey as well as other items as may be present within the domicile and not listed on the survey." This was standard wording as a catchall, meaning everything in the home whether on the list or not. The price for the home was £1 million and with the contents, the total price was £2,275,000.

All the paperwork was in order and the filing was now complete. For the tidy sum of £2,275,000, plus 4% government property sales assessment and registration, and all the fees for solicitors Hawkes and Bean, James completed the purchase of the Thompson estate and its contents. The total cost of £2,450,000 or approximately $4 million, was no small amount of money for a university professor, but thanks to Great-grandfather Christopoulos, James was able to afford the purchase. The contents were most likely worth even more than the amount which Solicitor Bean certified, but it was important to Robert that the house with its contents be paid in full. Robert Thompson and James both agreed they did not want any bureaucratic hassle with which a lien on the house might bring. They also wanted the price to be high enough to not draw undue government attention to the sale.

For Robert Thompson, insuring the contents of the home were transferred with the sale was essential. Neither James nor Robert placed any significance on the amount of the transaction. For James, it represented the first time for him to use any significant amount of his inheritance. And while he was now a property owner, he really didn't feel any different. For Robert, the money meant little, for he didn't expect he would be alive much longer. What it did do was make Robert a potential philanthropist. With his other holdings, Robert's personal worth was now valued at approximately £4 million. Now he needed to decide where he would leave his money.

Edwardian Heathrow Hotel

James arrived back at the hotel around 3:30 p.m. Thomas and Matthew were in the lounge just off the lobby having a cup of tea. He spotted his two friends, who now looked refreshed and alert, and joined their table.

"Jimmy, you are positively beaming. Don't tell us you've fallen in love again?" asked Matthew.

"Well, maybe—but that has nothing to do with the moment. Right now I am pleased to introduce myself to you as a brand new English land baron."

Thomas responded, "You know Jimmy, you truly are an enigma. Maybe it's time for you to tell us the whole story. I know there has to be a whole lot more to tell which is not in the Joseph of Arimathea report you sent to us. By the way, you don't by chance happen to know a priest named Frederick Fulgrum, do you?"

"Funny you should ask. A couple of weeks ago, just before Christmas, I got a call at my London flat from a man who introduced himself as Father Fulgrum. He said he was friend of yours from the seminary and he just wanted to introduce himself. We got together to talk. He acted like he was available and wanting to help me with my research, saying something about his job with the Vatican where I got the impression he's sort of a gatekeeper to Jesus.

"He wanted to know how my search for the Holy Grail was progressing and asked in a way which implied my search was widely known. He wanted me to know I could contact him directly if I had any questions about how to portray Jesus, if my research findings took me in that direction. Strange fellow, I felt like he was on a fishing expedition. You two weren't actually friends in the seminary, were you?" asked James.

"No, far from it, but he seems to have developed a habit of telling people we are friends, as if that's going to open doors for him. I don't know what he's up to, but I sense he knows more than he's letting on. What does he know about your research?"

James moved a little closer and spoke in a hushed tone, causing Thomas and Matthew to lean in to hear more clearly. "I don't know what he knows. Everything in my report was completely accurate; but Tommie, you're right it's not complete. There's so much more I need to tell you, but I just didn't want to run the risk of the report falling into the wrong hands. Maybe Fulgrum is the wrong hands I was unknowingly thinking of."

"Fulgrum is trouble, and most definitely the wrong hands," responded Thomas.

James began to tell all, "Guys, I have been convinced for some time Joseph of Arimathea is the key to locating the Holy Grail, but he's also the key to an artifact which is much more important. In the non-canonical Gospel of Nicodemus, I learned St. Phillip sent Joseph of Arimathea to Great Britain to carry the Lord's message to the British Isles. Jesus entrusted what I believe to be the Holy Grail to Joseph when he was held captive by members of the Sanhedrin. But equally as important as the Grail are the instructions Jesus gave to Joseph. I'm confident the Grail never left Joseph's side and he brought the Grail with him to England. The Grail is not a cup or a chalice as has been popularly believed—it is something much more significant."

"What is it?" asked Matthew.

James answered, "Let me tell you a story which I hope explains what I mean. Joseph of Arimathea was approximately sixty when Jesus was crucified and roughly 63 or 64 when St. Phillip sent him to Great Britain. He was the perfect choice to start the Christian Church in Great Britain, because in his earlier merchant days he frequented the British Isles many times and was known and respected by the Celts as an honest man. During that time he found favor with Britain's King Arviragus and was given land at Glastonbury to build the first Christian Church in Great Britain. He married a Scottish Celtic woman and, at age 65, fathered a child, a girl named Josa. He stayed in Britain and continued to minister to the people until he died in his nineties."

James reached into his briefcase and pulled out a photograph of a stained glass window from St. John the Baptist Church in Glastonbury. The photo portrayed a saintly Joseph of Arimathea bearing a halo. "Take a close look.

In his right hand he is holding a staff. Cradled in his left hand are two cruets legend says contained the blood and sweat of Jesus. Those two cruets are what I seek."

The expressions of Thomas and Matthew showed confusion, not disbelief. They had just been told something they had not heard before and each was processing the information. James recognized their expressions, because he had the same reaction when he came to grips with this new information.

"Let me tell you more," continued James. "After Joseph claimed the body of Jesus, he and Nicodemus took the body to the tomb and washed it, anointed it with precious oils and wrapped it in clean linen. As he washed the body of the Christ, Joseph filled a small bowl or an earthen jar with the blood and sweat of Jesus. The hour was late and they had to hurry to finish their work before the Sabbath. Joseph and Nicodemus left the tomb and rolled the stone in front. In their hurry, they left behind the jar containing the blood and sweat of the Christ.

"Two days later, when Jesus had risen, he visited Joseph who was imprisoned in a guarded house. You may recall that was in my report. What I didn't tell you was when Jesus visited Joseph, he gave Joseph the jar holding His blood and sweat. Jesus entrusted the container to Joseph and instructed him to separate the blood from the sweat and to save each in separate cruets. Joseph obeyed the Lord and brought those two cruets with him to England.

"Over the past two years, I've visited Glastonbury several times to see for myself what I had read about or been told. The town is different now than it was two thousand years ago. Back then Glastonbury was an island in a marshy area, but the marsh has since dried up. Today Glastonbury has become a Mecca for young people who are into mysticism. They are there ostensibly searching for a way. Not 'The Way' offered up by Jesus—that would be too traditional. There are, in essence, two Glastonbury's, one for the young and the other for the gray hairs who know what they believe and are secure in their faith. The problem is time is not on the side of the gray hairs. I have attended Sunday services at St. John the Baptist Anglican Church and there were fewer than 100 attendees, more than half senior in years. The same is true at the smaller St. Mary's Roman Catholic Church.

"The legends of Joseph of Arimathea and the boy Jesus coming to Glastonbury 2,000 years ago are regarded by many residents of Glastonbury as true, by others as no more than legend. Sadly, there are many who haven't a clue about Joseph or Jesus."

Thomas and Matthew remained quiet. "I've spent quite a bit of time in and around Glastonbury, so the locals are getting used to me. About seven or eight months ago I was in a pub in the small town of Priddy, a few miles from

Glastonbury—a place called The New Inn. I hang out there a bit, but that's another story. I got into a conversation with a couple of the boys over a pint or two of Guinness. I bought—it's the price for information. They told me about an old man they referred to as the Old Scot. They said he knew more about the traditions and legends of Glastonbury than anyone, and suggested I pay him a visit. Margo gave me his address and directions."

"Margo? Who's Margo?" asked Matthew.

"Margo Webster, the manager of The New Inn. Lovely woman, quite attractive. She's mostly Irish and has a lovely Irish brogue. She has been most helpful."

"Could this be your new interest?" quizzed Thomas.

"I will admit I enjoy her company, but back to the story."

Thomas and Matthew were grinning.

"Okay, I know what you're thinking. I simply enjoy her company," James said grinning.

"Well, apparently Margo knows the old Scot quite well. His name is Robert Thompson. In fact, it's his home I just bought, but I'll get to that later. Robert is now in his 90's and about ten years ago he stopped his B&B business. Margo used to manage the Thompson B&B back then and now she has taken over management of The New Inn. She and Robert remain friends.

"Margo shared a lot with me about Robert and the time she worked for him. He is quite a character. She told me Robert would entertain guests in the evening having them all come together in the parlor. He would wear his kilts and regale the guests with stories about Scotland, World War I and World War II. She said she often heard roars of laughter as Robert would tell a story. It wasn't just the story that was funny, but the telling of the story as only Robert could.

"Anyway, I confided somewhat in Margo as to what I was doing and what I was searching for. She wanted to know if she could help by way of an introduction to Robert. I readily accepted and she phoned to set up an opportunity for me to meet him.

"The next day, I paid him a visit. The house is a large two-story, which is much more than enough for one person. I could see how it would have been a lovely upscale B&B. The exterior is well maintained with a lovely parade of flowers on both sides of a serpentine walkway. It's painted in a mild pastel yellow, making it stand out against the gray stone, which is representative of many homes in the area.

"When I arrived I knocked on the door and heard someone moving about. As I stood there, waiting for the door to be opened, I thought it interesting that a passage from Mark popped into my head: 'seek and ye shall find, ask and it will be given unto to you, knock and the door shall be opened unto you.'

"Finally the door was opened and standing there was a tall, handsome older gentleman—somewhat slowed by age, but still a magnificent figure of a man. He had a welcoming smile, a friendly countenance indeed. He said, 'Welcome, you must be Dr. Christopoulos; please come in.' His voice was low and melodious, with just the slight waver of an older man. He led me to his parlor where a woman greeted me, probably in her early fifties, a little plump but pleasant and nondescript, the kind of person who can easily go unnoticed.

"Robert's tone in his introduction of Estelle was most courteous as if to say, while Estelle may be common, she is nonetheless an important human being. He said, 'Dr. Christopoulos, this is Estelle Higgins who keeps both the house and me in working order. You will see her and her husband Henry often. Henry keeps the outside and Estelle keeps the inside.' I thought the comment to be a bit odd. I just met Robert and already he was telling me I would see Estelle and Henry often.

"Then he put his hand to his mouth in a gesture of forgetfulness and said. 'Please excuse me; I didn't introduce myself, I am Robert Thompson.' He then pointed to another room, his library, and a large dark brown leather chair for me to sit on. Estelle excused herself only to return in a few minutes pushing a teacart with two cups, a pot of tea, sugar and cream and a plate of scones. Robert asked if I would care to join him and I accepted."

"A plate of scones sounds like a great idea," interjected a hungry Matthew.

James, seeming not to hear Matthew's request for food, took a sip of tea and leaned back in his chair. "Oh, excuse me. Are you hungry? I apologize for this rather long monologue, but there is so much you need to know and short of writing all this down, I can't think of any other way to bring you two up to speed."

James continued, "This may be a good time to pause. Let's have dinner and then I will continue to tell you more about Robert and my plan for the days ahead."

The dinner conversation was off the subject of Robert and was pleasant banter about what's going on in their private lives. After dinner, the three retired to the hotel parlor. There was no one else around and James was able to speak less guardedly.

"Let me pick up where I left off," said James. "Robert and I were sitting in his library having tea and scones. I explained who I was and that for the past two years I'd been researching Glastonbury. I told him of my conversation with some of the boys and Margo at The New Inn and they told me Robert knew everything about Glastonbury and the surrounding area. I stayed away from specifics, just asking generally about Glastonbury and Robert himself. I learned he was 91 and was born in Scotland. Long ago, his friends, all of whom have now passed, called him 'Bobby the Scot.' After we finished our tea in the parlor, he offered to give me a tour.

"I want to tell you about his house. The interior of Robert's house is simply beautiful, very clean with highly polished dark wood; mementos of his past are everywhere. All around were framed photos of Robert in his RAF, Royal Air Force, uniform with his comrades. His favorite room is his library. It's a fairly large room with a functioning fireplace where a fire is kept going most of the time. I don't know if you are aware, but the English don't have roaring fires like people do in the States. Rather, their fires are kept low. Often you will see a peat brick burning slowly keeping the low fire going for hours, mostly just to take the chill out of a room. Peat has an odor that stays with you for a while. It smells a little like a combination of wet wood and charcoal. He had classical music, mostly Beethoven and Mozart, playing softly, just audible enough to add to the ambiance."

The mention of a peat fire and choice of music triggered Thomas's memory of his grandfather.

James continued, "Opposite the library's entry is one large wall-to-wall bookcase. Several of the books are quite old and some are possibly first editions. Robert has books on science, history, linguistics, religion, and World War I and II. Robert is a fan of Sir Arthur Conan Doyle. He told me he has all 56 Sherlock Holmes short stories and Conan Doyle's four full-length novels. Doyle, like Robert, was a Scot, and also a renaissance man, a physician and a writer."

"Fascinating, I don't know if you know this, but I'm a Sherlock Holmes fan. I would love to see his collection," interjected Thomas.

James acknowledged Thomas's comment and continued his description. "The other walls of Robert's library contain a collection of paintings from primarily British artists. Robert is fond of fox-and-hounds themes as well as paintings of dogs and horses. There are tables and cases displaying souvenirs and artifacts, swords, old rifles and pistols, bullets of different caliber, military insignias and badges of rank. There is a special display case in a different room, his study, which I will not even attempt to describe, except to say his private study is one hundred percent filled with things that bring Robert joy. In many respects, Robert's home is like a museum.

"We sat in his library and continued our conversation. We talked for over three hours on my first visit and because I'd arrived in the afternoon, I could tell Robert was tiring. I suggested I should go so he might get some rest and he agreed, but asked if I would return so we could visit some more. I said I would and that there were many things about Glastonbury I wanted to know. He suggested when I came back, I might want to spend some time in his library. He surprised me when he said, 'what you seek may be found among my books.' It was a strange comment since I hadn't told him what it was I was seeking or that I was seeking anything at all. He just seemed to be able to read my thoughts.

"I left him, went back to my flat in London and began compiling my notes on what I'd learned about Glastonbury. I was having an unusually difficult time focusing my attention on the task at hand. I kept thinking about Robert and what a pleasant diversion it was to visit with him. Everything about Robert had a calming effect on me. His home was quiet and comfortable and seemed oddly familiar—as though I'd been there before. The time in his library in particular delighted my senses. There was the comfortable ticking of his large grandfather clock, the aroma of fresh flowers and taste of sweet herbal tea, the softness of the gently worn leather chairs, and the visual delight of the different colors and sizes of books that filled his bookcase. I felt at home.

"The following week I was back in Glastonbury and decided to pay Robert another visit. He was pleased to see me but wondered why I didn't return the next day. Apparently he brought out several things to show me but then I didn't return. There was almost a sense of urgency about him as though there were things he wanted to tell me and his time was short. He almost seemed hurt. I explained I had to focus on my research and didn't have time to visit, which was a lame excuse. I felt like I was talking to my father and coming up with reasons for why I didn't visit him more often. Worse, it wasn't true. I was looking forward to seeing him."

James apologized for rambling on. Thomas told him not to worry about it.

James picked up where he left off. "We sat in his library. He looked straight at me. He has a look, not a stare, which is penetrating but non-intimidating. He asked again if he could help me find what I was seeking. As before, I wondered how he knew I was a seeker. Maybe Margo told him, but then again maybe she didn't. Was Robert prescient? I wondered if he knew what I was searching for?

"I decided to unload my mind. Keep in mind this was only the second time Robert and I talked with each other. I told him about who I was and what I'd been searching and researching for my whole adult life. He nodded as though he understood everything I told him. I shared the stories about Joseph and Nicodemus attending to the body of Christ, about Joseph's imprisonment and his visit from Jesus and the container holding the sweat and blood of Jesus. I revealed my supposition that Jesus as a boy came to Britain with Joseph of Arimathea. I even told him of my belief that after the Lord ascended into heaven, Joseph was sent to Britain to start the first Christian Church. I must have rambled on for close to a half hour telling him what I knew about the cruets and showing him the photo of Joseph of Arimathea from the stained glass window of St. John's Church. I then finally revealed to him I was searching for the two cruets.

"I felt like a Catholic school boy going to confession and unburdening my soul to a kindly old priest. He looked right at me, past my eyes and into my soul and asked me why I wanted the cruets and what I would do with them if they were in my possession.

"What would I do with the cruets? It was a question that I was not prepared to answer. My whole life was always in the pursuit and I never really thought about what I would do with the cruets if and when I actually had them. I feebly explained I wasn't interested in fame or fortune—I really had enough of both. I described my scholarly work and my inheritance. I told him what you, Tommie, often said about the importance of finding something tangible, something real that was proof of Jesus being here on earth.

"Robert put down his tea and said, and I recall it as if it were yesterday: 'What you seek,' he said, 'is within your reach. But know this, finding those sacred relics will not provide you with the closure you so badly want. Only when you come to realize the responsibility to protect those sacred relics, will you truly understand their awesome value and purpose.'"

"There was a long pause and then he said, 'Your motives are honorable, but incomplete. Why is it so important to prove Jesus Christ was actually here in the flesh? Will it change the world? No, my young friend, it will not. Is it not enough for you to believe without seeing, or are you like the doubting apostle Thomas, who needed to put his finger into the Lord's hand wounds and his hand in the Lord's side in order to believe?'"

James took in a breath and held it. He exhaled saying, "What he said next cut to the quick. He told me he has never understood why some people who have the desire to believe and follow Jesus are the same people who require proof Jesus existed. He said many people believe and follow and are content to believe without seeing. He said these are people of great faith, but that I am not one of them. He told me I am not content to be a follower, and if I can't lead, then at a minimum I want to walk alongside God as an equal. He said I want to know God, not just in my heart; I want to know God in my head. Then he said, and I doubt I will ever forget his words, 'James, you want to know God on an intellectual level and that, my young friend, may be the highest form of arrogance. I don't mean that as an insult, but rather as a challenge. You may be strong enough to look the Devil in the face, but you are not meek enough, not humble enough to look God in the face.'"

James paused. "I was silent. This man who I had been with for only a few hours knew me better than my own mother and father."

Thomas dropped his gaze, rose and walked to the window. Matthew and James waited as Thomas stood looking out, but really not looking at anything. He was drinking in everything James said and he knew all too well what the old man said applied to him as well. Thomas returned to his friends. "I would like very much to meet this man."

"Oh, you will," said James, "I have told him about the two of you and how we three grew up together. I regaled him with stories about our childhood and our expeditions as kids with great imaginations. I even told him the story about how we found that old Civil War rifle and how we donated it to the museum. He seemed to be impressed, just like our fathers were back then. I explained who both of you are today and why I asked for your help. He very much wants to meet both of you and he even asked if he might be alone with you, Tommie, for a short while. Tommie, Robert is a Catholic who has lived the life of an Anglican and has not gone to Catholic Mass for some time. I think he wants you to hear his confession.

"Interestingly, Robert seems to know more about both of you than what I have told him. Tommie, Robert has read your article in *The Christian Scholar* on the Second Coming. I saw a copy on a table in his library. I hadn't even seen it before, much less read it—so much for how current I am. And Matt, in his library are copies of your books, *Interpretations of the Dead Sea Scrolls* and *Unveiling the Nag Hammadi Codices.* Something is afoot here, and I can't explain it. He knows more about the three of us than can be left to coincidence.

"You know guys, I feel like I've been bouncing all around with my story, so let me sum up what I'm sure of, and then together we hopefully will be able to fill in some of the gaps."

James began building the summation. "We know when Jesus died on the cross, He was taken down by His Uncle Joseph and fellow secret believer Nicodemus and carried to the tomb. They prepared the body and then left the tomb. The Jews were angry with Joseph and they locked him in a house and posted a guard. Jesus appeared to Joseph and took him to his own home in Arimathea. Jesus gave Joseph the bowl containing His blood and sweat—the blood and sweat Joseph and Nicodemus washed off His body and left behind in the tomb. He instructed Joseph to separate the sweat and blood and put them in separate cruets. After Jesus' ascension, Joseph was sent to begin the Christian Church in Britain. He married, had a daughter, died, and was buried in Glastonbury.

"You must let me tell you a little more," said James. "Where does Robert fit in this story? Are you ready for this? Robert is a descendant of Joseph of Arimathea. Remember I told you Joseph had a daughter named Josa. Robert has the genealogy of his family which stretches all the way back to Josa. Not only that, Robert showed me his family Bible with his genealogy chart, he's also related to the Scottish hero, William Wallace and to Arthur of Avalon. Yes, Robert is related to Joseph of Arimathea, King Arthur and William Wallace. While this is important, just know there are certain to be many more who claim a lineage to Joseph, Arthur and/or Wallace. Remember this is 2,000 years of history. England is littered with people who are related to saints, kings and heroes."

James stopped for a moment, "I know I've been rambling on and on, but if you can stand a little more, let me tell you a couple more important facts."

"Please continue," said Thomas.

James picked up where he left off. "Robert is very ceremonial and traditional—some of which may have to do with his RAF days. He's had much tragedy in his life. Robert is the last of his family. He was born in 1920 and joined the Royal Air Force at age 19 at the start of World War II. Before he left for the war, he married his childhood sweetheart, a woman named Jean, and they had a baby girl the following year. While Robert was away, his wife and daughter were killed in May of 1941 in the Blitzkrieg bombing of London. He had an older brother who was always sickly and frail. His brother also died during the war, but not directly from the bombing. Robert did not remarry. Later when Robert was in his 40's, his mother died. I don't know the cause. His father depended on his wife and simply couldn't live without her. He passed some four months later. According to Robert, the doctors said his father simply quit living when his wife died.

"All that remained of the Thompson Family were Robert and his Uncle Mason. Robert was close to his uncle and they often just talked and shared war stories. Uncle Mace was in World War I. His fondest story and the one Robert never grew tired of hearing was the famous Christmas Truce of 1914. Uncle Mace was there at Frelinghien, France. He was an 18-year-old soldier serving with the Black Watch, the 5th Battalion of the British Army, when soldiers from both sides stopped fighting on Christmas Day, 1914. It was a day of peace spontaneously begun when some British soldiers shouted Merry Christmas to the German soldiers hunkered down in a trench a hundred yards away. The Germans began singing *Stille Nacht* and the British responded by singing *Silent Night.* Uncle Mace loved to tell how finally a young German soldier climbed out of his trench holding a small fir tree with handmade ornaments. He shouted in broken English: 'Merry Christmas. We no shoot. You no shoot.'

"The British and the Germans came out of their trenches and laid down their weapons. They exchanged gifts such as the insignias they tore from their uniforms. The Germans rolled out some beer. The British had a soccer ball and they played soccer for hours, keeping but then not really keeping score. They shared pictures from home, exchanged cigarettes, drank beer, sang and tried their best to talk to each other. As night fell they went back to their own trenches. The truce lasted only a short while. The leaders ordered the resumption of fighting. What was important though was the truce was started not by presidents and prime ministers, but by the soldiers themselves—the most honorable and most fitting way a war should end. Not so unlike how two boys might end a fight between them.

"Uncle Mace told Robert that after the soldier's truce he was never the same. He'd seen the faces of the enemy, looked into their eyes and shared with them the same desire to go home. Uncle Mace never took aim at an enemy again. Yes, he fired his weapon only to be counted along with the others, but many of them also no longer aimed. They used up and replenished their ammunition, but Uncle Mace no longer wanted to kill someone he now knew. He wasn't alone; many of those who were there on that day rejected the urgency to kill. He remained convinced the only reason he survived was the Germans, no longer strangers, didn't want to kill him either.

"Uncle Mace died in 1980 and Robert inherited the family home which had been passed down from generation to generation for over 400 years. When I left you this morning, I finalized the purchase of the Thompson home and all its contents. Robert wanted me to own the home and he wanted to make it official by selling it to me. We agreed on £1,000,000 for the home plus £1,275,000 for all the contents, which is below its value, but high enough not to draw any suspicion from the government. I finally invaded my inheritance putting the money to good use. It was an odd feeling to spend that kind of money. I never felt like I was spending it, just transferring it from one bank to another. Buying the house and contents outright and limiting the paperwork will hopefully keep the snoops away."

"There you go again, Mr. Paranoid," said Matthew.

"No, not me, not this time," answered James. "Robert wanted it done legally so the house and especially the contents did not become property of the state. As I said, he has no one else. In the seven or eight months I have known Robert, I believe I have become like family to him. In all my visits, there never was anyone else around, save Estelle and her husband Henry and occasionally Margo. None of them was in a position to acquire the house and its contents. Robert told me what is in his will. He intends to leave some of his money to St. John the Baptist Anglican Church, as well as St. Mary's Catholic Church. He also will leave a tidy sum to Estelle and Henry. She has loyally served him, cooking his meals and cleaning his house for many years. He also asked me if I would help arrange his funeral with honors. You'll understand more about the funeral with honors when you finally meet him.

"But now the house and the contents are legally mine and you need to know this was at Robert's urging. He didn't want to see the house on the market with people wandering through touching artifacts which mean more to him than any price could compensate."

James leaned forward as one does when he is about to share a secret. "I believe within that house is the clue to what I've been searching for all my life. Robert's words keep ringing in my head—what I'm seeking is within my reach. Which is why I needed you here. Not just to search for a relic, but to help me understand and meet Robert's challenge to protect the sacred relics."

Thomas added, "Maybe Robert's challenge is basically a concern about what will happen to the sacred treasures once they're revealed? Who will want to possess them and why? I share your quest to prove Jesus walked upon this earth, but I also understand the proof needs to be protected lest it fall into the wrong hands."

Thomas continued, "We need to…no…wait…I need to look inward. Why do I want to prove Jesus lived and walked on earth 2,000 years ago? Do I have a crisis of faith those sacred relics can put to rest? Do I share the arrogance of wanting to know God on an intellectual level? Do I envy the apostles? What would I have done 2,000 years ago? Would I have been content to follow Jesus, or would I have insisted to walk alongside?

"Jimmy, these are questions each of us must answer. Maybe whatever we find will put us on the road to answer those questions. Maybe this is our road to Damascus—where, like St. Paul, we experience our own personal epiphany—where we begin to understand we are no more than humble disciples. I readily admit being humble isn't a trait I easily embrace."

James responded. "Maybe if we commit here and now to do what must be done to protect and defend the knowledge those artifacts may reveal, maybe then we'll be worthy of at least holding those sacred relics. But we must also be willing to put our professional reputations in harm's way. We risk being ridiculed or pilloried. Our standing in the religious and archeological professions may be challenged, and our peers and colleagues may ostracize us. If we have the mettle to stand fast, maybe we'll have served the greater good. Hopefully we'll continue to have the support of those who love us and who believe in us. If all else fails, at the least, we'll still have each other.

"I sense what we are about to embark on could be dangerous. When Christ overturned the moneychangers' tables in the temple, he sealed His fate. Matthew, you may be in the greatest peril. You're a Jew who may be called upon to defend Jesus. You have a family to support. I have plenty of money and Thomas is a bachelor and doesn't need much. Maybe we should call you Nicodemus."

Matthew said little during James monologue. "Sometimes I wonder what it was that made us friends and why we continue our friendship. Maybe as boys it was the spirit of adventure and our willingness to suspend reality so we could continue to play the game. However, I think it was and is much more. As kids, we were taught to be honest and not tell lies. As we grew, I think our early childhood experiences helped us to understand and value truth. I am not worried what might happen. Like you two, I value truth over comfort."

James and Thomas paused and then nodded agreement.

"What say you men? Are you ready to commit?" asked James.

"Aye, Captain," said Thomas.

"Count me in," said Matthew.

"May God have mercy on fools such as us," said James.

"Robert's is expecting us around noon tomorrow. Let's get together for breakfast at eight and leave by nine. And just so you know, Robert dresses like a retired gentleman, tweeds and ties. Tommie, Robert knows you are a priest, so please wear your collar. I hope you brought it with."

"I never leave home without it."

The men retired to their rooms to prepare for the next day. Thomas brought along a lot of reading material, but wasn't sure he brought the essay on the Second Coming James had seen on Robert's desk. Thomas searched through his files thinking it might be good to review what he wrote two years ago, just in case the mysterious Robert Thompson were to challenge him on his position. Thomas had been commissioned by *The Christian Scholar* to write a fictional account of a surprise visit by Jesus Christ during Easter week, 2008.

There it was; a somewhat crumpled copy of *The Christian Scholar* in his attaché case. In the quiet of his room, Thomas pulled out the copy and straightened it out. He bought a bottle of Jameson Irish Whiskey at Heathrow and he poured a couple of shots in a tall glass and poured a second glass with an equal amount of water from the bottled water in his room. This article earned Thomas his verbal scolding from the bishop and theoretically put him on a short leash. He hadn't looked at the article for some time. Although the world was much changed from Jesus' first visit 2,000 years before, the story remained true. Such is the way with truth.

The Christian Scholar – March 2008

Publisher's Message: As we enter this Easter Season, *The Christian Scholar* has commissioned Father Thomas Ryan, S.J., Ph.D., to write an article on a fictional Second Coming of Jesus Christ. Father Ryan's message may be difficult for some readers and challenging for others. Please be aware this story is fiction and there is no intent to portray any religious, secular or political figure. We invite your reactions and will publish a representative sample in the June 2008 issue of *The Christian Scholar.*

Mysterious Aircraft Alarms Residents
Two days of intense activity result from a golden sphere appearing in the sky over New York's Central Park.

Report and analysis by Thomas Ryan
To comment, contact the publisher at The Christian Scholar

A large golden sphere mysteriously appeared in the morning hours on Thursday, March 20, 2008, over New York's Central Park. The sphere hovered approximately 100 feet over the park. The precise time it appeared is not known. Reaction to the sphere ranged from near panic to mild concern among thousands of eyewitnesses. Myrtle Wahlberg was walking her dog near Central Park at 6:30 a.m. when she looked up: "It was just there. I have no idea where it came from or when it got here. One moment there was nothing, and then all of a sudden it was there."

According to several eyewitnesses, the sphere was completely silent and didn't appear to emit any exhaust. The President of the United States ordered the Department of Defense to scramble Air Force helicopters and Marine Harrier jets. The aircraft assumed a defensive position and immediately began monitoring the sphere's activity. U.S. Army ground forces cordoned off the area, and U.S. Navy warships were positioned in the Hudson River to assist as needed. New York City Firefighters, Police and SWAT teams were also sent to the scene. 9/11 protocols were activated. Because of the deployment of U.S. Military assets, the U.S. Department of Defense was in command.

Tensions were high. Terrorist activity had been detected in the previous weeks as the United Nations was preparing to go into general session. The President considered ordering the alert status to be elevated to Red Alert. Throughout Thursday morning, the sphere continued to hover and did not demonstrate any aggressive behavior.

Government sources admitted they had no knowledge of any aircraft (domestic or foreign) resembling the sphere. The air and ground forces continued to maintain a defensive posture. At 11:45 a.m., the sphere began a slow descent and at noon, landed in Central Park. Attempts to communicate with the sphere were not successful and authorities continued to maintain a wait-and-see posture.

The United Nations General Assembly was called into emergency session. Coincidentally the Pope arrived in New York the day before to prepare for the celebration of Easter Mass on March 23 at Saint Patrick's Cathedral. The Pope participated in the emergency session as he joined the Vatican's Permanent Observer Mission Delegation. The Pope pleaded for calm and urged all not to assume the sphere was hostile.

To prevent panic and to demonstrate that appropriate government agencies were on top of the situation, the White House quickly convened a press conference. The President's Press Secretary, the Secretary of the Department of Homeland Security and New York City's Police Commissioner were available to answer questions. The assembled press found they were in uncharted territory as they scrambled to come up with questions. Because space here does not permit printing all the questions and answers, the following synopsis represents the tone and substance of the press conference.

Question: "Mr. Secretary, can you tell us what the sphere is made of and do you have any idea what's on the inside?"

Answer: "We have not yet approached the sphere, so we are not sure what the sphere is made of. It appears to be metallic with an unknown propulsion system which allows it to hover silently and move about effortlessly."

Question: "Do you have any idea where the sphere is from?"

Answer: "We simply do not know at this time. It doesn't belong to the United States or any of our allies. Its advanced state of flight is something which the scientific community is not able to immediately explain."

Question: "Is it a UFO?"

Answer: "Well technically not at this moment since the sphere is on the ground. However, we have begun to assume it is extraterrestrial. Our science experts believe it's not from Earth."

Question: "What are you going to do? Will you try to open it?"

Answer: "We're taking a 'wait-and-see' approach. We've made no assumptions whether it's friendly or not. We're preparing for either scenario. We do not want to act provocatively."

Question: "Who's in charge of developing a strategy for whatever you decide to do?"

Answer: "The sphere is on United States soil and the U.S. will take the lead in deciding what to do. Our protocol calls for the Secretary of Defense to coordinate all assets. We are, however, in contact with our allies and all nations working through the United Nations."

As the Press Secretary was about to call on another reporter, an aide came forward to the podium and handed a note to the Secretary. "One moment, please."

The Press Secretary read the note to himself and then handed it to the Homeland Security Secretary. The Press Secretary returned to the podium and addressed the assembled reporters. "Ladies and gentlemen, I have just been informed there appears to be some activity emanating from the sphere. The sphere is emitting sounds and changing colors. The sounds appear to be known classical music, which we interpret as intended to send a benign signal. We cannot assume this is a friendly act; it may be designed to confuse us. We will suspend the press conference at this time and ask you to stand by for more information."

At approximately 2 p.m., Air Force One, carrying the President, landed and he was taken directly to the United Nations to confer with the Secretary General. The Secretary of State and their close advisors were already in New York City. The Vice President had been taken to a secure location in the event the sphere was hostile.

At 3 p.m., the sphere began a slow ascent stopping at approximately 50 feet above ground. Standing where the sphere had been moments before was a man dressed in a white robe. He was approximately 5'10" with a medium build and shoulder-length soft brown hair, a medium length beard and gentle brown eyes. The man raised both arms and the crowd, which gathered, fell silent. In a clear, soft, unamplified voice the man spoke to everyone in a language, which somehow each person could understand.

With a friendly countenance He began: "I am Jesus the Nazarene. Have no fear. I have come to witness to the world today. I am a man of peace and peace I bring you. I will be among you but a short while and I would like to speak to all peoples around the world. I would welcome the opportunity to address a forum of your leaders."

There was an eerie silence. No previous experience equipped anyone to respond to such a situation. As commanders on the ground looked at one another, no one knew how to respond or what to say. There was no protocol to deal with the situation. The Mayor of New York City and the Secretary of Defense were the highest-ranking government officials on the scene. They looked at one another. Something had to be done. Someone had to speak, but who should say what, and how should one address Jesus?

The two men stepped forward. Finally, the Secretary of Defense said: "Sir, may I introduce myself." Jesus raised his hand and said, "There is no need; I know you." After a short pause, the Mayor, realizing he did not need to introduce himself said, "Sir, would you like us to arrange for you to speak to the General Assembly of the United Nations? It is the body which represents all the people of the world."

Jesus answered, "Then I would appreciate it if you would so arrange."

The Mayor, a consummate politician, began to feel somewhat more comfortable. In his mayoral role as host, he inquired if there was anything the Lord needed? The Lord declined saying the sphere would provide for all He required. Jesus made a small gesture and the sphere began a slow descent covering and absorbing Him.

The Secretary of Defense and the Mayor were quickly ushered into a meeting with the President, the Secretary of State and their senior advisors. The media was promised a briefing would be held at approximately 6 p.m. and the President would make a brief statement. Heavily armed soldiers surrounded the sphere. Jesus remained "under the protection" of the U.S Army and New York City's finest.

The "protection" functioned more as a barrier to keep people away from the sphere than to keep Jesus from freely moving about. It was rapidly becoming apparent that there was little anyone could do to stop Jesus from going wherever He wanted to go or doing whatever He wished.

The meeting of the President and his advisors began awkwardly. There was a poignant silence for no one knew what to say. The President began, "I assume just about everyone in the world is aware of what has happened and is watching to see what we do. However, I'm really not sure what we decide to do will matter, because people, we are not in control of this situation. He is," the President said as he gestured to the outside. "So now people, does anyone have anything to suggest?"

No one in the room was eager to speak, but finally one of the President's senior advisors, Jack Daly, a devout Catholic, began. "Mr. President, I suggest we approach the situation without regard to the politics of the moment. By that, I simply mean if we approach this situation with an eye toward what we may stand to gain politically, we will have missed an opportunity unlike anyone has ever experienced."

A second advisor quickly countered: "Come on Jack, everything's political. Don't be naïve. We have an opportunity to solidify our hold on our offices for many elections to come."

Another chimed in, "Myron's right. We'd be crazy to let this opportunity go."

"Jack, I appreciate your strong belief and fervor, but maybe this isn't the time or place," said the President.

The Mayor jumped in: "I'm the only local in the room and this is my city. I hope you don't intend to hog the spotlight all to yourselves."

Once those assembled began to think about the current scenario from a political perspective, the room came alive with chatter. All except Jack Daly, who withdrew from the conversation and became an observer. His silence was hardly noticed as plans fell into place.

Myron offered, "This could be a great opportunity for you, Mr. President, to portray yourself as God's trusted advisor on earth."

The President chuckled. "Well, that may be taking it a little too far—let's just suggest I am one of God's confidants. After all, even God needs someone to talk to from time to time. Good work, people. Kissinger gave Nixon China; you have given me God."

Almost everyone in the room, save one, found reason to laugh.

"What about me?" was the Mayor's almost incessant refrain.

"Well, Bernie," responded the President, "you are the Mayor and this is your city. That makes you the host. How about if you accompany Jesus in the motorcade from Central Park to the UN? You can be Jesus' personal tour guide and point out the sites."

The Mayor jumped at the opportunity. "Agreed, I'll get my people on planning the route immediately." The Mayor's political instincts kicked into high speed when he began to consider the possibility his approval numbers among Christians could rise dramatically.

"And Mr. Secretary," the President said looking at the Secretary of Defense, "would you please go back to the sphere and inform our guest about the motorcade to the UN? Let's have the Mayor pick Him up at one o'clock. We'll arrange for a 2 p.m. speech at the UN. I will introduce Him, and we'll still be able to make the evening news."

Jack Daly reinserted himself in the conversation, looking at the Secretary of Defense, he said, "You don't need to go back and share your plans with the Man. I'm sure He already knows." Jack's comment produced more laughter around the room although that was not Jack's intent. His next comment made all in the room feel ill at ease as he chastised them for their lack of reverence. There would have been no reason for anyone to feel any discomfort had they exhibited a little more respect instead of treating the event like a circus parade.

The President broke the silence. "Thank you, Jack. I'm sure no one meant any disrespect. Okay people, let's get to work."

It was 6 p.m. and the President came to the podium for the quickly established briefing. "Ladies and gentlemen, I have a brief statement to make, copies of which will be circulated to you all shortly. I will not be taking any questions at this time."

The President continued using the teleprompter to make it appear spontaneous and sincere. "As most people around the world already know, we have been visited by a man, who descended to earth in a vehicle unknown to our technology. The gentleman introduced himself as Jesus the Nazarene, and has chosen this time and place for His Second Coming. We are humbled He has chosen to come to the United States of America, an honor for a country which is the last best hope on earth."

The President was anything but humble. He was first, last, and always a politician and this was an election year. The President continued, "There is much yet to do this evening and I certainly do not want to preempt anything Jesus Christ intends to say tomorrow at the United Nations." The President felt a bit smug giving the impression he was privy to what Jesus would be saying the next day to the UN General Assembly.

"Tomorrow afternoon, New York Mayor Bernard Cohen will join Jesus in a motorcade from Central Park, where Jesus' sphere now sits, to the United Nations Headquarters. The motorcade will begin around 1 p.m. tomorrow and the Mayor's staff is hard at work establishing the parade route. That information will be made public tomorrow in the morning newspapers as well as on the Internet. We intend to have Jesus speak before the UN at 2 p.m. I expect His speech may last an hour. We have not finalized all events as of this time." Another cool hint the President was privy to what the Lord would say. "Now, if you will excuse me, my press secretary will remain to answer as many of your questions as we can at this time. Certainly all will be made known by tomorrow morning." With that the President smugly exited the podium.

Throughout the evening hours and on Friday morning, Jesus wandered among New Yorkers to listen and learn. He dressed in jeans, a flannel shirt and sandals. None of the security personnel was even aware Jesus left the sphere. He spoke to no one and no one recognized Him. He merely eavesdropped on the conversations of those around Him. Much of the conversation on the street was about the appearance of the sphere. Many were certain the government leaders would screw up Jesus' visit and make it impossible for average citizens to hear Jesus without all the political spin, which would surely take place.

The racial and cultural diversity among the residents makes New York City a microcosm of the world. Jesus moved freely through several ethnic neighborhoods listening to the people, as He was able to understand all languages and all dialects. Despite the cultural differences, one commonality among the people was the distain and disgust for the political class. Those in office were being ridiculed for doing nothing to improve living conditions in the neighborhoods while profiting off the efforts of the people.

In the home countries the new New Yorkers left behind, human rights were nonexistent. What caused these immigrants to leave was lack of freedom, disregard for basic needs, and, in some cases, brutal treatment. Life in America was an improvement over the old country, but the politicians were the same, just more sophisticated, and possibly even more sinister. High taxes, corruption, kickbacks and mounting national debt held dreams of a better life hostage, making old New Yorkers just as angry as the new New Yorkers. The "haves" ignored the "have-nots" denying hope for the young and dignity for the old and infirmed.

Jesus was not surprised at the level of anger nearly all the people demonstrated. He knew all too well the pain those in power can inflict upon the innocent. The people did what they were told to do not out of respect for those in power, but out of fear. Jesus noted to himself the anger was palpable. If the political officials did not regain the trust and respect of the people, a very real revolt could be on the horizon.

At one o'clock on Friday afternoon, March 21, Jesus, dressed in a white robe, joined Mayor Bernard Cohen in an open limo to begin the motorcade which would pass by shining towers on their way to the United Nations building. The Mayor was beaming from ear to ear as they left Central Park following a route with sidewalks overflowing with people 15 to 20 deep. With cameras rolling for use in future campaign footage, the Mayor pointed out the gleaming buildings as testimony to the goodness, which is his city as well as to his adroit leadership.

Jesus leaned over and asked the driver his name.

"Nick, sir, Nick Kostas."

"Well, Nick, would you please turn right here." Nick did as he was instructed.

The Mayor, waving to the crowd, didn't immediately notice the change in the planned route.

After a few blocks, Jesus said, "Nick, please turn left here." Nick did as the Lord asked.

The Mayor's smile changed to a look of confusion over what happened to his carefully choreographed parade route.

With a few more turn requests by Jesus, the limo drove into some of the worst, rundown, rat-infested, crack-head neighborhoods with burnt-out houses and young children playing in the streets.

It was March and there was still a chill in the air, but the children wore no coats. There were young men sitting on steps playing dice for money they could only earn by selling. And what did they sell? Stuff they lifted, drugs, their sisters. No one there was expecting a motorcade. Instead of looking up to see who was in the motorcade, most of the young men saw the police cars and just took off. There were old men drinking and talking, some playing cards. Old, beyond their years. Poverty has a way of disguising age. Rumpled clothes, wrinkled faces, and missing teeth—they had reason to run, but they no longer did.

The Mayor was furious. He ordered the cameras stopped. He was lost in his own city. The Mayor barked a command. "Take me to City Hall right now and then drop this man off at the UN." The Mayor sat quietly until they extricated themselves from the neighborhood where he clearly did not belong. He exited the limo without saying farewell.

Nick said to the Lord, "I'll take you to the UN." Then with a wry smile, Nick said, "Welcome to New York." Jesus smiled.

"Would you like me to wait?" asked Nick.

"Please," said the Lord, "I won't be long."

The General Assembly Hall was filled to overflowing. None of those present was aware of the motorcade snafu, not even the President. The President, still preening for camera face time with Jesus, walked Him to the podium. This was the first time they met. They hadn't even spoken and yet the President paraded alongside Jesus as though they were old friends.

When the President reached the podium, he began: "Yesterday was the most important day for all of us on planet earth. Most important for all of us, but second for this Man who has come again. In the 2,000 years between visits, we have witnessed too many wars with too much suffering for far too many people. But we have also grown wiser and have more means than ever before to help those in need."

Some in the audience were squirming. They were not there to listen to a mortal—they could listen to him any time. It was an introduction that was not necessary, but made necessary by an ego that required constant massaging.

The President, feeling exalted said, "Delegates to this world assembly, I give you Jesus Christ, the Nazarene."

Jesus approached quite possibly the largest number of microphones ever bundled together.

The General Assembly Hall filled with applause like never before. Even those whose beliefs were different stood and joined in respectful recognition.

Jesus demonstrated He understood something about speechmaking when He opened with the famous line, "You may want to hold your applause until the end." That comment brought forth laughter but it proved to be most prophetic.

"I do not need an hour to tell you what I see and how I feel." Jesus wasted no words. He decried the deplorable treatment of people, especially the poor and the children, who are among the powerless. "Years ago, I asked you to feed my lambs, to take care of the children, the old, the infirmed and the weak.

"I have watched from afar for way too long. My heart weeps for the people who you disregard—the very people who you treat as nothing more than steppingstones in your desire for even more power. I have moved among the people and I can tell you they despise you. If they ever gain power, they will throw all of you out into the darkest reaches. And they will be right to do so, for there is no excuse for what you have done to them. There is no excuse for how you have injured this beautiful planet, a world that has been given to you to enjoy and share. You have demonstrated your evil intent to prey upon the weak and powerless. But worse, you have demonstrated your willful disregard for those in need. Your actions have revealed you for what you really are, vicious and despicable miscreants who deserve the hottest fires of everlasting hell."

There was no applause and no laughter, just stunned silence and an uncomfortable feeling of being undressed for all to see. Jesus' speech ended and He left the podium. He'd been offered one hour. What He said took just one minute. All who were present were frozen in place. No one moved. No one made a sound. They were all guilty, and they fittingly shared their dark company.

For Jesus, the anger He displayed inside the U.N. building was eerily reminiscent of 2,000 years before when He overturned the tables and chased the moneychangers out of the temple.

Jesus left the building and got back into the limo. "I listened to your speech on the radio. You really gave them hell. Good job. Way to go," said Nick.

"Thank you," said Jesus.

Nick drove Jesus to the sphere. "Jesus, how long are you going to be here?"

It was three o'clock on Good Friday and Jesus sighed, "Been there, done that—no need to do it again." Jesus said goodbye to Nick. The sphere gathered up its passenger and departed.

Thomas closed the magazine with a smile. *Not bad. No wonder I get in trouble.* He finished his drink, turned out the light and looked forward to tomorrow.

Chapter V

Beware the Sheep, Beware the Shepherd

Thursday, January 6 – The Feast of the Epiphany

James was seated in the busy lobby, sipping coffee and perusing the *London Times* as Matthew and Thomas got off the elevator. The modern Edwardian Heathrow catered to business-class clientele and it was the start to another busy day.

"Good morning, gentlemen."

"Good morning, Jimmy," replied Matthew.

"You're up early," added Thomas.

All three were appropriately dressed. Thomas wore his priest's black suit and semi-shiny black shirt and Roman collar. Matthew wore a blue blazer with light brown slacks and a light blue sweater over a white collared shirt and tie. He followed the tradition of wearing a dark-colored kappa Jews wear in recognition there's someone "above" who watches over them. James was in his professor's tweed sport coat with leather elbow patches and his favorite Sherlock Holmes bowler-styled hat by his side. The deerstalker hat, often associated with Holmes, was made famous by Hollywood when Basil Rathbone played the famous detective in several movies. However, the bowler hat was more authentic Holmes attire.

"I was reviewing some notes I prepared for our visit with Robert, when it suddenly occurred to me why he was so joyed that today be the day he meets you for the first time. I love the way his mind works. Today is January 6—the Epiphany. And we are the magi, the three wise men. I know Robert well enough to know he couldn't let the irony of today pass without putting it to some good use. I don't suppose either of you happen to have any frankincense or myrrh on you?"

"You're not suggesting Robert thinks he's the baby Jesus," joked Matthew.

"No, not Robert, he has no delusions about who he is. He's a Scottish gentleman and very traditional. I'm not sure which Epiphany Robert is embracing. I'm sure he's not celebrating the holy day when the wise men commemorated the birth of Jesus. I think his epiphany is what the word has come to mean. Epiphany is Greek, actually Koine, for that 'eureka' moment of understanding, like Newton's apple and gravity."

"Or like Paul's epiphany on the road to Damascus," offered Thomas. "I'm really looking forward to meeting this man."

With breakfast finished, the men gathered their luggage and prepared to leave for Glastonbury.

James's Mercedes was larger than most of the cars on the English roadways, but it proved to be just the right size for the three travelers and their luggage. James was fairly proficient at navigating the omnipresent English roundabouts. Washington DC has several circles, the American equivalent of English roundabouts. The English penchant for roundabouts at nearly every major and minor intersection, coupled with driving on the left side of the road, can initially be daunting for American drivers to negotiate.

James took M3 toward Southampton and exited onto A303, a less traveled route that would take them past Stonehenge and through the Salisbury Plain, home to England's crop circle country. They stopped briefly at Stonehenge to catch a somewhat long-range glimpse. They decided not to buy tickets, which would allow them the chance to do a closer walk-around of the ancient monument. They could do that later during their time in England. The view from the narrow two-lane blacktop road gave them nearly as good a view as inside the monument grounds. Since 1978, visitors could no longer wander through the maze. Thomas recalled stories his grandfather told him about wandering in and out of the stones and how truly massive the stones are.

Stonehenge is laid out as a circle within a circle. The inner circle consists of the smaller Bluestones, which are believed to come from the Prescelly Mountains, approximately 240 miles away, at the southwestern tip of Wales. There are 80 Bluestones each weighing up to four tons. The giant sarsen stones, which form the outer circle, weigh as much as 50 tons each. They were brought from Marlborough Downs, which is approximately 20 miles to the north. Studies have estimated at least 600 men would have been needed just to get each sarsen stone to where it stands today.

Stonehenge may be one of the world's most recognized ancient icons. While there is much speculation as to its original purpose, the ancient structure symbolizes mystery and power. Some people have theorized it was a temple built to worship ancient gods. Others have suggested it is an astronomical observatory for measuring significant recurring events, or possibly even a rocket launch pad. The gaps between the large stones could have allowed the escape of rocket exhaust. While no one is certain what Stonehenge was for, it surely wasn't built for any casual reason. The physical effort it took to transport the stones from far away and then to lift them into position would have been worth the effort only for some rather significant purpose.

Sharing the Salisbury Plain with Stonehenge are some of the most intricate earthen art works created by either human pranksters or alien visitors. While crop circles are a worldwide phenomenon, the main concentration is found in southern England near the ancient sites of Stonehenge, Avebury and Silbury Hill. As is true with Stonehenge, there are theories as to where crop circles come from. Despite the admission by some English farmers that the crop circles are manmade, many people believe the intricate and complex patterns are simply too difficult to be created by men with boards strapped to their feet trampling down grain fields in the dark of night.

Leaving Stonehenge, they arrived an hour later at the Glastonbury home and were welcomed at the front door by Estelle, and then led to Robert's library. Robert was seated such that he could see when his guests arrived. As they entered the room, Robert rose to greet them. To James's surprise, Robert was dressed in his formal kilts wearing his military blouse and RAF medals.

James opened: "Why, Robert, I've never seen you in your formal military attire. You're quite handsome. I bet the good women of Glastonbury can't keep their hands off of you."

Robert, smiling, responded. "Maybe I should go to town more often."

"Robert, allow me to introduce you to my two closest friends, Rabbi Matthew Halprin and Father Thomas Ryan. Gentlemen, I am pleased to introduce you to Robert Christian Thompson."

Robert smiled and extended his hand in a gesture to enter. "I'm so pleased to finally meet both of you. I've been looking forward to this visit for a considerably long time. Please come in. The tea is ready and Estelle has made some of her special scones which are delicious."

Estelle rolled in a cart with teapot, cups and all the trimmings. "Gentlemen, may I pour for you?"

Robert responded, "Thank you, no, Estelle. I believe we are all capable. We appreciate your care. You need not stay if you have other responsibilities. Thank you."

"My pleasure gentlemen. I will be in the kitchen."

Matthew looked around. The library was as James described—soft leather chairs, highly polished dark wood and a bookcase covering the entire eastern wall surrounding a fireplace. The bookcase was filled but not crammed and the differing colors of the book bindings did add texture to the room.

Robert gestured with the wave of a hand, "Gentlemen, please be seated." Robert waited to seat himself after his guests had done so. The three gentlemen took their seats close to the fireplace.

Thomas looked at Robert and thought, *what a magnificent looking gentleman.* Age may have shortened Robert's height somewhat, but he still stood a stately six feet, two. His face showed signs of wisdom, not just lines of age, and his hair was a combination of soft black and silver. His blue eyes were clear and warm yet direct, almost piercing. Thomas wondered how many men his age could still put on his military uniform and not have it pinch or sag. It was as though his uniform was recently tailored and pressed.

A fire was gently burning and the sweet pungent smell of peat filled the library. Robert had his peat bricks, which are made from decomposed plants, imported from the vast peat bog in the Wicklow Mountains south of Dublin, Ireland. The bricks, about the size and weight of a mason's brick, are sliced out of the bogs, stacked to dry in the sun and wind, and then burned like logs in fireplaces and stoves. They are inexpensive and plentiful, and were Ireland's standard heating fuel for centuries. The interesting odor still has many, such as Robert and Thomas, nostalgic for the smell of a good peat fire.

"What a beautiful room," said Matthew, "so very comfortable. I can see how one could spend a lifetime here."

"Thank you Rabbi, I'm honored to have you here. Actually, this room, as well as the house and all the contents, now belong to James." Turning to James, Robert continued, "I trust you were able to get all matters resolved regarding the purchase?"

"All went as exactly as we planned," said James, "but I must admit I'm still somewhat overwhelmed by it all."

"James, I'm a good judge of character and the friends you have chosen demonstrate your judgment. I'm comfortable knowing you will take care of her; she's been in the Thompson family for over 400 years.

"Gentlemen, as James noted, I'm dressed a bit more formal than usual, but today is a special occasion. It's January 6, the feast of the Epiphany, and I wanted you to know how grateful I am you three wise men have made your pilgrimage here on this day. I decided to honor this occasion with my formal military dress kilts. I believe your visit here on this feast of the Epiphany will prove to be most prophetic."

"We realized too late that today is the Epiphany. So I'm sorry to say none of us has any gold, frankincense or myrrh," said James. His comment was met by laughter all around.

Robert was eager to begin what he hoped and prayed would be the most significant discussion for the remainder of his time on earth. "I'm not sure how much James may have told you about me, but I am a bit of a writer. I have written several poems and essays I've had bound and placed in my library here. They are all unpublished, which is my wish, but I have no objection to you reading any you choose."

Robert's comment begged the question, which Matthew offered, "May I ask why you prefer to be unpublished?"

"Mostly because the pieces I've written can really never be finished to my complete satisfaction. I regularly return to each and modify them based upon what I've learned. I prefer it that way. If you publish a piece, it's gone from you and beyond your reach. It is finished and can no longer be changed or improved upon. It's as though what you have written has stopped living."

Thomas had not yet said a word. He was drinking in the room's atmosphere and was experiencing a déjà vu moment. The library, the house, the ticking of Robert's seven-foot grandfather clock and even Robert himself, all reminded Thomas of his grandfather. Not that his grandfather's parlor was anywhere near as grand as Robert's library, but the similarity was uncanny. His mind drifted back to his youth, sitting on his grandfather's lap as the old man read to him. Seldom did his sense of smell play such a meaningful role in a memory. The peat burning in the fireplace had an aroma unlike any other—a sweet and yet pungent perfume. Thomas's grandfather would have a load of peat shipped to America from Ireland. It was not cheap, but it may have been the old man's one luxury.

"Stops living? I think I know what you mean, but please continue," begged Thomas.

Robert responded, "When something written is published, it moves to a different state of existence. No longer can it be modified. No longer can it be changed and, therefore, it can no longer grow. It becomes static. In my mind it dies, so to speak."

"Interesting perspective—one which I really hadn't considered," responded Thomas. "Robert, if I may call you Robert, please tell us more about your kilts and the medals on your blouse."

"Please do call me Robert, or Bobby if you wish, Father Ryan. I will explain my uniform and medals in a few moments.

Turning toward James, "With your permission, may I show your friends around and for one more time, show the treasures this house holds? Treasures that are now yours, my friend."

James nodded a somewhat embarrassed yes.

"Gentlemen, this is an old house, over four centuries old. It has been modernized as conveniences became available, you know, indoor plumbing, electricity. It was done so well the changes can barely be seen. The entire house is an architectural delight, but please allow me to introduce you to my two favorite rooms.

"This room where we are is my library where I have entertained guests over the years. The bookshelves are filled with my favorite works. Please feel free to take them off the shelves and review them. They have little value if they are never read. I know you will recognize some are fragile and I trust you will be gentle. When you put them back, please put them in a different place. If you do, it will change the look of the bookcase and help keep my wits sharp."

"Robert, that's very interesting. It reminds me of how the dynamics of a meeting are affected when someone decides to sit in a different chair after returning from a break. That always requires others to then sit in different chairs. Almost like the game, 'musical chairs.' Some people are uncomfortable when it happens," added Matthew.

"Quite the opposite for me," responded Robert. "I often look at my bookcase from across the room. From a distance, it almost appears to be a massive painting or a mosaic. Since I like to see change, moving the books about always presents a different image. Then when I want to review a book again, I have to go searching for it. Searching keeps my wits sharp, but more so, as I search, I invariably come across a title I had not visited in some time. When I find what I am seeking, I not only have a sense of satisfaction, but almost a relief in finding an old friend. I'm not sure who said it, but I believe a book once read is a friend for life. I'm sure you three understand far better than most what it means to search.

"Now, if you three seekers will please excuse me for a few moments. While I'm gone, please look around and feel free to touch things. We need to exercise all of our senses. To me, antiques have no value if you cannot sit on them, touch them or use them as they were intended. Some have described this house as a museum. If that is so, then I would have it to be a living museum."

The three wise men rose showing their respect and remained standing as Robert left the room.

Thomas went to the bookcase as Matthew and James sat back down.

"Jimmy," said Matthew, "you were right about Robert on so many accounts. He is an interesting person. Virtually everything he says reveals an understanding about life in a very personal and uplifting way. To find simple pleasure in the rearrangement of his bookshelves tells me he's a man at peace with himself. You were also right about how he understands people. He knew we three are seekers, and I bet he even knows more about what we are seeking than even you know."

Thomas ran his fingers across some of the titles. Somewhat amazed and taken aback, he said: "Jimmy, you were right—some of these books may be first editions." The bookcases contained the complete works of Shakespeare along with authors as diverse as St. Augustine, Josephus, Homer, Chrétien de Troyes, T.S. Elliot, Dante, Chaucer, Upton Sinclair, Thomas Malory, Thomas Moore, Miguel de Cervantes, C.S. Lewis, J.D. Salinger and more. It was an eclectic collection. One book was sticking slightly out as though it had been recently read and not put back completely—almost inviting Thomas to take it. Thomas removed the book which had a bookmark inserted in it.

Thomas was familiar with the book although it must have been over twenty years since he read it. *But why was it sticking out inviting me to pick it from the shelf? Odd,* he thought, *in many ways this book was my bible, bible with a small "b." It might be one of the reasons why I am who I am. Or maybe, because of who I am, I could be comfortable with the book.*

The book was *The Cynic Epistles,* by A.J. Malherbe. People who are not familiar with the cynic philosophy might be confused by the title. The book is not "cynical" in the modern sense of the word. Some of the more influential Cynics were Diogenes, Socrates, and Hippocrates. Originally written in Koine Greek, *The Cynic Epistles* are among the few Cynic writings, which have survived from the time of the Roman Empire.

The Cynics were an influential group of philosophers in first century, CE. Their philosophy espoused life was to be lived as virtue in agreement with nature. They rejected all the conventional desires—power, wealth and fame. They lived a life free from all possessions. They neither possessed anything material nor allowed anything material to possess them. The Cynics believed, through the power of reasoning, people could gain happiness by rigorous training and by living in a way that was natural for humans. They believed the world belonged equally to everyone, and suffering was caused by false judgments of what was valuable. They rejected the worthless customs and conventions surrounding society. People today who strive to be "minimalists" are emulating the Cynic philosophy.

Diogenes was always the most flamboyant and controversial of the Cynics. He practiced and made a virtue of extreme poverty. Not only did he beg for a living, but he also slept in a large tub in the marketplace. He became notorious for his strange behavior and philosophical stunts, such as carrying a lamp in the daytime claiming he was looking for an honest man.

Thomas's mind drifted back to his seminary days with his friend and roommate, Michael Moriarity, some twenty years before. Michael and Thomas were hooked on the television adaptation of Ray Bradbury's *Martian Chronicles*. They used to think the television adaptation fit nicely with the Cynic philosophy. Near the end of the television series, a Martian ghost gave his answer to the question about the meaning of life.

Thomas remembered the philosophy as one would remember a favorite poem: *Life is its own answer. Accept it and enjoy it day by day. Live as well as possible. Expect no more. Destroy nothing. Humble nothing. Look for fault in nothing. Leave unsullied and untouched all that is beautiful. Hold that which lives in all reverence. For life was given by the sovereign of the universe. Given to be savored—to be luxuriated in—to be respected.*

Thomas remembered how Michael seemed to embody the Martian's philosophy of life and of the advice Thomas received from Michael long ago. He could still hear his voice: "There are mysteries in life put there, I believe, by the Almighty—put there to challenge your faith, not your intellect.

Someday you will face a moment that will challenge both your intellect and your faith, which you will not fully comprehend. My advice friend, listen to your heart for that is where the soul resides."

The book fell open to page 43 where the bookmark was placed. Thomas's eyes focused on a few underlined words. He read to himself: *"For me, a Scythian cloak serves as my garment, the skin of my feet as my shoes, the whole earth as my resting place, milk, cheese and meat as my favorite meal, hunger as my main course. Accustom yourself to wash with cold water, to drink only water, to eat nothing that has not been earned by toil, to wear a cloak, and to make it a habit to sleep on the ground."*

He snapped out of his trance when he heard Matthew calling his name.

"Where have you just been, my friend?" said Matthew.

"Long ago, far away," sighed Thomas as he replaced the book exactly where he found it, leaving it to stick out slightly from the rest.

Thomas chose another book with a beautiful handcrafted leather binding, but without a title. It was a delicate, almost fragile book. He opened it and found it to contain a collection of handwritten poems—essays on different subjects, each with different handwriting. There was one poem in particular which caught his attention. It was a draft with lines crossed out and other words inserted. The lined through title was "The Last Charge." In place was a new title, "The Brigade's Charge." At the bottom of the poem were the handwritten initials, "A.T." Thomas's eyes opened wide when he realized he was holding an early draft of *The Charge of the Light Brigade* in the hand of Lord Alfred Tennyson.

Robert reappeared and smiled at Thomas. "Father, I sense you know what you're holding."

Thomas whispered "Tennyson" and Robert nodded.

"As I was saying, when you publish a work, you can never change it and therefore it dies so to speak. I sense if Lord Tennyson were alive today, he might want to revisit his poem and make some more changes."

Robert continued. "I believe you would agree the handwritten poem you are holding is quite valuable. But I have no way of deciding its value. Tennyson and my grandfather were good friends when Tennyson was the Poet Laureate of Great Britain and he gave my grandfather that early draft. Both my grandfather and father cherished the poem and believed it was priceless and could have fetched a fair amount of money on the antiquities market. But why sell it? Who could appreciate it more? The buyer? Probably not, to the buyer it would have been an asset, an acquisition—probably one of several in a collection. If my grandfather or father would have sold the poem, it could never again be priceless."

Matthew asked for clarification on what Robert meant if it had been sold, it could no longer be considered "priceless?"

Robert was clearly enjoying the intelligent conversation Matthew, James and Thomas brought with them. "I can't begin to tell you how much I value this and more discussions to come. I don't get out much anymore and the opportunities to stimulate my mind are way too few. Just to be able to talk with such brilliant minds is the greatest gift you could have brought here on the Epiphany. But, to your question Matthew, if the poem were to be sold, a monetary value would have to be agreed upon by the seller and the buyer. Then once the poem had a price affixed to it, it could no longer be priceless."

Robert continued. "Tell me, Father Ryan, what do you find more interesting? Tennyson's final product or the unfinished poem you hold in your hand. Tell me if you feel as though Tennyson is still alive in the text you're holding. His work isn't finished and therefore neither is he."

Thomas nodded agreement yet his face revealed questions.

Robert sat down and sighed, "Except what I just said is really only a wish—an old man's wish. At some point, we are all finished." It was one of the only times Robert bowed toward reality.

"Father Ryan, you've written a few works. I've read them and son they are quite good. I especially like your story about the Second Coming in *The Christian Scholar*. It's as true today as it was 2,000 years ago. I bet you got in trouble for that work." Robert gave an approving laugh. "Given the chance, would you go back and change anything?" Robert asked rhetorically.

Before Thomas could answer, Robert continued, "I suppose there are occasions when changes are necessary. I generally don't mind if an editor suggests a minor style change, but I tend to bristle when someone suggests serious content change." Thomas was relieved Robert liked his work. He just met the man, and already Robert's acceptance of his writings was strangely important to him.

Robert paused and changed the subject. "Now, Estelle, the woman who looks after me, has prepared a lunch of soup and sandwiches. While she's preparing the table, let me show you my other favorite room on our way to the dining room."

Robert led the three to his private study. It was a cozy room, smaller than the library. "This is my study/trophy/collection room, if you will." The room had an old wooden roll-top desk and two leather easy chairs and a leather couch. Robert gently brushed his hand over a blanket that was draped over the back of the couch. "This is the MacTavish dress blue tartan. We Thompsons are Scots from the MacTavish clan and are descendants of Mac Giolla Chriost." Robert's comment meant little to his three guests, but he said it with such seriousness and emphasis it must have been important.

"Robert, I am of the school which says there is no such thing as a dumb question. Could you please explain what you mean by Mac Giolla Chriost?" asked Thomas, stumbling somewhat over the pronunciation.

Robert smiled and said, "Mac Giolla Chriost, not an easy name to say is it Father, even for an Irishman. I shall write the name down for you and you can research it at your leisure. I think at the right moment of your search, you may find it to be enlightening." A smiling Robert wrote "Mac Giolla Chriost" on a card and handed it to Thomas with a wink and a nod. Thomas realized he had just been taught a lesson. Robert was not going to give him an answer and Thomas understood. More value would be achieved if it were earned.

Robert's study was neatly full and regularly cleaned. James was thinking, *poor Estelle, this has to be a dusting nightmare.* There were three display cases filled with military artifacts. There were swords, flags, pistols, cannon-balls, letters, caps, old yellowed photographs, a World War II German Potato Masher hand grenade, insignias and more, from old and more recent conflicts.

The room was well cared for, not dusty, musty or messy. Robert paused, looked at James and said, "Lucky you have Estelle, for this has to be a dusting nightmare." James never ceased to marvel at Robert's ability to recognize and respond to questions before they were asked. In this particular case, James had been wondering to himself who would attend to the Thompson house once the ownership of the house would legally and emotionally pass from Robert to him.

One of the cases held mementos from Robert's Uncle Mace, including his insignia from the 5th Battalion (the Black Watch) of the British Army, along with some German insignias, a German World War I helmet with the pointed top and a Broomhandle Mauser pistol.

Another display case held Robert's personal military mementos. Robert had a distinguished career in the RAF and earned many decorations. He chose that moment to remove the medals he was wearing and return them to their positions in the case, taking the time to explain what each of the medals meant. He first removed a star with a tri-colored ribbon with a gold rosette attached. It was called the 1939-45 Star and was awarded to Robert for his participation in the Battle of Britain. Next, Robert replaced the Atlantic Star and the Italy Star awarded for Service against the Enemy at Sea in the Atlantic and the Mediterranean.

Finally, there was a place of honor in the display case for the Victoria Cross, personally awarded to Robert by King George VI. Next to the Cross was a photo of Robert with the King and a letter commemorating the award. The bronze Victoria Cross, with Crown and Lion superimposed, carried the motto: For Valour. The Victoria Cross is the highest military decoration awarded for "most conspicuous bravery in the presence of the enemy." Robert earned his Cross for exceptional valor during the Battle of Britain where the RAF defeated the German Luftwaffe in October 1940. Robert had been shot down. He parachuted safely and made it back to base, only to then climb into another plane and continue the fight. Later in life, Robert wondered if the award should have more aptly said, "For Conspicuous Stupidity."

The name of the battle was derived from a famous speech delivered by Prime Minister Winston Churchill in the House of Commons: "The Battle of France is over. I expect the Battle of Britain is about to begin..." The RAF handed the German Luftwaffe its first major defeat and it became one of the crucial turning points in the war. Had German forces succeeded in destroying Britain's air defenses, Britain may have had to negotiate an armistice or an outright surrender.

Thomas, Matthew and James stood silently as Robert conducted the ceremony of returning each medal to its proper place. He paused over each medal rubbing each gently, remembering a time long, long ago. He closed the glass cover slowly with a barely audible sigh as if this were the last time he would conduct such a ceremony. He then told James to feel free to change things and replace his mementos with whatever he wanted to put on display.

James responded, "You know Robert, we haven't really discussed this, but I want you to stay here as long as you wish and I would be honored to have the study remain as a depository of your personal effects now and in the future. This will always be the Thompson house."

"Why, thank you, James; that is most kind. I guess I didn't want to give any thought to where my stuff goes when I go. The contents of the house are yours and I do appreciate your willingness to make a distinction. The medals do mean a great deal to me."

"Then it's decided. The medals and the mementos stay, and you Robert stay as long as you want. This will always be your home."

"Again thank you, James. I appreciate your generosity."

Robert continued, "Gentlemen, there are six bedrooms on the second floor. Estelle has prepared a room for each of you. They're all quite comfortable, but James's room is a little larger and has a working fireplace. He's the new lord of the manor and deserves the extra comfort. James knows I want you all to stay. We have much to talk about and not as much time as I would like.

"Now let's have a bite to eat and then if you don't mind I'll take my nap. It's a habit of mine. You can use the time to move your belongings into your rooms and then we can get back together this afternoon for a conversation about what it is you three are seeking."

There he goes again, thought James.

Lunch was pleasant and the dining room, like the rest of the house, was beautifully decorated and well maintained. The conversation was light and mostly focused on the house. Robert's ancestors had it built around 1600. It had been remodeled several times to stay current, and it had been only slightly damaged during World War II. A bomb shelter was added during the war and then after the war was converted into a wine cellar, which Robert kept both secret and well stocked. Robert ended his day with a glass of red wine, generally Burgundy.

Robert, Estelle, Henry and Margo were the only ones who knew about the converted bomb shelter and they were also the only people who knew how to gain access to the hidden wine cellar. After lunch Robert led the men back to the library to show them the secret mechanism that allowed one to gain entry.

"Lads, the process is fairly simple. Facing the bookcase, you will find the release mechanism on the far left hand side, third shelf from the top. Remove two or three books to reveal the wood paneling. With the paneling visible, all you need do is push on the panel which appears more darkly stained," Robert demonstrated. "The panel is hinged and when you push, it will swing inward revealing a handle."

Robert reached in and lifted the handle releasing the lock. One half of the bookcase easily swung out revealing a hidden staircase leading to the wine cellar. Now James, Thomas and Matthew were also in on the secret.

Robert excused himself, adjourning to his first floor suite for his customary afternoon nap. The three friends took the opportunity to move into their upstairs bedrooms. Their rooms were as pleasant and comfortable as Robert described. Each room was an en suite, having its own private bath and shower. It was easy to see how the house had been used as a bed and breakfast.

After the three moved in, they returned to the library to talk while they waited for Robert to return. Again Thomas perused the titles on the bookshelves. There was an entire bookcase dedicated to religious works—mostly Christian, but also Jewish, Orthodox and Moslem. There were some beautiful ornate Bibles, including an early King James edition. There also was an English language copy of the Koran.

Some of the books were new to Thomas. He called Matthew over to review some of the titles. Among them were books titled: *In the Language of the Lord—a Study of Ancient Aramaic;* and *Aramaic, Koine and Hebrew Sayings of Jesus*; and yet another, *Translating Ancient Aramaic into Modern English.* "Matt, it appears Robert has more than a casual interest in ancient text. None of these would qualify as light reading."

There were works on genealogy, King Arthur, the Round Table, the Knights Templar, History of Glastonbury, Joseph of Arimathea, Opus Dei,

Dead Sea Scrolls, Constantine and a half dozen leather bound Bibles. One was in a special glass cabinet built into the bookcase. It was a large beautiful edition with gold leaf lettering identifying it as the Thompson Family Bible.

Thomas remarked to both Matthew and James, Robert seemed to have an insatiable thirst for knowledge. "He's one of the most inquisitive people I've met."

Robert rejoined his three guests around two o'clock. Thomas was struck by how easily Robert inserted himself back into the group. It was almost as though the three were simply marking time waiting for him to return, which to some extent they were.

"James has told me the three of you grew up together and now, some thirty or more years later, you are together again and all on the same quest. If you do not mind, Father Ryan, let me ask you a question: why do you continue to search for proof that a man named Jesus walked on earth?"

Thomas inhaled deeply thinking Robert really cuts to the chase, but in a non-threatening way. "Maybe because my name is Thomas, and early in my life I related to the apostle who doubted—to the man who needed proof. Part of me believes Jesus exists. I know I said exists, not existed. I believe who Jesus is and how He lived is as real today as it was 2,000 years ago. But I'm also a scientist and to find the truth I must peel away myths and legends from reality.

"I search for the man so I can know God better. For the very reason His simple way is so appealing; it's so hard to comprehend, so hard to believe. He lived life without worry about what He would eat and where He would sleep. He believed the Father would provide. How beautifully simple His life was. Not easy, but simple. No cars, no cell phones, no internet, no 401K plans and no concept of the defining oxymoron of our time—virtual reality.

"Robert, I think you understand what I'm saying." Thomas was still standing next to the bookcases. He reached in and pulled out *The Cynic Epistles.*

Robert smiled, "Good job, I knew you would find what I left for you. Your seeking abilities will reward you sooner than you know."

Thomas replaced the book back on the shelf, but this time in a different position. He smiled and said, "There, now doesn't that look nice?"

Thomas sat down. "Robert, you mentioned you read my article about what might happen if Jesus were to visit us today. I was surprised you read it; *The Christian Scholar* magazine is not widely circulated. It was more difficult to write than I expected, but shortly after I started I realized just how poorly Jesus would be received if He came back to Earth today. His presence would be so inconvenient. We'd feel compelled to stop whatever we were doing to listen to the Man. What an interruption He'd be to our everyday lives. In the United States, we certainly wouldn't want Him to come during the World

Series or the Super Bowl. When could we fit Him in? How long would He stay? When could we get back to our lives as usual?

"In that article Jesus was only here for a day and a half and then needed to leave. The political leaders were about to run Him out of town for being such an irritant to the system. So I search for Him to tell Him it's okay for Him to come again. I want Him to know what many of us know—that we have made our lives too complicated, that so much of what we do, we do for tomorrow, not today. We work so someday we can quit and enjoy leisure. Our lives today are much like the story Jesus told about the rich man who tore down his barns to build bigger barns to house more and more grain. In the parable, the rich man dies that night, never enjoying what he worked so hard to store up."

Thomas stood up. He felt he needed to stand to give the answer he wanted to give. "Why do I search for Jesus the Man?" Thomas paused. "We live in a world poor in faith—we live in a world which requires proof. If I could hold an object in my hand for all to see," Thomas held up an empty hand, "I could say look at this, Jesus is real. He was here. He walked on this ground. He died on the cross for us. He is our one true friend." Thomas stopped. He was almost embarrassed, as he stood empty handed after delivering his impassioned sermon.

"I like your answer," said Robert. "You were ready for the question. I sense you have asked yourself that question before."

"Yes, I have," answered Thomas. "But, I'm afraid people would ask, what does He look like? What color is His hair, His eyes, His skin? And they would walk away from Him because they didn't feel He is like them. How could I convince people He's a little bit of everyone? How could I convince them He had to choose a form compatible with the times? What is truly important is the message, not the visual form of the messenger. If I could hold in my hand just one thing proving Jesus was here, I'd be able to satisfy even my own doubts."

"Father Ryan," responded Robert, "I appreciate your honesty. At my age, I'm prepared to take things on faith; I don't require proof. However, I do understand your quest and I'm confident what the three of you seek, you will soon find. I'm more comfortable than ever you three will be able to hold, appreciate and, most of all, honor that which you seek."

"Robert, I believe you know what we are seeking and I believe you know where it is. But you aren't going to tell us where to look, are you?" asked James.

"James, this isn't a game. You already know more than you think you know. However, you must conduct your search; for only by being a seeker will you find the answer and so much more. Your quest does not end when you find what you seek. You must be prepared to protect what you have found.

When the three of you assemble all the clues, you three and you three alone will know where to look. But I want you to be sufficiently prepared for what will come after. I warn you to steel yourself against your enemies, and even against your friends who will turn on you when your embrace of change makes them uncomfortable."

"Robert," asked Matthew, "Thomas and I are coming late to the game. Sorry for the figure of speech, for I know it isn't a game. Please tell us more about what you sense will happen."

"Once you find what you are seeking, be prepared, for not everyone will be pleased. Those who you would expect to celebrate with you may be the ones who work the hardest against you. Be careful whom you trust. You may be holding that which can turn everything upside down and there will be many who like things just the way they are. Beware the sheep, beware the shepherd. They may be wolves, not sheep. Gentlemen, you may think I'm talking in riddles, and to some extent I am, but when you find what you seek, all will be clear.

"I thank God every night that eight months ago James paid me a visit. I was beginning to worry what would become of this place." Robert waved his hand to indicate the house. "I was ashamed for having waited so long. I am no longer a young man and I know my time on this earth is short. Without a plan to carry on, this place, this house would have gone to the government and I have no idea what would have come after. Now I can rest. I have come to know, appreciate and trust James. And if there was any doubt, you two have reinforced my confidence in him."

Thomas had a sense Robert wanted to say more, as though Robert was burdened by some thought. But Robert remained silent. Estelle beckoned them to the dinner table. The meal was oddly quiet, as though each man was privately reflecting on the day.

After they finished, Robert invited them back to the library for a glass of wine. "James, why don't you go with Estelle to the wine cellar so you might be able to do the same by yourself later on?"

James went to the bookcase and saw how simply disguised was the lever that allowed Estelle to open the bookcase like a door.

Robert said, "Seek, ask, knock."

James accompanied Estelle to the cellar and returned with a bottle of Burgundy. Estelle brought out the glasses and Robert poured.

"Robert," said James, "Matthew, Thomas and I would like to take a spin around Glastonbury tomorrow to see some of the legendary sites. We would very much like for you to accompany us and be our personal tour guide. My vehicle can easily accommodate four. What do you say? Would you care to join us?"

"Thank you, I'd love to. It's been a while since I have been on the Tor grounds. There's no way I could make that climb, but it would be fun to see it again up close. I'm a little slower, but if you do not mind an old man coming along, I would really enjoy the outing."

"Good, let's begin in the morning after breakfast. We can have lunch in town and still get you back for an afternoon nap."

"James, I'm not that old. I can skip an occasional nap. Let's make a day of it and take it all in."

Robert finished his glass of wine and begged leave so he could retire. "I'm going to need a good night's sleep if I'm going to be able to keep up with you boys. Our conversation about what you are seeking can wait another day. Goodnight gentlemen."

The three friends rose to say goodnight and remained standing until Robert left the room.

"Well, Jimmy," said Thomas, "this has been quite a day. It's been fun. Almost like when we were kids playing our detective games. Only this time, it's a real live adventure."

"It's a bit too early to turn in. If you don't mind, I'm going to my room to give Sara a call. It's only about 2:30 for her. I'll meet you back here in 45 minutes," interjected Matthew as he headed toward the door.

"Not a bad idea," said James. "I'll call my landlady in London and see if I have any messages."

"Are you sure you're not going off to call Margo?" asked Thomas.

"After I call my landlady, I may give Margo a call," answered James, with a smile.

"Well, poor me," said Thomas. "I have no one to call. I think I'll just spend some time in the library. See you two in an hour."

Matthew and James went off to their rooms leaving Thomas alone in the library. There was only a little wine left in the bottle, which Thomas poured into his glass. He then began to examine the bookshelves. Just for fun, he removed several books with the more colorful bindings and then returned them to different places on the shelves. He backed up to see if he changed the mosaic. With his thumb held up like an artist inspecting his model, Thomas had to admit to himself he really didn't see much difference. *I guess I don't have the old man's eye for change.*

Thomas took the last sip of wine and set down his glass. *I think we'll have one more glass of wine together before we retire*, he said to himself. Thomas went to the far left end of the bookcase. *Now, where is that lever?*

He removed a few books so he could see the wood panel. He pushed and nothing happened. He repositioned, pushed again. Again, nothing. He removed a few more books and continued his futile search. But found nothing. He removed about eight or nine books. *That should've been enough,* he thought. He backed up to see if he could make sense of his efforts. *Ah, wrong shelf.* Thomas removed books from the fourth shelf from the top.

He put back the books and then removed three books from the shelf above. He could see the wood paneling and could see the one panel that was slightly darker. He pushed and the hinged panel opened. Thomas lifted the lever and the left side of the bookcase was freed. He pulled it open enough to reveal the stairs to the wine cellar. He descended the twelve steps and found himself in a room that was roughly 12' by 12'. All four walls were lined with wine racks. *This would've been one hell of a bomb shelter. One could've gone down here and gotten bombed and waited out the war.* There were wine bottles in each rack, and each rack was about three-quarters full. There was one rack for Burgundy and Bordeaux, one rack of claret, one of Blanc and Chardonnay, and one rack of Pinot Noir and cordials.

I'm going to have to talk to the butler about getting some Jameson down here. Thomas grabbed a bottle of Burgundy and went back upstairs.

As he was closing the bookshelf, Matthew came back into the room.

"Matt, you have got to see the wine cellar. Most impressive. How are Sara and the kids?"

"They're all fine, missing me and hoping I'm having a good time. Jackson had a pretty major collision in a soccer game and has a chipped tooth and an epiphyseal fracture on his right wrist. A growth plate fracture for a kid can be serious, so it looks like this soccer season is done. Sara is taking him to the orthodontist to get his tooth capped."

Matthew continued, "Kyla is miserable. As the kids say, she kind of likes a boy, but he doesn't seem to even know she is there. I told Sara about our trip so far. She's interested in hearing more about Robert. Hannah wants to know more about Stonehenge and asked if we have seen any alien crop circles. Otherwise, not much else happening,"

"Sounds like Sara has everything under control," Thomas answered.

James entered the library.

"How's Margo?" asked Thomas.

"She's just fine, thank you. I had an interesting call from your buddy Frederick Fulgrum."

"Freddy called you? What did he want?"

"Well, according to my landlady, Freddy, as you call him, stopped by to see me. I guess getting my address is not difficult," explained James.

"What did she say?" asked Thomas.

"Well, he told her he called my home phone and left a message. He also told her he was a friend of a friend. I assume meaning you. She told him I was on a research trip and I was meeting a couple of friends and would be going to Stonehenge. Apparently he's going to call her back in a week, so she wanted to know what she should tell him."

James continued, "I told her to tell him all she knew was we three had gone to Stonehenge. I asked her not to tell him anymore.

"She also questioned whether he was really a friend of yours. Pretty astute of my landlady. I'm guessing Freddy has the kind of personality nobody really likes. So I called my voice mail to see if he called. Listen to this."

James redialed his home phone voice mail and put his cell phone on speaker for all to hear.

"Hello, this is Father Frederick Francis Fulgrum." The voice enunciated each syllable in tight staccato fashion. "I trust you remember me. I'm an old seminary friend of Father Thomas Ryan and I'm in London for a few days. I was hoping I might catch up with you, have a cup of coffee and talk with you about how your research is going. I think I may have told you I work for the Vatican and we're all thrilled with your efforts to find the Grail. As I am sure you know, many have searched, but none has been successful. I'll stop by your flat to see if I can catch up with you and then I must get back. If I don't find you this trip, I will be back in a couple of days and I'll try again."

The message from Freddy ended and James added, "What do you make of that?"

Thomas pressed two fingers above the bridge of his nose, squinted and exhaled. "I don't know. Something is going on, and I'm at a loss."

James and Matthew waited for Thomas to say more.

"I don't think Freddy is acting solely on his own behalf. And I don't know whether the Vatican is watching me or watching you, Jimmy. Freddy's no mule; he's smart and devious. I'm sure he won this assignment because he knows me, but I'm also fairly sure the Vatican was aware of you and your research, independent of me. So, we must be getting close to something that has the Vatican worried. The fact we're together probably has them doubly worried."

"Maybe triply worried," interjected Matthew. "Sara received a call about you, Tommie. She presumed it was from Georgetown. The caller wanted to know if Sara knew where Father Ryan was. Sara asked if it was an emergency and the caller, a woman, said no, they just wanted to know where to forward any mail. Sara thought it was a bit strange; she was sure you would have left forwarding instructions with people at Georgetown."

James looked at Thomas and said, "I think you better open that bottle of wine, and let's toast whatever comes next."

"Agreed," said Matthew. "Let it unfold and we'll follow wherever it takes us."

"To whatever the future may hold," said Thomas with his glass raised in toast. "And with that, I think it is time to retire. For tomorrow, Louie, could be the beginning of a beautiful friendship."

"Great Schwarzenegger," said Matthew.

"Bogart," said Thomas with a feigned sigh of exasperation.

Chapter VI

Bless me Father, for I have sinned

FRIDAY, JANUARY 7 – THOMPSON HOUSE

Estelle prepared an ample English breakfast anticipating a busy day for her four gentlemen who would be spending the day in Glastonbury. The plan was for James, Matthew and Thomas to start the day hiking the Tor while Robert met with Heather Bean, his solicitor.

James parked in front of Heather's office on George Street in time for Robert's ten o'clock appointment. "Robert, we'll be back to pick you up at noon."

THE TOR

Most people who see the Tor for the first time think it's manmade. While it is a natural formation, it does show signs of having been artificially shaped long ago by someone cutting seven terraces. The terraces are now worn and weathered, but still traceable over long stretches. The walk up is a strenuous spiral ending at the summit where St. Michael's tower still stands. Many believe the terraces disguise a labyrinth, which is intended for ritual purposes. One legend describes a hidden entrance, followed by a long and twisting approach to an open center where a waterfall cascades sacred water giving everlasting life.

James, Thomas and Matthew took the trail starting on the north side of the Tor and continued clockwise to the top. It was a steep climb, which included several switchbacks. The day began chilly and overcast with a stiff breeze out of the west. During most of the trail up the Tor, the three seekers were protected from the wind, but occasionally their ascent would swing them out of the hill's protection and the blast of cold air against their slightly overheated bodies was an unpleasant shock to the system.

There were several people ascending the Tor or already at the top, but it was hardly crowded and each person moved at his or her own pace. With several stops along the way, the walk up took roughly 45 minutes. The view from the top was a breathtaking 360-degree panorama. The windchill was brutal and one needed the little protection St. Michael's Tower afforded. All that remained was the Tower; the rest of the old church building burned hundreds of years before. The Tower rose another 80 feet and was of solid granite, which resembled weathered steel.

The tower did not have a stairway, and was open from the base to the top. About eight to ten visitors huddled inside the ten feet by ten feet space. Two women in long hippie-styled dresses were looking skyward and chanting. A third woman, a friend of the other two, was taking collections. No one knew what is was for, but James tossed in a £1 coin.

The men stayed at the top for about thirty minutes just enjoying the view. Matthew finally said, "This place is supposed to be magical, but I don't feel a thing. Do either of you feel anything?"

"I feel cold," said Thomas.

"And I'm cold and hungry," offered James. "Let's go down, pick up Robert and I'll buy lunch at the New Inn."

Heather Bean's Office

Since Robert sold the Thompson home to James, he needed to make sure his will was in order. He was ready to make some significant changes with solicitor Bean's assistance. In addition to being a solicitor, Heather Bean was also a valuer and Robert engaged her to set the value on the contents of his home. She saw virtually everything Robert owned and she objectively valued each item. Some items, for example his medals and commendations, had a book value ridiculously low compared to what they meant to Robert.

"Robert, I trust you are well. I mean you're still in good health, aren't you? You have me a little worried, the sudden selling of your home and the adjustments to your will. Are you trying to send a signal?"

"Heather, there comes a time in everyone's life when, if they are smart, they prepare for the inevitable. My friends and family are all gone and I have accomplished almost all of what I have wanted to do. Life has not cheated me. But I will have cheated life if I do not have my affairs in order."

Heather nodded agreement. "You are a wise man."

He was also a fairly wealthy man. With his other holdings added to the home sale, he now had nearly 4 million pounds sterling or approximately 6.5 million U.S. dollars. Robert converted all of his investments into cash to make their dispersal to the beneficiaries easier. He decided he wanted to make a limited number of bequests so each gift might make a difference. He would reward Henry and Estelle for her service over the past 20-plus years with a bequest of £750,000. Both Estelle and Henry had done much to make Robert's life better and fuller.

He wanted to honor both his Catholic roots and Anglican membership by leaving £200,000 to St. Mary's Roman Catholic Church on Magdalene Street and £300,000 to St. John the Baptist Anglican on High Street.

Both churches were in need of some significant repair and the funds would be a big help. Robert hesitated for a moment over his gift to St. John the Baptist because he really didn't get along very well with Vicar Carol Dunmore. He stopped going to church at St. John's two years before. He could blame it on mobility issues, but truthfully, it was more of a personality issue. Vicar Dunmore replaced the popular Vicar David MacPherson, who passed away after nearly thirty years of service. When Vicar MacPherson was there, the church was filled every Sunday. MacPherson was capable of fire and brimstone as well as sweet and gentle sermons, and he seemed to know just which style his parishioners were in need of the most. One always knew where the good Vicar stood on any issue and he was always able to rally support for the good of any cause. For Robert's sake, it didn't hurt that he was also a Scotsman.

However, Vicar Dunmore was more private and hard for Robert to get to know. She was in her 40's and divorced, and was driven to succeed as if she had something to prove. Robert and some of the older boys thought she probably didn't like the hold men have on the Church hierarchy. He felt he had given her several chances, but they just couldn't connect. He didn't blame St. John's when the fault was his and hers.

Robert asked Heather to help him develop a letter of specific instructions to be read immediately upon his death. In the letter, he stipulated he wished to have his funeral celebrated at St. John the Baptist. Robert also asked Vicar Dunmore to find a way to involve Father Thomas Ryan in the service—the result of the immediate rapport he developed with Thomas.

Shortly after Robert and James's relationship began, Robert had Heather file the required government applications to establish a nonprofit organization. The organization was intended to serve as a research and educational venue with a focus on the impact of religious teaching on society. It was to be known as The Epistolic Institute. Several months ago, Robert asked James to serve as The Institute's president and James accepted, not knowing precisely what Robert had in mind.

The Institute's application for nonprofit status had been approved, and Robert and James had just begun to establish some goals for The Institute. All that was needed was money to get it started. "Heather, I want to make a change in my will. I would like to leave the balance of my estate to The Epistolic Institute. After the gifts to Estelle and Henry, St. John's and St. Mary's and whatever may be required for funeral expenses and related fees, I'm assuming the balance of my estate will be approximately £2.75 million. I want all that is left to go to The Institute."

"Robert, we can do what you wish, however I should point out you currently have The Doorway in your will. Are you now telling me you want The Institute to replace The Doorway?"

"Yes, Heather that is precisely what I want. I hope it doesn't upset you?"

Heather looked confused. "Excuse me Robert, but why would you think it would upset me?"

Robert pointed to The Doorway's replica clock on her desk. "That's the more expensive Rolex replica. I assume you are a life member."

Heather waved her hand. "Oh, that thing. One of my clients gave it to me as a gag gift. I'll tell you honestly, sometimes it makes me want to gag. I would gladly give it away or toss it in the trash, but my client might be offended."

Heather made notes of what Robert wanted. "I will make the changes you request."

"Heather, I have a couple of last minute items regarding The Institute." Robert explained, "I would like to name Father Thomas Ryan and Rabbi Matthew Halprin as two of the five members of The Institute board of directors. I haven't asked them as of yet, but I sense they will accept the post. Then, along with James, they can fill out the remaining three positions."

"I will see to it."

"Heather, one last item. You've done a wonderful job for me, and your efforts these past several years are truly appreciated, but I have a confession to make. When you valued my possessions for the sale along with the house, I did not show you everything. Heather, I have a few artifacts, which have been in my family for hundreds of years. They are truly priceless and they aren't in your valuer's report. They have, in fact, not been viewed outside of the Thompson family lo these many years. I want these artifacts to also become the property of The Epistolic Institute. How do I make sure these artifacts are transferred appropriately?"

"Robert, you have no need to confess anything. What you need to do is describe the artifacts in a letter and in sufficient detail as to be verifiable. I'll then add that letter as a codicil to your will bequeathing those artifacts to The Institute."

"Can their complete description and whereabouts remain confidential until the reading of my will?" asked Robert.

"Yes, certainly. To avoid any problems, let me suggest you write a letter, in your own hand, describing the items and their location. We will have you sign and date the letter in my and another person's presence. The other witness and I will verify the authenticity of your signature and include the original in your will. I will add a codicil to your will right now noting the existence of this sealed letter."

"Heather, how specific need I be regarding the location of the artifacts? Would it be sufficient to say the artifacts are in my library?" Robert asked.

"That would be fine, just be as specific as you can about the artifacts." Heather paused. "Robert, let me also suggest you inform The Doorway in writing. I can draft a letter telling them they have been removed from your will. You can sign it and I along with another person can witness you signing the letter."

"I will be back in town tomorrow. I know it is Saturday, but can we finish the task then?" asked Robert.

"I would be happy to meet with you tomorrow for one final review of the will, and to witness your signature on the codicil and the letter to The Doorway. Shall I have my secretary here or can one of your associates be a witness?"

"I will ask Father Ryan to serve as witness. I am sure he will be agreeable."

"How does 10 a.m. sound?" asked Heather.

"That'll be just fine; we'll see you tomorrow then."

THOMPSON HOUSE

It was after 4 p.m. when the four somewhat weary tourists returned home. All agreed there was simply too much to see and do in one day. Robert had not done all he needed to do, so he exacted a promise they would return the next day.

As they entered the house, Estelle had the expression of a worried mother. "Mr. Thompson, you look tired; allow me to pour you a nice hot bath." She looked at the other three with a bit of a motherly scowl.

"Now Estelle, not to worry. I've been in good hands and had more fun today than any time I can remember. However, a hot bath does sound very good indeed," responded Robert.

"Did you have lunch?" asked Estelle.

"A fine lunch and a most unexpected treat. The boys took me to Priddy. I can't remember when I was there last, but I directed the boys to where we would go on the hunt. I told them back in the 60's I was a Huntsman in the Masters of Foxhounds Association and joined in fox hunts all over England, Wales and Scotland. Toward the end of my hunting days, most of my time was spent around Priddy. The hunt is not the same today. No more foxes, just the scent of the fox—animal rights, you know.

"We lunched at the New Inn and I took a ribbing from the lads about whether I wore a red coat with tails. I tried to explain the scarlet, not red, coat was only worn by Huntsmen and Masters. I told them about 'being in the pink,' which only seemed to induce more laughter at my expense." Robert was enjoying the moment for he was once again the storyteller as he had been when the Thompson house was a B&B and he was the entertainment.

Robert continued, “I went into a bit of detail telling the lads ‘in the pink’ gained its meaning from fox hunting, and was a combination of the colour of the coat, and the pink and healthy glow gained by outdoor exercise. They wanted to know more about what I wore. I told them on hare hunts, I would wear a forest green rather than a scarlet coat. Both my green and scarlet coats had the five brass buttons to signify I was a Huntsman. The colour of my breeches was always white, and my boots were English dress boots without laces. And of course this was topped off by my black hunt cap. They wanted to know if I still had them, and I promised to model the coat and hat while we are all together.

“Margo Webster was there at the New Inn and she sends her regards. And guess what? It seems Margo and our James here may be a bit of an item. Seems they have been carrying on behind my back.” Robert was beaming as he saw James show signs of embarrassment.

“Clearly, James received the best service while we remaining three bumps could only watch as Margo saw to his every need. What say you James—is the fair Margo your lady?”

James’s grin and slight blush revealed the secret to be true.

“I have a splendid idea.” Robert paused and pulled down slightly on his lower lip, striking a thinking pose. “James, why not invite Margo to dinner here with us all tomorrow? And you too, Estelle. I would like you and Henry to be my guests for a change. In fact, I will prepare dinner. I’m a pretty good cook you know.”

Estelle was taken aback. Over the past two decades she never dined with Robert. She would prepare his dinner, but he would dine alone. She would then clean up and head home. “Mr. Thompson, I don’t know what to say. I’m embarrassed,” she said as her cheeks turned a rosy shade of pink.

“Estelle, it would please me if you would say yes.”

Estelle paused, “I am at a loss. If it will please you sir, then I accept and I will bring Henry. But you must let me clean up.”

“I’ll help with the dinner,” offered Matthew.

“Very well then, dinner will be at 7:30 p.m. tomorrow and Matthew and I will be the cooks. Matthew, we will do some shopping tomorrow while we are in town. Now, I think I will take Estelle’s advice and soak in the tub.”

“Tonight’s dinner will be at seven,” acknowledged Estelle, as she left to pour Robert’s bath.

“I don’t know how Robert does it, he’s virtually twice my age. I’m going to my room and stretch out for a short while,” said James, “and give Margo a call.”

“I’ll do likewise, except I’ll call Sara,” said Matthew.

"And I'll go to my room and just lie down for a moment," added Thomas.

In the dark and quiet of his room, Thomas fell fast asleep. But he awoke with a start. It was dark and he fumbled for his watch. *I can't remember when that happened last. I guess I must have needed the sleep*, Thomas thought. It was almost six o'clock. He refreshed himself in his adjoining bathroom and made his way downstairs.

The house was still and the lights were low. He passed the kitchen and saw Estelle getting dinner ready. She waved. *Good*, he thought to himself, *mother isn't angry*. Matthew and James had not yet come down. Thomas could see a light emanating from Robert's study. He gently knocked on the half-open door. Robert looked up and beckoned him in. "Please come in and sit with me Father, and would you please close the door behind you."

Thomas did as he'd been asked and took a seat across from Robert.

"I want to tell you what a wonderful day today was and how much I appreciate the three of you. I can't recall the last time I felt this joyful and at ease. And my Lord, what a wonderful feeling it is, like a heavy burden has been lifted off my shoulders. I've worried about who would follow me and be the steward of the sacred secret I have been privileged to hold in my hands."

"I assume all the introductions you made in town today were made to remove any doubt that James has the legitimate claim to your home and contents?" responded Thomas.

"Yes, and I intend to do more of the same tomorrow."

Robert raised his right hand and closed his eyes for a brief moment. The pause allowed Robert to move on to a new subject. "Father, I asked the door be closed because, if it would not be too much of a burden, I should like to make my confession. It has been a long time. Many years ago I was a devout Catholic, but for more than twenty years I have been an Anglican and member of Saint John the Baptist congregation. We Anglicans make a community confession, not a private one-on-one. It's not the same—not nearly as painful." Robert smiled a knowing smile. "I don't think God will find too much of a difference with an Anglican confessing to a Catholic priest. Our two religions have more in common than not."

"I trust God will note this as a distinction without a difference. Please give me a moment." Thomas reached into his suit pocket and retrieved his stole. He kissed the stole and placed it about his neck. Thomas bowed his head, closed his eyes and silently prayed: *God, grant me the garment of immortality, which was forfeited by our sinful first parents.*

"Go ahead my son," Thomas said to Robert. It was not uncommon for Thomas, or any priest for that matter—to be younger than his confessant; but this time was different. For Thomas, Wordsworth's Ode, "And the Child is the Father of the Man," took on a new and sharper meaning. Thomas was not prepared for what would come next.

"Bless me Father for I have sinned," started Robert. They sat together for close to an hour with the door closed.

James and Matthew came downstairs and exchanged pleasantries with Estelle. Seeing the light under the closed study door, they knew not to knock. They went to the library and waited for Robert and Thomas to join them. Estelle wheeled the teacart with tea, scones and clotted cream into the library and returned to the kitchen.

"Father," began Robert, "I am guilty of a most grievous sin." Robert paused. He found the words to be painful and the task of finding the right way to express his transgression arduous. "Father, I lost faith. And worse, I took an action, which was an outward sign of my loss of faith. I want to explain what I was thinking and what action I took. I need to do so, not as an excuse, but as a full and complete unburdening of my soul."

Robert began his story. "Not long ago, before I met and came to know James, I began to despair. I knew my time on earth was drawing nearer and nearer to its end and I did not know what would become of the sacred secret, which I alone had in my possession.

"I lost hope and trust in the Lord. When would the next protector arrive? How would I know who it would be? How much time did I have left to transfer the secret? A man of faith would have realized God would send the next protector and defender in plenty of time. But I was without faith. I decided that I alone would need to take action to compensate for our Lord's lack of action. My first sin was my lack of faith and trust in God, but that was only the beginning.

"Father, it was then I decided to join The Doorway—which was my second sin. I decided that when the end-of-days finally came, I would carry the sacred secret with me through the portal to the other side. I still had not decided what to do if I didn't live long enough to go through the portal. I would have to find someone who could be my surrogate to carry the secret."

Thomas remained silent.

Robert continued, "I did not realize at the time, but I should have. I have been on earth long enough to know these things. Father, The Doorway is not a harmless organization invented by some misguided person. The Doorway is evil. There is much I can and will tell you about The Doorway, things we can discuss outside this confessional.

"My second sin is not just that I joined The Doorway, but I didn't quit when I became fully aware of The Doorway's mission. That was a sin of arrogance. I believed I could face down the Devil to get through the portal to the other side while carrying the sacred secret with me. I now realize what a foolish old man I have become. I know where the portal leads—I know what is on the other side."

It was time for Thomas to intervene. This was a confession unlike the thousands that Thomas heard before. It began as a conversation between two men without the usual veil or screen meant to keep the confessant anonymous. Thomas was not sure what to say and as the words rolled out of his mouth, he realized his response to Robert was stern, but time was short and the stakes were high. He felt his response to Robert was right.

Thomas knew more about the Devil and his power than just about anyone on earth. As one of the few priests schooled in the dark art of exorcism, Thomas knew many ways the great deceiver stalks and captures his prey. The evil one has time—he is eternal and we, his prey, are not. One man's lifetime is but an instant to the devil and he will toy with his quarry like a cat with a mouse for as long as he enjoys the game. And when he is done with his game, he will reel in his catch and move on to the next. Some victims mean more to him, but no victim means all to him. There are many prizes to collect yet a capture like Robert would be of some satisfaction.

"My son," began Thomas, "whether The Doorway is evil is not as important as is the fact you believed The Doorway was evil and yet you haven't quit. Remaining as a member when you were convinced of its evil intent was, as you have said, an act of arrogance. Believing your power is stronger than Satan's is foolish. Lucifer, Baal, or whatever name he uses, along with the other fallen angels, will create a howling wind against which no man can stand alone. Only by the grace of God can you survive. The evil one is powerful, but he is not all-powerful. The only way for a human to out game the Devil is to let the Devil outsmart himself, and when he is beating his chest with pride, by the grace of God the prey may slip away."

Robert nodded his assent to Thomas's scold.

"Robert, recognizing your sin and then renouncing it while begging for God's forgiveness for your lack of faith is what is required for absolution. What have you done regarding your membership in The Doorway?" asked Thomas.

"Quitting the Doorway is far more difficult than joining," answered Robert. "It isn't even a matter of no longer paying your dues. They count you as theirs and they don't intend to let go. I am fortunate for not having taken the next step. I had not yet accepted the mark."

"Could you please explain what you mean?" asked Thomas.

Robert continued, "When you join, you are given a white plastic card with a barcode on it—you cannot see the barcode, but it is there. The card resembles a credit card, but it's really your ticket through the portal to the other side at the precise moment of the end-of-days. When you receive your barcode card, you are almost one hundred percent part of The Doorway—almost. The next and final step is when you accept the mark on your person. You are told it is easier and safer to enter the portal when your barcode is embedded on your left hand. You won't need to worry about losing your card or not having it on you when the time arrives."

"May I see the card?" said Thomas.

Robert reached into his pocket, pulled the card out of his billfold and handed it to Thomas. "I don't know of anyone who has quit the Doorway and refused the mark. I understand the mark is not visible to the human eye—not until the day draws near. It is just expected; once you have the card you will eventually have the barcode embedded in your left hand. Father, I need your help. I need to return the card. I also need to inform them I have taken them out of my will. My solicitor, Heather Bean, wants me to present them with a witnessed letter."

"Robert, do you know how the barcode on the card is transferred to your hand?" asked Thomas.

"I am not sure exactly how it is done," answered Robert.

"Robert, this is important, please tell me all you know about the transfer process."

Robert lowered his head into his hands, "I believe I was told they will send a signal to all members that will activate a mechanism which somehow transfers the number on the card to your left hand. You don't even need to have the card in your possession when they send the signal to transfer the bar code to your left hand. When you join, you are required to send them a print of the thumb on your left hand. In the materials they send for you to join, they include a small pad where you place your thumbprint. I believe when you receive your membership card, your thumbprint has been transferred to the card with your barcode. Thomas, I can't claim to understand the technology they use, but nothing surprises me anymore."

Thomas had known Robert for little more than a day. When they first met, Robert was a man afraid of nothing, a man in complete control. However, at this moment, Robert had shrunk. He was old and vulnerable.

Robert reached out for Thomas's right hand. "Will you come with me tomorrow when we go to the city centre and make sure they don't try to pull a fast one on an old man?"

Thomas closed his eyes and inhaled a slow and deep breath thinking of what would be required of him on the following day. "Robert, I will do as you ask. Now, I will need some time to prepare. As for now, let me suggest we do not speak of this to anyone, not even James or Matthew—at least for the time being."

"Father, I am sorry I have made my burdens yours," started Robert, "but I have one additional request."

"What is it, my son?" asked Thomas.

Robert responded, "Father, I want to give you a letter. While it is not part of my confession, I ask you keep it in sacramental confidence until the right moment. You will know when the moment is right for it to be opened and its contents to be revealed."

Thomas accepted the sealed letter and placed it in his suit coat pocket.

"Now let us pray together the prayer that Jesus taught his apostles. When we have finished the Lord's Prayer, I will wait as you silently beg God's forgiveness."

The prayer was said together in unison and for a few minutes Robert buried his head in his hands. When Robert rose up, Thomas placed his hand on Robert's head. With his thumb, he sketched the sign of the cross on Robert's forehead saying, "Go and sin no more."

With the confession ended, Thomas rose, removed his stole, kissed it and put it back in his pocket.

Both men exchanged a look and there were tears in Robert's eyes. Robert clasped Thomas's right hand in his. "You are a strong man Thomas; you have a fighter's hands."

As they exited the study, Robert placed his arm around Thomas's shoulder, and they made their way to join the others in the library.

Matthew noticed, but said nothing about how at ease Robert appeared, as though a big burden had been lifted off his shoulders. Matthew thought to himself *that may be what is so beautiful and compelling about the Catholic confessional. The penitent always has the burden of sin lifted from him.* Conversely, Matthew also noticed Thomas looked as though he was deep in thought and might be harboring a headache.

As Robert and Thomas joined the other two, Estelle called them to dinner. She prepared Robert's favorite, rack of lamb.

"What's the celebration?" Robert asked Estelle.

"Nothing in particular sir, just the joy of having the Thompson house once again filled with guests," responded Estelle.

Robert answered, "I agree. This house has not been so joyful for years. This day and tomorrow will be the best days I will have had in a long, long time."

After dinner the four men moved to the library for a glass of wine. Henry built a fire and opened a bottle of Burgundy to let it breathe.

Robert said, "Gentlemen, I wish to make a toast. These past two days have been a good omen. I feel as though I know Thomas and Matthew nearly as well as I know James. I feel at peace."

Robert raised his glass. "Fine wine, a warm fire and good friends. Salute."

Each took a sip of wine and sat down—all except Thomas, who was again standing beside the bookcase.

"Robert," asked Thomas, "I was wondering if you would mind if I looked at your family Bible? It appears to occupy a special place amidst all your books." The door on the glass box, which held the Bible, was not locked; but since it could have been, Thomas did not want to err and intrude on anything personal.

"By all means, please take it out of its case and review it. It means much to me and will also for you."

Robert continued, "Everything in this house is to be sat upon, hoisted up or otherwise used for its intended purpose. The artifacts and antiques I have collected have no value if they are not put to use. None of these possessions are off-limits. All are meant to be touched or used. If these things cannot be handled, but only admired from afar, then as far as I am concerned they are worthless.

"I had an elderly aunt who was a spinster librarian and she was only happy when all the books had been returned to the library and put back where they belonged. She died with few friends. Ironically, or maybe even joyfully in her case, she died in the library by falling off a ladder while returning a book to its proper place on an upper shelf. Maybe subconsciously she is my motivation for always varying where I place books on my bookshelves."

"I'm sorry to hear about your aunt," said Matthew.

Robert laughed heartily. "Don't feel bad. I made that up, but I thought it was a good way to explain what I mean about using everything that's here. I know people look at antiques and say something like 'don't touch; you might break it. It's an antique.' However, I assure you the 100-year-old cups and plates were used regularly 100 years ago. Back then, they were plates and cups, not antiques."

Of the three, Thomas showed the greatest interest in Robert's collection of books. Whenever they all were together in Robert's library, Thomas would stand in front of the shelves looking at the titles and running his hands over the ancient leather bindings, while the others remained seated.

Robert's comment that the Thompson Family Bible would have special meaning to Thomas was another message from the elderly Scot with a hidden meaning. Thomas went to the shelves reserved for Bibles and other religious works and opened the glass door protecting the aged leather bound book with engraved silver clasps and gold gilded pages. On the inside cover, it read: *Holy Bible, Oxford, Printed by Thomas Baskett, 1778, London. Printed for Roman Christian Thompson.*

The first few pages were allocated to a family history. It began: *This Bible given to Spencer Wallace Thompson by his mother upon her decease having died April 28, 1817, in the thirty-ninth year of her life.* Also included was a birth and marriage entry: *Spencer Wallace Thompson born April 2, 1805, and Mary Pellinore, born May 31, 1810. Marriage solemnized August 16, 1826.* The several notations and charts demonstrated the Bible had been kept current. The last entry was: *Family Bible presented to Robert Christian Thompson, born April 7, 1920, left to him at the reading of the Last Will and Testament of Mason Roman Thompson on November 1, 1980.*

Robert took only a sip of his wine and said, "Good night gentlemen and thank you for today. I look forward to tomorrow. Please excuse me, I want to say goodnight to Estelle before she leaves."

The three stood. "Good night, Robert. Sleep well," said Thomas, as he returned the Thompson Family Bible to its glass case. *I will review the Bible later*, Thomas thought to himself.

Robert smiled, turned about and left the room.

"Jimmy, this has been a fascinating and very full day and a half. Your Robert is an interesting man." Matthew continued, "He seemed to really enjoy introducing you to all the good townspeople. I'm sure you noticed how he told everyone you now own the home? I'm guessing he wants no questions asked about who owns the house when he passes, and hopefully that's a long time off. By introducing you as the new owner, he legitimizes the transfer. Even though you've been around Glastonbury for almost a year, you're still a stranger. While no one else could lay claim to the house, I am sure there are several who covet the place and especially its contents."

Matthew continued. "I have a suggestion. It might be wise for you to keep Estelle and Henry on. Lord knows you can't cook and as far as cleaning goes, well let's just say you cook better than you clean. And you'll still need Henry to take care of the garden and the yard."

"Excellent idea," said James. "Robert sure looked at ease tonight. More at ease than I can ever remember seeing him these past nine months I've known him."

"Some of the credit belongs to Thomas and the power of the Catholic confessional," offered Matthew. "We have our own Jewish confession tradition. It can take place anytime, but we tend to focus our confession on Yom Kippur. There is a big difference, however. The Yom Kippur confession is public and communal even though we don't speak our sins out loud. That's much easier than sitting across from another person confessing your sins. It is no small wonder the penitent Catholic exudes so much relief."

Thomas was strangely silent all evening, saying little at dinner, and mostly just responding to questions. James and Matthew looked at Thomas for a comment. Finally Thomas offered, "Well, you're half right. Actually, the priest is standing in place of God, and when the priest gives absolution, the sin is erased. The burden is lifted and the penitent is instructed to go and sin no more. Of course that rarely happens unless the penitent dies before he sins again.

"We have another sacrament that is closely related to the cleansing power of the confessional" continued Thomas. "The sacrament of extreme unction, also called last rites or anointing of the sick, is the absolution given to those who are gravely ill, especially those in danger of death. Catholic chaplains on the battlefield administer last rites to Catholic soldiers who have been shot and lie gravely wounded. I know we Catholics have a bunch of mumbo jumbo secret rites and ceremonies, which are often ridiculed, but when one is on their deathbed the rituals are mighty comforting. Even for Martin Luther; on his deathbed he is reported to have said: 'It is good to live as a Protestant, but better to die as a Catholic.'"

"Well, hopefully no one is dying. Not tonight, anyway," said James.

Thomas added, "If you don't mind, I would like to turn in. I need to collect my thoughts and I want to do a little reading before I go to sleep."

"Is everything okay?" asked James. "You seem a bit preoccupied."

"No, all's well," answered Thomas. "I just have a couple of things on my mind and we've been on the go ever since we got here. Tomorrow may be another busy day, so I need a moment or two to reflect." Thomas finished his wine and set the glass on the teacart. "See you in the morning."

James and Matthew responded, "Good night, Thomas." The two remained seated.

Thomas left for his room and James leaned over toward Matthew, "Is everything all right? Tommie hasn't said much all evening."

"I think so, but it does seem as though his mind is somewhere else. I have seen him like this before, generally after he has been hearing confessions. Since we Jews have a personal, silent confession, I can't really relate. I would suppose Thomas has probably heard it all, but still the penitent is freed of his or her sins when they give them over to the priest. The priest ends up with the sins and although he is not responsible for their commission, he still possesses them until he can let them go. He'll be fine in the morning."

During Robert's confession, Thomas asked to see the white membership card Robert received when he joined The Doorway. Thomas still had the card in his possession. He sat down at the desk in his room and took it out to examine it. There was nothing remarkable about it. It was a plastic card, the size of a credit card with nothing on it visible to the naked eye. He looked at it from several angles, but still could see nothing.

Thomas set the white Doorway card on his desk. He took out a permanent ink marker from his computer bag and tried to make an "x" on the card. But the card would not hold the marker's ink. *Nothing unusual there,* he thought, *sometimes ink doesn't adhere to plastic.* Next he took out a small pocket knife to scratch the card. He pressed the knife's edge into the card, but he still could not leave a mark. Finally, he took a scissors from the desk drawer to cut the card. He squeezed firmly only resulting in braking off one of the scissors' blades, again without leaving a mark.

It appeared the card was impervious to alteration. *What I expected,* thought Thomas. He finally took out a small vial of holy water that he always carried with him. Although one of the powers of a priest is the sanctification of ordinary water into holy water, the vial, which Thomas carried with him was special. He received it as a gift from Michael Moriarity when they were in Rome. A Carmelite nun, who belonged to an order dedicated to Saint Theresa of Avila, gave the vial to Michael. Michael then gave Thomas the holy water in appreciation for making it possible for him to go to Rome.

St. Theresa believed strongly that holy water could be used for protection from the "powers of darkness." She reported visions of Jesus and Mary in mortal combat with demons and devils, and she wrote about the power of holy water to repel evil. She wrote: "I know by frequent experience there is nothing which puts the devils to flight like holy water."

Holy water sounds like a card trick. Because any priest can sanctify ordinary water into holy water, it could be so plentiful as to be virtually meaningless. Yet, when belief in its power is present, holy water can become a powerful force against the power of darkness. In the infrequent application of exorcism, the exorcist counts heavily upon the power of holy water as part of his armamentarium in confronting the devil.

With the card on the desk, Thomas opened Michael's vial of holy water. This was the final option and Thomas feared that if it failed, he was unsure of what to do next. As he poured just a drop from the vial, he said, "By this holy water and by your precious blood, wash away all the sins from the man whose soul is written on this card." The drop of water turned smoking hot and burned a hole clean through the middle of the card, precisely where the invisible barcode would have been.

This was exactly what Thomas hoped and prayed for. But as the power of the water did as it was ordained to do, Thomas felt ashamed for his lack of belief. *Why do I always need a sign,* he asked himself? *Why can't I just believe?* Thomas knelt down and prayed. *I am unworthy and yet you always come to my aid. I beg your forgiveness.* He prayed for the strength he would need in the days ahead. He prayed for forgiveness.

Saturday, January 8 – Thompson House

The morning sun awakened Thomas, still kneeling. He slept the night on his knees, his head resting on his bed. He rose and stretched, feeling empowered and remarkably rested thinking to himself *that had to be one of the better night's sleep I've had in some time.* Thomas showered, shaved and dressed and went downstairs for breakfast.

Estelle felt obliged to see Robert's guests were well cared for, and even though Robert told her she need not come to the house on Saturday, Estelle insisted. She and Henry were there at half past six in the morning. While Henry attended to the yard, Estelle was in the kitchen gathering ingredients for a breakfast of eggs, toast, sausage, kippers, and oven-broiled tomatoes for all the manor's guests.

Thomas arrived downstairs before the others. He said good morning to Estelle and retired to the library to prepare for the day. Within moments, Estelle wheeled in the teacart. Estelle liked Thomas and she wished him "good morning" with coffee and a scone. The others wouldn't be down for another hour.

Finally around 8 a.m., the four men were seated at the dining room table as Estelle brought out the traditional English breakfast. "If you are spending another day in Glastonbury, you will need a good breakfast," she said.

"Thank you Estelle. This will most certainly hold us until lunchtime," said Robert.

"You are most welcome. If anyone wants more, please let me know," Estelle said as she returned to the kitchen.

Robert suggested the itinerary for the day. They would take separate cars. James and Matthew would go grocery shopping in Street, a city a few miles west of Glastonbury. Robert prepared a list of what he needed to make for the evening's dinner. James knew just where to go to get what Robert wanted. Since Matthew would be the cook's helper, he would go along and make the final selection.

Thomas would accompany Robert to a ten o'clock meeting with Heather Bean to authorize final changes to Robert's will. Thomas would drive Robert's Range Rover. "Lizzy needs a bit of a workout," Robert said referring to his car.

Robert did not mention their plan to stop at The Doorway headquarters. Thomas suggested to Robert they "not speak of this to anyone—at least for the time being." Not anyone, in this case, included James and Matthew. It had nothing to do with trust, but everything to do with the confidentiality of the confessional. The time would come later when Robert could lift the veil of secrecy allowing James and Matthew in on what was going on.

Robert suggested the four of them meet at noon for lunch at the old George and Pilgrims Hotel, and then pay a visit to St. John the Baptist Church to meet Vicar Dunmore. He also wanted his three guests to spend some time on the Glastonbury Abbey grounds and at the Chalice Well.

Heather Bean's Office

Robert and Thomas arrived at 10 a.m. and Heather was waiting for them. Heather had not yet met Thomas so Robert made the introductions. Heather had the documents ready to be signed and witnessed. She suggested Robert take his time reading his revised will. "Robert," she said, "please review your will carefully. It is not a complex document; regardless, we want to get it right. If you wish any changes, please let me know and I can make those changes easily."

Robert studied the document and all appeared in order. "I have prepared a letter which you need to sign and Father Ryan and I will witness. I will make another signed copy and will place it in your will noting the change. You can then hand deliver the other copy to The Doorway to inform them they are no longer a beneficiary of your estate."

Robert asked Thomas to review both the will and the letter to The Doorway. "Two pair of eyes is better than one, especially one old, tired pair of eyes."

Thomas reviewed both documents and noted, "I've not been privy to other conversations, but both your will and letter are what you and I discussed."

"One last item," said Robert as he produced the one-page, handwritten letter from his suit coat pocket, which would be a codicil to his will. Heather and Thomas watched as Robert signed and dated two copies of the letter. "You must pardon me but the contents of this letter must remain confidential until my death and the reading of my will."

After Robert signed, Heather and Thomas both witnessed and countersigned both copies without reviewing what Robert had written. Robert put a copy of each into separate envelopes, sealed both, and handed one to Heather to be included with his will and the other to Thomas for safekeeping. With the codicil attached, Robert then signed the will with Heather and Thomas as witnesses.

Robert stood erect, nodded his head and said with a sound of satisfaction, "Done."

"Heather, I appreciate everything you have done for me," said Robert as he and Thomas prepared to leave.

"Thank you, Robert. You two have a good day and I hope to see you soon."

☙The Doorway❧

The Doorway's headquarters was only a few blocks away. It was a fairly warm and sunny January day and Robert was up for a walk.

As they walked, Robert grabbed Thomas's arm to steady himself. "Father Ryan, there are no words for me to express how much I appreciate what you have done for me so far and what still must be done. Son, I am not sure I could stand up alone against our next foe."

"Robert, I did something last evening to make this next meeting a little easier. Now I know without a doubt what we are up against."

When they entered the headquarters, the receptionist immediately recognized and warmly greeted Robert. "Why Mr. Thompson, it is so good to see you again. It has been a long time. Please be seated. I will make sure President Niccolo and Mr. Collier know you are here."

"Thank you Mary, we'll stand. Getting up and down can be a bit of an effort for a man my age," responded Robert who was starting to look a bit ashen.

"Are you okay?" whispered Thomas.

"With you, yes, but I am a bit afraid. As long as you are by my side, I'll be all right."

Mary, not paying attention to Robert's condition said, "And your associate's name? I'm sorry; I don't believe you have visited here before."

Thomas smiled and said, "I am Father Thomas Ryan."

"Welcome Mr. Ryan," said Mary. "I am not sure I can let you in with Mr. Thompson. You are not in my book."

Robert said, "Mary, I am sure it will be okay. You see we are here together as though we are one. There is no other way. I am sure Mr. Collier won't mind."

Mary was a bit flustered. She called the director's office leaving the phone on speaker. "Mr. Collier, Mr. Thompson is here, but he is not alone. There is a Mister…"

Thomas interrupted, "Father…"

Mary said, "There is a Father Ryan with him who wants to be let in with him."

There was a pause. Collier said, "Let them both in, Mary."

Father Ryan and Robert signed the log, received their badges and were let in by a security guard. The Doorway Director, Malcolm Collier, met them in the lobby and escorted them into his office. It was a spacious room with a large window overlooking the Glastonbury Abbey historic grounds. The Abbey grounds occupied over 35 acres of land in the center of Glastonbury. Although the remaining Abbey buildings were under constant renovation, the grounds were open for business. There were five fully restored buildings, several open ruins and well manicured grassy areas. The view Collier could enjoy on an everyday basis was there mostly to impress visitors to The Doorway.

Collier was a tall, thin man in his mid-fifties with a trimmed beard. He was wearing a brown robe, hemp belt and sandals. Thomas, not wanting to reveal a smirk, covered his mouth with his hand as the image of Obi Wan Kenobi from the movie, *Star Wars* flashed into his mind.

In Collier's office, standing looking out the window was a tall, thin man with short blond hair wearing a dark suit. Collier introduced him as Niccolo, the president of The Doorway. Niccolo gave the guests a sideways glance but made no gesture to come forward.

Thomas nodded his head asking, "I'm sorry, is it Mr. Niccolo?"

Niccolo looked directly at Thomas, yet said nothing.

"I'm sorry," said the more conversant Collier, "President Niccolo merely goes by Niccolo."

Collier, speaking in a friendly manner said, "Robert, it is good to see you. What can I do for you?"

"Good morning Malcolm," said Robert. "I have come to return this." Robert was carrying a small bag. He opened it and produced his Rolex Countdown Clock.

Collier, looking a bit surprised said, "Robert, I don't understand? Is the clock broken?"

Thomas was looking straight at Niccolo who continued looking out the window refusing to return his stare.

"Malcolm, I will no longer be a member of The Doorway. I have come to return this clock and to give you this letter." Robert set the clock down on Collier's desk and handed him the letter.

Collier slowly read the letter. He then walked over and whispered to Niccolo as he handed him the paper. After Niccolo read it, he folded it, whispered to Collier and handed it back. Collier returned to speak to Robert.

"Robert, why don't you please be seated?" suggested Collier.

Robert replied, "Malcolm, we really won't be here long. I would prefer to stand."

Collier walked behind his desk and took a seat. "As you wish."

Collier, seated, held the letter. "Robert, we fully understand your decision to no longer include us in your will. That is your decision and your decision alone. And we, of course, accept your decision. We really don't want your money, we really want you."

Thomas, his eyes still fixed on Niccolo, witnessed a grin flash across Niccolo's face. Niccolo turned again to look out the window.

"Robert, there is no benefit in you resigning from The Doorway. Your dues have been paid in full, your membership card has been prepared and your membership number assigned. We never had anyone leave us. You can certainly return the clock if you wish; it alone has no significance. The important thing is your membership card."

Collier leaned forward. "Let me explain how it works. When you joined, you were given a number, actually a barcode, which was embedded in your membership card along with the thumbprint from your left hand. A special number was assigned to you and you alone. We have the technology to transfer the number on the card to your left hand. When it is done, you will be a member, regardless of whether you change your mind or not. Now, it may be true we are not interested in all who join, but you are special. As long as your membership card is intact, there is nothing more…"

Niccolo gestured to Collier and he stopped speaking. Collier rose and went to Niccolo who whispered to him. Niccolo appeared to be upset at Collier and Collier was nodding like a puppet apologizing to the puppet master. It would appear Niccolo scolded Collier, who maybe said too much—especially in the company of Father Ryan. Collier left Niccolo's side and returned to his desk. He took a moment to compose himself, sat down and then smiled a weak smile.

"Well, Robert, I have told you all you need to know."

Robert was feeling somewhat overwhelmed by the one-sided conversation, wondering when Father Ryan would come to his aid. Weakened, Robert slumped into a chair in front of Collier's desk.

Thomas waited to learn as much information about The Doorway as he could from Collier. Thomas finally intervened, speaking slowly and confidently: "Mr. Collier, Niccolo, I think there is a misunderstanding. Hopefully you can clarify this for both of us. Robert has indicated he no longer wishes to be a member of The Doorway and you are telling him, if I get this right, he essentially cannot quit. You are saying his number, his barcode, has been issued to him on a membership card, and as long as the membership card is intact, you have the technology to transfer the barcode to his left hand. Is that correct?"

Collier first looked to Niccolo who nodded. "Yes, that is essentially correct," said Collier, who was apparently affected by Niccolo's scolding and was not going to offer any more information.

"But you see," said Thomas, "his card is no longer intact." Thomas removed the card from his pocket, with the hole burned through the middle and placed in on Collier's desk.

Collier backed away as if Thomas just put a snake on the desk.

Niccolo gestured and Collier rose, picked up the card and took it to Niccolo. The two men spoke only in whispers, but their expressions spoke volumes. Niccolo's face expressed anger, while Collier looked confused.

Thomas thought he heard Niccolo whisper the word, "worthless."

Collier returned to his desk and smiled a fake smile. "Robert, President

Niccolo has pointed out to me we truly only want happy members and he concurs we will honor your wishes as your number apparently has been voided. I believe that concludes our business. You may leave the clock and what is left of your card. I believe you know the way out." Collier rose and went to stand next to Niccolo as they turned their backs and both looked out the window.

With Collier and Niccolo no longer looking at Thomas and Robert, Thomas picked up the altered card and put it in his pocket. He smiled and winked at Robert. He could see Robert's color coming back. Robert rose and both left Collier's office. They said farewell to Mary and stepped outside. The sun was shining.

"Well done, my boy, well done," said Robert. "The Good Lord sent you without a moment to spare. You saved my life. I will release you from your oath of confessional secrecy so you may tell James and Matthew. But before you do, allow me this day to savor this victory. Let us celebrate at the old George and Pilgrims. It is nearly noon and I feel as though we have already done a full day's work. I am as hungry as a horse."

Robert was beaming at how Thomas played the game and defeated Collier and Niccolo. Robert was repeating, "Well done, well done."

Robert and Thomas entered the George and Pilgrims and could see James and Matthew already seated. Robert and Thomas joined the other two as the waitress promptly arrived.

"Why 'tis you, Mr. Thompson," said Margaret, a waitress who had been so long at the George and Pilgrims she was an institution.

"Margaret, it is so good to see you looking so well," answered Robert.

Thomas, James and Matthew could see how Robert's comment affected Margaret. Robert was still a handsome man and his effect on women had not lost its luster.

James commented, "Robert, it doesn't seem to matter if you are wearing your military blouse and medals, you still have a way with women."

Robert smiled and offered, "Why thank you. Thomas and I had a good day, a very good day indeed. Let us order a round to celebrate and then a hearty lunch. This celebration is most definitely my treat." Robert signaled Margaret and she was promptly at his side.

"Margaret, I would like a glass of Chardonnay."

"Same for me," said Matthew.

"Same also," said James.

"Margaret, I hate to be different, but I would like a glass of Jameson, straight up, no ice, with a glass of water on the side," said Thomas.

"Margaret, that is not quite true, Father Ryan here, loves to be different," offered James.

With the drinks delivered, Margaret collected their choices for lunch. As the four chatted joyfully, the passage of time went unnoticed until Margaret returned with their meals. Thomas, still somewhat drained from his recent encounter with the dark side asked all to bow their heads in prayer. "Lord, please bless this food so it may renew within us the strength to continue to do your work. Amen."

As they finished their lunch, Robert said, "Boys, I would like to take you over to St. John the Baptist Church and see if we might be able to tour the building. Then, if time permits, we can take a tour of Glastonbury Abbey, the Chalice Well and, finally the Glastonbury Thorn."

When they first entered St. John the Baptist they were greeted by Agatha Niblett, one of the church's volunteer docents, who offered escorted tours of the restored fifteenth century church. Agatha was thrilled to see Robert. "Mr. Thompson, I haven't seen you for way too long. It is so good to see you again. You are looking well."

"Thank you Agatha. It has been a while and it is good to see you also. I brought some friends who have not yet seen the church. Well, James here has. Let me introduce you to my three American friends. Agatha, you know Dr. James Christopoulos. He is now a new resident of Glastonbury. James purchased my home and everything in it and has been gracious enough to let me stay rent-free. I think we have a couple good reasons to make him a permanent resident."

"I see. Would this be the gentleman who is seeing our Margo Webster?"

"Ah, the joys of a small town," answered James. "Yes, Margo Webster and I are…friends."

"I would also like to introduce Rabbi Matthew Halprin and Father Thomas Ryan. These gentlemen are boyhood friends of James. I'm hoping we can entice them to spend more time here with us. Gentlemen, Agatha and I have known each other for….well, let me just say for a while. She was the right arm and invaluable assistant to Vicar David MacPherson."

"You are too kind, Mr. Thompson. I did what I could, but Vicar MacPherson rarely needed any help. He was a saint and he is greatly missed. Maybe a saint who also used some colorful language, but a saint nonetheless."

"That is true Agatha, but you always knew what he meant."

"Amen."

"Agatha, these gentlemen and I are meeting with Vicar Dunmore at 1:30. But since we have some time, maybe you can show them around."

"I doubt I could do it as well as you, sir."

"Well then, let's do it together."

"It would be an honor."

Thomas grabbed hold of James's arm and with Matthew by his side said, "Robert is incredible. He is 91 and has some of the best pickup lines I've ever heard. Everywhere we go women virtually swoon over him."

Robert started the tour. "Gentlemen, St. John the Baptist Church is over 500 years old. It was built in 1475 around the time Christopher Columbus began his efforts to get someone to support his lunatic voyage to the new world. I have often thought Queen Isabella gave in simply to get him out of the royal hall. Maybe she thought having him sail over the edge was a good way of getting rid of him.

"Sorry for the aside," Robert chuckled, "back to the church. Over the years, there were fires and there were wars and the grand church went through periods of disrepair. While all the mechanical elements are currently functioning, the church could use some serious upgrading."

"Mr. Thompson, you are so right, but in this economy money is tight," offered Agatha.

"Well, since our time is also a little tight, let me guide you to the one place which has captivated our James's attention."

Robert led them to the north window, which he described as a tribute to St. Joseph of Arimathea.

"Notice the window consists of four stained glass window panels and each features Joseph of Arimathea. Some have conjectured having a window with four stained glass panels is symbolic of the fact Joseph of Arimathea is mentioned in all four Gospels. I am certain you three are well aware of how important Joseph was in the life of Jesus Christ. I also find it curious a man as significant as Joseph is a relative unknown to so many who proclaim to be Christian. My suspicious side has me wondering if there is a purposeful intent to keep Joseph in obscurity."

Robert's comment about his "suspicious side" was not lost on Thomas, who made mental note of Robert's suggestion that Joseph of Arimathea may hold the key to a better understanding of Jesus Christ.

Robert continued. "Each panel tells part of Joseph's story. The first panel shows Joseph of Arimathea protesting the condemnation of Jesus Christ. Panel two shows Joseph at the Lord's entombment. Panel three is the one that has James most excited. It shows Joseph of Arimathea cradling two cruets, which many have suggested held the blood and sweat of the Lord Jesus Christ. The fourth panel shows Joseph planting his staff in the soft ground of Wearyall Hill, which by the following morning turned into the Glastonbury Thorn Tree."

James interjected, "Legends, such as these, can play a role as we seek corroborating information to help prove our supposition. The Gospels of Matthew, Mark, Luke and John tell the story about Joseph's role in the burial of Jesus. The non-canonical Gospel of Nicodemus tells a story about Joseph collecting the blood and sweat of Jesus and placing both in cruets. These stained glass windows portray those sacred cruets—all corroborating evidence.

"Clues like this are overlooked by the casual and even the devout believer. Ask yourself, has anyone ever said to you, 'Gosh, have you ever noticed Joseph of Arimathea is mentioned in all four New Testament Gospels?' These and more clues support the supposition Joseph and Jesus had a much more significant relationship which may have played an important role in the Passion of the Christ."

"Welcome to St. John the Baptist," a female voice could be heard from the back of the church.

All turned toward the source.

It was Vicar Dunmore in her slightly off-white High-Mass vestments. "Please allow me to introduce myself. I am Vicar Carol Dunmore and I am pleased to welcome you to St. John the Baptist Church."

"It is good to see you Vicar," responded Robert. "It has been awhile. Allow me to introduce my associates. You may have met Dr. James Christopoulos. Dr. Christopoulos is an archeologist whose main interest is in the death and resurrection of our Lord, Jesus Christ. Rabbi Matthew Halprin and Father Thomas Ryan are lifelong friends of Dr. Christopoulos. They are here on holiday—old friends reconnecting." Robert did not want to reveal more than was necessary. "Incidentally, Dr. Christopoulos has just purchased my home and intends to make it his primary residence and we believe he has another important reason for calling Glastonbury home. Wouldn't you agree Agatha?"

"Absolutely," responded Agatha.

"I see," said Vicar Dunmore. "Could this be the gentleman who is spending time with our Margo Webster?"

"I seem to be hearing that a lot lately," said James.

There was laughter all around.

"I am pleased you have come to pay a visit. Please come join me in our boardroom. I have tea and coffee," continued Vicar Dunmore.

Agatha said her goodbyes and returned to her post as the four followed the vicar to the boardroom.

Thomas attempted to get the conversation started saying, "Thank you for taking the time to visit with us. It is not our intent to monopolize your time. We just thought it to be professional courtesy to let you know we are in town."

"And it is my professional courtesy to welcome you," responded Vicar Dunmore.

They did not seem to get off on the right foot. The professional courtesy stuff sounded stiff and way too formal.

Thomas attempted to lift the formality veil. "I understand you are fairly new yourself to St. John the Baptist. It's an honor to be charged with this flagship. I would imagine this appointment caught you off guard."

Thomas could have kicked himself before the last word left his lips. *Way to go Ryan, another subtle insult*, he thought. "I meant to say such a prestigious appointment so early in your career."

Matthew to the rescue. "Thomas and I are from America where much of our history spans less than 250 years. By comparison your religious institutions are three times as established as ours." Matthew's deference was disarming and Vicar Dunmore was smiling and more openly engaged.

Thomas thought, *Shut up Ryan. Let Matthew carry the conversation. You can try again another day.*

Matthew continued: "Vicar, if your time permits, I would welcome your assistance in trying to connect with my past. I believe the Halprin's have a connection with this area of England."

"Rabbi, I'm not a genealogist, but I would be happy to assist. How long are you going to be visiting with us?" answered the vicar.

"Unfortunately, I'll be here only another week," Matthew responded, "but it looks as though I may be coming back fairly soon. Thank you for offering to help. I'll check with my father when I get home about anything he recalls about his ancestors."

Matthew changed gears to try to get Thomas back into the conversation. "Father Ryan has told me he too may have some English roots. His grandparents came to America from Kinsale, Ireland and probably vociferously denied any English heritage."

Vicar Dunmore laughed. "Sometimes I think the Irish in America are more Irish than the Irish in Ireland."

"I accept that as true. My grandfather was very proud of his lineage and he left no doubt about his love for the old country," said Thomas.

Robert wanted to let the Vicar know about Sunday, "Vicar, Thomas, James, Matthew and I will be coming to the nine o'clock service tomorrow."

"Thank you, Robert. I look forward to seeing you all."

When they exited the Vicar's company, Thomas apologized for his comments. "That certainly did not come off well. The conversation with the Vicar was stilted and my weak attempts to strike a connection only seemed to widen the gap. We, I mean, I will have to try again tomorrow. Maybe I should just shut my mouth and watch how Robert does it."

The temperature was in the mid fifties, but the sun was shining and the absence of any wind made the afternoon most pleasant. The four men walked the two blocks to Glastonbury Abbey.

The abbey grounds are peaceful parklands with ponds, an orchard and a wildlife area. It was winter, but the crocuses were already out, and the four had a pleasant stroll through the ruins. Legend says King Arthur died at Glastonbury, and he and Queen Guinevere were buried on the Abbey grounds. Occasionally people lay flowers there to honor the mighty king whose life has given birth to so many myths and legends.

James and Thomas walked back to pick up the cars. They planned to drive Robert over to the Chalice Well for it would have been too much of a walk. Like the Glastonbury Abbey grounds, the Chalice Well area has several well-manicured gardens with a perfect view of the Tor.

A natural spring still flows orange-red waters, which it has done for hundreds, maybe thousands of years. Legend claims Joseph of Arimathea buried the chalice from the Crucifixion beneath its waters causing the waters to flow red. Miraculous cures are ascribed to the waters, but with little documented proof. There are also several Glastonbury Thorn trees, which flower twice a year—at Christmas and Easter. The first Glastonbury Thorn tree, according to mythology, sprung to life when Joseph of Arimathea stuck his staff into the ground. The following morning, Joseph's staff became a flowering thorn tree.

The hour was getting late and after a brief visit at the Chalice Well, Robert suggested it was time to head home.

The four arrived around 4 p.m. from a somewhat quixotic day. They managed to see what they missed the day before, but the day seemed to fly by way too quickly.

Estelle brought out whatever cooking pots and pans Robert and Matthew might need to prepare dinner.

"Estelle, I trust you had a good day. Anything of interest happen?" asked Robert.

Estelle paused, "Well, yes actually. There were two unusual phone calls. The first was for you Mr. Thompson. A man called introducing himself as a realtor from West London. He wondered if the Thompson home was for sale, suggesting he had a potential buyer. I did not think it was my place to discuss your affairs. But the man was most insistent, wanting to know if the household belongings would also be included in the sale. I explained the house was no longer for sale.

"The man kept probing saying things such as, 'Oh, so the house has already been sold? Were the belongings included or will they be on the market separately?' I apologize, but I couldn't get him to stop, and I didn't think to just hang up—I have never done that. It was a most unnerving call. And finally, the man hung up. He would not give his name and number.

"Then no more than 15 minutes had gone by, and Dr. Christopoulos received a call. This was a call from someone who said he knows the doctor. The caller announced himself as Father Frederick Fulgrum and said he was calling from Rome just to talk to Dr. Christopoulos. He said he was pleased he finally tracked you down with help from some of your colleagues at the University of Athens. He wondered when you and he might get together. He suggested the two of you get together here in Glastonbury next week. He also wanted to know if Dr. Christopoulos knew the whereabouts of Father Ryan, saying Father Ryan was a friend of his.

"I must say for some reason or other, the two calls seemed connected. The sounds in the background were much the same. They just seemed odd coming so close to one another. I hope I didn't say anything wrong. The calls just made me feel uncomfortable."

"Don't worry, Estelle. Your response to the callers was most correct," responded Robert.

"Thank you, sir. Henry and I will be going home now for a short while and will return around seven if that is all right?"

"That would be fine, Estelle."

Estelle and Henry had just left when Robert turned and said to the others. "Something is afoot and we better get on top of it."

James added, "Father Fulgrum is getting a little too close if you know what I mean?"

"Yes, I think we all do," said Thomas. "I think it might be a good idea if we were to sit together and try to figure out what is happening."

"Agreed," said Robert.

Chapter VII

A riddle wrapped in a mystery inside an enigma

LATE AFTERNOON SATURDAY, JANUARY 8 – THOMPSON HOUSE LIBRARY

Robert, James, Thomas and Matthew met in the library for a brief strategy session. Robert needed to get something off his chest. There would be more time tomorrow for discussion, but he had some things he wanted to say that couldn't wait.

"I've never met your Father Fulgrum, but from what you've told me, I know his type. I've seen this story before. People like him who are not well liked seem to think by bringing others down, they somehow elevate themselves. We need to keep him away from here at all costs," cautioned Robert.

Robert, Matthew and James were seated in the library while Thomas took his normal position standing in front of the bookcase. Thomas responded. "I have to agree with Robert, we may have a big problem in Fulgrum. It's beginning to look as though the secret we have yet to discover is no longer a secret. But all's not lost; we may be able to turn this to our advantage."

"What are you thinking?" asked James.

Thomas offered, "Let's assume Fulgrum is aware we have a secret, but at the same time he doesn't know what the secret is. In fact, we don't even know what the secret is or where it is; only our host knows. In a way, it's similar to how Churchill described Russia during World War II: *a riddle wrapped in a mystery inside an enigma!* Robert, you may be the exception, which proves the rule. Benjamin Franklin once said: 'three can keep a secret, if two of them are dead.'"

Thomas continued, "My boss at Georgetown, Dean Carroll, told me Fulgrum is a special assistant to the Vatican finance officer, Cardinal Pietro Castillo. Among other duties he is responsible for Church patents and copyrights. Dean Carroll felt compelled to remind me the Vatican is deeply concerned about its image. Besides the image problem, Father Fulgrum's job is to monitor how people within the Church portray Jesus.

"We know Father Fulgrum is telling just about every person he meets he and I are old friends. He's using this ploy as a way to discover what I'm doing with James and what James's research is all about—although James's search for the Holy Grail is hardly a secret."

Thomas continued, "We also know he's using surrogates to capture whatever information he can. For example, the call earlier today from a phony West London realtor, inquiring if the Thompson home was still for sale, and then inquiring if the household contents were included in the sale. That had to be at Fulgrum's direction. I think he's fishing for whatever he can lay his hands on."

"What concerns me most," added Robert, "is his questioning whether the household contents were sold along with the house."

"The fact he was able to track me down to Glastonbury, and even more specifically to Robert's home, is also very troubling," added James.

"On top of what everyone has said, let me add, Freddy seems to have picked up the pace of his investigation," noted Matthew, "making it seem critically urgent."

"It is critically urgent," stressed Robert who was fully engaged in the conversation.

Thomas responded, "You know, he's really going about this in a ham-handed way. Either he thinks we're unaware of his efforts or he's intentionally beating the bushes to let us know he's watching us. Freddy isn't stupid. I think he's trying to force us into making a mistake.

"Let me place a call to an acquaintance and see if he has any idea what Freddy's up to. He's probably not in his office, but there's no harm in trying."

"Who are you going to call?" asked Matthew.

"Do you remember after our Georgetown lecture, during the Q & A, one of the questions came from a *Washington Post* reporter, Randy Cross?"

Matthew nodded affirmatively.

"Cross is a former priest. We used to be fairly close. He left the priesthood on principle and later met a woman and married. He wasn't lured away as others have. He was fed up with the Church bureaucracy and the way the Church restricts and almost censures honest inquiry."

Matthew interjected, "I remember. He was the one who asked if we felt our Churches were meeting the needs of the faithful."

"That's him," said Thomas. "I'm thinking he may be gathering information to do a story critical of the way the Church uses secrecy and the mantle of infallibility to protect transgressors. Cross is no friend of Fulgrum. Actually, no one is, but that's beside the point. I'm guessing Cross has sources in the Vatican who slip him information. I don't know if he knows anything, but there's no harm in asking."

"Can you trust him?" asked Robert.

"I won't give away any secrets. I'll just see if there's anything on his radar," Thomas's replied.

"If you're comfortable, go ahead," affirmed Robert. Robert was solidly in Thomas's camp and trusted him completely.

"Are you comfortable using your cell phone?" asked James. "I'm afraid none of our phones are secure."

"What choice do I have?" asked Thomas.

"I guess none," answered James.

Robert offered, "Why not use my cell phone. It gets precious little use and I doubt it's tapped."

"You have a cell phone?" asked a somewhat startled James.

"Yes, James, I have a cell phone. I may be old, but I'm hardly ancient," replied Robert.

All four men laughed.

"All right then," said James. "We'll use Robert's cell phone. He'll just have to show us how to work the crank."

Robert retrieved his cell phone from his coat pocket and handed it to Thomas.

Thomas dialed the international operator for help in getting connected to the *Washington Post*. It was Saturday morning in the States and the Post's automated receptionist instructed Thomas to type in "Cross" on his phone pad.

"We'll see if he's in."

Cross's telephone extension rang.

"Randall Cross."

"Randy, this is Tom Ryan."

"Wow, a voice from the past. Are you calling to give me grief about my question to you and Halprin?"

"No Randy, that wasn't a problem. I know I seldom call, but I was wondering if I could ask a favor?"

"Seldom call! You never call. This has got to be important. What may I do to help you this fine Saturday morning?" Cross' tone revealed sarcasm.

"Randy, I'm in England with Matthew Halprin and James Christopoulos, and a gentleman who is helping James with his research. You do remember James don't you?"

"I do, but it's been a long time. He doesn't call me either."

"Touché. Randy, do you remember Frederick Fulgrum?"

"Ichabod Fulgrum? He's not easy to forget—the weasel."

"That's him," acknowledged Thomas.

"Okay, Ryan, you never call me, but now you are in England with a couple of your old friends and you decide to call to see if I remember Freddy Fulgrum? I'm glad you're paying for the call. All right, you got me, what would you like to know?"

"This is a bit off the wall, but Freddy was at the lecture last week, and he seemed to be paying very close attention to my every word. And for the past week or so, he keeps popping up all over the place telling people he and I are old friends. I'm just wondering if you have anything on what he's doing at the Vatican which might cause him to be so interested in my work?" asked Thomas.

"That kind of depends. What kind of work are you into?"

"Right now, I'm simply helping Jimmy with his research, along with writing a piece on the lost years of Jesus," answered Thomas.

"You're helping Christopoulos chase the Holy Grail!" was Cross' retort.

"Randy, the Grail is not a UFO. Jimmy is doing some important scientific inquiry. And how do you know Jimmy is looking for the Grail?"

"Sources, my friend, sources."

Cross continued, "Ryan, you are really serious aren't you? Okay, I will do a little digging for you. But I'll tell you what I know already. I try to keep tabs on Fulgrum because when he appears, a story is never far away. Freddy and his minions play in the muck a lot. He's sort of the leader of the Vatican disaster cleanup crew. It's a dirty job and he's good at it. That makes him important; not well liked, but important. The transgressions by priests you hear about are really just the tip of the iceberg. Freddy keeps most of the stories under wraps, either through buyouts or intimidation. It's no secret he keeps extensive dossiers on several people, especially people of some power or notoriety, so he can bribe them later. You better believe he has an open file on you, Thomas.

"Fulgrum works for Cardinal Castillo, the finance officer at the Vatican. Castillo is old and very much a figurehead. Freddy has a band of merry investigators, four priests, three of whom are also canon law lawyers and one who is a former New York City cop who worked the vice beat. Castillo has given Freddy fairly free rein. Along with cleanup detail, his team also has a proactive job as watchdog over the way the Church is portrayed. More specifically, Fulgrum's main focus is on how Christ is portrayed in the media or in literature. This all got started 25 or so years ago, way before your time and before Freddy and his team was in place. You may remember the uproar over the art exhibit by photographer Andres Serrano. One of the centerpieces in the exhibit was his photograph titled *Piss Christ*. The photo depicted a small plastic crucifix submerged in a glass of the artist's urine.

"Some called Serrano's work an art form, but not me. Some people are just dark and mean. I have quarrels with the Church, not with Jesus Christ. Even though the Serrano controversy predates Freddy, the Vatican has set up a line of defense to ward off future attempts to denigrate Christ and they have made Freddy the point man. For example, there are a couple of new movies coming out which put Jesus in a negative light—movies focusing on that Mayan thing and the end of the world. The group putting it together is The Doorway. You touched on them during your Georgetown lecture, but you didn't go far enough. You should have asked me about The Doorway. I could have helped spice up your lecture. That's a story for another time. The Vatican's intent may be justified, but putting a zealot like Freddy in charge of prosecution is overkill."

"Well," interjected Thomas, "let's not put The Doorway too far on the back burner. They are headquartered here in Glastonbury and they just may play a part in what's going on."

Cross finished his thoughts: "There was a lot of conversation a couple of years ago about your fairly harmless, from my perspective, fictional piece about the Second Coming in *The Christian Scholar*. Personally speaking, I enjoyed the article. And, I know for a fact your piece on the lost years of Jesus has got them plenty worried."

"How do you know about their interest in my work on the lost years?" asked Thomas.

"Ryan, you cannot be that naïve. Take my advice. Be careful. Nothing would please Freddy more than to whack you over this article. Now if they see you involved in the search for the Holy Grail, watch your back! I'll keep my eyes and ears open and let you know if I hear anything. Where can I reach you?"

"You have my cell phone number. Just call there or email me and I'll get back to you right away. Thanks Randy, I really do appreciate the information, and I'll repay the favor with a real scoop."

"Now you've got my attention. Take care, Ryan. Bye now." Cross hung up.

"Did you learn anything new?" Robert wanted to know.

"Yes, I think so. For one, I didn't know The Doorway was in the movie-making business. That may come in handy later." Thomas gave a knowing glance to Robert. "Nothing else really new, but he did validate our concerns. Fulgrum is tenacious and he's on a mission to catch a crook, so we better take him seriously. He's a climber in the Church hierarchy and doesn't have much of a social life. He already has acquired more power than he needs. If he senses he can profit more personally, he won't let go."

"I hate to have to change the subject, but we have guests coming this evening and Matthew and I need to get dinner ready," suggested Robert. Robert wanted the conversation about The Doorway to end. He gave Thomas permission to reveal his confessional statement about The Doorway, but didn't want it to come out this evening.

"I'm not much of a cook, but I'm a pretty experienced gofer. I'll set the table and help wherever you need help. What are you making?" asked Thomas.

"Something an Irishman like you will love—Shepherd's Pie," answered Robert. "But this is my Scottish version which makes it better. You Americans make it with beef, but we Scots prefer lamb. I add corn, peas, carrots, tomato,

Worcestershire sauce and garlic, covered over with mashed potatoes and baked until golden brown. Okay, gofer, in addition to setting the table, you can select the wine. Matthew, I need you to make the salad."

"Aye, aye captain," said Matthew.

Thomas saluted, did an about-face and headed for the wine cellar.

"And I gentlemen, am off to capture and return with the fair maid Margo," said James.

Thomas returned with a bottle of Burgundy and opened it. "This is for the kitchen staff. It should make for happy workers!"

The three were having a grand time and decided to enjoy the moment. They could discuss Frederick Fulgrum some other time.

The Vatican

Father Frederick Fulgrum was a citizen of the Vatican, the smallest sovereign city-state in the world—an area of just over 100 acres. All 800 Vatican citizens are employed by the Vatican, as was Freddy, or they are otherwise related to the Holy See in some fashion. The Holy See employs about 3000 people, more than all the citizens in the Vatican. Frederick Fulgrum held dual citizenship in the United States and the Vatican.

Fulgrum was in an enviable position—a position he was intent on maintaining. He was part of Cardinal Pietro Castillo's inner circle of investigators and prosecutors. Even though he was not well liked by others in the cardinal's circle, he managed to keep his position because he was willing to do the dirty work. He had no real friends and it really didn't matter to him. He was socially awkward and content to pour himself into his job. The dossiers he kept on people included those who worked for him as well as his bosses, including Cardinal Castillo.

He appreciated the benefits of his job and was always looking out for himself first. His Vatican employment opened up the opportunity to rent an apartment at far below the market in the San Calisto apartment and office complex—the high-rent and trendy district of Trastevere. He had a fairly generous expense account and his boss, Cardinal Castillo, was a hands-off manager. He told his men what he wanted done and didn't want to hear any details on how they accomplished their assignments.

Freddy's entertainment was found in a bottle of Grey Goose vodka and he was quite comfortable being by himself. His paranoia caused him to shop at a fairly large store about five or six miles from his apartment where he regularly and anonymously purchased his vodka. He was certain the proprietor was unaware he was a priest. Freddy was wrong, he had the look of a loner priest. The shopkeeper knew, but couldn't care less.

Frustrated by his inability to catch Ryan in some religious transgression, Fulgrum convened a meeting of the four priests on his investigative team, each of whom were assigned a jurisdiction over one of four targeted areas: literature, film, archeology, and art. Fulgrum decided he would use his entire team to capture whatever information they could about the activities of Father Thomas Ryan and company. While the Church only had jurisdiction over Ryan, the priest, Fulgrum expanded his investigation beyond its limits and decided to also investigate Rabbi Matthew Halprin, Professor James Christopoulos and a private British citizen, Robert Thompson.

The animosity Fulgrum had toward Ryan went all the way back to their seminary days. They were polar opposites. Thomas Ryan was well liked and a celebrity of sorts. His pairing with the equally likable Michael Moriarity made his circle of friends all the more popular. The boxing business Thomas and Michael formed was known by all the seminarians, even by the dean, who decided to look the other way. However, when Freddy blew the whistle, the dean had no choice but to shut down the business. The effect was opposite of what Fulgrum hoped for. Ryan and Moriarity became martyrs to the system and Frederick Fulgrum became known as "the snitch." Even the dean disliked what Freddy had done. Truth be known, the in-crowd at the seminary was proud of Michael's boxing prowess and the dean won more than a few bets on Michael with some of the other senior clergy.

Fulgrum's decision to involve all four of his investigators was most unusual, but Freddy decided this might be his best chance to catch Ryan. Three of his investigators, with Father Peter Vacini as the team leader, were instructed to do background checks on the four suspects. Vacini, born in the United States to parents who were both born in Italy, spoke fluent Italian and was the favorite of Fulgrum's boss, Cardinal Castillo. This irritated Fulgrum; it always seemed someone else was more favored than he.

Prior to their expanded assignment, the investigators had gathered information concerning the activities and whereabouts of only Father Ryan. Although Ryan committed no crime, his refusal to allow Church officials to edit his article on the lost years of Jesus Christ had many at the Vatican concerned about how he would portray Jesus. The fact he joined Dr. Christopoulos in his search for the Holy Grail only heightened Church concern, making Ryan a priority.

Ryan had excellent rapport with many in the media and Fulgrum knew there was little he could do to prevent him from releasing information. If Ryan's work turned out to be harmless, Fulgrum could back off. But it was the fear of the unknown that motivated Fulgrum. If Ryan's article turned out to be a bombshell, the Church would be caught in a reactive posture. If Ryan's past was an indicator of things to come, Fulgrum was certain Ryan would not shy away from controversy. What made him so popular with the media was his edgy presentation skills and his willingness to give candid responses to questions.

The last option for neutralizing or controlling Ryan was one that Fulgrum's superiors did not want to use. They referred to it as the "nuclear option"—basically discrediting Ryan and denying the legitimacy of his work. Freddy would have loved to have this option, but his bosses were less inclined. Ryan was extremely valuable when kept on the team. If they were to discredit him, his value would be lost, which is why it was so essential for Freddy and his team to learn where Ryan was headed. Cardinal Castillo was willing to look the other way on how Freddy proceeded, as long as Freddy did not implement the nuclear option without prior approval.

The team acquired some, but not enough, information. Fulgrum reviewed the videotape of the Georgetown lecture, which was of little value except for Ryan's response to one questioner. Ryan revealed he and Rabbi Halprin "have a close friend, a preeminent archeologist, who believes there is a Holy Grail." That close friend could be none other than Dr. James Christopoulos.

Fulgrum also found Ryan's reference to Saint Joseph of Arimathea while answering a different question to be most interesting. Joseph of Arimathea was an important person in the early establishment of Christianity, but he was hardly a person who would be known even by most Christians. In fact, Church leadership preferred that Joseph of Arimathea remain out of the spotlight. Joseph was the key to much information about Jesus, but the leadership did not want the faithful to know just how pivotal he was. That Joseph would stay in the background was what the leadership hoped for. Scholars outside the control of the Church knew of Joseph's connection to Glastonbury, England.

Fulgrum learned from Dean Carroll that Ryan was spending his sabbatical with Christopoulos in Glastonbury. Somehow Rabbi Halprin was also involved. One of Fulgrum's investigators learned Dr. Christopoulos just bought the home of Robert Thompson in the city of Glastonbury. Of interest was the fact the contents were sold along with the home and their value exceeded the value of the house itself. They knew next to nothing about Thompson except he was a senior citizen, an Anglican, a decorated World War II veteran, a proud Scotsman and a well-respected member of the Glastonbury community.

Fulgrum played the DVD of the Georgetown lecture for his investigators. "I have marked two comments by Father Ryan which seem significant to me. It's not only significant for what he says, but watch closely the passion he displays." Fulgrum advanced the disc stopping at the marked passage. There was Father Ryan standing, both hands outstretched and upright resembling one making a prayer request to God.

The passage had Father Ryan saying: "Ask yourself, what would it prove if the Holy Grail were found? For me, I have no doubt. For if a discovery is made of an object proven to be from or of Jesus Christ, I believe it would be the most significant historical find of all time."

Fulgrum continued, "Ryan also said some disparaging things about the Church." Fulgrum fast-forwarded and stopped the DVD again. "This was his answer to a question about how we are doing in response to the needs of our members. Clearly the man is not a team player. Again notice his passion."

The DVD showed Ryan as he responded to the reporter: "This will not sit well with traditionalists in the Church and I may disagree slightly with my friend Rabbi Halprin, but I believe Jesus did not come to build a church or to start a religion. He came to start a revolution. He came to change the order of things."

Fulgrum continued, "I am going to get closer to what is happening on the ground. I'm leaving for London on Sunday. I've taken a flat in Bath near the Abbey on York Street, which is only about 35 kilometers from Glastonbury. I'll do some quiet investigating from there first. I want to be careful so when I go to Glastonbury, I'll know where I'm heading. I don't want to bump into Father Ryan on the street having to say, 'what a coincidence running into you here.' Your assignment is to analyze what I have presented and call whoever you feel will be of help. We have got to know what these people are up to. Any questions?"

"How much pressure should we apply to get complete answers?" asked Father Jerry Fletcher. Father Fletcher was Freddy's best investigator as he used to be a New York City police officer working the vice squad. He worked vice for three years and had his fill. He quit the force and entered the seminary. Freddy recruited Fletcher when he was in his final year at the seminary. The fact his approach was often heavy-handed didn't matter to Freddy. Freddy could count on Fletcher to "get his man" every time.

In answering Fletcher's question, Freddy was a bit cautious. "Use your discretion, depending on who you're talking to. Don't scare anyone, but make sure they know they'll be doing God's will by telling you all they know. We're on the side of truth." Fulgrum sounded so believable his investigators, like Fletcher, wanted to believe. Then, Fulgrum was off and running.

GLASTONBURY

It was 7 p.m. and Estelle and Henry arrived with James and Margo right behind. Robert, enjoying the role of host, welcomed the two couples. He was dressed in his Thompson clan tartan kilts but this time he left his medals in the display case. He ushered them into the library where Thomas stood, dressed in Robert's scarlet Huntsman coat. The coat was a bit long for Thomas, as Robert was two inches taller.

Matthew finished setting the table in the dining room and joined them with a couple bottles of wine. Matthew was wearing Robert's green Huntsman coat—the colour he wore for the Hare and Hounds hunts. Matthew was a good four inches shorter than Robert and he could have easily rolled up the coat sleeves, but that would have ruined the effect.

The guests were enjoying the royal treatment as Thomas poured the wine and Matthew carried and offered hors d'œuvres. Robert was in his element, telling story upon story as he had done many times before.

At 7:30 they adjourned to the dinner table where they all enjoyed shepherd's pie family style. Henry, who most likely had taken his meals throughout his life in the kitchen, managed to relax and join in the conversation. The wine may have helped. Much of the talk was about the old days when the Thompson House bed & breakfast was the place to be.

Robert's bed & breakfast differed significantly from other B&B's in the area. While the others offered a room and breakfast and mostly left the guests alone, the Thompson House guests were invited to the library each evening for cheese and wine before they would go to dinner. Robert, wearing his Thompson tartan kilts, got the conversation going by telling a story or two, and then it would take off from there. Some nights the guests had such a grand time they would skip dinner and just enjoy the conversation.

The Thompson House charged two pounds more per night per guest than other B&B's in the area. The extra charge covered the wine, cheese and breakage. In all the B&B's years, Robert and company only remembered one guest who overindulged. Most people who stayed at the Thompson House would tell their friends, thus insuring they were busy most of the year. Staying at the Thompson House was an attraction in its own right. So much so, the bed and breakfast guidebooks often featured the Thompson B&B with a picture of Robert in his kilts on the cover.

After dinner, Estelle and Margo cleaned up the table and did the dishes as the men retired to the library for one more glass of wine. Around ten o'clock Estelle and Margo reappeared. The cleanup was complete and it was time to call it a night. James took Margo home and returned about an hour later. Robert was tired. The nonstop activity had gone on for three days and even though Robert was in his element, enjoying and living every moment, he had enough for the evening.

SUNDAY MORNING, JANUARY 9
ST. JOHN THE BAPTIST ANGLICAN CHURCH

Estelle spent more time at Robert's home this past week than she normally did. She cherished Robert and would do anything for him, and she knew he could not have been the host he wanted to be for his special guests had she not been there to help. Estelle did not eavesdrop, but she could tell nonetheless how much Robert was enjoying the company and the activity.

However, on this Sunday, Estelle went with Henry to her church, the Glastonbury Methodist Church on Lambrook Street. She told Robert the previous evening she would be available for him if he needed her, however he assured her he was in good hands and wanted her to spend some time at home with Henry. He also expressed how much he enjoyed preparing the evening meal and serving her for a change. Estelle remarked she was not really surprised he was quite a good cook.

As the four men scrambled to make their own breakfast, James gained more appreciation for how effortless Estelle made it all seem. This morning cornflakes and juice would have to do.

This would be the third day in a row for Robert to go to town. He could not remember when he last attended Sunday service at St. John's. Since he gave up his driver's license three years before, he depended on others for rides. Being as proud as Robert was, he just wouldn't ask for help. The one time he hired a car and driver to take him to services at St. John's brought just too much attention for this gregarious yet private man.

Attending service at St. John's gave Robert yet one more opportunity to introduce James as the new owner of the Thompson house. Of course, many of the townspeople wanted to know if this was the James who won Margo Webster's heart. The attention, which Robert received as person after person stopped to say hello, reminded one of a receiving line at a wedding.

By the time all the greetings concluded, it seemed as though half the population of Glastonbury knew James was the new lord of the manor. One person said to James, "So, you are the one who bought the old Thompson house," almost as though there were no Thompsons remaining.

Robert took Communion with the rest of the congregation, only this time his conscience was clear, not by a public confession, but by the more personal one-on-one confession between a man and a priest. His confession was barely two days old and Robert had been way too busy to have sinned. At 91, the opportunities for sinning were considerably diminished. He enjoyed himself the last few days so thoroughly he neither said a curse word, nor even had one enter his head. As he received the Communion host, he felt he was in a state of grace with the innocence of a child. Robert and the boys exchanged only passing greetings with Vicar Dunmore. Sunday was her busiest day and she needed to be available to all her parishioners.

When they returned home, Robert begged leave of the three with the excuse of needing to complete some paperwork. They, of course, obliged his request and returned to the kitchen to scrounge for food to make up for their meager breakfast. Robert went to his study and somewhat uncharacteristically closed the door. At his desk, he took out paper and pen. He wrote:

Dear James, Thomas and Matthew:

Please accept my sincere appreciation for these past few days, for you have made it possible for me to say goodbye to so many dear friends and acquaintances. Your act of kindness has brought great comfort to my heart and soul. For I now know the responsibility I alone bore for so many years is now safely transferred to your stewardship. I began to fear I had failed my responsibility as protector and defender of God's secret here on earth.

I feared I waited too long to find my replacement. That was a most grievous sin. But the sin was not in the waiting; rather, it was in the arrogance it would be me who would be the one to choose my successor. My arrogance overwhelmed my faith, for in the end, it was not me, but He who chose the next protector and defender. I have shared this with Thomas during my confession and I now release him from his oath of confidentiality so he might share with you one of the dangers that lie ahead. May God bless you Thomas. You have saved my life in the hereafter.

Keeping the secret hidden is not a game; rather, it is for your safety's sake that you must discover where to look. The clues are there and in a short time, you will find them. This letter is for you three and you three alone. You must destroy this letter so no one else may learn of my message to you.

My Last Will and Testament has been duly executed and notarized. A copy with a codicil letter is in the Thompson Family Bible. The original is with my solicitor, Heather Bean. The will is simple and brief. For with the sale of the home and all its contents, I have transferred all my assets entirely into sterling.

As you will discover, the amount of money in my estate is fairly substantial. I have decided to have just four beneficiaries. I limited the number so the impact of the gifts could be larger and hopefully could make a difference. I am leaving significant amounts to St. John the Baptist Anglican Church and St. Mary's Catholic Church and an even greater amount to Estelle and Henry who have served me so loyally for many years. Estelle is not aware of my bequest to her. I look to the three of you to explain my wishes and help Estelle understand how much she has meant to me. Lastly, I am leaving the largest amount to the Epistolic Institute that James and I formed this past year. It is my wish that both Thomas and Matthew join you James as members of the Epistolic Institute's board of directors. James will be able to tell you more about The Institute and its mission will become clear when your search is complete.

My final wish is for a simple yet dignified funeral, whereupon I wish to be cremated and have my ashes spread on the Tor. I have made arrangements and paid the funeral managers. They know of my wishes. The funeral manager is the Boyle family in Bath. Sean Boyle is the son of my best friend who I served with in the RAF. He is in several of the photographs you see about the house. My friend Shamus Boyle died in 2005. Sean, his son, is his spitting image.

Lastly, the burden I have transferred to you will give you great joy and great sadness. Great joy in knowing God lives. Great sadness in knowing how God's love is ignored by so many. I am at peace in the knowledge I have done all I could. I leave it to you three to take God's secret and make its message known to all who will listen.

May God's grace shine upon each of you.
Sincerely,
Robert Thompson

Robert folded the letter and placed it in an envelope addressed to Dr. James Christopoulos, Father Thomas Ryan, and Rabbi Matthew Halprin. He sealed the letter and set it in the center of his desk, then leaned back, closed his eyes and with a sigh, simply let go.

It was past two o'clock—the time Robert normally woke from his nap. But, he had not gone to his bedroom; he'd gone to his study and the door was still closed.

Thomas said to James and Matthew, "I think we need to check on Robert."

Thomas knocked on the door. There was no answer. He opened the door and called out: "Robert is everything all right?"

There was no answer.

The three men entered the study and found Robert leaning back in his chair, with eyes closed and a gentle smile on his face.

Thomas approached and took hold of Robert's hand and checked for a pulse. There was none. Thomas paused and bowed his head in prayer. James and Matthew followed Thomas's lead. "Lord, Robert Thompson was your loyal and faithful agent here on earth; we pray you now take him home. In Jesus' name, Amen."

The three men stood in silence for several moments as they looked upon Robert's serene countenance.

James broke the silence with barely more than a whisper. "People need to be notified." Without hesitation the three friends began working their phones. It was Sunday and one could not be sure who was on duty, but all calls were successfully placed and received.

James called Margo to break the news and stayed with her on the telephone to receive her tears. She was not hysterical, just deeply saddened. She thanked James for coming into Robert's life and for bringing Thomas and Matthew to him. She told him she had not seen Robert so happy in years. James asked her whom he needed to call.

"Dr. Benjamin Christian is the regional medical officer. He is a physician here in Glastonbury and was Robert's doctor. He is the one to certify the death." Margo said she would be right over to help. "Has anyone called Estelle?"

"Matthew is doing that right now," answered James.

Matthew had just broken the news to Estelle. He heard her call out to Henry who came to her side. As Estelle sobbed deeply, he heard Henry say, "There, there, Stelle, there, there." Henry took the phone and told Matthew they would be over shortly.

Matthew's next call was to Vicar Dunmore, who was in the church narthex and had to be called to the phone. She took the news politely and professionally saying she was ready to assist however she and St. John the Baptist Church could help. She said she would tell the parishioners who were presently in the church for Bible study. Most of them knew Robert and would be able to spread the word.

"Word spreads quickly in Glastonbury," added the Vicar. "I will be over later this afternoon."

Thomas's first call was to Heather Bean, who best knew Robert's final wishes. Unable to break away due to a previous engagement, Heather apologized and suggested Thomas call Sean Boyle, the funeral manager in Bath, who would make the necessary arrangements. After giving Thomas Sean's home phone number, she thanked him for being there.

"Having you three in the house must have been a comfort to Robert. No one should die alone," she said.

Thomas called Sean Boyle. Sean's response was somber. He knew this day was approaching. "You may not know this, but my father and Robert Thompson were the best of friends. They served together in the RAF and stayed close till the day my father died. I regret this responsibility like few others. Robert is the last of an era when Britain was still a great nation. I know his wishes and I will have my people there shortly. Has anyone called Dr. Christian?"

"He's on the way," replied Thomas.

"Most of all," Sean continued, "Robert wanted this done in a dignified way. If you can, please move his body to a couch and cover him with his tartan blanket. I'll come there myself, but my men will arrive before me."

"It will be done. Thank you, Sean. I know your concern for Robert's dignity will be appreciated by all," said Thomas.

Thomas and James lifted Robert and laid him on the couch. Matthew retrieved his favorite Thompson formal tartan blue blanket and covered Robert as though he were asleep.

Thomas retrieved a small container of holy oil from his coat pocket. With his right thumb he placed a drop of oil in the shape of a cross on Robert's forehead saying, "We commend to you, Dear Lord, the soul of your servant, Robert. May his devotion to you here on earth now reap the reward of his eternal salvation." Thomas made the sign of the cross. "In the name of the Father, the Son and the Holy Spirit."

James and Matthew joined in, "Amen."

It was only after they moved Robert that James saw the letter addressed to the three of them sitting in the center of the desk. He showed the envelope to Thomas and Matthew, opened it and shared its contents with his two friends. He was somewhat amazed at how they managed to make the right phone calls even before they read his letter. Robert must have clearly impressed on them his desire for dignity. James came upon the passage that urged the letter be destroyed.

"We need to read this again when we have a moment. I'll keep the letter safe and we'll come back to it when we have time."

People started to arrive. First was Margo who was immediately followed by Dr. Christian. Margo offered to receive guests. James stayed by her side as Dr. Christian, Thomas and Matthew went to the study to officially record Robert's death.

Estelle and Henry arrived just as Dr. Christian, Thomas and Matthew exited the study. It was now 3:30 p.m. Thomas and Matthew offered to relieve James and Margo so they and Estelle and Henry could have some time alone in the study to pay their final respects.

Sean Boyle's two men arrived appropriately dressed in dark suits. They brought with them a dark oak casket to remove Robert's body—a much more dignified way than on a gurney. Thomas instructed them to wait until Margo, James, Henry and Estelle left Robert's study. Ten minutes later, the four emerged and Matthew escorted Sean's men into the study. They lifted Robert's body into the casket, closed it, and moved the casket to their vehicle.

Word spread and the townspeople began to arrive to pay their respects. Margo and Estelle, instead of sitting and grieving, busied themselves with creating a memorial. Margo gathered up several fresh floral arrangements, which could always be found in the house. Robert loved flowers, especially stargazer lilies, which give off a beautiful aroma. Estelle found a framed photo of Robert wearing his RAF uniform with his friend Shamus Boyle, along with a book used previously as the Thompson House Bed & Breakfast registry, and placed both on a small table with the floral arrangement—a dignified memorial and guest registry was quickly established.

It was now 4:30 p.m. and James decided to allow Robert's friends to visit until six. Sean Boyle arrived and was moved by the simple beauty of the makeshift memorial—a spontaneous and dignified tribute to a man who was both well known and well loved.

James, Thomas and Matthew met briefly with Sean to discuss arrangements for the memorial service. Sean knew Robert's preference was to be cremated and not to be put on display in an open casket. According to Sean, Robert believed putting a dead body on display was one of the more macabre traditions of a modern society. "What purpose is served by dressing up and putting makeup on a dead man? Postponing the inevitable? Cremation is much more dignified than having a loved one's body rot away for years." James and Thomas agreed to meet with Sean in Bath on Monday.

Just before six, Vicar Dunmore arrived. The last of the townspeople left, 33 having signed the guest register. The Vicar, Thomas, Sean, Matthew, James, Margo, Estelle and Henry sat together around the dining room table. It was agreed Robert's ashes would be consecrated at a memorial service on Wednesday morning at St. John the Baptist. The vicar would preside. A memorial reception would be held in the back of the church. Pictures of Robert were collected, along with his RAF medals—the Victoria Cross to be borne on a velvet cushion, as is the British military tradition. The British Union Jack flag would also be present at the church, and a Scottish bagpiper would begin and end the service.

Vicar Dunmore noted that spreading ashes on the Tor is not legal. "I'm not saying it hasn't been done before. It's just not legal."

"Understood," said James. All knew they were going to do it anyway. Thomas was comfortable with the fine line difference between breaking the law and sinning. He equated a misdemeanor as a venial sin and a felony as a mortal sin. Thomas pictured a late-night stroll on the Tor with his friends, fulfilling the wishes of a dignified old Scot who had done more than his fair share for the Crown.

The vicar departed leaving Robert's six friends to carry on the discussion. James turned his attention to Estelle. Not yet ready to let her know she was in Robert's will, James did tell her he wanted both she and Henry to continue in their service.

"Estelle, you and Henry know the house better than anyone. You know where things are and what this house needs. This is a grand house and it needs to remain a joyful place. But more importantly, I need you," said James.

James's request for Henry and her to stay was a relief for Estelle. She had been in Robert's employ for more than twenty years. Taking care of Robert meant more than just a salary, she truly loved Robert and caring for him was her calling. Knowing that James needed and wanted her to stay was as important as the job itself.

Estelle could have been bitter. She cooked and cleaned for Robert for years. She could have viewed James as a wealthy interloper and been resentful of his good fortune. But he said, "I need you," which gave her the freedom to mourn the loss of her friend and employer and not worry about where her next pound sterling would come from. James presented Robert's tartan blanket to Estelle noting he was sure Robert would have wanted her to have it. Estelle tearfully accepted the blanket and held it close to her chest.

It was 8 p.m. when Henry, Estelle and Margo left and at last the house was quiet. The three friends reconvened in the library, which was now the focal point and designated meeting spot.

"Gentlemen, I know how tired we all are. It's been an exhausting day," said Thomas. "Yet we have much to discuss, and let me suggest we get started right now."

James went to the wine cellar and returned a few moments later with two bottles of Cabernet. "Once we start talking, we don't stop. I'm just making sure we have enough lubricant."

The house was amazingly quiet compared to an hour before. No Estelle in the kitchen. No light banter. James uncorked both bottles and poured a glass for each.

"Well, Jimmy, when you invite a couple of friends on an adventure, you do not disappoint. Let's try to figure out what to do next," said Thomas.

Matthew responded, "Before anything else, I need to call Sara. I'm going to tell her I'll be here another week and hopefully she and the university won't have a problem."

"Good idea Matt, but wait—it's still early back home and we ought to at least figure out what's going to happen the next few days," noted James.

"What are you expecting?" asked Matthew.

"I not sure," said James, "but I think our search has become more complicated by the loss of our guide."

"Matt, what time is it for Sara? Six hours different?" asked James.

"No, it's five. So, it's about 3:30 in the afternoon."

"Good, we have time to talk before you need to call," added Thomas.

James began to lay out the events for the coming week. "The funeral will be on Wednesday at St. John the Baptist with a reception following in the church narthex. Considering our experience today, I think the turnout will be substantial."

Thomas added, "When I spoke with Heather Bean, she said she had specific instructions from Robert that his will be read immediately after his death. She also said since there are only four beneficiaries and they are all local, convening a meeting for the reading of the will can be done without much difficulty. She suggested Thursday afternoon and requested Jimmy also be there. Both St. John's and St. Mary's are aware they are in Robert's will, but Estelle doesn't know yet. Matt, you're doing a great job consoling Estelle. I think it best you tell her she's in the will and she needs to be prepared because the amount of money is substantial.

"Heather also mentioned the largest gift is to The Epistolic Institute. Jimmie, I understand you're the president. What was Robert's purpose in forming The Epistolic Institute?"

James answered, "Robert described its purpose to me as a place for research and education. The Institute was formed just this past year and Robert's bequest will make it possible for it to get started. I do admit I am unclear about what kind of research and education The Institute will be doing. I agreed to be president to help Robert get it off the ground. Unless Robert has more to say in his will, it may be up to us to define its purpose. I'm going to need your help as we move forward. Robert apparently wants both of you to serve on the board of directors."

Thomas was up and pacing in front of the bookcase. "Jimmy, do you think Robert established The Institute to serve as the protector of the secret. The word epistolic is interesting. If it means what I think it means, an epistle or letter, then we have a few candidates. We have Robert's final letter you have in your coat pocket, there is a letter which is a codicil to his will, and I have a letter Robert gave me after his confession."

James and Matthew looked at each other and simultaneously said, "What letter?"

Thomas answered. "Friday night, Robert gave me a letter and told me I would know when the time was right to open it. I wish I could say I feel this is the right time, but I know it isn't. We have much to do in the next couple days and I sense Robert's letter is going to help at the right time. I just wanted you two to know about it."

Matthew responded, "Maybe, just maybe, one of those letters contain directions which will lead us to the secret."

"Let me sum up where we stand," interjected James. "Tomorrow Thomas and I will meet with Sean Boyle at the Boyle Funeral Manager's office in Bath. He said his office is easy to find; it's near the Abbey on York Street. I have been to Bath several times. The road pattern is a bit odd, but I know where the Abbey is. So I don't think we'll have much problem finding it."

"Bath," said Matthew. "Isn't that where our friend Robin lives?"

"Robin, who's Robin?" asked James.

"A perfectly lovely woman, a flight attendant we met on the way over," answered Thomas. "However, that's a story for another time."

James picked up where he left off. "Okay, Monday Tommie and I will go to Bath to firm up the funeral arrangements. Matthew, you stay here. I am certain people will be stopping by to pay their respects. Robert will be cremated on Monday or Tuesday in Bath, but that doesn't involve any of us. Wednesday will be the funeral and Thursday will be a reading of the will. Maybe on Wednesday evening, we three can take a late night stroll along the Tor."

Thomas added, "It looks like Tuesday will be a good day for us to begin our search for the hidden treasure. Jimmy, I think it would be a good idea to read the letter Robert left for us one more time."

"You are so right, I nearly forgot." James took the folded letter from his pocket and read it aloud.

After he finished reading, James offered his reaction, "Virtually half the letter is about the sacred artifact, 'God's secret here on earth,' we are charged to protect and defend—an artifact we have not found and are really not at all sure what it is or where it is. Most of the rest of the letter is about his will and last wishes. Lastly, he wants this letter destroyed so God's secret cannot be found by anyone other than us."

James paused, "Let me read it aloud one more time and then I think we should burn it before it accidentally falls into the wrong hands. I know you guys think I'm a bit paranoid, but try to remember why I asked you to come here. I feel strongly we are on the verge of a major discovery and based on what Robert has told us, it's a discovery that will probably not please everyone. Robert wants this letter destroyed."

"Jimmy, you're right. Is there anything in the letter we cannot commit to memory so we can destroy it without losing any clues?" asked Thomas.

Matthew agreed, the letter needed to be destroyed. He then summed up his sense for what happened over the past few days: "We came here to help

Jimmy find his holy grail and instead we've been caught up in a drama which has taken on its own life."

"I agree we must burn the letter," said Thomas, "but it just seems a shame to lose Robert's poetry."

"I understand Tommie. It's a beautiful letter, but as for helping us find the secret, it offers nothing new. One more thing we must not lose sight of is Frederick Fulgrum. He's breathing down our necks and I suggest we start looking for the secret in earnest," suggested Matthew.

"I agree," offered James, "the letter offers no more clues than what we already knew, but I think we know a whole lot more than we think. I believe Robert has dropped enough clues for us to find what we seek. So, here's the plan for tonight. Matt, you call Sara and tell her you'll stay for one more week. Tell her about Robert's passing, but be discreet in discussing our search for the secret."

"Well, shall we burn the letter from Robert?" asked Matthew.

"All agree it's time?" asked James. Both Matthew and Thomas nodded their agreement.

James placed the letter on a smoldering peat brick. They stood for a moment in front of the fireplace watching the letter ignite and quickly turn to ashes.

With the letter burned, Matthew went to his room to make his call in privacy. "Sara, so much has occurred in the last few days I hardly know where to begin. I'm going to need to stay here another week and then I will come home. However, I will need to come back right away and stay for at least another two to three weeks, maybe more."

"What's going on Matt? Are you all right?" asked Sara.

"Sara, I need to be cautious in what I say. At the risk of sounding like Jimmy, I cannot be sure this line is secure. I don't think it wise I discuss too much over the phone. Let me tell you what I can. Most importantly, I sense Tommie and I may have become involved in something quite significant. Our host, Robert, died earlier today—nothing sinister or unnatural, the man was ninety-one. But this changes things."

Sara was calm despite the startling news. "Matthew, your host died! Are you sure you are okay?"

"Yes, I am fine, but Robert was more than just our host, he was our guide. We were about to begin James's search—the search that brought Tommie and me here in the first place. I'm going to send you an email and attempt to fill you in as best I can, but I also need a favor. Would you get a hold of Dean Weiss at Towson and tell him I'll need to be gone another week and I'd like to get together with him on Monday the twenty-fourth?

Matthew spoke with Sara for about a half hour before he rejoined his friends in the library. "All's fine with Sara and the children. I told her about Robert's passing, but I didn't elaborate on what we'll be doing after the funeral. Sara will get a hold of the dean of my department, and get me a week extension. I'll send her an email and tell her only what is safe to tell her. I'll meet with my Dean on the twenty-fourth and ask him to grant me an open-ended leave so I will have enough time to complete our work."

"That sounds like a good plan," said James. "When you email Sara, tell her we will be staying at the house here in Glastonbury and why. Until we find the secret, we cannot leave the house unprotected, so she will always be able to reach one of us here.

Bath

Frederick Fulgrum's flight from Rome to London had been delayed for nearly three hours by an on-again, off-again pilots' union slowdown. Once he landed, he got his rental car and drove 180 kilometers to Bath. Since he didn't arrive until well after midnight, the flat manager left a key for him in a lockbox. The Boyle Rental Managers, located next door to the Boyle Funeral Management headquarters, supervised and managed several Bath area flats. Freddy's was right around the corner.

Freddy retrieved the key and let himself in. He decided he would sleep in.

Glastonbury

It had been one of those days. The kind of day when events take on a life of their own and change the plans of everyone they touch—the kind of day that starts with a smile and ends in a somber mood.

Then, as quickly as it began, the frenetic activity stopped—as though the earth stood still and anything upright just toppled over. It was the kind of day, when done, those still standing heave a collective sigh of relief. Three friends sat in stillness. Finally, Matthew broke the silence, "We made it through the day, and I think we did it well."

James offered his thoughts. "It's just starting to sink in—I own this house and everything in it. I've never owned a house before, and while Robert was alive, it was his house. I didn't really feel like I was the owner. But now this is all mine, and I'm responsible to make sure it's maintained. I know Estelle appreciates being needed. I really do need both her and Henry.

"In time, I'll move my own belongings here. Come to think of it, I really don't have many things. I promised Robert I'd care for his possessions and

I intend to do just that. I'll ask Estelle and Margo for their help in keeping Robert's spirit alive here. I know he would want me to make this my home. At some point I'll move to the first floor bedroom suite, but not until it feels right," concluded James.

Thomas raised his glass of wine. "Let me offer a toast to the challenge which lies ahead. May we be guided by the truth and not by what we want."

As they each finished their wine, James concluded, "And with that, gentlemen, I think it is time to go to bed. The adventure begins tomorrow."

Chapter VIII

Jesous Christos, Theou Uios, Soter.
Jesus Christ, Son of God, Savior.

MONDAY, JANUARY 10 – THOMPSON HOUSE

The previous four days at the Thompson house bubbled with activity—Estelle, busy in the kitchen singing softly to herself, while the four men carried on with lively discussion in the library. Today all was quiet. Robert's body was at the funeral managers in Bath and final arrangements were made. Robert would be cremated on Tuesday and the memorial service was scheduled for Wednesday.

Estelle took the day off and stayed at home with Henry, so Thomas, James and Matthew were left to themselves. The atmosphere in the house changed drastically. The mood was surreal, almost dreamlike—as though the house lost its meaning, its identity. It was still, and always would be, the Thompson house, but for the first time in more than four hundred years, there was no Thompson living there.

James and Thomas rose late, and were surprised to see Matthew in the kitchen, apron on, preparing a full English breakfast, much like the one Estelle provided.

James commented, "Matthew, I am impressed. You really are an accomplished cook."

"Why thank you, I like to think of myself as somewhat of a gourmet. I actually enjoy inventing dishes."

"You may regret revealing that," joked James. "The job's yours until Estelle returns."

"Actually, I do a bit of cooking at home when it's just family and close friends. I may also regret admitting I enjoy washing the dishes. Moses knows we rarely see an end to our work. I manage to gain some satisfaction in transforming a pile of dirty dishes into a clean stack—a little immediate gratification."

As they sat at the kitchen table finishing breakfast, Matthew inquired, "What's next?"

James responded, "Tommie and I will go to Bath to meet with Sean Boyle. We hate to abandon you, but I'm afraid you're going to be plenty busy responding to inquiries from Robert's friends and neighbors about the memorial. I don't expect we'll be in Bath very long and should be back around noontime. What's for lunch?"

"Ah, the way to a Greek man's heart is through his stomach. I found some goat cheese in the refrigerator. I can build an awesome salad with what we have here. Will that be sufficient for you hungry working men?" joked Matthew.

It was the first bit of humor since the tragic events of the weekend and it was most welcome.

"We better get going," suggested Thomas. "I don't want to return to wilted lettuce."

"Tommie, when you are in Bath, why don't you call Robin? She asked, almost pleaded for you to call her."

"I doubt she's there, but I'll call," answered Thomas.

"Sean Boyle is expecting us at ten o'clock. I know roughly where his office is. It's near the classic old Bath Abbey. Bath is a fascinating city, founded by the Romans over 1,500 years ago. I swear, there's so much to see and do, so much history in this part of England, one could spend a lifetime here and not see it all. I'm taken by the area and could see myself settling down here, especially now that I own a home," said James.

"Maybe you can tell us more about your plans when you two return. Drive safe. See you back here for lunch," answered Matthew.

Thomas joked, "Look at that, will you? The man puts on an apron, makes breakfast, and now tells us to drive safe. Maybe we should call you mother Matthew?

"You better get going before I grab a rolling pin," said a grinning Matthew.

The drive to Bath was only 35 kilometers, but with traffic and parking, James allowed an hour to get there.

James and Thomas kept their conversation more about personal things as they drove to Bath instead of discussing the past few days' events.

"I hear what you say about the area. There is so much here to see. I'd love to explore it more myself. Jimmy, what are you going to do with the Thompson house now that you are the owner?" asked Thomas.

"I've been giving it some thought. Not just about the house, but what if I find what I've been seeking? What if I find the Grail? That's been my life's work. What would I do next? I'm just beginning to realize how my life could change. Not just with the notoriety which would follow the discovery, but more so what it would mean to hold and protect those sacred artifacts."

James continued, "It's not the kind of find one can simply stick in a ruck sack and move on. It will need further research and analysis. It may be, if and when I find it, my real work will begin. The University of Athens has been generous the past several years in letting me pursue my goal. However, I'm there so seldom, I feel like a guest lecturer at a course I'm supposed to be teaching. The University could do quite all right without me. I have my inheritance, which is still worth plenty; and then there's The Epistolic Institute.

"Maybe that's why Robert had it formed and asked me to be president. The Institute is supposed to be for research and education. Maybe Robert was mapping out my future knowing I'd need a vehicle to fully explore the findings. With The Institute and the house, Glastonbury may become my home."

"Could there be another reason?" asked Thomas.

"If you mean Margo? Yes," answered James. "The past few days have made me appreciate her all the more. To watch how she cared for Estelle and interacted with all who came to pay their respects. She is genuine. Besides the fact she's a beautiful woman, she has a real interest in my work. I've struck out twice in marriage; maybe three times is a charm.

"What about you, Father Ryan? What are your plans for the future? And, if I might ask, who is this Robin Matthew mentioned?"

"Jimmy, to be honest, I just don't know. I think I may be wearing out my welcome at Georgetown. Oddly, not really with Dean Carroll, and certainly not with the students. But, I bring baggage and the Dean has to defend me to his bosses. Maybe the bureaucracy is getting to me. I'm still free to speak and write, but I'm scrutinized more than ever. There are several things I can do on my own. I can write, give lectures and speeches, consult, and if you offer me a part-time position at The Epistolic Institute, I might be able to get along quite well."

"Part-time? Would you consider full-time?" asked James.

"I really don't think so. No offense, but if I'm going to strike out on my own, I'd really like to be on my own. If you offer me a consultancy, I think I could be happy living in two places. I love D.C. and the Georgetown area."

"And now, what about this Robin?" asked James.

"Jimmy, Robin is simply a beautiful woman who was very cordial to Matthew and me on our flight over. Matt mentioned giving her a call because she lives in Bath. If you are asking if she's a temptation, the answer is no. I have been true to my vow of celibacy, even if some in the Church like Freddy, especially Freddy, would love to prove the opposite. I'm true to my vow, but there's nothing that says I cannot appreciate beauty. Robin is one of God's children and God was on target the day he made her."

Thomas continued, "Robin ask me to call her, actually it was more like a plea, but I don't think it was my dazzling charm she found attractive; I think she may have spiritual needs. It's a shame when people only want a pretty woman like Robin to be nothing more than a pretty woman. I have known many women who were beautiful on the outside and wretches inside. I spent only a few moments with her, but I sense inside the shell of a beautiful woman is a little girl who may have questions. I'll give her a call and help her as I would anyone."

"Tommie, you're spot on. That may be what's so endearing about you. You're true and you always have been. I'm glad you're my friend and that you and Matt are here. This is one adventure I couldn't do alone."

The conversation flowed so smoothly, James and Thomas were hardly aware of the passage of time. They arrived at the funeral manager's office early. Jimmy parked across the street.

They were about to exit the car when Thomas said, "Wait!"

A gangly priest exited the Boyle Funeral Manager's office and entered a building a few doors down.

"It's Fulgrum!" said Thomas. "What the hell is he doing here?"

Fulgrum was out of sight when James and Thomas exited the car and continued into Boyle's, where Sean immediately met them.

"Thank you for coming gentlemen. This won't take too much of your time. Please come into the conference room. We have coffee and tea."

"Thank you Sean. Before we start, I'd like to ask about the priest who just left here a few minutes ago. Do you know who he is?"

"I don't believe I do. Let me ask Carolyn, our receptionist.

"Carolyn, the gentleman who just left, who is he?"

"His name is Father Frederick Fulgrum. He's rented flat 2G in the Abbey building for the balance of January and all of February. He wanted me to invoice the Vatican, but when I explained we couldn't do that he finally produced an American Express card. That's really all I know."

"Thank you, Carolyn."

Sean led Thomas and James into the conference room.

"Sean, I'm a bit confused. Do you also lease flats?" asked James.

"We do. When I took over the business after my father died, the building next to us was put on the market for sale. I thought it might be a good way to expand the business with little extra effort. May I ask why you ask? Is there a problem?"

Thomas replied, "No. I'm sure Father Fulgrum will be a fine tenant. I know him and had just not expected to see him, that's all."

"Is he a friend of yours?" asked Sean.

"No, just someone I know from long ago. Sean, I would appreciate it if you didn't tell Father Fulgrum about us."

James and Thomas met with Sean for close to an hour to discuss the memorial service, as well as the cremation and Robert's request to have his ashes spread on the Tor.

"I'm sure others have told you, it's illegal to spread human ashes on the Tor. I don't want to know if that's your intent, but if you do, let me suggest the east side," Sean said as he winked and leaned forward. "That's where my father Shamus' ashes are, and it would be fitting that two old friends be reunited. You might just want to take a stroll on the Tor some evening."

Sean became serious again. "I'll provide you with an urn which can be sealed and kept at the Thompson house, or if you'd prefer to bury the ashes, we could secure a burial plot. I'll deliver the ashes to you in a leather carry bag. However, I must repeat I don't want to know, officially that is, what you plan to do."

"Sean," asked Thomas, "before we leave, may I use a phone? I need to make a local call."

Sean led Thomas to his office, "This will be more private."

"I really don't need privacy. I expect I will just be leaving a message," answered Thomas.

Thomas dialed the number Robin gave him. After a few rings, a male voice answered.

Thomas began, "Hello, I am Father Thomas Ryan and I was calling Robin Potter. Did I call the correct number?"

"Yes, but unfortunately Robin isn't here. I'm one of her roommates. Can you give me your number and I'll pass it on to her."

"Actually this is a courtesy call. Robin has my cell number. If you'd be so kind as to leave her a message that Father Ryan called, I'd appreciate it," said Thomas.

Thomas heard the male voice call out, "Bryan, when will Robin be back?"

The male voice returned, "Robin is on an extended trip and will be home next week Tuesday. Is this urgent?"

"Not at all," said Thomas. "Please just leave word I called."

"Yes, I will."

Thomas exited Sean's office: "Thank you Sean."

With their business in Bath finished, James and Thomas carefully left the funeral manager's office making sure not to run into Freddy.

"That weasel is getting way too close for comfort. It would appear Freddy has set up camp in Bath. We have only one advantage over him and it's not much of an advantage," said Thomas.

"What's the advantage?"

Thomas answered, "We know he's here and he doesn't know we know."

"Do you think he's aware Robert has died?"

"It's possible, but I doubt it. Clearly he didn't come to attend Robert's memorial. Seeing him is one hell of a coincidence, which is only momentarily in our favor. When we get back, I suggest we begin our search for the cruets in earnest."

James suggested, "I have an idea. We can close up the house in honor of Robert and have the place even more to ourselves than we would otherwise. I'll call Margo and tell her we won't be receiving visitors this afternoon. She can spread the word which will buy us some time."

They arrived back at the Thompson house and were not surprised to see several Glastonbury citizens in the house paying their respects. Thomas took Matthew aside to explain the plan while James began to graciously ask callers to end their visit. With the last of the guests gone, Matthew created a sign and placed it on the front door:

We appreciate your desire to pay your respects to Robert Thompson. The memorial service will be this Wednesday at 11 a.m. at St. John the Baptist Church. We are not receiving visitors at this time. We appreciate your condolences and hope you will be able to join us on Wednesday.

With the note attached to the door and the shades drawn, the house took on the quiet appearance of mourning. Anyone stopping by to pay his or her respects would surely understand.

James said, "Let's go to the kitchen, have lunch and fill Matthew in on what occurred in Bath."

"Was there a problem?" asked Matthew.

"Yes," said Thomas, "but nothing to do with Robert or the memorial plans. The problem is Freddy. We spotted him coming out of the Boyle Funeral Manager's office. He didn't see us. At first I thought, how could he possibly know about Robert's death and his transfer to Boyles? Turns out to be quite a coincidence. Sean Boyle also has a flat management service in the same office. Freddy has rented a flat there in Bath for the next couple months. It must be his base camp."

"What do you think he knows?" asked Matthew.

Thomas responded, "I'm not sure. He must be getting orders to find out what we're doing. It's unlikely he knows Robert has died. He's never met Robert, so what he knows is based on what he's been told by others. He's moving too fast for my comfort. I wish I knew what he knows. Then again, he may just be stumbling ahead, turning stones over in hopes of finding something useful."

Thomas continued, "Here's what I think. Freddy knows Jimmy is in pursuit of the Holy Grail, but I don't think he knows Jimmy's Grail is really the Joseph of Arimathea cruets. He knows we three are old friends. We must assume he also knows Jimmy has bought the Thompson house and all its contents."

Matthew offered. "He knows Thomas and I have an interest in Jimmy's research, and that that's why we're here."

James added, "Thomas, he also knows you're writing about the lost years of Jesus and may assume Matthew and I are assisting you in some way or other."

"Freddy's smart and he has a staff to help him do his investigations. I'm confident he's started collecting information. Even though we know much more than he could possibly know, we're still piecing the puzzle together. He can't be ahead of us, but I don't think he's too far behind," said Thomas.

"Well, let's not delay. After lunch, we'll start in earnest," said James.

Bath

"Damn it, Peter," said Freddy. "Oh, it's not your fault." Freddy was whining. "But every time we make some progress we get a setback." Father Peter Vacini, one of Freddy's investigators, just reported Robert's death.

"I'm changing plans. I'm going to Glastonbury right now to see what more I can find out. Call me on my cell the moment you learn anything," grumbled Fulgrum.

Glastonbury

With lunch finished, Thomas and James brought their plates to the counter as Matthew was cleaning up. James heard a car door slam outside. Thomas, James and Matthew quickly moved to the parlor where they could look out without being seen. It was Freddy scurrying up to the front door. He stood reading the sign Matthew posted, then without ringing the bell, just turned, went back to the car and drove off. He could only follow the one lead the note offered. He was off to St. John the Baptist Church to find out whatever he could about Robert and Robert's memorial service.

"He's a persistent little bugger," said James.

Thomas added, "And now even a bit more dangerous. He's not normally a risk taker. He's more of a plodder, a grinder. He must have sensed he's lost ground and is trying to make it up quickly. I wonder if he even knew what he was going to say if someone answered the door."

"What's next?" asked Matthew.

"Next," answered Thomas, "we begin to do what we came here to do—find Jimmy's grail. Only now, it's more than just your life's quest Jimmy—it's a race against Freddy to get there first."

Thomas added, "This isn't a race to win a prize. It's a race to protect and save the truth. Freddy and those he represents are not evil, they're just lost.

They've been following a path for over 1,500 years. They intended to do good, but along the way they got sidetracked. They felt persecuted, and they were. So they set up defenses, and those defenses became walls. Once they became the establishment, they didn't take down the walls, they retreated behind them. They defend the walls, because the walls protect them from harm."

"What do you mean by walls?" asked James.

"All the laws and rules. All the mysteries. All the ceremonies designed to comfort the afflicted are now designed to sustain the comfortable. When those who are protected by the walls do harm to others, they should be punished; but instead they're protected, moved about so they cannot face their accusers. Pedophile priests are criminals and they should go to jail. Instead, they are moved about and sheltered. They're treated more like they are the victims and not the miscreant vultures they really are."

Thomas continued, "And what are they behind the walls most afraid of? They're afraid of the truth. Because the truth may upset all that has been established over the centuries. All the treasures, all the churches, all the basilicas, all the art, all the gold, all the wealth. All of these vast resources could be used for good, to feed the hungry, to clothe the naked, to shelter the homeless. All the resources locked away, and for what? Sadly, they who have locked away those resources may not even know why they do what they do, why they preserve traditions that no longer matter. Which is why I believe they're lost."

James and Matthew sat quietly following every word as Thomas continued. "When our Lord broke the bread and gave it to His disciples and said, 'take ye and eat, for this is my body,' He was saying the bread of life is meant to be shared with all. It was not meant to be reserved only for the few and used only as a ceremony. The Church could do much good, but to admit they are not doing all they could is to admit they are failing.

"They've become prisoners behind walls built to keep others out while they keep themselves safe. Freddy's job is to patch any cracks when they appear. If a crack appears and it's not immediately fixed, the walls will tumble down. They can't let that happen because if those walls come down, all the world will see the truth."

There was silence. All were surprised, even Thomas, at what came out of his mouth. It was as though those thoughts were locked inside him and needed to be set free.

"We have the advantage. We have Robert on our side. When I was alone with him, the sense of urgency on his part to find the next protector and defender of the sacred secret was palpable. Once he realized we three would take on that role, he seemed to let go. He was confident we would find the secret and would be worthy of the task before us," said Thomas.

"Well, where do we start?" asked Matthew.

"Gentlemen, let us take our coffee to Robert's library and begin the search," responded Thomas.

"Why there?" asked Matthew.

"Because libraries are where most research is done and Robert has hinted many times the books hold the clues. Shall we begin?" said Thomas.

In the library, Matthew and James took their customary seats as Thomas stood next to the bookcase as though he was about to start a lecture.

Thomas began, "I noticed something on Saturday but didn't bring it up at the time. Come over here and take a close look at the floor next to the passageway to the wine cellar. Do you see the fine scratches on the floor caused by the bookcase as it swings open to allow entry to the wine cellar? Now come over here and look closely at the floor on this end. Similar scratches, just barely visible."

"By God, Thomas, that is some good sleuthing!" remarked James in a tone of surprise and respect.

"So," said Matthew, "the door swings both ways, or in this case, it's both ends of the bookcase."

"That is precisely the point. I noticed something else." Thomas took the Thompson Family Bible from the bookshelf. "Let me ask both of you something. Did either of you take this Bible out in the last two days?"

Their response was in unison, "No."

"Why?" asked Matthew.

"Because someone did. And if it wasn't either one of you and it wasn't me, then it had to be Robert," answered Thomas.

"How do you know someone took it out?" asked James.

Thomas opened the Bible to a place where a bookmark was inserted. "This bookmark was not here two days ago when Robert invited me to look over his family bible. I believe our friend Robert has left us a clue."

Thomas removed the bookmark, and in its place he inserted the letter Robert gave him after his confession. He remembered Robert saying, "You will know when the moment is right for it to be opened and its contents revealed." Thomas ran his fingers over the envelope and contemplated opening it, but he did not "feel" the moment was right and left the letter sealed.

On the bookmark placed in the Gospel of Luke were three numbers. "The bookmark Robert left merely says 11-9-10," reported Thomas.

Thomas held the large Bible cradled on his left arm and scanned the page with his right hand. "Gentlemen, let me read to you. Luke, chapter 11 verses 9-10: 'So I say to you, ask and it will be given you; search and you will find; knock and the door will be opened for you. For everyone who asks receives, and everyone who searches finds, and for everyone who knocks, the door will be opened.' Robert placed that bookmark there sometime in the last two days."

Thomas continued, "We have asked and we have been searching; I think it is time to knock. Jimmy, would you go to the other end of the bookcase and locate the panel that releases that side. Now tell me precisely where the secret panel is."

James went to the side of the bookcase that reveals the wine cellar entrance. "Third shelf from the top, two panels from the end."

Matthew surveyed the two men insuring they were at equivalent positions.

Thomas removed three books from the end of the shelf, reached in and gave the panel a push. All three heard the same "click" they heard before on the other side. Thomas reached in, spotted the lever, lifted it and the bookcase swung free.

The three men stood silent, each understanding the gravity of the moment.

"Thomas, James," said Matthew in a near whisper, "before we go any further and before what we are about to do takes on a life of its own, let's pause for just a moment. Let's remind ourselves who we are. We are more than just secular scientists. We are hoping for and praying for a special result, but we must maintain our scientific discipline and not have our desires override the truth. We must let what we discover reveal itself without imposing our wishes."

"Matthew, you're right. Thank you," said Thomas.

Matthew began again, "Please give me the opportunity to offer a prayer before we continue. And if you don't mind, let me borrow the Thompson Family Bible."

James retrieved the bible from the table and handed it to Matthew who opened it to the book of Psalms—to Psalm 118.

Matthew read, "Open the gates of righteousness that I may enter through them and give thanks to our Lord. For this is the gate of the Lord; and only the righteous shall enter through it."

The three stood in silence, each offering their own silent prayer asking the Lord for the power which comes with the virtue of righteousness.

The moment passed and James pulled open the bookcase. There it was—a combination lock safe built into the wall.

Thomas said, "I believe I know the combination. Jimmy, this has been your life quest. You do the honors. Go ahead and enter 11-9-10."

James spun the dial to the left to clear. Turning more slowly to the right, he stopped at eleven, then a turn to the left stopping at nine, then a turn to the right again stopping on ten. The tumblers audibly clicked into place, James lifted the locking arm and moved the safe door into an open position.

James said, "Listen, guys. Things are moving too fast and I'm a bit unprepared. Give me a few moments. I'll be right back."

James hurried to his room and retrieved a black bag resembling a doctor's medical bag that contained the tools of his trade: several pairs of surgical gloves, a large silk cloth, a few small hand tools, spray bottle with bleach water and another spray bottle with just water, towels, tape measure, flashlight, camera, tape recorder, along with a few other items.

James returned to the library. "Help me clear this table so I can lay down this silk cover, and then please put on these gloves. I have no idea what's in the safe, but I don't want us to contaminate it with anything on our hands."

Matthew and Thomas cleared the table and spread the silk cloth as James donned his gloves. James was breathing heavily. Years of research flashed in his head, not unlike the flashes of memories of a dying man. In those few moments, he remembered all the dead ends and all the disappointments. This time felt different. He knew in his heart that behind the door was what he searched for all his life.

James stood there, eyes closed, drinking in the moment. Matthew and Thomas understood and allowed their friend the time he needed to prepare himself. Eyes now open, James approached the safe.

Matthew and Thomas watched as James methodically slipped into his archeologist persona. Camera ready, note pad open, small hand-held recording device, and plastic bags readied to hold whatever he might find. James was in his element. He made the first entry in the tape recorder: "Monday, January 10, 1 p.m. Greenwich Mean Time. A wall safe was discovered in the library behind the bookcase. The combination, 11-9-10, was taken from the Gospel of Luke and entered. The wall safe was successfully opened in the presence of Father Thomas Ryan and Rabbi Matthew Halprin, witnesses and fellow searchers, both."

James looked at Matthew and Thomas, "Well gentlemen, are you ready?"

"We are at your service, Dr. Christopoulos," said Thomas as he and Matthew donned their surgical gloves.

James offered the following instructions, "Matthew, would you please photograph each step and Thomas would you make a note of each photo. Having you two here is enormously helpful. I'll be able to concentrate on the artifacts. You may recall one of my favorite movie lines from Indiana Jones and the Last Crusade when Indiana said: 'archeology is the search for facts, not truth.' Jones was incorrect; archeology is not the search for facts, but the search for artifacts.

"Gentlemen, more pictures and notes are better than less. Before we begin, Matthew would you please put the camera on the tripod so we can take a picture of all three of us? Thomas would you please hold up the copy of today's London Times and the three of us will need to stand next to Robert's grandfather clock. Even though each picture taken has a date stamp this will validate the date and time in a more personal way."

Matthew and Thomas were intrigued with both the good humor and the discipline James displayed and they were only too happy to assist.

After the group photo was taken, James clicked on the small digital recorder to capture their conversation and mental notes as he began to inspect the safe. He was not sure of the safe's age, but he was comfortable that it seemed both substantial and in good working order. The front was slightly oblong, about two foot wide and three feet high. James noted, "It appears that the safe has been well maintained and with the absence of dust, it has probably been used recently."

James continued, "Matthew, after I open the door, wait a moment and I'll let you know if it's okay to photograph. I don't think the flash will do any harm, but it's best to be sure."

James carefully opened the door. The safe appeared to be about two feet deep. In the center was a container that filled most of the space. James turned to Matthew. "Okay Matt, please take a couple photos of the container as it is in the safe. Then switch the camera to video and record me removing it. Switch back to photo mode and take another couple shots of the safe after I have removed the container. Thomas, please make note the safe holds a container estimated to be approximately one foot long, and a little less than one foot wide and one foot high."

James reached into the safe with gloved hands, he took hold of the container, and as Matthew filmed, carefully removed it and placed it on the silk cloth. "It's heavy," noted James.

"The container appears to be made of pewter," said James still speaking into the recorder. "Pewter, that makes sense, we are in the heart of tin mining country. Pewter is nearly 95 percent tin."

It was a simple pewter box with the ancient Christian symbol of a fish on the lid. The box was in excellent condition. Matthew took pictures from all angles and Thomas took a tape measure from James's archeologist bag. The pewter box measured approximately thirteen inches long, ten inches wide and ten inches tall. The lid was approximately three-quarters of an inch thick with a recessed edge cut around the rim about one half inch deep. The box was not hinged; rather the lid fit over the top of the box and was kept in place by its own weight.

As the three stood in quiet awe, Thomas broke the silence. "Notice the symbol on the lid; it's a fish, not a cross. That's important—the ichthys, or fish symbol, was used by early Christians as a symbol of Jesus Christ. The symbol of the cross came much later in Christianity around 300 AD—sorry CE.

"It was the Emperor Constantine who caused the cross to be the Christian symbol." Thomas did not elaborate, but decided to notate a longer explanation of the fish symbol in James's notebook. He would later enter the following historical anecdote:

The night before the battle of the Milvian Bridge outside Rome in 312 CE, Constantine claimed to have seen a cross in the sky with the inscription: 'In Hoc Signo Vinces' or 'In This Sign Conquer.' The next day Constantine's armies defeated his Roman rival, Maxentius. Maxentius drowned in the Tiber River during the battle. Legend has it Constantine's cross was his personal epiphany resulting in his conversion to Christianity. He declared Christianity to be the official belief of the Roman Empire and he had the Roman eagle replaced by the cross on all battle standards. He became so strong in his support for Christianity he is often referred to as the "thirteenth apostle."

Thomas thought, how poetically ironic it was two of the most vicious persecutors of Christians (Paul and Constantine) did more to establish Christianity as a religion as a result of their personal epiphanies—Paul's on the road to Damascus, and Constantine's before the battle of the Milvian Bridge.

As Matthew photographed the pewter box, Thomas entered a description in the log. James's camera was configured to include a date stamp on each photo taken, but in this case redundancy was better than relying on a single source. Great care was being taken to insure the integrity of the find. It was now time to lift the lid.

James's forehead was damp, beads of perspiration were forming and his temples were throbbing. This was the moment, the reward, for all the time and effort he invested. He knew the box would not be empty, but he was hoping and praying it might contain that which he so long pursued. Thomas and Matthew could feel James's hesitation. Was this the end of a quest, or another dead end with the heavy burden of having to start over again? This was the moment. This was James, not Paul, on the road to Damascus and James, not Constantine, standing before the Milvian Bridge. This was the moment when the world could become a different place. James neither wanted to hurry the moment nor impede its arrival.

James was deep in prayer. Tears formed and his hands trembled. He raised his head and looked at his two friends. There was silence, yet all three shared the moment as though they were one body, one mind, and one spirit.

"It is time, my friend," counseled Thomas.

James nodded and placed his hands on the box. He carefully removed the lid and set it on the silk cloth. Again, Matthew videotaped the moment. Inside the box were three objects wrapped in what appeared to be fine linen.

James took the first item out. It was small and light and for a moment James wondered if the linen wrap was empty. James carefully unfolded the cloth to reveal a single coin. It was a Roman denarius, sometimes referred to as a "Tribute Penny."

James asked Thomas to enter a notation about the coin. "Note, the first artifact removed from the box is a coin, more specifically, a denarius with the likeness of Emperor Tiberius, a coin of the period around 30 CE. The coin appears to be in uncirculated mint condition."

There are several Bible passages mentioning the "Tribute Penny." Matthew, Mark and Luke, the three synoptic gospels, all tell the same story in essentially the same way. Several Pharisees and Herodians tried to trap Jesus when they asked him if Jews were required to pay taxes to the emperor and would it not be a sin to pay Roman taxes with the Jewish shekel.

Jesus was not to be fooled by such a crude trick. Jesus asked to be shown a denarius. He did not ask to see a shekel. The shekel was used by the Jews to pay the Jewish Temple tax, and it had the face of Hercules on it. So to get His point across, Jesus asked for a denarius, which had the face of Caesar. Jesus then asked, "Whose head and whose title does it bear?"

The Pharisees answered, "The Emperor, Caesar."

Jesus deftly avoided the trap by then saying, "Give to the emperor the things which are the emperor's, and to God the things which are God's."

"Isn't it ironic," James said smiling. "We used a newspaper and a clock for proof of the date of our find. Whoever put together the contents of this box did the same by using a coin. This coin was among the most common denarius in circulation in the early 30's CE. It's in remarkable condition. The likeness on the coin is Emperor Tiberius who reigned at the time of the ministry of Jesus Christ."

Matthew took several photos of the coin as Thomas logged it in the record book.

James reached into the pewter box to retrieve the second linen-wrapped article. He could feel the irregular objects through the linen. His heart raced as he closed his eyes, which only enhanced his sensation. He could feel two objects and he knew what they were. Eyes still closed, he unwrapped the objects and sensed them first with his gloved hands.

He opened his eyes and there they were—the two cruets, which at one time held the sweat and blood of our Lord, Jesus Christ. James genuflected,

Thomas followed suit and Matthew bowed his head. All rose and simply looked upon the cruets. They were empty, of course. The sweat and blood long ago evaporated from these 2,000-year-old amber colored vessels. James pulled from his bag a copy of the photo he had taken of the stained glass window in St. John the Baptist Church which pictured Joseph of Arimathea holding the two sacred cruets. "Remarkable," he said, "they're perfect."

James held one of the cruets up to the light. There was a faint stain line near the top. He held up the second and there too was another line of discoloration slightly more pronounced than the first. It was a color similar to rust. The three looked at each other. They knew the rust-colored stain could be the remnants of blood and could most likely be dated by a carbon-14 test and possibly even a DNA test.

James placed the two cruets on the cloth. With a faint smile and tears in his eyes, he sighed, "Gentlemen, I need to sit down for a moment."

Matthew videotaped James with the cruets. When James returned them to the silk cloth, Matthew photographed each several times from different angles.

"I think you know what we have discovered—what I have searched for my whole life. This is the Holy Grail. The Grail is not the chalice from which Jesus drank or the cup that caught his last drops of blood as he hung on the cross. These are the two vessels, which once held His sweat and blood. These cruets prove Jesus was a man—His toil produced sweat and His torture produced blood. This is proof of the Passion. A simple test could provide a date, but I don't need the test. I know in my heart what we have found."

Tears welled up from James's eyes. They were tears of joy, of fulfillment, of sorrow for the Man who gave His life for all humanity. James felt so unworthy, so inadequate. Yes, this was his life's mission, but that alone did not grant him the right to hold these precious artifacts. James sank in a chair and heaved a deep sigh. Again, Thomas heard a voice inside him reciting Paul's letter to the Romans—*a sigh too deep for words.*

Thomas and Matthew sat with their friend as he retold story upon story about his many searches. At times, James would laugh over an incident only time could makeover as humorous. After fifteen minutes of respite and reflection, Thomas brought them back to the moment. "James, we are not finished. There is another item in the box."

Thomas and Matthew rose and stood next the box.

James remained seated, "I've had more than enough for today. Thomas, would you please retrieve the final item?"

James was not slighting Matthew by asking Thomas to retrieve the final item. Matthew's dedication to his faith and his devotion to science was on a par with both James and Thomas, but Matthew's quest was to be found in the

Old Testament, where the answers to Thomas's searing questions could only be satisfied in the New Testament.

Now it was Thomas's heart that began to race. He was feeling that which his friend just experienced. He searched his memory for the prayer seeking righteousness he prayed moments before. What right did he have to reach into that box? What right did he have to hold something St. Joseph of Arimathea may have held, or more so, to even touch something Jesus Christ may have touched? Thomas knew himself all too well. If ever there was a man more unworthy, he doubted it. How could he, a man who was in constant conflict with what he was supposed to believe, be afforded this opportunity?

But who else was there? James acquired all for which he searched his whole life. Matthew was one of the most open and accepting non-Christians, completely unafraid of whatever challenge this find might bring to his beliefs, but it was not his place to uncover that which was hidden. Who else of Thomas's faith should be the one to retrieve this final artifact? Who throughout the Catholic Church hierarchy was willing to accept whatever the linen wrapping hid? Would the artifact validate the Church or would it challenge the Church at its core? Who would be intellectually honest enough to accept that which might overturn all he believed? No, for all his failings, Thomas was the one. His life was both a blessing and a curse. Despite his ecclesiastical indoctrination, he was a man who forcefully protected his free will. And no trait greater than a truthful protection of free will would qualify.

He reminded his two friends of Robert's warning. He could almost hear Robert's Scottish brogue. "Not everyone will be pleased. Those who you would expect to celebrate with you may be the ones who work the hardest against you. Be careful whom you trust. You may be holding that which can turn everything upside down and there will be many who like things just the way they are. Beware the shepherd."

Thomas stood before the pewter box in much the same way he had many times before in front of the tabernacle holding the consecrated Eucharist as he prepared for the sacrament of Communion. In the box was one more object, tightly wrapped in linen. It appeared to be in the shape of a book about nine inches wide and twelve inches long. Thomas took hold of the object and removed it from the box placing it on the silk covering.

He gently unwrapped the linen and revealed not a traditional book, but a codex. The codex before him was similar in appearance to the Nag Hammadi Codex. The front and back covers were each about three-quarters of an inch of thick, dark leather and were meant to protect whatever was inside.

The cover was beautifully hand-tooled with the ancient Greek letters ΙΧΘΥΣ and the early Christian symbol of the fish. James rose from his chair and was standing next to Thomas. James read the letters Iota, Chi, Theta, Upsilon, Sigma. Then translating from Greek to English, "Jesous Christos, Theou Uios, Soter. Jesus Christ, Son of God, Savior."

The Codex had three silver clasps holding the contents safely together. Thomas carefully undid each clasp and opened The Codex revealing several pages of varying sizes and different kinds and color of paper. The individual pages were not bound together; rather The Codex was used to protect their individuality. Thomas, with gloved hands, carefully turned each page. There appeared to be no more than fifteen individual pages. The pages appeared to be the work of multiple authors as there were noticeably different writing styles.

The first twelve pages were written on various high-quality papers in several styles of English, some quite old. The paper quality and writing style changed every three pages. The last three leaves were vellum, a very high quality parchment. The words were Aramaic and the handwriting was the most beautiful Thomas had ever seen—elegant, strong, flowing, graceful and confident. Thomas was one of the most capable translators of Aramaic to English, however, that did not mean he could read it fluently. A translation would take time.

Thomas was sweating and breathing heavy. The moment arrived. "James, Matthew, this is the time to read the letter Robert gave me when I heard his confession."

Thomas retrieved the Thompson Family Bible and removed the letter from where he placed it earlier. He slid his finger along the seal and removed the letter addressed to Father Thomas Ryan. He read the letter aloud to his friends.

Father Ryan:

Please extend my best wishes to James and Matthew. I cannot find words to adequately express my appreciation to you three for the sharing of your time with an old man and for the great burden you have lifted from me. You have freed me so I hopefully can join Our Lord in Heaven.

I trust you have now found that which you have sought for so long. I knew you would follow the clues. Yours is now the sacred honour and responsibility to protect that which you now hold. Protect it from anyone who wishes to deny the existence of Our Lord, Jesus Christ and what his life here on earth meant to those then and to all, now, and for generations to come.

It has been the life work of my family to preserve and protect the message from Our Lord. My ancestors and I have done our best to translate our Lord's message even though we were never schooled in the art of translation. The several books in my library, which explain Aramaic, the language of Our Lord, have served as our guide these many years.

Father Ryan, you are the foremost world scholar in Aramaic. You will be the judge if our meager efforts have done justice to Our Lord's work. Yes, Father Ryan, the Letter you hold was written by Our Lord, Jesus Christ in his own hand. Some over time have questioned whether Our Lord was literate. How could He not be literate? Jesus Christ is God. He is omnipotent. It is not possible for one who is omnipotent to be illiterate.

Thomas stopped, closed his eyes for a few moments—he was breathing heavy, He open his eyes and looked down at the letter and reread the one sentence: *Yes, Father Ryan, the Letter you hold was written by Our Lord, Jesus Christ in his own hand.* Thomas looked at James and Matthew. Nothing was said; nothing needed to be said.

Thomas picked up the letter and continued.

Because we Thompsons never felt confident we correctly translated His word, we never made the existence of The Letter known outside our family.

The message in The Letter is needed more today than ever before. The knowledge the three of you now possess is sufficient to make the Word known to all.

I must warn you not all will be pleased with your findings. The message may be much more than uncomfortable for those who prefer things remain as they are. Father Ryan, when you wrote the fictional account of Our Lord's Second Coming, you wrote that all were initially pleased with the Second Coming. It was only after they heard and understood Our Lord's message that they once again turned on Him. Be prepared for that to happen again, for this Letter is not a fictional Second Coming.

I must give you one final warning. Be most careful whom you trust. The powerful within the Church are aware of The Letter. It is one of three documents offering proof Jesus Christ was a man who lived and walked among the people. The powerful do not know what The Letter says, but they know it exists and they want it. Until they have it under their control, they will continue to deny it exists.

My ancestors have kept another secret, passed down from generation to generation. It is known by a small group of people that the Vatican has the private papers of Pope Petrus, St. Peter. In those private papers is a letter from Pope Petrus to Joseph of Arimathea requesting the return of The Letter, which is now in your hands. That is the second document proving Jesus was here. The third document is the legendary "Q" Gospel—the source document for the Gospels of Mark, Matthew and Luke. The message in "Q" is further proof our Lord was personally present here on earth. They want all three and will do almost anything to get them.

May God bless and keep the three of you safe from harm and may God grant you the strength, courage and wisdom to carry out this mission. In many respects, I have not done you a favor, for the future will not be easy. Stay noble and the Lord will protect you from harm.

May God bless you,
Robert

The three sat in stunned silence. Robert's words etched in their minds. *Yes, Father Ryan, the Letter you hold was written by Our Lord, Jesus Christ in his own hand.*

For what seemed like an eternity, no one spoke.

Thomas finally broke the silence: "There is a rumor."

He paused to collect his thoughts and then continued speaking haltingly: "I am aware of the possibility that a letter from Jesus Christ did, at one time, exist. At least I have heard it spoken about in some small circles. The story tells of a letter from Jesus given to St. Joseph of Arimathea as St. Joseph left on a mission to carry the message to the British Isles.

"No one knows if the story is true, but presumably there was also a letter from Pope St. Peter later sent to St. Joseph asking him to bring the letter back with him to Rome. And then, nothing more—at least nothing more that I am privy to. That's all I know."

Thomas collected the pages and leaves and put them back in The Codex. He shut the cover and closed the three silver clasps. Without a word said among the three men, James rose and began to rewrap the cruets in the linen, while Matthew did the same with the Tiberius coin. The items were returned to the pewter box in the order in which they were removed. James lifted the box and returned it to the safe, closed the safe door and spun the combination dial.

With the bookcase pushed back to its normal position, the three men sat down.

Matthew began. "When the Dead Sea Scrolls were discovered, there was great hope of finding the mention of Jesus Christ by name. I can assure you those eleven caves of the Qumran have been thoroughly and exhaustively investigated. The fact no such reference has been found is a great disappointment to believers in the Christ. If what we have just seen is authentic, it may be the most significant discovery of all time."

After another fairly long pause, James cautioned, "The credibility of our discovery is based on words from of a man speaking on behalf of 400 years of his ancestors. Robert is an extremely credible source, but that alone is not proof. Furthermore, he's dead. We can run tests and date the find, but proving authorship is an entirely different story. We three may be prepared to accept things based upon faith, but faith is not enough for a skeptical public. Based on what Robert has shared with us, the message in *The Letter* may not be well received. I don't think we will get much support from the Vatican."

Thomas added, "We may never be able to state with absolute certainty by whose hand *The Letter* is written. However we may be able to discern its divinity through its message. By that I mean if the message is prophetic, and it can be shown the prophecy has occurred, we may be able to show the hand of the divine at work. However, the prophecy would need to be specific and significant. It cannot be vague, like Nostradamus. Asserting divinity would be similar to beatification—one of the steps in the process whereby sainthood is decreed. There, a miracle must take place through the intercession of the one who is being considered for sainthood."

James added another thought. "I now understand Robert's purpose in the formation of The Epistolic Institute. The ownership of the artifacts needs to be transferred to The Institute. Private ownership brings up too many questions about conflict of interest and investigative integrity."

"Excellent thought," said Matthew, "but how do you transfer ownership to The Institute? Won't you have to show ownership in order to have the right to transfer ownership to The Institute?"

Thomas added, "Maybe Robert anticipated that. It wouldn't be difficult for Robert to show ownership because the artifacts have been in the Thompson family for more than 400 years. I suppose a case can be made James acquired ownership when he bought the Thompson house and contents, but I can also see it challenged by the one organization with the money and power to present a challenge."

"Tommie, if you mean the Vatican, you have an excellent point." James continued, "They could build a case stating the artifacts are too important, too universal in their potential impact, that only an organization like the Vatican can safely house the artifacts in their archive. They would mouth some platitudes about making the artifacts available to the scientific and religious communities. And then they would find a way to limit access based upon the document's fragility until the masses forget or lose interest…"

"…and the message would be forgotten and status quo maintained," Thomas finished James's sentence.

St. John the Baptist Church

"Good afternoon Vicar. I appreciate your willingness to meet with me."

"The honor is mine Father Fulgrum. We are not often visited by the Vatican. Not only not often, but never. What can I do for you?" said Carol.

Freddy was not a good liar. With all the practice he had, one could expect more. However, when he was lying or otherwise embellishing the truth, his words came out as if they had been rehearsed—poorly rehearsed at that. His presentation was stiff and lacking emotion. "I am an old friend of Father Ryan and an acquaintance of Rabbi Halprin and Dr. Christopoulos. I have been trying to meet up with them. I was also hoping for the opportunity to meet Robert Thompson, but sadly, it appears I am too late."

"Yes," said Carol, "Robert Thompson was a prominent person here in Glastonbury. He had many friends and many more who wished they had known him. His passing is a great loss. There will be a service said in his honor on Wednesday at 11 a.m. and you are welcome to attend. Your three friends will be there."

"Thank you. I would like to pay my respects. Does Mr. Thompson have any family here?"

"No, equally as sad, he was the last of the Thompsons. It may seem strange to many around Glastonbury not to have any more Thompsons living here."

"That is sad. Did he have any heirs?"

Carol stiffened at this question, which seemed inappropriate. "I really know nothing about Mr. Thompson's estate."

"Excuse me, I didn't mean to imply I was…"

"No apologies necessary."

"I wonder if you might know where I would find Father Ryan."

"I would assume he is at the Thompson house. He has been staying there this past week with Dr. Christopoulos and Rabbi Halprin."

"Ah yes, I met Rabbi Halprin just a little over a week ago at a lecture at Georgetown University. That's in Washington, DC." Freddy's conversational style was often condescending and was all the more apparent when he spoke with women.

"Yes, I know Georgetown." The Vicar really did not like being treated like a schoolgirl being provided information as though she were unaware.

"The Thompson house?" asked Freddy.

"Yes, except now the house belongs to Dr. Christopoulos. You should find all three there, unless they're out and about making funeral arrangements."

"I won't take up any more of your time, Vicar. It was a pleasure and I look forward to seeing you this Wednesday."

"I hope you are able to catch up with your friends."

THOMPSON HOUSE

The glory and awe of their discovery was beginning to sink in.

"I'll give Heather Bean a call and see if we can meet with her tomorrow. She helped Robert incorporate The Institute and maybe she can advise us how we can transfer the artifacts," said James. "I need to find out more about administrative details if I am going to run the organization. Maybe she will be able to tell me if Robert had plans to transfer the artifacts. Regardless we will need continued legal assistance and I assume she would be happy to help with that."

"Jimmy, I want to get high resolution photographs and electronic copies of the pages in the Glastonbury Codex. In doing a translation, I would rather work off copies and not the originals," stated Thomas.

"Glastonbury Codex. I like the sound of it. The name fits," interjected Matthew.

"Tommie, I have all the equipment you need to photograph and scan documents. All brand new state-of-the-art stuff. Just one problem, all the equipment is in my flat in London."

"Is there any way we can get your equipment here ASAP," asked Thomas?

"I'm willing to drive over and get it," offered Matthew.

"I hate having you do that Matt. It will take up the better part of a day to go back and forth. I have an idea. Let me call the man I bought all the equipment from and see if I can get him to help—see if he can bring it over."

James dialed the number.

"Marconi Electronics, this is Patrick."

"Pat, Dr. Christopoulos. How are you doing?"

"Just fine Doc. What can I do for you?"

"Pat, you remember all the photographic and computer imaging equipment you sold and set up for me?"

"I sure do, chief. Is there a problem?"

"Not with the equipment. It's precisely what I wanted, but I do have a problem. The equipment is in my flat in London and I've taken up residence in Glastonbury. I need the equipment moved here, and even more Pat, I need the equipment in Glastonbury right away. I'll make it worth your while if you bring it here and set it up."

"You mean right now?"

"Precisely."

"I can do it, but I'll have to shut down my office for a day."

"Tell me what you want and I'll pay you."

"OK, you got a deal. What do you want me to do?"

"I'll call my landlady and tell her you will be stopping by to pick up some equipment. Pat, if you can pick it up and bring it over this evening, I will pay you for your time and put you up for the night. You and I can set it up tomorrow morning and you can be back on your way home by noon. Will you do it?"

"Consider it done, doc. I'll see you this evening."

"Thank you, Pat, you're a lifesaver."

"You're welcome. I'd better get going."

James called his landlady and filled her in on the plan.

"Is everything set?" asked Thomas.

"Yes, Pat Marconi will pick up all my equipment and bring it here so we can begin in earnest tomorrow morning."

"Terrific," said Matthew.

Thomas interjected, "While you were talking to Marconi—by the way great name for someone in electronics—I called Heather Bean. She'll meet us at eleven tomorrow morning. Perfect timing. I want to be around when Marconi sets up the equipment and also meet with Heather."

BATH

Unable to accomplish more, Freddy went back to Bath to place some calls. He stopped in the manager's office to see if he had any messages. While he was waiting for Carolyn to get off the phone, Freddy noticed Carolyn's desk was full of memorial cards she was cutting and folding. He couldn't help but notice the memorial cards were for Robert Thompson.

"Carolyn, may I ask you a question? Why are you preparing memorial cards for Robert Thompson? I mean, I was just in Glastonbury and met with the vicar of St. John the Baptist and she was preparing for his memorial service. I don't understand the connection."

"Oh Father, our office not only manages rentals, but we are also the headquarters for Boyle Funeral Managers, and we are responsible for Mr. Thompson's funeral arrangements."

"Quite a coincidence. Tell me, have I any messages?"

"Well, Father, not really a message. When you left this morning after making the rental payment on your flat, two gentlemen came in who are involved in the Thompson funeral. One of the gentlemen was a priest. He saw you leave, but you must have missed him."

"Do you know their names?"

"Yes, Dr. James Christopoulos and Father Thomas Ryan."

"Thank you Carolyn."

Back in his room, Freddy placed a call to Father Peter Vacini.

"Peter, this has been a day full of coincidences. I will fill you in later, but for now I need you to do some investigative work. Get everything you can on Vicar Carol Dunmore. She's the Vicar of St. John the Baptist Anglican Church in Glastonbury. Also search the databases and get me as much information as you can about Robert Thompson. Let's see if we can get the information working for us for a change."

Thompson House

Patrick Marconi arrived around 9 p.m. in his bright orange and dark blue Marconi Electronics Volvo lorry.

"Welcome, Pat, thank you for coming. Did you have any problem at my flat?"

"No problems, your landlady was nice, let me in and stayed with me while I removed the equipment. I may have sold her a new computer system. This trip may end up being worth my while after all. Oh, she gave me your mail. Not much there of any interest."

"Thank you," said James, a little put off by Marconi's evaluation of his mail.

"Pat, I want you to meet Father Thomas Ryan and Rabbi Matthew Halprin. They, especially Father Ryan, are going to need your help setting up."

"Pleased to meet you, Reverends," said Pat as he handed each one a business card.

"Nice to meet you," said Matthew, stifling a laugh.

"Same from me, it's an honor meeting a Marconi," continued Thomas.

"Well, chief, where's my bunk, if you don't mind? A bit tired—long drive, you know."

"Let me show you to your room; we can get started in the morning," said James.

"Right you are, chief."

James showed Pat to his room. Matthew and Thomas waited for James in the library. Thomas looked at Pat's business card. "Patrick Marconi, III, Esq., Master Electronic/Computer Specialist." His slogan read, "No one knows Electronics like a Marconi."

James returned and raised his hand before either Thomas or Matthew could speak. "He's really good. Trust me."

"How could he not be? He's a Marconi," said Thomas.

"All right, enough sarcasm from you reverends; back to business.

"I was thinking we would set up the equipment in Robert's study. It's the least used room and less will be disturbed. We can move a few things around and create a good workspace. What do you think?" asked James.

"It should be perfect. I can use Robert's desk to review the scans and photocopies. You know, I think Robert would have liked that," said Thomas.

Matthew added, "I'll collect all the relevant books on Joseph of Arimathea, Aramaic, Koine, and the Dead Sea Scrolls from Robert's bookshelves and create a makeshift resource center in the library. We each have much to do. My suggestion is James and I research the literature Robert has here, as well as our online sources, while Tommie begins the translation process. Jimmy, you and I'll use the library and Tommie can use the study; he's going to need privacy."

"That sounds like an excellent strategy. What do you think Tommie?"

"It's good. It'll work."

"So, tomorrow, we'll get Pat going early so we can get him out of here by about ten. We have an appointment with Heather at eleven. After we meet with Heather, we can get started. I must be losing my mind. Why are we meeting with her again?" asked James.

"We wanted her help in making sure the artifacts are legally transferred to and owned by The Epistolic Institute," answered Thomas.

"This has been quite a day. I'm exhausted," said James. Let's stop for this evening and get started early tomorrow. Sweet dreams guys. I know what I'll be dreaming about."

"Me too," echoed Thomas. "By the way, what's for breakfast?

"Good night all," said Matthew. "I'll be in the kitchen in the morning."

Chapter IX

Thy will be done

TUESDAY, JANUARY 11 – THOMPSON HOUSE

When Matthew entered the kitchen at seven the next morning, Patrick Marconi was already foraging for food. Matthew suggested he have a cup of coffee and be patient.

"Coffee, nah. Now a spot of tea, that would be fine."

Marconi was an interesting type—high energy, always moving about and talking rapidly. He was a squatty fellow, standing maybe five feet eight, with a fairly long graying beard. He was just one of those people who had a passion for computers. His social skills were lacking and his choice of attire was a mix of clashing colors, just like his dark blue and bright orange lorry. When it came to electronics though, no one was more skilled than Patrick Marconi.

James and Thomas arrived as Matthew was preparing tea for Patrick.

"Pat, let me suggest you go with Father Ryan and Dr. Christopoulos and take a look at where they want the equipment set up. If you do and bring in the equipment from your truck, I will have breakfast ready and more tea."

"Okay, I'll go out to my lorry first and bring in the equipment. I could use a hand if you two gents could help out."

Patrick, Thomas and James went out to Marconi's truck to bring in the photography equipment.

In the daylight, Thomas caught his first glance at the orange and blue lorry. "That's a colorful rig you have there," said Thomas.

"If you want business, you gotta be seen," answered Marconi.

James led Pat to Robert's study. While Marconi unpacked the equipment, James and Thomas rearranged some furniture to provide a good working space. With the equipment unpacked, they took a break for breakfast.

Matthew just put breakfast on the table and immediately Pat started and finished eating before the rest barely began.

"That was good chief. I better get started. I gotta get back so I can call on your landlady and see what she might need. I gave her my card, but it's always smart business to call back."

Patrick busied himself in the study, while Matthew, James and Thomas finished breakfast.

Patrick set up the camera, mounted on a tripod to steady the picture. Since the study was well lit, Marconi recommended using a longer exposure without a flash. This would help eliminate any harsh shadows created by a direct flash and better capture the subtleties of the pages and leaves.

The photo images would automatically be transferred to the tethered computer making them ready for analysis. This would resolve Thomas's major concern about excessive touching of the manuscripts as he would now work exclusively on copies and not on the priceless originals.

"None of my business what secret documents you boys got to transfer, but this setup is good enough for MI-5, if you know what I mean," said Marconi with a smile and a wink.

With the equipment in place, Marconi gave Thomas, Matthew and James a rapid, yet thorough, orientation. The process was fairly straightforward, and within 30 minutes the orientation was complete and Patrick Marconi was on his way.

"Jimmy, you were right," said Thomas. "Your Marconi guy is a bit strange, but he does know his stuff. We better leave for our meeting with Heather."

Again, Matthew stayed behind at the Thompson house. They decided not to leave the house unguarded.

Heather Bean's Office

"Welcome gentlemen, I'm glad you could come by today. I have something rather important I need to share with you."

"Likewise Heather," said James, "we have something to discuss with you, and we need your advice. But why don't you start."

"Certainly, Robert asked me to help him develop a letter of specific instructions to be read immediately upon his death. One of Robert's directives was for Vicar Dunmore to invite Father Ryan to participate in the service. I've informed her and she was most agreeable, but she wants to discuss with Father Ryan what his role should be. She asked you give her a call; there's no need to stop by."

Heather continued, "This will be covered in more detail during the reading of the will, but you need to know Robert has left a portion of his estate to The Epistolic Institute. The exact amount will be revealed on Thursday, but I can tell you it is substantial. In addition, Robert stated he would like to have both Father Ryan and Rabbi Halprin serve on The Institute board of directors. He noted he had not asked them, but was hopeful both would accept the positions. The Institute is to have five board members and a president, which is you, James. Robert further suggested the three of you could name the remaining three members. He felt you would know best whom to appoint once you understood The Institute's mission.

"Lastly, Robert has also left a substantial amount of money to Estelle and Henry. Robert's wish is you three assist her in understanding the value of the gift, and why Robert wanted to reward her so. He was also concerned this sudden wealth could be a life-changing event for Estelle, and he wanted her to have support from people she could trust, and not be taken in by some charlatan. Robert did not set up any investment vehicle; rather, he left it to you to counsel Estelle. You should be aware Henry is on disability. He was a miner and has some pulmonary problems. I know the cost of his care often puts a strain on their finances. This will be a blessing if they manage the money well.

"I think that pretty much covers what I had for you," finished Heather.

Before we begin," said James, "I want you to know I've asked Estelle and Henry to continue in their service at the Thompson house in their same positions. I didn't do this out of charity; I really do want and need their help."

"I think that will be good for them and for you. I commend you," responded Heather.

"Thank you." James continued, "Heather, what we're about to tell you must be kept in confidence. We've made a discovery in Robert's library of some religious artifacts Robert had securely hidden away. If these artifacts are genuine, their value would be priceless—beyond priceless, if that's possible. We haven't completed any tests to determine the authenticity of the objects; that may take some time. However, we have every reason to believe they are authentic.

"The problem is the ownership of these artifacts since they were hidden and not on your valuer's list. I question whether I own them, even though I bought all the contents of the home whether it was on the valuer's list or not."

James continued, "Artifacts such as these should not be owned by a private individual. I would like these artifacts to be the property of The Epistolic Institute."

"James," Heather interjected, "I believe Robert may have already addressed that issue which will also be made clear when we read his will. He revealed to me he had a few artifacts that have been in the Thompson family for hundreds of years, and he also told me they are priceless and not in my valuer's report. He said the artifacts had not been outside the Thompson family and he wanted to make these artifacts the property of The Epistolic Institute.

"I had Robert draft a letter describing the artifacts in detail and I added his letter as a codicil to his will. Last Saturday, Father Ryan and I cosigned the letter as witnesses to Robert's signature without knowing what was in the letter. Robert requested I not reveal the contents of the sealed letter until the reading of his will. It must be somewhat comforting to know Robert and you are on the same page in thinking about these artifacts and The Institute," responded Heather.

"It is an enormous relief. Thank you for all your work. We truly appreciate your advice and hope we can call on you for help with The Institute," said James, as he rose concluding the meeting.

"You're welcome. By the way, welcome to Glastonbury," answered Heather as she saw them to the door.

In the car, on the way back home, James sighed, "What a relief. God bless Robert. He thought of everything."

Thomas said, "Let me call Vicar Dunmore before I forget." Thomas entered the number Heather gave him not realizing it was the Vicar's private line.

A voice answered, "Carol Dunmore."

Thomas was caught off guard by the informality and hesitated before answering, "Car…Vic…Dunmore…. Father Tom Ryan."

"Father Tom Ryan, nice of you to call. Please feel free to call me Carol."

"Thank you, Carol, and please feel free to call me Tom or Thomas—I answer to both. We just left Heather Bean's office and she suggested I give you a call. I understand Robert requested I be involved in his funeral service. This may be a bit awkward, since I've only just met him."

"Tom, it will be fine—nothing to worry about. I was wondering if I could call on you to give a two or three minute homily?"

"Carol, that would be perfect and something I'd be comfortable doing. Thank you."

"Tom, while I have you on the phone, I thought I would mention a friend of yours stopped by the church yesterday, a Father Frederick Fulgrum. He said he stopped by the Thompson house and must have just missed you, but said he would come to the service." Carol paused, then said, "Tom, he really isn't a friend of yours, is he?"

"Carol, no he's not a friend."

"I thought that would be the case; you and he don't seem to be cut out of the same cloth. Oops, that really was an unintended pun. Why don't you come to St. John's around ten, tomorrow morning? I can show you where to stand for the homily and we can go over the ceremony."

"Thank you, Carol. I'll be there. See you tomorrow. Bye now."

"So, sounds like you and your buddy Carol are getting along much better," said James.

"Very funny, Jimmy. Carol is a little tough to get to know, but once you do get to know her, you realize she's very warm and friendly. Oh, another surprise; my best buddy Freddy Fulgrum stopped by to visit with Carol, and he'll be attending the funeral."

"How nice. Finally, you two old pals will be able to get together. Margo's going to stop by this evening and prepare a dinner for us. I don't think she knows Matt is vying for Estelle's job. She will be over around six tonight. That gives us the whole afternoon to begin our work."

Thomas's cell phone rang. He didn't recognize the number on the Caller ID "It's probably Matt at the house."

It wasn't Matt. It was Robin, who had gotten Thomas's message from her roommate.

"Father Ryan," started Robin. "Thank you for calling me yesterday. I hoped you would. I got the message from Walter you called."

"Walter?" Thomas responded.

"Oh, I'm sorry. Walter and his partner Bryan are my roommates in Bath. We're all flight attendants and we seldom are in the same place at the same time." Robin paused leaving space for Thomas to respond.

"Robin, I understand you are on a long trip. What can I do for you?"

"Father, I don't want to intrude, but I was hoping I could see you and ask you some questions?"

"Robin, please feel free to call me Thomas or Tom or whatever you're most comfortable with. I'd be happy to spend some time with you. However, the situation I'm in, for the present, is a bit frenzied. Please don't think I'm brushing you off, I'm not. Some events have occurred making scheduling my time a bit difficult,"

"Father Ryan," began Robin. "I'll be on this trip for about another week and when I'm finished I'll be back in Bath for a little more than two weeks. I could come to Glastonbury, if it would save you some time?"

Robin's choice of calling him "Father Ryan" made him realize Robin was seeking spiritual, not temporal, help and her plea sounded somewhat urgent.

Thomas tried to see if he could help by telephone. "Robin, is there anything I can help you with now?"

"Father," Robin paused, "I need to talk to someone in person. It's too hard to do it on the phone."

"Let me take a closer look at the obligations I have and see when I can free up some time. Please don't get the impression I'm so busy I'm trying to push you away. It's just the circumstances of the moment," said Thomas.

Thomas suggested, "Robin, when your trip is nearing completion, give me another call at this number and let's see what we can arrange."

"Thank you, I will. Goodbye Father."

"Goodbye Robin."

"Tommie, that was an interesting one-sided telephone conversation," started James. "Would you care to share what's going on?"

"Jimmy, Robin was the attendant on our flight over and she took really fine care of Matthew and I. We struck up a conversation and she seemed to be interested in us. I sense she needs help. And for some reason, she seems to think I'm the one who can help her."

Thomas paused, "Jimmy, there is something about her which is hard to describe—she is a mixture of innocence and worldliness. She is a stunningly beautiful woman—not the runway model kind. You know the type I mean, the ones who always look bored or aloof. I know this may sound out-of-place coming from me. I'm supposed to be dedicated to the Church and not paying attention to the secular world, but she has me a bit baffled. She'll call again in a week or so and we'll see where it goes."

Bath

Freddy placed a call to his Vatican office. "So Vacini, what have you discovered?"

"I'm not sure, sir. I need to do more digging, but here's what I have so far."

"Vicar Carol Dunmore is a homegrown product living her whole life in England. She was born in London in 1966. She received her master's degree at the London School of Theology and her doctorate at the Oxford University School of Divinity. She has been practicing for approximately 20 years. She served at churches in Leeds, Liverpool, and Taunton and has been the Vicar at St. John's for the past three years. As far as I've discovered, her whole career has been, in a word, unremarkable. She was married to a man who was an elementary school teacher, but was divorced two churches ago. She doesn't have any children."

Vacini paused to see if Freddy had any questions, but since he remained silent, Vacini continued.

"Robert Thompson, on the other hand, is a very colorful character. He comes from an established Scottish family. Along with being a decorated World War II hero, he was also a successful businessman. The pictures I've seen of him when he was approaching 60 years show a tall, handsome, strong and confident gentleman. The kind of man you'd want on your side in a disagreement. After he retired from his import business, he owned and ran a successful B&B in Glastonbury. We have information on his family going back a long way. Some of his family records claim a heritage to King Arthur and later to the Scottish hero, William Wallace. And sir, Robert Thompson is a descendant of St. Joseph of Arimathea."

"Good work Peter," responded Freddy. "The few people who I've talked to about Thompson support what you've found. You can forget about Vicar Dunmore. I met her and she is, as you say, unremarkable. Get me everything you can on Robert Thompson, his family's lineage and standing. See if there is any truth to the Arimathea connection. Concentrate on the family. If a family is considered noteworthy, they must be recognized for something, even if it's rescuing Irish Setters. The key here is his family.

Freddy continued, "I'm going to spend tomorrow in Glastonbury and will be going to the Thompson funeral. I learned our friend Father Ryan will be part of the service. He has surely ingratiated himself quickly into his surroundings. Also, I need more info on Rabbi Matthew Halprin and Dr. James Christopoulos. The three are in this together and I want to know what they're up to. There's also a reading of the Thompson will on Thursday. I'm sure there has to be a public record released after the reading. Find out what Thompson had and who got what. We may have a few more people to investigate. Stay on it, Peter. I need this stuff ASAP."

"Yes, sir, I'm on it," answered Father Vacini.

"Good boy. I'll talk to you tomorrow. Oh, I'm bringing Jerry Fletcher up here immediately. I need to put a tail on these guys. I'll let the Cardinal know what I plan to do."

Freddy thought about snooping around the Boyle Funeral Manager's office, but figured that was just a time waster. He decided to email his boss on progress to date.

To: Cardinal Pietro Castillo, Vatican Finance Officer
Date: January 11
Subj: Status Report, Case File #VI-2010-33

Your Eminence:

Attached is a status report on the events that have unfolded to date. The report is quite comprehensive. Allow me to highlight some of the key points that are in the report.

It appears Father Thomas Ryan, Dr. James Christopoulos, and Rabbi Matthew Halprin (an odd mix, if I am allowed an aside), are staying together in a house in Glastonbury, England. The house is the former home of Robert Thompson (a person of interest). Mr. Thompson is now deceased, having died this past Sunday.

The house and all its contents were purchased, in cash, by Dr. Christopoulos. Records indicate the transaction was finalized last week, on January 5. Attempts to find out the exact price have been rebuffed, but I have learned the total price was close to £2.5 million (that's approximately $4 million). It is my assumption Dr. Christopoulos may have used chicanery to convince the aged Mr. Thompson to sell him the home and contents. I emphasize contents because I believe the contents may be what these three have conspired to control.

I have instructed Father Jerry Fletcher to come here immediately. I will have him follow these three individuals of interest whenever they leave the Thompson house.

Lastly, I am assuming that which they have been searching for may be in the house. We may have an opportunity to learn more about the contents while they are all away tomorrow at the Thompson Memorial Mass at St. John the Baptist Anglican Church, which is why I require Father Fletcher immediately.

There is more in the attached report about some of the other characters in this cabal including Vicar Carol Dunmore of St. John the Baptist Anglican, who appears to be an unwitting accomplice. We are attempting to learn more about Robert Thompson. We will also be investigating Malcolm Collier, Director of The Doorway, a nefarious organization. It appears our Father Ryan along with Robert Thompson met at The Doorway last Saturday, January 8. I believe this is significant and intend to interview Collier myself.

In service to the Holy See, I remain,
Father Frederick Francis Fulgrum

THOMPSON HOUSE

James and Thomas rejoined Matthew. “We have roughly five hours before Margo arrives. Will that be enough time to photograph and download the pictures from The Codex?” asked James.

“I believe so, if we don’t delay. I’d like to get it done in one attempt so we disturb The Codex as little as possible. Matthew, while James and I are retrieving The Codex from the safe, would you make sure the photographic equipment in Robert’s study is ready?” asked Thomas.

“Absolutely, I’m on it,” responded Matthew.

James and Thomas returned to the library and again opened the bookcase to reveal the safe. James dialed the combination 9-11-10 and opened the safe. The two observed the same reverence as before. After donning surgical gloves and spreading the silk tablecloth, James removed the pewter box and set it on the table. Both men genuflected and made the sign of the cross.

James paused as Thomas offered a brief prayer.

"Dear Lord, if this be your will that we uncover these sacred secrets and share the message that Jesus lives, then we humbly offer ourselves in your service."

Together they said, "Amen."

James removed the lid and set it aside and removed the wrapped coin and set it aside. He next removed the cruets and lingered while he held the wrapped package.

He took a deep breath, exhaled and set the wrapped cruets on the silk cloth next to the coin.

As before, Thomas reached in and retrieved The Codex and kissed the linen wrapping. The two men proceeded to the study with the wrapped codex in hand. Matthew had already cleared a place and laid down a silk runner he took from the parlor. Thomas laid The Codex on the runner, and gently removed the linen wrapping. Thomas genuflected and made the sign of the cross again. He then undid the three silver clasps to reveal the pages of The Codex.

Working as a team, the three men photographed the 12 pages and the three vellum leaves. It appeared the 12 pages were four distinct documents, each three pages long. Each was written in a different hand and each appeared to be a translation of the Aramaic letter. After each translation was photographed, it was time to photograph the three page Aramaic document.

Thomas bowed his head and whispered, "Thy will be done."

The same protocol was used on the delicate vellum leaves. Each leaf was photographed and each photograph verified for pinpoint clarity. The three leaves and 12 pages were returned to Codex in the correct order.

Continuing cautiously and with careful precision, the process was completed in three hours. The three men had not yet discussed a carbon-14 test of any of the pages in The Codex. If that were to be done, a small cutting would be made later and sent off for analysis.

The three men returned to the library. Thomas carefully replaced The Codex into the pewter box. James added the cruets and Matthew followed with the coin and replaced the lid. James placed the pewter box in the safe, closed the safe door, spun the dial and then closed the bookcase.

James gathered up his tools of the trade, the silk cloth and the surgical gloves, while Matthew returned the silk runner to the parlor.

At 5:30 all was complete to their satisfaction and the three men smiled proudly at what they accomplished in an expeditious, yet reverent manner.

Matthew noted, "You know, we barely talked to each other the whole time."

"I suggest we celebrate with a glass of wine," offered James.

The three retired to the library for a brief celebration.

As the three men were seated, James said, "I'm worried about tomorrow and the safety of the artifacts while we're all at the funeral. Even though only we three know of their existence, somehow having removed them seems to have changed things. Somehow, they just don't seem quite as safe as before."

Matthew asked, "What do you suggest?"

James replied, "I would feel better if someone were here while we're gone."

"How about if we ask Sean Boyle and his two big men," offered Thomas?

"Great idea," said James.

"Well, gentlemen, good work," Matthew said with glass raised.

Thomas and James responded, "Amen."

"Margo will be here shortly. Excuse me while I freshen up," said James.

"While you do that, I'll give Sean a call," said Thomas.

Sean answered his phone and was pleased to hear from Thomas. "How's everyone holding up?"

"I think all's well Sean, but we do have a favor to ask of you and your men. Robert's home, as you know, is full of many valuable items. Rarely has the home ever been left without someone to care for and watch over it. We're concerned when we all attend Robert's memorial service, the home will be left unguarded. Most everyone will know the house will be empty and it could be a welcome target for thieves."

"Good point, Father. My men and I would be honored to keep watch," offered Sean before he was asked. "In fact, it'll give me the chance to look at some of the old photos of my father and Robert. While I have you, Father, we forgot one item from yesterday. You didn't choose an urn."

"Sean, we trust your judgment. You knew Robert well. Please go ahead and select an appropriate one," answered Thomas.

"I'll pick one Robert would have felt is understated and dignified. We can always change it if you wish," said Sean. "I will bring the ashes in a leather pouch and you can decide what you wish to do when we get together. What time would you like us to be there?"

"Would nine be too early? I need to be at the church by ten," was Thomas's reply.

"Nine o'clock it is, Father. See you tomorrow."

Margo was at the door, but James was still freshening up, so Thomas and Matthew let her in and chatted with her in the dining room about how she was feeling, about Estelle and the funeral arrangements. They continued the small talk until the "freshened" James appeared. Thomas and Matthew retired to the library as James and Margo went to the kitchen.

"Look at that, will you? Our James has become kitchen help. Before long, he may be as good a cook as you," said Thomas.

"That I'd love to see," replied Matthew with a broad smile.

Bath

"Just be sure you get here tonight, Jerry. I have an important assignment for you in Glastonbury tomorrow. By the time you get to Bath, it'll be too late to get a key from the manager's office. I'll get a key for you and have it at my flat. Come to 2G and I'll give you your key. Plan on an early start on Wednesday. We'll have breakfast at 7:30 at a café around the corner and be on our way by nine," said Fulgrum, explaining the short-range objectives to Jerry over the phone.

"Yes, sir," was the snap military response from Father Jerry Fletcher. Father Fletcher was a former New York City police officer and one of Freddy's best investigators. His police training and experience caused Freddy to call Fletcher his best "bloodhound," someone who could sniff out anything suspicious. As a vice squad officer, he often skirted the laws he was called upon to uphold. Having developed an anything-goes attitude where the ends justified the means, he believed and acted as though he was above the law. Even though he was now a priest, Fletcher was still a rough man who knew his way around. His years away from police work softened Fletcher somewhat, although he could still handle himself in most situations.

Fletcher left the vice squad after he was involved in a particularly nasty undercover operation. The unfortunate incident involved a rookie police officer, unaware that Fletcher, who was disguised as a drug dealer, was also an officer. The rookie happened on the scene of a drug buy between Jerry and a big time pusher. When the rookie tried to make an arrest, the pusher pulled a gun and shot him. Jerry acted instinctively, drew his weapon and shot the pusher. After handcuffing the pusher Jerry went to the aid of the rookie, who was bleeding profusely, while at the same time calling for backup and emergency help. Fortunately the young officer lived, but the pusher was dead and Jerry's cover was blown and his ability to work the streets was over.

It was then, as he sat in the street holding the young officer, covered in the young officer's blood, that Jerry "got religion." Ironically the drug buy, attempted arrest and shootings occurred on the steps of St. Jude the Just Catholic Church. The first to come to his aid was a priest from the church who coordinated the emergency calls and may have helped save two lives. After the drug dealer's body and the rookie officer were taken from the scene and other officers arrived, Jerry was given the opportunity to use the church to get cleaned up and have his wounds cared for.

Jerry realized all the drug transactions he was involved in over the years were taking place in front of a church Jerry had never noticed. He spent so much time working vice he became hardened. Sitting in the church vestibule, Jerry reflected on how dark and dangerous his street life had become. As he sat in the quiet sanctuary of St. Jude the Just, the patron saint of desperate cases and lost causes, he knew it was time for a change.

Father Fletcher hoped he'd left that sordid life behind when he accepted a position working for Father Fulgrum. He told others he traded the vice squad for the virtue squad.

Anticipating a late arrival for Jerry Fletcher, Freddy went next door to talk to Carolyn, the manager, about getting a room key for Father Fletcher.

"Is he also a friend of Father Ryan?" asked Carolyn.

"Not yet, but they'll be getting to know each other shortly," said a smiling Father Fulgrum.

"I can put him in the flat next to you or in the next building over, whichever you prefer."

"The next building over would be fine."

Carolyn gave Freddy the key to 3H and Freddy returned to his room to make more calls. After calling information for The Doorway Headquarters in Glastonbury, he placed the call and Mary the receptionist answered.

"Hello, my name is Frederick Fulgrum, and I wonder if I might be able to make an appointment with Malcolm Collier for sometime tomorrow afternoon?"

"May I ask what it is regarding?" inquired Mary immediately followed by, "Excuse me, but would you please hold?" Mary returned moments later.

"I am from the Vatican in Rome and I would like to have a conversation with Malcolm Collier about..." Fulgrum started.

"Hold please." When Mary returned, she said, "I can work you in for 45 minutes at one o'clock. Hold please."

Freddy was getting irritated.

Mary was back. "Would 1 p.m. work for you?"

Before Freddy could say yes, Mary again said, "I'm so sorry, hold please."

She came back on the line and Freddy said quickly, "One o'clock would be fine, thank you," and hung up.

Freddy busied himself preparing for Wednesday while waiting for Father Fletcher.

It was just after 11:30 p.m. when Father Fletcher arrived and knocked on the door of 2G. He waited, hearing clumsy movement inside. Father Fulgrum opened the door wearing a pair of light blue silk pajamas and bloodshot eyes.

"I was reading and must have fallen asleep," he burped. "Here's your key. See you tomorrow."

Jerry took his key and left. Being the good investigator, he thought to himself, *Hmm...I guess the good Father Fulgrum likes vodka.*

Wednesday, January 12

At 8:30 a.m., Sean and his men arrived at the Thompson home. "We're a bit early. I hope that's not a problem."

"Sean, thank you for coming. I know we'll all feel better with people in the house while we're gone," said Thomas.

Sean brought Robert's ashes in a leather pouch and an understated yet dignified urn. James thought burying an empty urn was ridiculous on its face so he placed the urn and leather bag in Robert's study.

Moments later, Margo arrived with Estelle and Henry. They were using the Thompson house to gather so they could all go to St. John's together.

Always most comfortable when she was working, Estelle, with Margo's help, decided to prepare breakfast for all the men, including Sean and his two assistants.

After finishing his breakfast, Thomas excused himself, borrowed Robert's Range Rover and left for St. John's to meet with Vicar Dunmore, who was waiting for him at the front door when he arrived.

"Good morning, Tom. How's everyone holding up?"

"Fine, Carol, thank you for asking."

Carol showed Thomas where to stand for the homily and then reviewed the order of the service, all fairly standard. "Well, Tom, you arrived just a week ago tomorrow. This must be one of the strangest weeks of your life."

"Carol you have no idea. Sometime, when we get a little more time, I hope to be able to fill you in," responded Thomas.

St. John's was filling up with friends and Glastonbury residents. Robert was better known than even he would have assumed. Estelle, Henry, Margo, James and Matthew were seated in the first pew along with Thomas. Freddy sat way in back, trying not to be noticed.

Carol thought to herself, *I wish Sundays were as well attended.*

The strains of Scottish bagpipes announced the beginning of the service. The bagpiper's introductory song itself was unknown, but the melody and message were familiar—one part mournful and two parts triumphant.

Vicar Dunmore organized the memorial as a celebration of a very full life. She called upon three of her parishioners to come forward to share their stories about Robert. The stories were rehearsed and were deftly woven into the religious ceremony.

She called upon Thomas for a homily and he did not disappoint. He spoke about feeling as though he knew Robert his whole life, not just the past five days. He described Robert as a special man who had seen and lived through generations of change, yet managed to be current and involved his entire life. He spoke about Robert's sense of humor and his zest for life and how it would be well for others to emulate him. He closed with an explanation of Robert's wish for the same dignity in death he earned in life.

With the sometimes sad, but mostly uplifting sound of "Amazing Grace," the service came to a dignified conclusion. It was a memorial celebrating the earthly life of an amazing man who achieved his own unique sense of immortality.

As people gathered in back of the church to pay their respects, one attendee left, avoiding an awkward encounter. Freddy was off to meet with Malcolm Collier at The Doorway and get to the bottom of this unholy cabal.

The gathering in St. John's narthex lasted about an hour. People viewed a very well done memorial for Robert: pictures, flowers, and his well-earned medals of honor, including the Victoria Cross on a velvet cushion. When the last of the mourners were gone, the "family," Estelle, Henry, Margo, James, Thomas and Matthew returned to the Thompson house. Carol Dunmore planned to stop by later.

The Doorway

Freddy arrived a little early at The Doorway's headquarters. Mary was working the phones and Freddy was relieved to know there was nothing personal in the brief conversation he had with her the day before, as each caller received the "hold please" treatment. Freddy reviewed The Doorway literature as he waited for Collier.

"We don't get many priests in here," said Mary, "and now two in one week."

"What do you mean?" asked Freddy

"Well, last week...pardon," as she answered another call.

Freddy was starting to regret he asked.

"The other priest was with Mr. Robert Thompson—a wonderful elderly gentleman who just passed. He, the priest, and Mr. Collier did not...pardon."

Freddy was relieved to be ushered into the director's office before Mary could say "pardon" one more time.

Malcolm Collier dressed in his Obi Wan robe met Freddy in the hallway and invited him into his spacious office. Freddy didn't know how much Collier knew or to what degree he might be involved in the goings-on at the Thompson house. He probed with some general questions and received some general responses. Their conversation was going nowhere—either Collier was being cagey or he was out of the loop.

Freddy tried a more direct tack. "I understand you recently met with a colleague of mine."

"You know about that? I really hope I didn't offend him, because I feel maintaining a good rapport between our two organizations is important. There are so many souls out there and so little time. We differ on ways and means, but in the end, we each offer a way out of these difficult times. I would like the opportunity to meet with him again. If you are a friend of Father Ryan's, perhaps you can facilitate another meeting?"

Freddy thought he had the opening he was looking for. "Well, it is true Father Ryan and I go way back. Maybe I can carry a message from you if you wish."

Collier was being disingenuous. He and Niccolo knew Father Ryan had the knowledge to undo what The Doorway planned. In an odd sort of way, and for different reasons, both Collier and Fulgrum wanted to discredit Ryan. "Father Ryan and I had a bit of a disagreement about the rapture, and I was hoping he and I would have another chance to talk," responded Collier.

"Could you elaborate?" asked Fulgrum.

"Well, we here at The Doorway are concerned with the living, while Father Ryan seems to be more interested in reuniting the dead with the living." Collier responded.

Freddy was certain Collier's statement had to be important, but he didn't know what the tie-in was. He would have to do some research when he got back to his flat in Bath. He brought a copy of the videotape of the Georgetown lecture and wanted to review what Thomas said about The Doorway.

Freddy tried a different direction. "I just came from Mr. Thompson's memorial service. It was quite moving—quite a tribute to the man. I wish I could have met him before he died. I wonder, how well did you know him?"

"We are all saddened by his death," responded Collier. "I considered Robert to be a friend. He was one of our members, but sadly his death brought that to an end." Collier continued his half-truth.

"I hope you don't mind all these questions, but I am just trying to understand The Doorway. Do you consider The Doorway to be a Christian organization?"

"I believe we at The Doorway, as well as many of our members, are very much in agreement with Christianity. As I understand it, Christians have a belief system they call 'The Way.' We call our belief system 'The Doorway' and our members follow the Seven Principles of The Doorway."

Collier continued, "I really believe our Seven Principles are congruent with your ten commandments. My sense is the differences are really more semantic than substantive. I trust Father Ryan will come around. After all, we all benefit by getting along. We all are in pursuit of the same goal. I trust you know what I mean."

Freddy nodded as though he understood, but was not at all sure he knew what Collier meant. "If you don't mind, may I ask one last question? How long have you known Father Ryan?"

"We just met, in a physical sense that is, for the first time on Saturday. However, based on his level of knowledge about us, we would consider him a friend of The Doorway. I truly hope we will be able to work with one another in the future. Cooperation and sharing is the key. We are close to enjoying the fruits of our search. I trust Father Ryan would agree it's best we work together," was Collier's response.

"May I ask why the questions? Is Father Ryan under some sort of investigation?" asked Collier.

Fulgrum fumbled for an answer, "Let me just say Father Ryan is a free spirit which is something we value, but with freedom comes responsibility. We all are accountable to one another. My job is to make sure we continue to enjoy that freedom. Well, Mr. Collier, I feel as though I have taken enough of your time. Maybe we can have another conversation in the future?"

Collier responded, "Please extend my best wishes to your colleague and the hope all of us will be part of that joyful moment of discovery."

Freddy thanked Collier for his time and left The Doorway headquarters somewhat mystified by Collier's responses to his questions. What did Collier mean about "enjoying the fruits of our search" and "that joyful moment of discovery?" Oh, Collier knew much more. Freddy was sure of it. Collier was testing him to find out what he knew. It was beginning to make some sense. Ryan was having a spat with Collier over the "secret" whatever the "secret" was. It seemed to Freddy more than a few people were in on "the discovery." He would review the Georgetown tape and see what his investigators uncovered.

Freddy planned to meet Jerry Fletcher at the George and Pilgrims Hotel Pub at 2:30 to compare notes before they headed back to Bath. When Freddy arrived, Jerry was already there.

"Any luck?" asked Freddy. "What did you find at the Thompson house?"

"Nothing. I almost got busted. I thought you said the house would be empty. I went to the front door and found it open. I thought, 'Great, I won't have to break in.' Well, I pushed open the front door and was about to go in when I was set upon by two big guys in dark suits. A third guy showed up and I think I was able to convince him I thought people were gathering at the house. He directed me to St. John's and I left. I don't think he caught on. How did you do?"

"I went to the service at St. John's and found out Robert Thompson was well known and greatly admired. I also learned our Father Ryan has established himself rather quickly. He had a role to play in the service, which was well received. That's one of the things so dangerous about him—he is easily likable. He has been like that since the seminary."

Jerry looked a bit puzzled about the likability factor being dangerous, but decided not to say anything. "How did things go at The Doorway?"

"I'm not sure. I let the director, Malcolm Collier, believe I was a friend of Ryan's. I need to review the Georgetown tape to see what Ryan said about The Doorway. I know there is an angle here; I just don't know what it is. But as the saying goes, 'follow the money.' The Doorway is big and they have money. And Collier is either brilliant or a boob."

"Could it just be an unrelated sideshow?" asked Jerry.

"Not with Ryan. I don't trust the man. The Doorway plays some role here; I'm just not sure what it is. Let's get back to Bath and review the Georgetown tape. I'm hoping Ryan may have accidentally given away some hint during his lecture. I'll give Vacini a call on the way back and see what he's learned."

Thompson House

Sean was telling how he and his men foiled Father Jerry Fletcher's break-in. To the laughter of all, Sean continued, "...and then he says, 'Oh, I thought we all were supposed to meet here.' He had that expression you Yank's say, 'like a deer in the headlights.' So, I directed him to St. John's and he scurried out of here."

"That's only humorous because you foiled him. It's a good thing you were here," said Thomas.

"Listen," said James, "you are all invited to stay for dinner. Vicar Dunmore will be joining us later and Estelle and Margo have requested you all stay."

One of Sean's men whispered to Sean and he said, "My two men wish to get back, but I will be happy to stay."

It was close to four o'clock and starting to get dark. Vicar Dunmore wouldn't arrive for two more hours. After Sean's men departed, James said to Sean, "Thomas, Matthew and I are going to take a walk. Would you care to join us?"

"I'd love to. It's been awhile since I've said hello to my dad."

"Margo, Estelle, Henry; Sean is going to join us on a walk. We should be back in about an hour or so," said James.

The Tor was quiet and there was a seasonal chill in the air. Those on the Tor were working their way down as the four men made their way around to the east side. Along the way, Sean told the men stories about his father, Shamus, and Robert.

"I can't imagine a world without either one of those two men. They belonged to another era—to a simpler time, not an easier time, but to a time with greater clarity."

As they approached the east side of the Tor, Sean said, "Ah, this is where dad is."

All four paused, Sean was first to speak, "I'm sorry Dad. I know I should visit more often, but at least I brought along a friend. You won't be lonely anymore." Sean's eyes welled up and his voice cracked. He looked at the ground and in a quiet voice said, "I have spread my dreams under your feet. Tread softly because you tread on my dreams."

Sean raised his head and looked at the others and answered the question, which wasn't asked, "Yeats, one of my dad's favorite poems."

James opened the sack and gently scattered some of the ashes next to where Shamus' ashes had been spread years before. He passed the bag and each man poured out some ashes until the bag was empty. James handed the bag back to Sean who would take it back to Bath.

With the deed done, Thomas asked the men to gather around for a prayer.

"Dear Lord, we commend to you the ashes of a man who has been in your service these many years. He joins his friend Shamus in eternal rest. We ask you to allow your perpetual light and grace shine upon both of them. In Jesus Christ, Our Savior's name, Amen."

With a sense of satisfaction at having completed Robert's ceremony with the dignity he earned and requested, the men left the Tor to return to the warmth of the Thompson home.

Carol Dunmore arrived shortly after the four men returned from their stroll.

After dinner, James let it be known he wanted to make an announcement.

"I have discussed this with Margo and Estelle and they've agreed. So I'm pleased to announce my intention to reopen this home as the Thompson Manor Inn. Margo has agreed to leave the New Inn in Priddy to be the manager. This will be a slightly different kind of inn as we will market it as primarily a conference center for small groups. With six guest rooms upstairs, we will cater to the professional and business community and rent the entire Manor to small gatherings. When not sold to an organization as a conference site, we will open the Manor to the public as a B&B."

"Jimmy, you're becoming quite a businessperson," said Matthew, "or maybe you're just the front man and the real brains behind the outfit is sitting at the table," a clear reference to Margo and Estelle. "Nonetheless, I applaud your decision and I think Robert would be honored."

"There's still much to be worked out. We very much want Robert's personality to shine through, so we need to make some decisions about all his memorabilia and its proper display. It may be we'll set out different items depending on the audience."

"Great idea," said Carol. "I know with Margo and Estelle behind the venture, it's bound to be a success. I'm fairly sure I can steer some Anglican gatherings your way."

James added, "We already have one client. I intend to have the quarterly board meetings of The Epistolic Institute here."

"The Epistolic Institute?" asked Carol.

"I'm sorry," said James. "Let me explain. Six months ago, Robert formed a nonprofit scientific and educational institute dedicated to studying and reporting on religious artifacts."

"Scientific and educational, how interesting. I'd love to know more when you're ready to share."

"Certainly. We're still working out details, but we'll keep you up to date," replied James.

As the guests prepared to leave, Estelle thanked James, Thomas and Matthew for coming into Robert's life. "You made a big difference in his life. From the time he first met James and then Thomas and Matthew, I saw him become more at peace. Thank you."

It was late when everyone was gone, but there was business yet to be conducted. James, Thomas and Matthew retired to the library for more conversation.

"Guys, I'm sure we're all beat, but we have one more day of obligations tomorrow," said James.

"You know Jimmy, if you don't mind," said Thomas, "I would prefer to stay here and get to work and not go to the reading of the will. Besides, we need someone to stay in the house, lest Freddy's goons attempt another break-in. I have everything up on my computer. I can begin my review.

"You're right," said James.

Matthew added, "I spoke briefly to Estelle about tomorrow's reading of the will. I told her Robert left a substantial amount of money to her and Henry and I would sit with them tomorrow and in the days to come to help them figure out what it may mean for them."

"Is there anything you'll need from us or can you handle it on your own tomorrow?" James asked Thomas.

"No, I'll be fine. In fact, I need the quiet. Oh, there's one thing. It doesn't have to be done tomorrow, but soon. I've been thinking about a carbon-14 test. Can you get ahold of your friend at Cambridge and get the process started? Just find out how much material he needs and we can make the cuttings tomorrow when you two get back. I don't mind as much taking a cutting from the translations, but let's keep the cutting of the parchment vellum to the minimum."

"I'll give him a call tomorrow morning. I know the average turnaround time is around two to three months at his lab. However, since it is his lab, he might be willing to move us up. The actual test only takes a couple of days," answered James.

"Well, guys," said Matthew, "another long day. Let's pack it in and get ready for one more. I want to get ahold of Sara and bring her up-to-date without mentioning what we've found."

"Agreed, it's bedtime," concluded Thomas.

Bath

"Peter, what have you got for me?" asked Fulgrum.

"Sorry to say, sir, not as much as I would have liked, but I do have some interesting information," answered Father Vacini.

Vacini continued, "First, I can't get any information for you on the will until later this week or early next. The reading isn't until tomorrow. I'm using some insiders where the will is to be registered and I'll get it for you the moment they have it.

"I know you said to forget about Vicar Dunmore, but I went back and took one more look at her graduate work. I'm not sure if this is relevant, but she did her doctoral work on the Dead Sea Scrolls. More specifically, she focused on the Jeselsohn Stone."

"Peter, I don't want you to think less of me, but I really don't know everything about everything." Freddy's attempt at humor fell flat.

"Oh no, sir, I never thought you knew everything about everything," answered Vacini.

"Peter, go ahead tell me about the Jeselsohn Stone."

"Yes, sir, the stone used to be called the Dead Sea Stone and was often referred to as 'Gabriel's Revelation.' It supposedly tells the story about the resurrection of Jesus, but the stone is incomplete and one cannot be sure the stone is referring to Jesus. It's estimated to have been written around the time of Jesus' birth, but, as you know sir, the dating process isn't exact. What makes it interesting and unique is it's not a scroll, but a stone. The writing is Hebrew and it's actually ink on sandstone."

"And why, Peter, is this stone relevant?"

"Well, sir," Vacini continued, "the writing is an apocalyptic prophecy attributed to the angel Gabriel. Gabriel was the angel who visited the

Virgin Mary to let her know she had been selected by God to give birth to the Messiah. As I said, the stone is incomplete, but what still remains is the message someone 'will rise from the dead after three days.' There are many who believe the 'someone who will rise' is the Messiah, Jesus Christ."

"Peter, it's getting late. Would you please tell me why you feel this is relevant?" asked Fulgrum.

"Yes, sir, the great disappointment about the Dead Sea Scrolls is they nowhere mention Jesus Christ. If what people say about the Jeselsohn Stone is true, then there would be a reference to Jesus in material discovered which is associated with the scrolls. We know Father Ryan believes such a revelation would be earth shattering, but the Jeselsohn Stone is not enough. Anyway sir, I found it curiously coincidental Vicar Dunmore and Father Ryan may have a common interest."

"Yes, I see. Good work as always, Vacini. Have you any more on Robert Thompson's family?" Fulgrum wanted to move off of further conversation about Vicar Dunmore.

"Yes, sir, quite a lot. I'm assembling it into a report, but suffice it to say the Thompson family was an important Scottish family. There's little doubt Robert's ancestors include, among others, Joseph of Arimathea, King Arthur, the Scottish hero, William Wallace and several other people of prominence. I'm not sure exactly how much information you want, but it could fill a small book," noted Vacini.

"Peter, we may have enough information on Robert Thompson. I could tell by the funeral service today he's both well known and well regarded. The information may be useful in the end, but not as critical as I first thought. He's obviously an important personage, so let's move on to more urgent issues and people," explained Fulgrum.

"What would you like me to do, sir?" asked Vacini.

Fulgrum gave Vacini his next assignment. "Peter, concentrate on getting the will. But in the meantime, see what you can scare up on Malcolm Collier, the director of The Doorway. We need to know what The Doorway is all about, and let's also find out if there is a connection between Collier and Father Ryan."

"Will do, right away, sir," was Vacini's usual response.

Fulgrum ended the conversation: "Peter, Jerry is here and we're going to compare notes from today and review the Georgetown videotape where Father Ryan talks about The Doorway. You're doing a great job. Keep it up and I'll call you tomorrow."

Jerry Fletcher came to Fulgrum's flat in Bath to review the Georgetown videotape. Fulgrum cued up the tape to see and hear Father Ryan make the following statements:

"How can we criticize organizations like The Doorway when we have acted in the same way? In the past, the Catholic Church had been guilty of selling salvations and granting dispensations and annulments in return for money or favors.

"The Doorway could attract tens of millions or possibly hundreds of millions of people looking for answers to the vexing questions of this ever increasingly complex world. Organizations like The Doorway succeed because many of the faithful have lost their trust in organized religion. They have lost trust in us because of our transgressions."

"Jerry, I'm an honest man and I guard against making judgments based on personalities. If I have any bias against Father Ryan it is because I believe in what we're doing, and I don't want people like Father Ryan distorting the truth we have worked so hard to produce. I want your honest answer. Listening to Father Ryan just now, I sense what he would like to pass off as criticism of The Doorway actually comes off as mild praise. He refers to them as a new religion, calls them ingenious and doesn't refute what they purport to do," stated Fulgrum.

"I see your point, sir," responded Jerry Fletcher. "Let me offer one more. Father Ryan appears to be quite knowledgeable about The Doorway. Maybe he had to prepare for his presentation, but the fact he knows so much about the organization may be more than just casual knowledge."

"Good thought, Jerry." Freddy loved it when people agreed with him. "Why don't you go ahead and call it a night? You've been on the go for the better part of the last 24 hours. We can pick up on this in the morning. Peter is collecting some good information we can also review in the morning and develop a new game plan. I'm going to review the tape one more time."

"I'm sorry, sir; I don't think I accomplished much today."

"Not to worry, Jerry. We'll start again tomorrow."

Jerry left and headed for his room and stopped. He searched his pockets for his room key. "Darn it, I left it in Father Fulgrum's room."

Jerry knocked on the door and heard what sounded like ice falling on the floor.

"Who is it?"

"Jerry sir. I left my key on your table."

"One moment."

Freddy opened the door and handed Jerry his key. On the counter was a bottle of Grey Goose.

Jerry left and headed back to his room. "At least the old man has good taste."

Chapter X

When the Devil turns 'round

~ THURSDAY, JANUARY 13 ~

Thursday began with activity on all fronts. Frederick Fulgrum and Jerry Fletcher headed to Glastonbury in separate vehicles. Jerry's assignment was to stakeout Heather Bean's office and record who was present for the reading of Robert's will. Freddy would attempt to find out more about Vicar Dunmore and Robert from Agatha Niblett, the docent at St. John the Baptist. Freddy struck up a conversation with her about the church before Robert's memorial service so he planned to use that as an entrée to gather more information.

Henry and Estelle Higgins prepared to go to Heather Bean's office, ever thankful that Margo Webster and Matthew would be there by their side to offer support. Vicar Carol Dunmore, as well as Father Ricard LaRouche from St. Mary's Catholic Church, would also be attending the reading as beneficiaries. And, of course, James would be there. Thomas opted to stay behind to begin his review of the Glastonbury Codex and guard the house.

James placed a call to his friend Tobias Merten, director of the Cambridge RadioCarbon Analysis Laboratory. To his friends, Tobias Merten was "Toby," and just about everyone who met Toby became his fast friend.

James began, "Toby, I really need your help. Along with Tom Ryan and Matt Halprin I have been involved in an unbelievable find here in Glastonbury."

"I've heard of both gentlemen, but have never had the pleasure to meet either. What on earth are you doing in Glastonbury?" asked Toby.

James nodded slowly as if in agreement, "Well, to say it's a long story may be the understatement of the year. I'll fill you in, but not on the phone. It would take too long and you never know if someone might be listening."

"Okay, you have my attention. Just tell me what you can, and what you need from me."

James was being more cautious than ever. "Toby, we may have made a most remarkable find, unlike any before. I believe what we have found to be true, but we need to validate its authenticity. I need you to run some carbon-14 tests and it has to be done with absolute confidentiality and as quickly as possible. I'd like to get some test strips to you, but don't want to cut too much. I need you to tell me how much material you need to run a test."

"Well, that's a little tough to decide over the phone," answered Toby. "It would help if I could see the material you want tested. You'll need to bring the material to me."

"Toby, we really can't and if you knew why, you'd understand," replied James.

"Jimmy, you're really serious, aren't you? I owe you plenty of favors. I guess if the mountain won't come to Mohammed..." Toby paused. "Would it work if I came to you, saw the materials and made the cuttings myself?"

"I didn't want to ask and take you away from your work, but if you could come, we all would be truly grateful." James's was apologetic.

"I run this place. I have good people doing the work. I can pretty much come and go as I please. When do you want me to come to Glastonbury?"

"As soon as you can. Today, if possible," pleaded James.

"Wow, when you cash in favors you don't mess around. I have a brief eleven o'clock meeting this morning in London, but my afternoon is open. I could leave London around noon. What's for dinner this evening?" joked Toby.

"Matt Halprin's been the designated cook for the last few days. He's actually quite good, but my friend Margo will do the honors tonight," answered James.

"Your friend, Margo? Sounds like this may be some story. Email your address and directions and I'll see you later this afternoon."

"Thank you, Toby. You're a prince. I'll send it. See you for dinner," answered James.

James turned to Matthew and Thomas. "I've been blessed with some of the best friends. None come any finer or smarter than Toby Merten, except the two of you. Toby knows more about carbon-14 testing than just about anyone else on this planet. He practically wrote the book and he built the laboratory at Cambridge as almost a one-man endeavor."

James explained Toby would be coming over that evening to do the cuttings himself from The Codex documents. James planned to ask Toby to conduct the tests in private and authenticate the dates while protecting absolute secrecy until the time was right.

"Jimmy, what's Toby like?" asked Matthew.

"Well, if I could choose just one word, I would call him jolly," answered James. "In fact, each year he plays St. Nick for children in hospitals and gives each a present, mostly teddy bears which he buys himself. He has to add a little padding to his girth, which is already ample, but the padding makes him look more realistic. He has an absolutely exquisite Santa suit, beautiful. He's about five feet ten and has his own beard, which is getting a little gray. If he lets it grow, he wouldn't need to add a fake beard. You're really going to like him."

"I know you have faith in your friend, and I don't mean this as an insult, but I hope I'm correct in assuming we can trust him. Remember, we have a lean and hungry Freddy out there," cautioned Thomas.

James replied, "Toby isn't only intellectually honest and trustworthy, he's deeply religious and a believer in Jesus Christ. In fact, I was going to tell both of you that I'd like to invite him to serve on The Institute's board. We have three spots to fill and he'd be my choice. Have either of you decided who you want on the board?"

"I've given it some thought, but I'm not ready to say yet—soon, maybe even later today," answered Thomas.

Matthew joined in. "Odd you should ask right now, because I was thinking about telling you who I'd like on the board. I don't think you know him personally, but I'm sure you know of him. He's an excellent archeologist and without his help, I could never have completed my book, *Interpretations of the Dead Sea Scrolls*. Bennu Hasani is an Egyptian and knows his way around the Qumran caves. He's extremely well regarded and trusted in the Egyptian antiquities community, and that community, as you no doubt know, is rife with suspicion."

Matthew continued, "Once you meet him, you will know why I want him to serve on The Institute's board. He's comfortable in both worlds. He did his graduate work at Berkley. In the western world, he goes by 'Benny,' and if we ever have to go back to Qumran, he's the man to lead the effort. In several ways, he's perfect, and he's a heck of a nice guy."

"It sounds like Benny and Toby might help give The Institute instant credibility," Thomas replied.

"I think you're right," said Matthew. "Jimmy, you and I need to get going to Heather Bean's office. Tommie, have you everything you need to get started?"

"I believe I do. Give my best to the others."

Heather Bean's Office

Everyone arrived on time for the reading. Heather explained the process they would follow and noted Robert's will was both current and valid, as it had been modified within the past few days and attested to by Heather and two of her assistants. She explained, although the will was complete, Robert added a codicil, also valid and attested to, which she would also read.

Outside in a small VW rental car, camera in hand, Father Jerry Fletcher stealthily photographed everyone entering Heather Bean's office. At just before ten the arrivals ceased, so Father Fletcher hunkered down behind the wheel. He felt like he was back on a New York stakeout as Officer Fletcher. And he came prepared. Not only did he have a camera, but also a thermos of coffee and a half pack of cigarettes.

The session inside the solicitor's office began with introductions since James and Matthew had not met Father LaRouche before. In fact, Father

LaRouche wasn't known to Henry, Estelle, Margo or Heather or even Heather's secretary. Father LaRouche had been the pastor at St. Mary's Catholic Church for the past year, but it was obvious to those present he did little to get to know his parishioners or even the city. The only person present who knew him was Vicar Dunmore.

After the introductions, the Vicar offered a brief prayer in remembrance of Robert. Heather let everyone know Robert made just four bequests and that he wanted his gifts to be substantial enough to make a difference to each beneficiary.

Heather first described the gifts to the two churches. Robert wrote of his pride in his Catholic roots and his later affinity with Vicar MacPherson at St. John the Baptist Church. Robert then stipulated that the bequests to St. Mary's of £200,000 and St. John the Baptist of £300,000, was to be used to advance the ministry and not be squandered on nonessentials. He was adamant the gift was not to be wasted on trivial uses such as a memorial to him.

Next was the bequest to Estelle and Henry Higgins. Estelle was seated between Henry and Margo and held tightly to their hands. Heather read that Robert's gift was in recognition of their years of service, but moreover because of Estelle's love which showed in all she did for him. When Heather revealed the gift of £750,000, Estelle bowed her head, tears falling to the floor. She clutched Henry's hand so hard she nearly broke the skin. She raised herself up and leaned into Henry. Henry, his arm around Estelle, gently said, "There, there, Stelle; there, there" and kissed her forehead. She composed herself and smiled faintly at Matthew as he placed his hand on her hand letting her know he was there for her.

Estelle, having regained her composure, sat up and received best wishes from all assembled. She didn't know who to thank, since Robert was not there. She expressed her appreciation saying she felt unworthy of such a gift, for her service to Robert was a joy and her love for him was real.

Finally, Heather revealed Robert's bequest to The Epistolic Institute. James was astonished to learn the remainder of Robert's estate, valued at nearly £2,750,000 (approximately four and a half million dollars), would be donated to The Institute. Heather noted it was Robert's wish The Institute be sufficiently funded to begin its work. Robert appointed Dr. James Christopoulos as the president and requested Father Thomas Ryan and Rabbi Matthew Halprin serve as members of The Institute board of directors.

Heather continued, "That is the full extent of the bequests stipulated in Robert's will, however there is also a letter from Robert which serves as a codicil to his will. Robert's letter has been witnessed and is valid. I have been under verbal and written instructions not to read the letter until the reading of the will."

Heather opened the sealed letter and began to read. Robert's letter began with a stipulation that the contents of the letter remain embargoed from release to the public until approved by The Institute. His letter required all present to sign an agreement not to release any information to the public. When Heather asked each if they were willing to sign such an agreement, all agreed. Heather paused to give her secretary instructions on developing an embargo letter which all parties would then sign before the reading was over.

Robert further stipulated the embargo letter be placed in the wall safe in his library. Estelle, Henry and Margo exchanged looks of surprise. They were unaware of a wall safe in the library or anywhere in the house. Heather continued to read Robert's brief one page, handwritten letter occasionally pausing to offer clarification.

In the wall safe in my library, which I trust has now been discovered, is kept a message from our Lord, Jesus Christ. For over 400 years, the Thompson family has been entrusted with the duty and honour of protecting three sacred relics of our Lord. As the last living member of my family, upon my death, I transfer that responsibility to The Epistolic Institute.

Heather paused to explain how Robert had her incorporate The Epistolic Institute as a nonprofit foundation several months prior. It was now becoming clear to James just what Robert had in mind when he formed The Institute. She read on.

In the safe is a pewter box tooled by the hand of Jesus Christ's great uncle, St. Joseph of Arimathea, around the year 35 CE. Inside the box are three relics preserved without aging by the grace of God. The relics contain a coin, a denarius with the likeness of Emperor Tiberius, a coin from the period around 30 CE. Next is a pair of cruets, which at one time held the sweat and blood of Our Lord Jesus Christ. St. Joseph of Arimathea brought those cruets with him to Glastonbury around 35 CE. The cruets are as they appear in the stained glass window at St. John the Baptist Church.

Lastly, in the pewter box is a codex protecting a letter on three vellum leaves written by Our Lord Jesus Christ in His own hand. In addition to The Letter are twelve pages of translation completed by members of my family. The most recent translation was started by my uncle, Mason Thompson, and concluded by me.

Heather paused, her normal businesslike demeanor visibly altered by what she just read. Her mind and heart were racing as she thought, *what did I just read—written by Our Lord, Jesus Christ in His own hand?* Heather was shaken. She was not a believer—a fact she kept from her clients, especially the older ones as they were strong in their support of their church. All in the room were silent, reflecting on what they just heard.

"Heather, please excuse this interruption," said James, "I need to interject something here which is most critical."

Heather was only too pleased to give up her convener role as she was still somewhat unnerved.

James closed his eyes as he composed in his mind what he wanted to say. He knew his words must be precise and unequivocal. Looking at each person assembled, James began, "What Robert has written is accurate so far. We have discovered the wall safe and its contents are precisely what Robert has written—a coin, a pair of cruets and a codex which contains four translations and a letter written in Aramaic on parchment which may be from the hand of Jesus Christ. We have no way of ascertaining that fact at this moment."

James, still in the role of scientist continued, "Father Thomas Ryan is one of the world's foremost experts in the translation of Aramaic to English. In fact, Father Ryan is back at the Thompson home beginning his analysis of *The Letter*. I also have a carbon-14 expert on his way over today to take some cuttings so we can authenticate the time from which it comes. If what Robert has written is correct, this may be the most significant event of our lifetimes, whether we are believers or not." James was looking unintentionally at Heather and she bowed her head.

"Let me be perfectly clear," continued James. "At present, we cannot say with certainty *The Letter* is from the hand of Jesus. The carbon-14 test will give us a date range. However that is not proof of authorship, only proof of when it may have been written. I am sure everyone here is aware of the controversy surrounding the Shroud of Turin. There have been many tests done on the Shroud and more tests will be done until all are satisfied.

"While a carbon-14 test which dates *The Letter* is extremely important, the contents of *The Letter* itself are even more important. To support the supposition that *The Letter* is from Jesus, the contents would need to contain prophecy as well as demonstrate they are consistent with what is known about Jesus and His life and times."

"Can you give a specific example?" asked Heather.

James responded. "Yes, let's assume *The Letter* describes a specific future event and that event has already occurred, we may be able to build a case that *The Letter* is prophetic. If the prophecies are of significant importance, we may be able to conclude *The Letter* is divine and may actually be by the hand of our Lord."

James concluded, "We've all agreed to embargo any public release regarding this letter and the other artifacts, but we'll also need to be patient. It may take some time to resolve these questions. Now since you all know the secret, I promise to let you know the test results before we go public."

"Thank you, James," noted Heather, who regained her composure. "Those are excellent points and we should all heed your caution. This letter from Robert is nearly complete. Let me finish his thoughts."

Heather continued with the reading from Robert's letter.

It is more ironic than intentional that the four translations mirror the four Gospels. The first three Gospels, Matthew, Mark and Luke, are known as synoptic, while the fourth gospel by John differs in revealing another side to Our Lord. I am not equating our poor efforts at translation with the divine work of the gospel writers, but merely pointing to the coincidence. The final translation Mason Thompson started and I finished is different from the first three, for Mason and I had the benefit of more recently published translation aids.

It is my hope that Dr. Christopoulos, Father Ryan and Rabbi Halprin will be able to complete the task started by my family over 400 years ago. If they are successful and what I believe to be true is really so, then what they hold in their hands may change the world. It is with great reverence and great faith they must continue their task. A mistake would be fodder for those who would ridicule Our Lord. But, if The Letter is true, as I believe it to be, we all must brace for the firestorm that will surely follow.

I go to my rest at peace in knowing I did my best. God bless you all.

Robert Christian Thompson

Those inside Heather Bean's office sat in momentary silence while Father Jerry Fletcher, parked outside, finished his last cigarette and patiently continued his stakeout. Vicar Dunmore broke the silence. "Let us all pray for the repose of the soul of Robert Thompson and for the grace, wisdom and courage to finish the work the Thompson family has begun. If it is Thy will the truth be told, then Thy will be done. Amen."

Heather reminded all of their pledge to embargo the information in Robert's letter from public release until The Institute is prepared to release

The Letter, and then gave Robert's letter to James to be kept with the other artifacts. The participants exited Heather's office one at a time, allowing Father Fletcher to snap several pictures of each with his long range lens.

As Carol left the office, she stopped Matthew to tell him of her graduate work and interest in the Dead Sea Scrolls. "Matthew, I continue to have more than a layman's interest and if I can offer any insight into Glastonbury or the Thompson family, I would be only too happy to help."

St. John the Baptist Church

While Jerry Fletcher continued his stakeout, Freddy attempted to extract information from Agatha Niblett by again posing as a friend of Father Ryan. He requested Agatha give him a tour of St. John the Baptist. During their walk, Freddy somewhat clumsily probed for what was of interest to James and company during their tour the previous Saturday. Agatha had been cautioned by Vicar Dunmore to be careful about any inquiries about Robert and his friends.

Their tour took them past the four stained glass windows, which depicted St. Joseph of Arimathea. Freddy stopped in front of the window and commented, "Those are the four panels which tell the story of Joseph of Arimathea coming to Glastonbury, aren't they?" Freddy was speaking rhetorically wanting to see how Agatha reacted. He pointed to the third window. "This shows the sacred cruets which according to legend once contained the blood and sweat of Jesus. I would think Dr. Christopoulos would find them to be of great interest."

Agatha, already on guard, showed no emotion. "Most people who know the legends enjoy viewing those windows in particular. I apologize, and I hope you excuse me, but I need to attend to some church matters for Vicar Dunmore. Please feel free to stay and view all St. John's has on display."

"Certainly, please go ahead and do what you must," responded Freddy with a slight tone of indignation.

"Good day, Father." Agatha bowed her head and walked away leaving Fulgrum standing by himself in front of the north window.

George and Pilgrims Hotel

Freddy and Jerry met for a fairly expensive lunch at the historic George and Pilgrims Hotel Restaurant to discuss what each learned from their morning espionage.

"Not much yet, sir. Besides the solicitor, there were seven others attending the reading of the will. Interestingly, Father Ryan was not among the seven.

I'm not sure what to make of it. He could merely have stayed back to guard the house. I was able, however, to get some good quality photographs of everyone as they departed."

Jerry turned on his camera to show Freddy the photos. "The first one to exit is a priest, but I don't know who he is."

"That's Father Ricard LaRouche of St. Mary's Catholic. I want you to pay him a courtesy call from the Vatican and see what you can find out. I had a tour of St. John's and the guide seemed to be a bit cautious, but she may have revealed something as we observed the stained glass windows of Joseph of Arimathea. I will head back to Bath and check in with Vacini. You go talk to Father LaRouche. Let's get back together for dinner in Bath."

Thompson Manor

James invited Margo, Henry and Estelle to come to the Thompson Manor later that evening, rather than immediately after the reading of the will. This allowed Matthew and James the opportunity to spend the afternoon with Thomas to learn what he may have discovered.

"Welcome back. Your friend Toby called and he's on his way," Thomas said rapidly. "I told him we have five documents we wanted dated, although it may be sufficient to just date the vellum leaves. The four translations are dated and the author of record is identified. The first three are similar, much like the Synoptic Gospels, whereas the last, which is partly Robert's work, is different only in several minor ways."

James raised his hand motioning Thomas to stop. "Are you interested in what happened at the will reading?"

"Sorry, I guess I'm a bit focused on this incredible find. I'll be quiet and you can fill me in," responded Thomas.

James identified who was present at the reading and recounted the bequests from Robert's estate emphasizing their need to help Estelle manage her newfound wealth. Lastly he revealed the incredible gift Robert made to The Epistolic Institute. £2,750,000 was certainly more than enough to establish The Institute and lend it the kind of credibility it would need to fend off efforts by others to wrest away control of the artifacts.

Thomas let out a quiet whistle when James mentioned the bequest for The Institute.

"Heather read the sealed letter from Robert, which I have with me, and you need to read. We'll put it in the safe when you are done with it. It's vintage Robert. I felt it wise to share a cautionary note with all in the room letting them know we have not yet scientifically determined the authenticity of The Codex.

All present agreed to an embargo on revealing the contents of *The Letter* to the public until such time we, The Epistolic Institute that is, is prepared to make a statement."

"That was wise. Was Freddy or any of his goons there?"

"I saw neither, unless they were hiding in the bushes."

"I had a nice conversation with Carol Dunmore after the session," offered Matthew. "She did her doctoral work at Oxford on the Dead Sea Scrolls, more specifically, on the Jeselsohn Stone and has stayed intellectually current. She offered to assist in any way she can."

"I'm not surprised she has that level of knowledge and interest. I sensed she did," responded Thomas.

"So it's your turn, tell what have you discovered?" asked Matthew.

St. Mary's Roman Catholic Church

"To what do I owe the honor of a visit from the Vatican?" said Father Ricard LaRouche, as he welcomed Father Jerry Fletcher into St. Mary's Rectory.

"I hate to disappoint, but I'm mostly here on holiday and like to visit churches in the fold whenever I get out and about. They don't let us out very often," Jerry joked. "I'd like a tour, if you care to show me around?"

"I'd be happy to, but could we talk for a while? I have some issues I need to discuss with someone like you. Would you care for a drink? It's cold outside and a little warm up is good for the body and the soul," offered Father LaRouche.

Jerry thought to himself, *it's not that cold out and it's a bit early to drink,* but LaRouche just opened the door. "I guess I have seen more than enough churches. A little afternoon libation sounds like a good idea."

Father LaRouche opened his bottom desk drawer and pulled out a bottle of brandy, added some ice to a couple of tumblers and filled each glass. He had a bucket of ice in his office, which Jerry found more than just a bit out of the norm. *Was this just a convenient anomaly or was this the way LaRouche began his afternoons?*

Father LaRouche was born in Lyon, France, but was raised and educated in the United States. His father was French and his mother was American. His parents divorced when he was thirteen. However his father, a well-connected established diplomat, used his connections to obtain an annulment. While LaRouche's mother had primary custody, Ricard spent his summers with his father in France enjoying the free time a lack of supervision often permits.

His mother's influence finally won out and young Ricard entered the seminary to become a priest. Now in his early 30's, Glastonbury was his second parish assignment in three years. He was unhappy being in a small town in England and seized upon this opportunity to talk to someone who might be able to pull some strings and get him to where he wanted to be.

LaRouche was short and thin, almost frail. His blond hair was parted on the right and appeared heavily oiled. His thin blond mustache was barely visible. "I really don't belong here. These are not my people. I've been here a little over a year and I don't feel as though I fit in."

"Let me guess. You might be more at home in France?" guessed Fletcher.

"Southern France. It's too cold here."

They whiled away the time. Jerry Fletcher, the wise cop, had just enough in his glass to keep LaRouche talking. They were well into the brandy bottle, mostly consumed by the good Father LaRouche, when Jerry began to apply the gentle squeeze.

"You know, Father, there may be some things I can do to get you transferred to...say... Marseilles. I can put in a good word for you which is often enough to make it happen."

"And in return, what can I do for you?" asked Ricard.

"Practically nothing, except maybe help satisfy my curiosity. I've been in Glastonbury just a short while and everyone here is talking about a Ronald or Robert Thomas and some sacred religious secret he has," probed Jerry.

"His name is Robert Thompson and, sad to say, the old man is no longer with us. I barely knew him—he being a member of St. John the Baptist Anglican. However, he did leave us a tidy sum in his will. I hope that goes in your report—my ability to raise money," responded LaRouche.

"So, St. Mary's was in his will? How much did he leave the church?" asked Fletcher.

"£200,000. Which is enough to complete the church building project. You could also put that in your report," stressed LaRouche.

Jerry poured another glass for Father LaRouche and topped off his. "£200,000! That's quite a bit of money. I'm guessing that had to be about the most anyone received."

"No, unfortunately not. But I wasn't here long enough to work on the old man. The old guy only had four benefactors. Had I been here sooner, I would have gotten much more." LaRouche was talking louder and slurring his words.

"Who got more?" asked Fletcher.

"Well, St. John the Baptist got a little more. They got £300,000. But look how long they have been here and the old man was even a member," stuttered LaRouche.

"You know Father, it's not my call to make, but I think we could use a man like you in France or possibly Rome. So, who were the other two beneficiaries?" Fletcher probed.

"The old man had a couple who took care of him—you know, cooked and cleaned, took care of the yard, that sort of stuff. They must have worked him pretty well because they pocketed three quarters of a million pounds," Father LaRouche sounded a bit sarcastic.

"Father, we need to meet again soon to discuss what would be the best scenario for you, where you would like to be, whether or not being a parish priest is what best utilizes your talents. Oh, did you say there were four beneficiaries? Who was the fourth?" Fletcher was being unnecessarily coy.

"Most strange, the largest beneficiary is a nonprofit named The Epistolic Institute. It's fairly new, formed just last year by Thompson. He named an archeologist, a Dr. James Christopoulos, as its president and then left it almost three million pounds. My father was an international banker. He would say a transfer like that smells like a shell game." LaRouche sounded angry.

"What is this Institute supposed to do? What's its purpose?" asked Fletcher.

"Frankly, I don't know what they do." LaRouche stopped talking as though he just remembered something. "I'm really not supposed to say anymore. We have all agreed."

Jerry gave a look of being annoyed, which Father LaRouche immediately recognized. He did not want the Vatican emissary angry with him, but he also knew he said too much and needed to end this conversation.

"All I know is The Institute may end up being the repository for some sacred artifacts. Right now, one of Dr. Christopoulos's colleagues is conducting tests to determine their authenticity. They're hoping to know fairly soon if they are real. I would be more than happy to tell you more when I learn what is going on."

Jerry sensed he might have gotten all he was going to get out of Father LaRouche. He didn't want the priest to develop remorse over talking too much. Jerry knew he would get more at their next meeting.

"Father, I'm having dinner later today with one of my colleagues who's well placed in the Vatican hierarchy. Let me discuss your wish for a new assignment with him and see what can be done. Maybe we can get together tomorrow or the next day and talk further?" responded Fletcher.

"I'd like that very much. Maybe I can find out more about The Institute and share that with you when we next meet." LaRouche was eager to prove he was on the team.

"I'll be getting ahold of you in the next day or so. Thanks for the brandy—it warms the body on a chilly day like today."

The men said their goodbyes and Jerry was on his way to Bath feeling as though he finally did something to earn his pay.

THOMPSON MANOR

"So tell, what have you discovered?" asked Matthew.

"Well," started Thomas, "I first read the four translations. As I mentioned, the first three, the oldest ones, are similar. The fourth one started by Mason Thompson and finished by Robert is a significant refinement. Mason and Robert had the benefit of some Aramaic translation texts the previous translators didn't have. Nonetheless, all four translations have significant gaps where the translators were stuck. I then took a close look at the original Aramaic document. As I've mentioned, it is the most beautiful Aramaic handwriting I have ever seen."

Thomas continued, "The style is artistic, yet bold and confident. I cannot see any hesitation or pausing by the author, which is why I call it confident. The author knew exactly what he wanted to say and just let it flow. It's also older Aramaic, definitely from the time of Christ. I can't just read it off like it's English, but I don't think the translation will take me very long. I'm guessing no more than a week to ten days. I want it to be complete before we make any public release concerning the artifacts. I hope we can keep this under wraps until then. I'm sure your friend Toby can complete his tests long before I'm done with the translations."

"I'm really sorry, but I'm going to need to go back home this weekend," said Matthew. "I'll stay for four or five days to get things straightened away and get my Dean to give me an open-ended leave of absence. I want to be back here before all the fun starts. I'll fill Sara in and tell my Dean just enough without revealing any secrets."

"Good, just do what you have to do. You're on The Institute's payroll now, but without pay," said James smiling. "We'll continue while you're gone, and keep as low a profile as possible until we have something definitive to release."

"Let me tell you more about the four translations," offered Thomas. "The first was completed in 1763 by Spencer Wallace Thompson. The middle name, Wallace, refers to the Thompson ancestor, William Wallace, the Scottish hero who fought for Scotland's independence from the English King William. Jackson Spencer Thompson completed the next translation in 1821 and the third was completed in 1910 by Roman Wallace Thompson. Those first three are what I refer to as the synoptic translations. I think the second and third translators relied heavily on the first."

Thomas continued, "The fourth and final translation was started by Mason Thompson and completed by our Robert in 2009. It's different in style and some detail from the first three, using more contemporary English. I think

Mason and Robert went back to the original Aramaic and didn't rely solely on the first three translations. All three are what I would call choppy; and there are occasional gaps where the translators just weren't sure which words to use. Aramaic is not easy. In some cases, the translators used poetic license to complete a thought. All things considered, they did an admirable job. You can tell by the reverence shown it was clearly a labor of duty and love."

Thomas continued. "When I do my translation, I'll work solely off the copies of the Aramaic and won't rely on the translations; I won't even look at them again. In fact, if I could I would like to completely erase them from my mind. Having them close at hand could tempt me to use their translations when I get stuck, and I will get stuck. Please feel free to read them if you wish, but if you do, please don't discuss them with me or ask for a clarification. From here on, I will work only from the original."

"Then I think it may be wise if we put aside the translations," offered James. "I would love to read them, but I will wait for the final. I'll still have Toby take cuttings in case we want to date them, but then we'll lock up the copies of the translations along with the originals."

"Agreed," said Matthew. "It will only heighten our curiosity. It'll also allow us to be honest if queried about what we have found. We'll all have the same response—we'll share what we know when the research is complete."

Bath

Jerry drove cautiously back to Bath. He'd had a couple glasses of brandy with Father LaRouche and didn't want to risk getting stopped. Excited to finally be able to report some progress for his efforts, he went back to his flat, freshened up and called his boss. Father Fulgrum suggested they meet in the café around the corner.

Jerry arrived first, secured a table in the corner away from others and ordered a pot of coffee. He then called the remote Vatican transcription unit to file a complete report, which would be put into a secure file.

Freddy arrived and was pleased to see Jerry with his notebook out ready to pass on his findings. "Well, can I assume you have something to report?"

"Yes, sir, a veritable gold mine."

"Well, should we celebrate?" Freddy answered his own question as he signaled the waitress.

"I'll have a vodka gimlet, Grey Goose. What would you like, Jerry? I have a fairly generous expense account."

"Jack Daniels on the rocks, I've had a couple cups of coffee, but I need to get the taste of brandy out of my mouth." Jerry thought his boss was becoming more familiar. He never saw Father Fulgrum drink in public before.

Jerry detailed his conversation with Father LaRouche. "What's the possibility we could get him transferred to France, Southern France to be specific? Because, if we do, I think I can get him to tell all."

"A transfer is simple enough, but make him think it's a big deal so you get everything from him. Finally," Freddy said emphatically, "we have a lead! Vicar Dunmore and her tour guide were of no help, I believe intentionally so. I may have misread her. And Collier at the Doorway may be just a talking head. I can't figure him out. Vacini is trying to get the details of Robert's will, but it's going to take some time. Father LaRouche may be quicker."

Jerry reported what LaRouche told him about the amount of money each of the beneficiaries received. "There was £200,000 for St. Mary's and £300,000 for St. John the Baptist, £750,000 for Estelle and Henry Higgins and over £2,750,000 for The Epistolic Institute."

Jerry continued "LaRouche said his father was an international financier and the gift looked like a shell game—like they were moving money from one pocket to the other. All he revealed was the existence of some sacred artifacts, and that one of Dr. Christopoulos's colleagues would be conducting tests to determine the authenticity, maybe a carbon-14 test, but I'm not sure."

"Sounds like you have the start of a good connection. I can make France happen. Make a deal tomorrow, Southern France for whatever was in Robert's letter."

Freddy signaled the waitress. "One more round and a menu, please."

Thompson Manor

Tobias Merten arrived around 3 p.m. James brought him into the library and introduced him to Thomas and Matthew.

"Please call me Toby," said the smiling Toby.

"What a charming home. So warm, so inviting—and its all yours. Jimmy, you're becoming an English landlord," said the cheerful Toby.

"Toby, so much has occurred in the last week and with Matthew and Thomas's help, I will try to bring you up to speed so you can better appreciate what I am going to ask you to do."

For the next hour, the four men discussed the events leading up to the present moment. Mostly they talked about Robert, his life, his secret, his death and his gift to establish The Institute. Thomas attempted to sum up the man. "Robert was a special man—so very perceptive. He just seemed to understand so much about each of us. It was as if he knew what was on our minds and in our souls."

"Toby, we would be honored if you would accept an invitation to serve on the Epistolic Institute board. We are not ready to pay a salary, but we can pick up your expenses," explained James.

"What would you have me do?" asked Toby.

James enthusiastically laid out the beginnings of a plan for The Institute. "Toby, we are dealing with antiquities, an area where you have considerable expertise. We have inherited some artifacts—artifacts, which will humble and awe even nonbelievers. I must caution you. What we have may be the most important find ever. I know that the word 'ever' sounds grandiose, but after you see what we have in our possession you may think we are being too modest."

Toby was sitting forward in his chair, listening to every word. "I've known you for some time, Jimmy. This may be the most serious and the most excited I've ever seen you. You have me, please show me more."

James removed the pewter box from the safe before Toby entered the library. Thomas approached the pewter box with the same reverence as before. He described the contents as they were removed; the coin, as a mechanism to date the contents, and the cruets, the object of James's lifelong pursuit. Thomas then carefully unwrapped The Codex from the linen to reveal the four translations and the three vellum pages. "Toby, what we have here may be the Word of Jesus Christ in His own hand."

Toby stood in wonder, devoutly reviewing all three artifacts. He recognized the writing on the vellum to be Aramaic and he marveled at its graceful strength.

He looked at Thomas as if to ask, *is this real*? "Gentlemen, I would be honored to serve on the board. I only hope I am equal to the task." Gazing at The Codex, he said, "I assume this manuscript is what you want tested. I have never seen anything ever before which even comes close in beauty."

Toby stood in quiet reverence saying nothing just admiring the delicate vellum leaves.

James added, "You know, gentlemen, we are going to need to establish an office for The Institute and create a room where we can keep these artifacts both secure from thieves and safe from environmental degradation. I think it best to keep the artifacts here in Glastonbury. Toby, do you know how to set up a room where we can keep these artifacts safe?"

Toby did not look up, he continued reviewing the vellum. "Yes, I can help with that, but first let me concentrate on the cuttings." His gaze never left the manuscript.

"I think I know someone who might be able to help us secure some good space in Glastonbury," said Thomas. "I haven't confirmed this, but I'm ready to name my choice for the board and am convinced she would be a valuable addition."

"She?" questioned Matthew.

"Yes, my new friend, Carol Dunmore."

"Toby, Carol Dunmore is the Vicar of St. John's Anglican; she knows the town and they know her. She's studied and continues to study the Dead Sea Scrolls. Her being a local will rally the good townspeople around us when the heavy lumber starts to come down," said Thomas.

"Excellent choice," said James.

"Heavy lumber? You mean Freddy?" asked Matthew.

Thomas continued, "No, Freddy's not the heavy lumber; I'm talking about the full force of the Vatican. As St. Thomas Moore told his lawyer son-in-law, Thomas Roper, 'I would suppose you would cut down every law to get at the Devil, and you are just the man to do it. But when all the trees are cut down and all the laws are laid flat and when the Devil turns 'round, do you think you could stand in the winds that will blow then?'"

"I'm not sure I understand the analogy. You are not equating the Vatican with the Devil, are you?" asked Toby.

"No, the Vatican is not the Devil. But we are about to cut down the trees that have protected them and they will tenaciously fight to hold onto what they control. We need to be prepared to stand fast. Having the good townspeople of Glastonbury standing with us will surely help," responded Thomas.

"Now if I may take some cuttings, I am sure you want to return these artifacts to the safe."

Toby, like a skilled surgeon, made his cuts taking only what would be necessary to do two independent tests, the second test intended to validate the first would be done on a different day. All agreed it was unnecessary to test the Mason/Robert translation for it was clearly contemporary. Toby then took cuttings from the three earlier translations. Each of the cuttings was placed in a specially labeled glass tube with an aluminum cap, which kept the sample from sticking to the top and possibly being damaged.

His cuttings complete, Toby explained, "We are able to date most of our tests to .03% or within 25 to 30 years. It only takes two days to complete the tests, but we have a two to three month backlog at the lab. I'll go back tomorrow and run the tests myself this weekend and give you the results no later than Tuesday. I need to put my samples someplace safe until tomorrow."

"Toby, before we put the artifacts away, I would like you to take a look at this." James had Toby inspect the cruet with the rust-colored stain. "Toby, we believe these two cruets at one time contained the sweat and blood of Jesus Christ."

Toby held the cruet up to the light revealing the stain. "I think your assumption this is from blood is correct. I've seen this many times over and that would be my guess. I hesitate recommending scraping it for a test though. I might have to take it all for a good sample, and then it would be gone forever.

My advice, don't do it. We'll get a good date off the vellum and the stains can be left to faith."

James said, "Toby, I must apologize in advance. Only Thomas, Matthew and I know the location of the safe that holds the artifacts. I admit it's a game, but if we keep that information just to us three, it allows you to be able to say, with total honesty, you do not know the whereabouts of the safe. How about if Thomas shows you to your room while Matthew and I secure the secrets, including your cuttings?"

Toby's jolly smile returned, "Don't be concerned. I love playing games, especially those which are mysterious."

James and Matthew returned the artifacts to the pewter box and placed it and Toby's cuttings in the safe, then closed the safe and the bookcase.

Friday Morning, January 14 – St. Mary's Catholic Church

Father Ricard LaRouche welcomed Jerry Fletcher to the rectory of St. Mary's Catholic Church where they sat in the parlor drinking coffee.

"Well, Father, I have some good news. A transfer to France is possible, but the Vatican has some serious concerns," said Jerry.

"I can't imagine what's wrong. I've always done as asked," answered a worried LaRouche.

"No, not you, Father. The Vatican isn't concerned about you. They're concerned about the Epistolic Institute as well as Dr. Christopoulos and his colleagues. The Vatican is concerned the artifacts they possess are in danger of being compromised. Only the Vatican can keep sacred artifacts safe and secure. I know you want to be part of our team. Am I right?" Jerry's words calmed LaRouche.

"Yes, but I've agreed to embargo any public release of what I know until The Institute releases the information first," said LaRouche.

"You can honor the embargo and still tell us what you know. The Vatican has no intention of releasing any information to the public. Our only interest is to protect valuable sacred artifacts," explained Jerry.

"I see your point. It was an embargo not to go public, not a request for confidentiality. What do you know about a transfer out of here?" LaRouche wanted to be sure he got paid in kind for whatever information he gave out.

"I can't say exactly where we will send you, but I can say it will be Southern France," promised Jerry. "You have my word. Can we count on you to help us?"

"That's good enough for me. What do you want to know?" LaRouche was ready to tell all.

"If you can detail what the artifacts are and where they are, we will be able to determine their value and safety. That's our number one concern—safeguarding of the sacred," explained Jerry.

LaRouche began, "Well, during the reading of the will, the solicitor revealed a handwritten letter from Robert Thompson as a codicil to his will. In the letter, Thompson detailed three sacred artifacts which are kept in a pewter box in a wall safe in the library of his house."

"What are the artifacts?" probed Jerry.

LaRouche continued, "The first relic is a coin, a denarius with the likeness of Emperor Tiberius, from around 30 CE. Next was a pair of cruets, which the Thompson family believed once held the sweat and blood of Our Lord, Jesus Christ. Thompson wrote he believed St. Joseph of Arimathea brought those cruets with him to Glastonbury around 35 CE. That is a long-standing belief in these parts. There is a famous stained glass window in St. John the Baptist which depicts St. Joseph of Arimathea carrying the cruets as he arrived in England."

"Father, the cruets sound both fragile and significant. That is precisely the kind of artifact, which is best kept in the vaults at the Vatican. I am sure you agree, don't you?" Jerry was attempting to make LaRouche feel important and part of a bigger team.

"Oh yes, I agree. But, there's more." LaRouche was just getting into his disclosure. "There is also a codex in the box which contains a letter on vellum along with some translations of the letter. Robert Thompson wrote that the vellum letter was written by Our Lord, Jesus Christ in His own hand. No one knows the contents of the letter, but presumably Father Ryan is attempting to translate the writing. It's Aramaic. They also have a carbon-14 expert who will be dating the letter. That is really the full extent of what I know."

Jerry did his best not to show surprise. "Father, I think what you have reported is quite significant. I need to get back to Bath and report this to my superior. I know he will be most pleased with you and may want to meet with you personally."

"And, France?" pestered LaRouche.

"Don't pack your bags just yet, but I believe your wish will be fulfilled," was Jerry's response.

Jerry left and headed back to Bath. He called Freddy on his cell phone and told him he had the goods and to be ready for a bombshell, but wouldn't say more on the phone.

Bath

Freddy invited Jerry into his flat. "Jerry, you sounded excited on the phone. What did you learn from Father LaRouche?"

Jerry was almost breathless. "Well, I finally got him to open up and he revealed the contents of a letter that Robert Thompson included in his will. When LaRouche got started, it just flowed and flowed. Here's what I got." Jerry took out his notebook making sure not to skip any detail.

"There's a wall safe in the Thompson house library. In the safe are three sacred artifacts. They include a denarius from around 30 CE, which was meant to serve to date the other artifacts. The second item is the Joseph of Arimathea cruets, the ones in the stained glass window in St. John the Baptist. These are the cruets legend says contained the blood and sweat of Jesus Christ after the Crucifixion."

Jerry purposefully stretched out his report because he wanted to enjoy sharing the news with his boss. "The third artifact, are you ready for this—is a letter on three vellum leaves written by Our Lord, Jesus Christ in His own hand."

Freddy's response shocked Jerry. He did not smile or say great job, Jerry. He just stood up. Jerry looked at him as though he was looking at a ghost. Freddy had no color. He looked as though he had been fatally wounded.

Jerry waited for his boss to respond.

Freddy closed his eyes. With fingers pressing the bridge of his nose, he said, "Damn!"

Freddy opened the door. "You have to leave. I must call Cardinal Castillo. We'll get back together after my call and I'll fill you in, but for now you must excuse me."

Jerry was left completely perplexed. He thought he brought good news and he couldn't understand his boss's reaction.

Freddy called the Vatican and got his aide, Father Peter Vacini. "Vacini, I need the Cardinal immediately and tell him to be on his secure line."

Freddy waited impatiently pacing back and forth until he heard a voice on the other end. It was the characteristically charming, almost sing-song-like answer, "This is Cardinal Pietro Castillo."

Freddy blurted, "Cardinal Castillo, Ryan has *The Letter*."

"Damn!"

Castillo and Fulgrum briefly discussed strategy. They knew if Thomas Ryan had *The Letter*, he would be able to translate it. Ryan was one of the most sought after translators of Aramaic to English. Under different circumstances, the Vatican would have called on him to do precisely what they now feared he would do on his own.

"Father Fulgrum, have Fletcher get that information in detail ASAP. I want you back here immediately," Cardinal Castillo was uncharacteristically sharp. Freddy had never seen this side of his boss before.

Freddy met Jerry in the pub around the corner from their flat.

"Jerry, I need your help; I'm going to tell you something you must keep in strictest confidence. If it gets out I told anyone, it would cost me my job and possibly more. Jerry, for two thousand years, there has been a belief there may be a Letter, in Jesus Christ's own hand. For years the Vatican has allowed and even quietly fostered the notion Jesus was illiterate. We needed to be prepared to deny *The Letter* if what it revealed was detrimental to the Church. Billions of people around the world depend on the Church and a message contrary to what has been established could only bring havoc to the fold.

"If *The Letter* does still exist, we know why it was written. It would be a Letter from Jesus to his Uncle Joseph of Arimathea. We don't know what's in *The Letter,* but there is cause for concern and the Vatican wants to see it before it's released to the general public. We must find out what Thomas Ryan knows. Does he have *The Letter*? Where is it? What condition is it in? Has he begun the translation?"

Freddy continued, "There is much more which I'll tell you later, but time is of the essence. I want you to find out who has been invited to serve on The Epistolic Institute's board of directors. Just get the names. I'll have Vacini find out more on each member."

Freddy's urgency was palpable. "Jerry, do whatever you must, but we need to have answers and we need them now. Time is of the essence. I can't emphasize that enough. I'm going back to Rome. Cardinal Castillo is sending one of the Vatican's jets to pick me up. I don't know when I'll be back but it won't be long—maybe just tomorrow or the next day."

"I'll do what I can, sir. If I go beyond, will the Vatican have my back?" asked Jerry.

"As always," answered Freddy.

"Sir," asked Jerry. "What about Father LaRouche? What can we offer him? I want to keep working him and I need some bait."

Freddy was exasperated. "The man's a pest. However, we might need him some more. Tell him we'll reassign him to Perpignan. It gets him back to Southern France and keeps him outside the limelight. We don't need him making any noise once we're done with him."

Saturday Morning, January 15 – Thompson Manor

Estelle was comfortably back in the kitchen as she and Henry returned to work at Thompson Manor. Matthew's tour as cook was over. Estelle prepared her traditional English breakfast. After breakfast, Toby left immediately to return to his lab and begin the carbon dating tests. Matthew and James planned to sit with Estelle and Henry to discuss their newfound wealth. Thomas left to meet with Vicar Carol Dunmore.

Thomas called ahead and so Carol was waiting for him. "Tom, good to see you again," said Carol. "You weren't at the reading of the will, but I understand you were quite engaged. It must be captivating work."

"It is Carol and that's exactly what I want to talk to you about. We're putting together the Epistolic Institute board of directors, and I'd like you to be a member. We have already confirmed some really solid people to serve on the board. Along with James, Matthew and me, we have a commitment from Tobias Merten, who is a carbon-14 expert and a friend of James. Matthew has selected Bennu Hasani who he collaborated with on his Dead Sea Scrolls writings. And I'd like you to be the final member. Feel free to take some time to think it through. I may not be doing you much of a favor. I think The Institute's going to be taking some heavy flak from the Vatican."

"I've never met them, but I know of both Tobias Merten and Bennu Hasani. You've acquired some high quality people. I really don't think I'm on that level. Are you sure you want me?" asked Carol.

"Yes, but as an equal. We're not looking for someone to take minutes. You have much to offer about the Thompson family and Glastonbury. One of the first tasks at hand is to secure adequate space for The Institute—space that can be made secure to protect the sacred artifacts from thieves and environmental degradation. But I'm getting ahead of myself. I want to caution you, we're going to disturb the traditional order of things and I know the people we will disturb. They can be very nasty," warned Thomas.

"Oh, they can't really hurt me. I'm an Anglican and I can always retreat into the girl world and claim you duped me," Carol said with a laugh. "Thomas if you really want me, I would be honored to serve and do whatever I can to advance the cause. I accept. Does this mean I'll see the actual Letter?"

"Yes, it does. Carol, Matthew is returning to the States for about a week, but when he returns he'll be on an open-ended stay. James wants to convene a meeting of The Institute board by the end of the month. Toby will have finished his carbon-14 tests and Bennu Hasani will fly in from Cairo. There is no salary at this time, but The Institute will pay whatever expenses you incur. At the first meeting, we'll spend some time on housekeeping issues, but the greater amount of time will be dedicated to the artifacts Robert left for us."

"Tom, I'm surprised. We really didn't hit it off when we first met. Thank you for including me. It's an honor and I look forward to all that lies ahead—the work, the controversy, the challenge," Carol said with pride.

"Good then. I'll let James and Matthew know you'll join us. I believe it's time to get started." Thomas was relieved.

Chapter XI

Peace be with you always

SATURDAY MORNING, JANUARY 15 – VATICAN CITY

Cardinal Castillo sent a Vatican jet to Bath to pick up Freddy—not one of the newer, nicer planes in the fleet, but Freddy was nonetheless impressed. It saved time by eliminating the drive to Heathrow and negated having to adhere to commercial schedules, plus it allowed Freddy to embellish his importance to whoever would listen that the Cardinal sent a plane to pick him up. Freddy got to his apartment in Rome on Friday evening and had a chance to freshen up and prepare for his meeting Saturday morning with the cardinal.

Freddy arrived at his Vatican office at 8 a.m. giving him roughly 45 minutes to see what might have been put on his desk before his nine o'clock meeting with his boss. Cardinal Castillo's office was just up one floor and down the hall. On his walk to Castillo's office, he greeted several colleagues who were buzzing about. Saturday's were always busy, but this day seemed much more hectic than most. He learned from Vacini that *The Letter* was the number one topic of conversation.

As Freddy arrived at the outer office, Castillo's secretary said, "Go right in Father, they've been waiting for you."

"They?" asked Freddy. "Who else is in there?"

"Cardinal Alvarez and I don't think he's in a good mood."

"Thank you," said Freddy, who now realized he had two rings to kiss.

Freddy entered and did his duty, bowing and kissing rings.

Freddy didn't know Cardinal Felipe Alvarez very well. He'd met him a couple of times in passing. Alvarez was young, just Freddy's age or a year or two older, but he was an aggressive climber—a trait Freddy admired. Alvarez was the director of security for Vatican antiquities.

Castillo began, "Father Fulgrum, please be seated. Cardinal Alvarez wants to ask you a few questions."

Alvarez smiled, and then looked back down at the file he was holding, "So you are from Texas?" He closed the file and put it on the desk. Freddy could only assume it was his personnel file. Alvarez looked up, smiled and said, "Well, we Texans have to stand together, right Father?"

Freddy responded, "Yes, your Eminence." Freddy thought, *I bet he uses that line on everyone.* Freddy was aware that Alvarez was from Madrid.

"Well, Father, let me get right to the point. You have reported to Cardinal Castillo that Father Thomas Ryan has a letter, which he claims to have been written by Jesus Christ. Have you seen this letter?"

"No, your Eminence. One of my investigators reported that to me," answered Freddy.

"Father you can drop the Eminence crap. Did your investigator see *The Letter*"

"No sir, he didn't. It was reported to him by a parish priest in Glastonbury," responded Freddy.

"Did this parish priest see *The Letter*?" asked Alvarez.

"No sir, he was told about it during the reading of a will." Freddy was becoming uncomfortable with the line of questions.

Alvarez looked at Cardinal Castillo and shook his head. He looked back at Freddy. "Do you know of anyone who has seen this letter?"

Freddy was embarrassed. "No sir, but we believe Father Ryan has *The Letter*."

Alvarez smiled an unfriendly smile. "Well, Father, you strike me as a man of great faith. You seem willing to accept this thirdhand story as gospel. Tell me, why do you believe it's so?"

"Well, your…sir, there appears to be other corroborating evidence which supports the belief..."

Alvarez raised his hand. "Relax father. I was just testing you to see how strong your convictions are. Cardinal Castillo's told me you have an exemplary record and you don't jump to conclusions. So tell me Father Fulgrum, if Ryan has a letter from Jesus Christ, what do you suppose is in it?"

"Sir, I have no idea and that is the part which is worrisome."

Alvarez stood up and walked to a window. He was running options through his mind. Alvarez was short, maybe 5 feet 8, and a little on the stout size especially in his robe. He had the reputation of being tough. He had to be, being responsible for the security of Vatican antiquities. Rumor had it Alvarez carried a gun.

Cardinal Castillo had not said a word since the introduction. Clearly this was Alvarez's meeting. Alvarez left the window and returned to his seat. "Is it true that you authorized the transfer of a priest in Glastonbury to a church in Perpignan, France?"

"Yes, sir, but the transfer paperwork has not..."

Alvarez raised his hand. "Did you get the information you were after?"

"Yes, sir."

Alvarez clenched his jaw and slowly nodded. "Good. You certainly didn't give away the store. Perpignan is not the Riviera. Good trade."

"Would you like to know what's in *The Letter?*" Alvarez said as he sat down.

"Yes, sir, by all means. I mean, sir, if you feel I should know…"

Alvarez raised his hand again. "Well, we'd like to know as well. Father, I'm going to tell you something you must not reveal to anyone. If I find out you have shared this information, well let's just say you know better."

Alvarez continued, "Okay Father, *The Letter* does exist. It is a letter from our Lord Jesus Christ to his Uncle, St. Joseph of Arimathea, which Jesus gave to St. Joseph shortly after the Resurrection. St. Joseph took that letter with him when St. Phillip sent him to Britain to establish the faith among the Celts. We have two documents safely preserved here in the Vatican archives, which reference that letter. Very few people know these documents exist and such knowledge is on a need-to-know basis. Cardinal Castillo knows, as do several others, but not all in the College of Cardinals.

"Let me tell you about the other two documents. One of the documents is a copy of a letter called the *Petrus Letter.* The original is most likely lost, but the copy is enough. Back then, when a letter was sent, they were careful to make an exact copy by hand with both the original and the copy signed by the author. No Xerox machines," laughed Alvarez.

Freddy smiled, but knew he was not supposed to laugh. Freddy's status was not sufficient to allow him to play along with insider jokes.

Alvarez explained, "The *Petrus Letter* is a letter from St. Peter, who took the name Pope Petrus, to Joseph of Arimathea. In that letter, St. Peter is requesting Joseph of Arimathea return to Rome for further consultation and to bring *The Letter* from Jesus Christ with him so it can be preserved with other early church records. We have no way of knowing if Arimathea ever received Peter's letter. I don't think 2,000 years have done much to improve the Italian postal service." This time Alvarez laughed heartily and was joined by Castillo. Freddy forced a smile and a quiet laugh.

"The other document we have may be one of the most important of all Christian writings." Alvarez continued, "It's fairly lengthy and mentions Jesus' letter to Joseph, as well as the *Petrus Letter,* requesting its return. Only the same few who are aware of the Petrus and Jesus Letters know this other document exists. It's known as the Quelle Gospel or simply as the Q Gospel. Quelle is German and means source. Q is believed to be the source document for the three Synoptic Gospels of Mark, Matthew and Luke.

"The translation of Q is quite fascinating and very revealing about our origins. I dare say, had Q been more widely circulated, our humble little church might well have gone in a different direction."

Freddy was curious and was hoping Alvarez would tell more about the Q Gospel. In a rather ham-handed way, he tried to get Alvarez to share more. "Is there anything in Q that I need to know as I attempt to get more information from Ryan about the Jesus letter?"

Alvarez leaned back and roared a hearty laugh. "Nice try, Fulgrum, I've been around the block before. I'll tell you what I want to tell you and no more. But since you are the curious sort, I will share a little background. Q was written by St. Matthias, the disciple who was elected to replace Judas Iscariot, who, as you know, betrayed our Lord and later committed suicide. Matthias was there from the beginning of our Lord's ministry. He was selected over Barsabbas, we believe, because he was one of the only followers of Jesus who was fully literate and kept an extensive diary. He was easily selected over Paul of Tarsus, who was not held in high regard, mostly because of his work among Gentiles and his attempts to portray himself as close to Jesus. Curious isn't it that Paul became so important to the establishment of Christianity while Matthias who recorded Jesus' message has been relegated to obscurity."

Alvarez looked sternly into Freddy's eyes. "So Father Fulgrum, you now know things you might be better off not knowing because you cannot share what you know and it's painful for humans to know something while at the same time knowing they cannot share what they know. You understand what I mean, don't you?"

Freddy was overwhelmed, but what good was it to know something so important, yet something you could not share?

Alvarez could see the inner turmoil as he watched Fulgrum absorb what he just learned. "So now, Father, we are sending you back right away. Your assignment is to find out what Ryan has and what he knows and assist us to do whatever is necessary to keep this from becoming public. Let me be crystal clear. We need that letter here so we can close the circle left open by Petrus and Q. But be absolutely certain what I've just told you never leaves this room."

The meeting was over. All three men stood up. Freddy bowed and kissed both rings and exited. On his way back to his office, Freddy was still processing what he learned about the *Petrus Letter* and the Q Gospel. He was now privy to information only a few knew, but he was not able to share it with anyone, not even anyone close. And, for a moment, he lamented there was no one close.

Freddy began to formulate a series of questions in his mind. *Why did Alvarez tell me about Petrus and Q? Why did he repeat the warning I must not tell anyone? Unless Alvarez knows to do my job I may have to tell someone to get what I want. That's it. He knows I have to use the information; but if it gets out I am the one who talked, then Alvarez can burn me.*

Saturday Midmorning, January 15 – Dulles Airport

The morning flight from London to Dulles was uneventful. Matthew was again in first class, but this time there was no Robin and really no time to doze off. Matthew reviewed papers, files, and memos from wheels up to wheels down. He was returning home to secure an extended leave of absence from the university and to tell Sara about the recent events in Glastonbury. He breezed through customs and was met by Sara, who was as happy to see him as he was to see her.

"Where are the kids?" asked Matthew.

"They are at my folks; we can pick them up later. I wanted to hear about your trip uninterrupted," answered Sara. It was mostly small talk until they pulled into their driveway. Once in the house, Matthew began to relax and finally confided to Sara what he simply could not share over the phone. Apart from issues of security, a telephone conversation on a subject so complex and sensitive could not substitute for face-to-face. But more importantly, Matthew wanted to explain all to Sara. She was not only his wife, she was his best friend. She understood Matthew and it truly pained him she couldn't be with him to share the experience.

Sara knew this was important work and Matthew was a pivotal player. She was proud of her husband and did all she could to let him know all was well with his absence. "Don't worry about us, we'll be fine. Throw yourself into it with all you have. I am so very proud of you," was Sara's sincere reaction.

"I have only one request," she stipulated, "this summer, if all is accomplished by then, I want you to take me and the children to Glastonbury so we can see these remarkable artifacts."

"That's been my plan all along," responded Matthew. "When you see what we have recovered, you'll realize how much grander it is than anything I could describe."

Matthew spent the next few hours answering questions. Sara was satisfied and together they picked up the kids and brought them home for pizza and a movie. As bedtime approached, Matthew thought about Thomas and how much he is missing, never being able to share the intimacy of a wife and the warmth of a family. This was a weekend to enjoy—no work, only family.

Matthew met with his dean on Monday morning to make sure he understood and approved of his time away. He told the dean the essentials only, not nearly as much as he shared with Sara. Both Sara and the dean saw the passion Matthew had for what he was doing and they understood the seriousness and even some of the danger involved. Matthew received an open-ended leave and agreed to line up replacements for the classes he taught.

Monday, January 17 – Glastonbury

Thomas was deeply engrossed in his translation of the Glastonbury Codex. He was a self-imposed prisoner in Robert's study, working all hours—sometimes sleeping on the couch so he could be near his work. He emerged from time to time for food and drink, and then returned to his cave with little interaction with anyone else.

Toby called excited to say he spent the weekend in his Cambridge lab and the results of his carbon-14 tests were complete. He said he would be over that afternoon and wanted to meet with James and Thomas.

Estelle and Henry were back at work at Thompson Manor. James and Margo spent the morning together in the City of Street shopping at Margo's favorite stores and just enjoying each other's company. Vicar Dunmore was at the hospital in the nearby town of Wells visiting ailing parishioners.

Freddy, feeling important, returned to Bath from Rome aboard a Vatican jet. He decided he, along with Jerry, would meet personally with Father LaRouche to extract additional information. LaRouche was mostly pleased with the promised transfer to Perpignan, France. It wasn't Marseilles, but he was happy to be leaving England and was willing to do whatever was asked of him. Freddy convinced LaRouche that by helping them, he would be doing God's work, while at the same time ingratiating himself with the Vatican. The plan they hatched called for Father LaRouche to pay an unannounced courtesy call to Father Ryan at Thompson Manor. LaRouche would say his reason for stopping by was simply to get to know Father Ryan, since Ryan had not attended the reading of Robert's will. The real reason, however, was to give him the opportunity to see if he could discover if Ryan was in the translation process, and if so, how far he may have gotten.

THOMPSON MANOR

It was a little past noon when James and Margo returned. Henry was outside tending to the yard and Estelle was in the kitchen preparing lunch. Thomas was hard at work on the translation. He worked late the last evening and slept in the study. His was a labor of love and he was unaware of the time and even the day. Margo was about to return to her job at The New Inn in Priddy and went to the kitchen to say goodbye to Estelle. All that was quiet was about to change.

As James approached the study to check on Thomas, there was a knock at the front door. Margo answered and found Father LaRouche standing on the front step. "Good to see you again, Father; welcome to Thompson Manor."

James turned around, halting his intended checkup on Thomas. "Father LaRouche, to what do we owe the honor of a visit?"

"I stopped by to see Father Ryan. He wasn't at the reading of Mr. Thompson's will and I haven't yet had the pleasure of meeting him. And I thought since I was in the neighborhood... Alas, I would have liked to have had the chance to visit with Mr. Thompson, but sadly I'm too late."

James did not respond, but thought to himself, *what a strange little man. He's been at St. Mary's for over a year and had ample time to meet Robert. This is not a spontaneous visit.*

Standing in the parlor next to James and Margo, LaRouche commented, "What a beautiful home. I'd love to see more if you'd care to show me."

Margo took over. "We're preparing the house to be a B&B and a conference center for small gatherings. I'd be pleased to show you the public rooms."

James gave Margo a look that said, "Thank you for taking him off my hands."

Margo took Father LaRouche to the dining room first.

"Beautiful," said LaRouche. "The wood is lovely and so well maintained.

Margo led him back through the parlor to the library.

"Ah, this must be the room with the wall safe mentioned in Mr. Thompson's will. It certainly is well hidden."

Margo thought the comment to be a bit strange. "Yes, in fact, I still don't know where it is," she responded with a note of indignation.

As she walked him back through the parlor, there was another knock at the front door. This time James answered. It was Toby Merten.

As Toby came in, Thomas, unaware of the arrival of guests, exited the study.

Simultaneously, the telephone rang. Margo answered, holding the phone aloft, she directed her words toward James. "It's Bennu Hasani calling to speak to Matthew."

Margo stood with phone in hand as Toby, Thomas, James and LaRouche stood silently looking at one another. The silence was broken by yet another knock at the door, which James opened to let in Vicar Dunmore.

"I was in the neighborhood and…" Carol noticing LaRouche, stopped talking and stepped in completing a circle of five.

After a somewhat uncomfortable pause, James said, "I'm not sure who knows who, so let me go around the room." Gesturing toward LaRouche, James said, "This is Father Ricard LaRouche from St. Mary's Catholic Church. Father LaRouche, this somewhat sickly looking person here is Father Thomas Ryan and this gentleman is Toby Merten, an old friend of mine from London." James, his paranoia kicking in, intentionally did not reveal Toby's affiliation with the Cambridge RadioCarbon Laboratory. "I think everyone knows everyone else."

Margo held the phone up and waved it at James.

"Excuse me one moment." James took the phone and said, "Benny, Matthew is back home in DC, but will be back here this weekend. I have some guests here, I'll call you back in a few minutes."

James rejoined the circle, gently clapped his hands and said, "Well, here we are."

LaRouche took the hint. "I should be going; you all look quite busy."

He reached out to shake hands with Thomas saying, "I look forward to seeing you again. I hope you'll be feeling better soon."

Thomas, still somewhat in a fog, just nodded and waved with his left hand.

"It was nice meeting you," LaRouche said to Toby as he exited with a faux French flourish.

Carol, Toby, Margo, Thomas and James stood in a circle looking at each other. James laughed saying, “What a cluster.”

Thomas muttered as he rubbed his eyes, “I need something to eat. What time is it?”

Margo said, “That was an interesting gathering. You’ll have to excuse me; I need to get to work. I still have a job there for another week.”

James looked at Toby saying, “Toby, I intentionally didn’t reveal who you are to LaRouche. I don’t know the man and he certainly doesn’t need to know what we’re doing. Let me call Benny back and then we four can talk about Toby’s carbon-14 tests. Why don’t you all go the library? I’ll be there right away.”

James called Benny’s phone in Cairo. “Benny, I’m sorry I had to cut you off, but we had an unexpected guest and I didn’t want to say anything in front of him. Matt went home for a few days, but he’ll be back here this weekend. I hope you’re good for a meeting on the 29th in Glastonbury? We haven’t set up a budget yet, but The Institute can cover your travel expenses.”

“Thank you James. I’m not concerned about expenses, I was merely calling to let you know I am available for the twenty-ninth.”

“Please feel free to call me Jim or Jimmy. I’m looking forward to having you join the team. I’ll be pulling together an agenda for the meeting which I’ll email to you shortly.”

“Well then, Jim, I accept. I am also looking forward to helping The Institute in any way I can. And please feel free to call me Benny.”

“Benny, I would really like to talk with you at much greater length, but I have an impromptu meeting of a few board members who just arrived. Please excuse me for cutting our conversation short. I am so looking forward to meeting you next week.

The New Inn

As Margo entered the New Inn, she was surprised to see two unfamiliar priests sitting at a table having lunch in the fireplace room. Freddy waved to her to come over. Their choice of the New Inn was not a coincidence; Freddy wanted to send a message he was around. Margo politely went over to their table.

“Welcome to the New Inn. I hope everything is satisfactory.”

“The food is very good and the atmosphere, especially in this room, is most comfortable. Please let me introduce myself. I am Father Frederick Fulgrum. I’ve just arrived from the Vatican and this is Father Jerry Fletcher. Father Fletcher is on my staff, and before he became a priest he was a New York City police officer. We heard all kinds of great things about the food at The New Inn and decided to give it a try.”

What an odd introduction, Margo thought to herself, *definitely trying to send me a message.* "Nice to meet both of you. But please excuse me; I have some functions I need to attend to in the office. Molly will take good care of you. If you need anything, just let her know."

As Margo left their table, Freddy said to Jerry, "Message sent."

Thompson Manor

James, Toby, Carol and Thomas continued their discussion in the library.

"Thomas, how's the translation going?" asked James.

Thomas, sipping on a cup of coffee said, "It's going fairly well. I may be finished with the first draft fairly soon. Once I finish that, I'll go back as often as I need to, but each time will move much quicker. I highlight words I've difficulty with. There really aren't many. This translation is much easier than any I have previously done. When I get stuck, I feel as though an invisible hand is showing me the way."

"And the message?" asked Carol.

"This is going to sound odd, but believe me, I haven't read *The Letter* for content, and won't until I've finished the entire translation. That way, I don't interject any of my bias. I translate letter by letter, word by word."

James turned to Toby. "I understand you have the carbon-14 results."

"I had enough material to run the test three times. I think I must have told you we're able to date most of our tests to .03% or within 25 to 30 years. The three tests I ran were identical. The vellum used for *The Letter* dates from 10 CE to 40 CE. I can't attest to what *The Letter* says, but I can tell you, not only does it date to the time of Jesus, but also the vellum used is most consistent with other documents of that area. The vellum is definitely Mediterranean."

"Thank you, Toby," said James. "Brace yourself, boys and girls. We may be in for a bumpy ride. If Thomas's translation is consistent with what we know about Jesus the man, coupled with the carbon-14 test, we may be able to make a case that *The Letter* may be divine."

"James, you were wise in not revealing Toby's identity while Father LaRouche was here," added Carol. "As I was leaving St. John's to make my hospital visits, I saw two priests entering St. Mary's rectory. Toby, St. Mary's is just down the street from my church. When I got back, I asked my docent, Agatha, to talk to her friend Nora, who is the St. Mary's parish housekeeper, about the visitors. She couldn't say what the meeting was about, but she did say Father Fulgrum and Father Fletcher met with Father LaRouche for about 45 minutes."

Carol continued, "Nora doesn't enjoy working for Father LaRouche. He's been at St. Mary's for coming on two years and is always complaining—about the parishioners, the weather, whatever. The parishioners don't care for him either. They think he's aloof, arrogant and condescending."

"Thank you Carol. I'm really glad you're on our team," responded James.

"One more thing," added Carol, "Tom mentioned The Institute is going to need space. Barclays built a new branch bank on Chilkwell Street, overlooking the abbey grounds. It's a lovely building, and it's never been used. When the economy softened, they abandoned plans to open the branch. It might be perfect for The Institute. It has a vault, which would certainly offer more security than the wall safe, especially now that the wali safe is no longer a secret.

"The local Barclays Bank president is one of my parishioners. I'd be happy to approach him. I can't help but believe they would jump at the chance to unload the building. There can't be many potential buyers for a building like that."

"Thanks again, Carol. Please do talk to him. It could be a perfect spot for The Institute."

Bath

Father LaRouche drove to Bath to tell Freddy and Jerry Fletcher what he just learned and to further demonstrate he was on the team.

Freddy began, "Father LaRouche, this is an unexpected visit. I assume you have information."

"Yes sir, I visited Thompson Manor as you suggested and may have stumbled upon some valuable information," LaRouche was puffing.

"Please go on," said Freddy.

"While I was there, two other people showed up and one called on the phone. I sense these are the people who will likely make up the Epistolic Institute board of directors. We know Dr. Christopoulos, Father Ryan and Rabbi Halprin are on the board. But shortly after I arrived, a gentleman named Tobias Merten arrived. He was introduced as Toby, an old friend of James's from London. Simultaneously, the phone rang and Vicar Dunmore arrived, saying she was in the neighborhood and was just stopping in to say hello."

"Do you know who was on the phone?" asked Freddy.

"Someone named Bennu Hasani. James spoke briefly to Hasani telling him he'd call him right back. Hasani was calling to speak to Rabbi Halprin, who I learned is back in the United States, but is expected back here this weekend. I don't know either Merten or Hasani, but when all were there, including Vicar Dunmore, the atmosphere toward me turned awkward and uncomfortable, almost secretive."

"And Father Ryan—did you see him?" continued Freddy's interrogation.

"He emerged from a closed room when everyone else arrived and he looked awful, almost as though he'd been on a weekend bender."

"Did Ryan say anything?"

"Not a word. He just nodded his head, when I addressed him. He looked like he hadn't slept, but there was no smell of alcohol on him. James said he was sick," continued LaRouche.

"Is this helpful to the cause?" LaRouche was fishing.

"Thank you, Father. Yes, it's very helpful and I'll make sure you get full credit for your help. I'm sure you need to get back. Please continue to find out whatever you can, especially about what Father Ryan may be up to."

LaRouche felt as though he had just been dismissed, which he was. He wanted to stay and be part of Freddy's team, however Freddy made it clear that was not going to happen.

With LaRouche gone, Freddy engaged Jerry in analysis. "LaRouche is not the sharpest knife in the drawer, which may be all right."

"What do you mean, sir?"

"Well, Tobias Merten is a well-known scientist; well known to those who stay informed. He runs the Cambridge RadioCarbon Laboratory and is one of the best at carbon-14 dating. Bennu Hasani collaborated with Halprin on his book about the interpretation of the Dead Sea Scrolls. LaRouche can be helpful, even if his reporting is incomplete. That's how you and he differ. Jerry you are good; you report not just the 'what,' but also the 'why' and the 'where.'"

Freddy continued, "I have to give Christopoulos credit though; he has assembled an excellent board of directors which is also quite ecumenical. Let me sum up who they have. Christopoulos, the president, is Greek Orthodox as well as a well-regarded archeologist. Thomas Ryan is a Jesuit priest and brilliant Aramaic-to-English translator. I dare say if he were on our side, we would be using him to translate *The Letter*. Matthew Halprin is a Jewish Rabbi, scholar, teacher and researcher. Bennu Hasani is an Egyptian Muslim and one of the best Qumran Cave investigators around. Together, Halprin and Hasani are a formidable team who know more about the Dead Sea Scrolls than just about anyone.

"Tobias Merten is a devout Christian and well-respected scientist who virtually built the Cambridge RadioCarbon Laboratory. Lastly, Vicar Dunmore is an Anglican priest who did her graduate work on the Dead Sea Scrolls. She is also part of the Glastonbury establishment. I may have underestimated her. She is sharp and resourceful. Quite a team. Christopoulos will be kept plenty busy herding these cats."

"What would you have me do, sir?" asked Jerry.

"First, let me call Vacini and have him begin to develop dossiers on both Merten and Hasani. We know the rest of the people. I'll also talk to Cardinal Castillo. We have a few options on how to proceed. I think we may also have to consider the nuclear option."

"Nuclear option?" asked Jerry.

Freddy was enjoying using his new knowledge as a game at Father Fletcher's expense. He could not reveal what he learned at the Vatican, but he found some perverse enjoyment in pretending he was calling the shots. He had already been authorized by Cardinal Alvarez to take Ryan down. Now as he presented the plan to Jerry, he pretended it was his idea.

"Let me explain what I discussed with the Cardinals yesterday at the Vatican. It's unfortunate, but I'm afraid Father Ryan may have gone over to the other side. The Cardinals agreed, we may need to discredit him as well as the rest of his team. They also agreed to hold a press conference to get the public on our side by explaining why it is so important that sacred religious artifacts be protected within Vatican archives. Jerry, I need you to monitor the scene. Stay on top of LaRouche; we don't need a loose cannon thrashing about. I think I hurt his feelings when I sent him away. Let him know he's part of the team, but also make sure he checks in first with you before going off on his own. Find out whatever you can about how far Ryan has gotten in the translation process. We know what they're up to, but we just need to force their hands to reveal how far along they are."

"I'll do my best, sir."

"I know you will, Jerry. You're a good man and I have confidence in you. Let's have dinner later this evening. There is a nice, albeit somewhat expensive, French restaurant I know in Bath. We can have dinner there and I'll bring you up to speed on what the Cardinals had to say."

Jerry left Freddy's flat to give Freddy privacy for his call to Vacini and Cardinal Castillo. Later that evening over dinner, Freddy revealed that Cardinal Castillo reluctantly agreed if all else failed, he would order the nuclear option.

Tuesday, January 18

James, Thomas, Toby and Carol held a lunch meeting at Thompson Manor. Estelle was happy to have so much activity going on. The excitement was palpable. While she didn't fully grasp the enormous importance of events about to unfold, she was sure what was taking place at the manor would have pleased Robert greatly. She was happy to work for James and was comforted by knowing she had a substantial amount of money wisely invested for Henry and her ultimate retirement.

Carol reported she had spoken to Keith Williams, her parishioner, about the possible acquisition of the empty Barclay's bank building. Williams was warm to the idea and promised to get Carol an answer quickly.

All six board members were available for the meeting on January 29. Toby would go back to his lab at Cambridge and return on the twenty-eighth. Benny would fly into London on the twenty-eighth and ride over to Glastonbury with Toby. James received an email from Matthew that all was well—he had been given an open-ended leave from Towson. Sara and the kids were okay with him being gone that long. He'd told her just enough so she could appreciate the seriousness of the work ahead. Matthew would be returning to Glastonbury on Saturday.

Thomas still had not gotten much sleep and was badly in need of a shower and shave. He was confident if he stayed at it he could complete a first draft of *The Letter* in a day or two. It would be a draft he could feel comfortable sharing with The Institute board members.

Carol was about to go back to her church and Toby was about to leave for Cambridge when Thomas's cell phone rang. He looked at the Caller ID and saw it was Randy Cross, the *Washington Post* reporter.

"Randy, you almost never call me," Thomas joked.

"No time for humor, Ryan. You and your friends are in danger."

"What do you mean?" asked Thomas.

"Ryan, you have *The Letter*, don't you?"

"Randy?"

"Ryan, don't be coy. Just listen. I know about *The Letter*; I just don't know what's in it. And if you have it, you can be damn sure the Vatican wants it. Watch your back Thomas."

"Randy, can I put you on the speaker phone? Four Institute board members, except Matthew Halprin and Bennu Hasani are here." Thomas identified who was on the call and how they became involved with The Institute.

"Go ahead and put me on the speakerphone. It's your decision," said Cross.

With the board members huddled around Thomas's cell phone, he restarted the conversation. "Randy, how do you know all this?"

"Ryan, it's my job to know this stuff. There are spies lurking everywhere; your phones, your computers, your mail—none of it is safe. I have contacts in many places. The Vatican is putting plans into action to neutralize any damage *The Letter* may cause. I don't think they've tapped your cell phone yet, but that technology is available to them. Fulgrum was called back to the Vatican. Castillo sent a Vatican jet to pick him up. Fulgrum had a meeting with Castillo and Cardinal Felipe Alvarez. Alvarez is responsible for security of their sacred artifacts. The man is tough and he doesn't play around. Rumor has it he carries a nine millimeter Glock. Castillo's family is part of the Sicilian network, if you catch my drift. Ryan, you're now playing with the big boys."

"Can I assume you know what's going to happen next?"

"I know some. Next Wednesday the twenty-sixth, the Vatican will convene a press conference. The purpose of that conference will be to discredit you, your compatriots, *The Letter*, the Epistolic Institute; all things related to *The Letter.* The Vatican will claim you and your friends fraudulently acquired *The Letter* from an unscrupulous antiquities merchant."

Cross continued, "They'll probably make one of two claims. First, *The Letter* is a fake, or second, if *The Letter* is real, it should be placed under the protection of the Vatican. It doesn't matter they don't own *The Letter*; they will attempt to create the impression such a find belongs to the Vatican. It won't matter that the Thompson family had *The Letter* for 400 years; the Vatican will claim it was probably stolen, and for the sake of all Christianity, must be returned."

"You're serious, aren't you?" asked Thomas.

"Not nearly as serious as they are. You're not playing with children. They have money and power and will attempt to develop support among their billions of followers. Over time, they will demand loyalty as an outward sign of one's faith," answered Cross.

Carol sighed. "A sign—that sounds eerily similar to Revelation's mark of the beast."

Thomas was silent as he pondered what was to come. "Randy, give me a little time for this to sink in. Can I call you back later this afternoon with The Institute board members?"

"We can do that, but we'll need to talk a little more abstractly in case someone is listening in. Do you have another number you can call from? A secure phone?" asked Cross.

"Randy, we'll find one. What number can I call you on?"

Randy Cross gave Thomas a number for a landline the *Post* maintained as a secure phone. Thomas had an idea where they could place the call.

"Randy, it's 1:30 p.m. here. 9:30 a.m. where you are, correct?"

"Yes."

"We will call you at 1 p.m. your time," stated Thomas.

"Okay, I will be standing by the number I gave you," answered Cross.

Thomas hung up. He summarized what Randy Cross told them, and then concluded: "I find it so hard to believe and so deeply personally painful that the Church leaders would put their love for the status quo and their positions above what it is they claim to believe in. *The Letter* may be the most important find ever. I don't say that because we have it, but because I believe it to be true. And they may be prepared to dump it in the trash because it may pose a threat to the status quo."

"What do you suggest we do?" asked James.

"Well, first, when we call Cross back we need to use a secure phone," said Thomas.

"We could use a phone at St. John's," offered Carol.

"I don't think so Carol. Your phones may have also been compromised," replied Thomas.

"Toby, can you stay? We need all the brainpower we can muster," pleaded James.

"Yes, I can. I'll email the office and let them know I won't be back until tomorrow."

"Okay, good. Now where do you suggest we get a secure phone?" James asked Thomas.

"How about if we ask Sean Boyle if he will let us use his conference room? I think we can trust him and there's no reason to believe anyone would have tapped his phones."

James explained to Toby, "Sean Boyle is a funeral manager in Bath. He was responsible for Robert Thompson's memorial and I think we can trust him."

Thomas called Sean using Toby's cell phone. Sean was only too happy to offer his office.

"Let's come up with a strategy before we call Cross back. Unfortunately, we're going to have to leave Matthew and Benny out of the loop. We can't risk calling them to bring them up to speed," suggested James.

For the next two-plus hours, the four continued planning for the conference call.

"Carol, would you feel comfortable speeding up the Barclays Bank building decision? I would love to move *The Letter* to their vault and out of here," suggested James.

"I'm not sure that's a good idea. It may bring more attention than we want. How about the St. John's Church safe?" offered Carol.

"Or how about my safe at Cambridge?" offered Toby.

Thomas responded. "I don't think either of those sites would work. St. John's would be the first place after here the Vatican would attempt to invade. Toby's safe would be better, but I just don't want the artifacts traveling all the way to Cambridge. No, I think we are better off here. At least the safe is still hidden and, for safety sake, I think it best not to reveal the exact location of the safe to anyone else at this point, even you Toby and you Carol. No offense, it just allows you to honestly say you don't know where it is. Neither Estelle nor Henry, nor even Margo knows."

At four o'clock they left for Sean Boyle's office in Bath, leaving Henry and Estelle to watch over the manor.

ঌBATHৎ

Freddy was gone, having left that afternoon for Rome leaving Jerry Fletcher behind. Jerry just returned to his flat when he spotted James's Mercedes pulling into a parking space in front of Boyle Funeral Managers. Jerry watched as the four entered the building. He waited about ten minutes then entered the office using the excuse of wanting to inform the manager that Father Fulgrum departed for Rome, but would be back in a few days.

Standing in the reception area, Jerry could see the four institute board members in the glass-paneled conference room, but they did not see him. It appeared as though Sean Boyle was showing them how to operate the telephone equipment. Sean completed his tutorial and left the room and it appeared that a conference call was underway.

Jerry noted which line was lit up on Carolyn's phone panel and jotted down the number. He would place a couple of discreet calls and hopefully discover who was on the other end of the conference call.

"Randy, we've been kicking this around for the last couple of hours and we're stuck. This is your area. What do you suggest?" asked Thomas.

"Come on Ryan, you're media savvy."

"Sure, when I answer questions or give speeches, but not like this."

"The best defense is a good offense," responded Cross.

"I thought it was the other way around," said Thomas.

"Maybe, but in your case it doesn't matter."

"Randy, we need your help. What do you think we should do?"

"Okay, here are a couple of suggestions. You're in a small city. Use it to your advantage. Make it appear an attack on you or your colleagues is also an attack on Glastonbury. Who do you have on your side in Glastonbury?"

"The Vicar of St. John the Baptist is on our board. Her name is Carol Dunmore and she is on the call with us now," answered James.

"Great. Vicar or Carol, which do you prefer?" asked Cross.

"Carol is fine."

"Carol, can you rally some Glastonbury officials to your side?"

"Officials?" asked Carol.

"Yes, for example, the chief constable or the chief of police," answered Cross. "Let him or her know you are concerned about a possible break-in by people who would try to steal what belongs to Glastonbury. Not what belongs to The Institute, but to Glastonbury. That's important."

"The chief constable is one of my parishioners," said Carol.

"Perfect, now what about some business leaders? In this economy, anything hurting local business hurts Glastonbury," continued Cross.

"I see where you are going," said Carol.

"Carol, don't limit yourself to just the city. Widen your reach to surrounding cities and towns. The more people who have a sense of ownership, the better," suggested Cross.

Thomas interjected, "We have been calling *The Letter* the Glastonbury Codex for lack of a better way to describe it."

"That's exactly what I mean. The Vatican will want *The Letter* and they will make the case they are rescuing it from five or six people. However, if it figuratively belongs to Glastonbury, then the Vatican has to take on a whole village of people.

"Second," continued Cross, "England, and I presume also Glastonbury, is primarily Anglican. The long arm of the Vatican ends at your gate. You don't want to get into an inter-Nicene war; just remember, even the Vatican has limits. Be respectful, but remind them of the limits of their jurisdiction. Clue in your bishop and get him on your side. Don't let him get blindsided by the press or by any of his professional colleagues and counterparts at the Vatican.

"Last, this is for Thomas. I meant it when I said the best defense is a good offense. You need to launch a preemptive strike. Call your own press conference for next Monday, two days before the Vatican press conference. You don't have much time, you need to get the word out you have made a discovery. Be bold; say you have made a discovery which will shock the world."

Cross paused. "In fact, Ryan you owe me a scoop. Let me break the story in Thursday's *Washington Post*. I will get it on the international wire and mention a press conference will be held next Monday, at 11 a.m. London time. Hold the press conference in Glastonbury. It's a little inconvenient for the press, but it will demonstrate your loyalty to the city. I'll see if I can get my editor to send me to follow up on my scoop. Maybe I can ask a well-placed question during the Q and A?"

"I thought you guys reported the news, not made the news."

"Hello Ryan—welcome to the twenty-first century. Just be sure, and this is critical, that you have some real news. Again, be bold. You know what you think you have. Say it."

"How do we set up a press conference? I have never done that before."

"Spend a little money, hire a P.R. person. Pay them a premium for fast action. Hold the conference at Glastonbury Abbey or at St. John the Baptist—someplace with a good backdrop. Listen to the P.R expert, but be prepared to do the following. Have a twenty to thirty-minute presentation prepared. Do it in PowerPoint if you can, but definitely have some visuals. Have a press release ready to hand out. Take questions for forty-five minutes to an hour. No more. Remember, you are busy translating *The Letter,"* replied Cross.

Cross was on a roll, "Someone will surely ask you why you are holding the press conference now. They'll ask if it isn't premature. Answer them directly. Tell them it's because the Vatican will be holding a press conference on Wednesday to challenge your find and you wanted to get the truth out before it gets muddied. You will be taking on the Vatican and you will have thrown the first punch creating controversy and intrigue. The press will eat it up."

"Wow, that's a ton of information we need to process," said a somewhat overwhelmed Ryan.

"Ryan, you don't have time to process; you only have time to act."

"This may sound like I'm back at the beginning, but where do we start?" asked Thomas.

"We just did. Are you ready to give me the scoop?" laughed Cross.

"Okay, I really owe you one. When the time is right, where can I reach you?"

"Use my cell phone," said Randy. "If the line is compromised, we can adjust."

Thompson Manor

It was nearly seven o'clock when they arrived back at Thompson Manor. Estelle had dinner ready and the four were most appreciative of her dedication to their needs. Estelle was part of the team. Her role was to provide support while not getting involved in the process. The board members continued discussing the day's events as they ate. Toby offered to contact the president of the P.R. firm he used to develop media materials for his radiocarbon lab at Cambridge. "I've done a lot of business with them. They understand the carbon-14 testing process. I'll see if I can get the president to fly over on the commuter from Cambridge to Bath. What do you think?"

"It sounds like a good idea. If they already understand and appreciate antiquities, we won't have to explain what we are all about. Go for it," said James.

Toby called the Trinity Media president, Helen Wickers, on her cell phone. "Helen, sorry to call after hours, but I need you ASAP." Toby explained as best he could without being too specific what was happening and what he knew of the Vatican's plans. He described the preemptive strike Randy Cross suggested and how Cross would announce the scoop in Thursday's *Washington Post*.

"Can we pull off a press conference next Monday in Glastonbury?" asked Toby.

"Anything is possible. It's a tall order, but I'm willing to try it," answered Helen.

"Can you catch tomorrow's first commuter flight from Cambridge to

Bath? I'll pick you up and take you to Thompson Manor. I'm sure we can use the manor as your remote command post," suggested Toby.

"I believe there's a 7 am flight. I could be in Bath by around eight. I'll get started here and get out a mass email to my British and Common Market news media file alerting them to the press conference. Where and when will it be?" asked Helen.

Toby put the phone down and asked the others where they should hold the press conference? Carol told him it might take too long to get permission to use Glastonbury Abbey. "We can use St. John the Baptist. I may get some heat, but what the hell."

Toby was back on the phone. "Helen, the press conference will be at 11 a.m. on Monday, at St. John the Baptist Church in Glastonbury."

"Okay, now I need a hook," said Helen.

"Hook?" asked Toby.

"Yes, I need something to grab the press' attention," answered Helen.

"Hold on, let me get Father Ryan on the line," said Toby.

Toby handed the phone to Thomas. "Thomas, Helen needs a hook, a grabber to get the press interested to attend the press conference."

Thomas took the phone. "Helen, this is Father Thomas Ryan. Nice to meet you. I understand you need a hook? How about something like, 'we may have made the most significant archeological discovery ever, a discovery which will shock the world.'"

"Not bad," Helen said somewhat mockingly. "Can you tell me more?"

Thomas took a breath and said. "We have discovered a letter written in Aramaic that we have reason to believe is written by the hand of Our Lord, Jesus Christ. *The Letter* has been rumored about in small circles for nearly 2,000 years. And we may have it."

There was a lengthy pause by Helen. "I apologize for the silence, but I am a bit overwhelmed and that almost never happens to me anymore. Oh my God! You have a letter from Jesus Christ? Have you translated it? What does it say?" asked Helen.

"I'm sorry, but my translation is not yet complete. I hope to have it done soon," answered Thomas. "We better not say anymore on the phone. We have already given someone a treasure trove of information if they are listening in."

"Say no more," said Helen. "You have given me a great lead. I'm excited. Let me have Toby again if you would, please." Thomas handed the phone back to Toby.

"Toby, I will email you with my travel plans. Can you secure housing for me? I am not familiar with Glastonbury."

"We'll take care of it. I'm sure you will be staying here at Thompson Manor with the rest of us," responded Toby.

After Helen hung up, James announced it was probably time for him to move downstairs to the first floor bedroom suite. Thompson Manor was starting to fill up.

"Now, if you will all excuse me, I have a bit of work to do," said Thomas.

James interjected, "I'll call Hasani to see if he can come this Saturday rather than on the twenty-ninth. Matthew will be back on Saturday. And Toby, if it works for both you and Carol, I would like to convene the board this Saturday afternoon."

Wednesday, January 19th

The next morning, Toby and James drove to Bath to pick up Helen. James told her about Robert, the Epistolic Institute and Robert's bequest to get The Institute started.

Henry and Estelle readied bedrooms for the new guests. They even prepared a bedroom for Carol, should she decide to stay if their meeting ran late.

Toby, James and Helen arrived at Thompson Manor around eleven. No sooner had they entered the house than there was a knock at the front door. It was LaRouche again, wanting to meet with Father Ryan. James told him Thomas was still not feeling well.

LaRouche stood in the doorway staring at Helen. James said, "Excuse me; this is Helen Wickers, an old friend from Cambridge."

Another old friend, LaRouche said to himself.

Thomas exited the study to get a glass of water and sure enough, he did look disheveled and "under the weather."

I'm sorry to bother you Father, I was hoping we could have a chat. I'll come back when you are feeling better."

Thomas nodded his head and gave a half wave. LaRouche, feeling out of place, offered his farewells and was gone.

Bath

Having been instructed by Jerry Fletcher not to use the telephone, LaRouche drove up to Bath to tell Jerry of his latest discovery. Jerry was a bit testy as he reminded LaRouche that he wanted him to check with him first before going off on his own. LaRouche apologized and then passed along his most recent information.

"We seem to have another new player. Her name is Helen Wickers from Cambridge. She was introduced as another old friend. I also saw Father Ryan again and as before, the man looked awful. I don't think he is sick or on a bender. I think he is spending some long days trying to understand what they have found," reported LaRouche.

"Thank you, Father. I will check out Helen Wickers. Sorry you had to drive all that way, but we do appreciate the information. Every piece we can add to the puzzle is helpful. Now, for the next few days, I want you to lie low. Plans are in place and we must not get in the way."

"I understand," said LaRouche. "Just let me know what I can do to help."

"Thank you Father, I will."

LaRouche headed back to Glastonbury as Jerry phoned Freddy.

"Father Fulgrum, I have some information for you. First, Father LaRouche was just here. He had another tidbit of information. Another person of interest has arrived at Thompson Manor. Her name is Helen Wickers and she is from Cambridge, presumably a friend of Toby Merten."

"I will have Vacini check her out. Jerry, we need to reign in Father LaRouche. I don't want him stumbling into something we have planned and messing it all up."

"I have just told him myself to lie low and wait for instructions from me. No more independent action on his part."

"Good. Have you anything else?"

"Yes, yesterday afternoon, the four we are watching came to Bath to the Boyle Funeral Managers' Office. I observed them from far enough away so they did not see me. They were in Boyle's conference room and appeared to be on a conference call. I was able to get the number they called and checked it out. It was a safe house secure phone number. I was able to find out that the phone number belongs to the *Washington Post*. Do you know anyone at the Post who might have been on the call?" asked Jerry.

"Yes, a few people—but one in particular. Good work, Jerry. Keep me updated."

Thursday, January 20 – The Vatican

Freddy was putting the finishing touches on a report he would deliver to Cardinal's Castillo and Alvarez, when a red-faced and exercised Father Vacini burst into Freddy's office with a copy of Wednesday morning's *Il Messaggero*, Rome's most read daily newspaper. The headline on the front page with the byline of Randy Cross from the *Washington Post* splashed "Letter from Jesus Christ Found?" The headline had a question mark, but it didn't matter.

Freddy sunk down deep in one of his office easy chairs, "Damn!"

He devoured the three-column story twice and then the phone rang. It was Cardinal Castillo.

"Yes, sir, I just read it."

"Damn!" said Castillo. "They've called a press conference for this Monday, two days before ours. There's no way we can move up our conference; it would look as though we're reacting. See what you can find out from your man there, and then come to my office as soon as you can."

Freddy called Jerry.

"I just saw it," said Jerry. "Do you know this Randy Cross?"

"Yes, Jerry, I do. He's a former priest and a friend of Ryan's. Clearly the conference call last night was with Cross. They are attempting to preempt us and they have been successful."

"We can't move up our press conference, can we?

"No, it would only make us look weak. They have enlisted some professional help. Vacini tells me that Helen Wickers is the president of a P.R. firm—Trinity, headquartered in Cambridge. Vacini found out Trinity does the P.R. work for Tobias Merten's radiocarbon lab."

"What's the next move, sir?"

"Jerry, I'm not sure. I have to meet with the Cardinal in a few minutes. We're going to have to make some adjustments. I don't know what yet, but keep me posted about events on the ground there and I will call you back after I meet with Cardinal Castillo."

"Sir, the *Post* article mentions their press conference on this Monday in Glastonbury. Do we have any reporters on staff we could send to grill whoever speaks on their behalf?"

"Good suggestion, Jerry. If we don't have a reporter on staff, we can dress up a priest to look like a reporter, maybe Vacini."

Glastonbury

Helen met Vicar Dunmore at St. John's and the two surveyed the site for the press conference. Helen wanted to be sure James and Thomas had the right background for their presentations. She was concerned with lighting and sound. Audio equipment was being readied and she did several sound checks to check the acoustics. Despite its historic significance, St. John the Baptist was showing signs of wear. Money was simply not available to spend on aesthetics. Rather, what money was available was spent on providing services to members of the parish. Robert's gift of £300,000 would make it possible to take care of some necessary repairs.

The setting was excellent. Helen switched gears to arrange the comforts of the media—everything from power hookups for video cameras to refreshments. It never ceased to amaze her how free food and drinks could put reporters in better moods.

Helen arranged for the Glastonbury Business Association to host a post press conference reception at the George and Pilgrims Hotel. Nothing heavy, just some light food and adult beverages to compensate for any inconvenience reporters may have suffered by coming to tiny Glastonbury. Several tour guides in period costumes would also be available for those who wanted to know more about the history of Glastonbury.

Helen flew back to her office in Cambridge to gather up some materials and get input from her staff on the upcoming press conference. She would return on Saturday in time for the Epistolic Institute board meeting.

Saturday, January 22

By Saturday noon, the Epistolic Institute board members, as well as Helen, had checked into Thompson Manor. For the first time, the manor served as the meeting venue for the Epistolic Institute with all six upstairs bedrooms occupied.

Matthew's flight arrived on time and Benny picked him up at the airport, which allowed the two an opportunity to get caught up on old times and current challenges.

Thomas spent most of his time in the study checking and double-checking to make sure his translation was as good as he could make it, but now he was able to be more social and share time with the other members of the board.

Thomas was tired and looked it. Tomorrow he would give *The Letter* one last review. He still had not read *The Letter* from beginning to end. Thomas focused all of his translation efforts at the words and sentences without attempting to appreciate or understand the content and context. Thomas spent most of his non-translation moments in prayer. The process reawakened his faith in God and in Jesus Christ. He no longer had time to have a crisis of faith—*odd*, he thought, *only the idle mind has time to lose faith.*

The board members, including Helen, gathered for the first time on Saturday at noon in the library of Thompson Manor. There was much to discuss about the purpose of The Institute, but this meeting's focus was on the forthcoming press conference. Helen detailed how she expected the press conference to proceed and what role each member would play. James and Thomas would be the primary presenters with the rest of the board sitting behind as a show of support.

Thomas's cell phone rang just as the meeting came to a close. He excused himself and moved to the parlor so he could better hear the caller. It was Robin. Her extended trip was cut short and she was back in Bath. She read the article in the *London Times* and called to say how proud she was to have met celebrities such as he and Matthew. She now understood why Thomas was so equivocal about meeting with her when they last spoke. She asked Thomas if he had time to see her, offering to drive to Glastonbury if he was available. Again, it seemed to be less a request and more a plea. He felt he should say no because there must be something else he should be doing, such as interacting with the board members. However, the board members were leaving to go to St. John's to review the press conference setup and he decided to stay behind and get cleaned up, so he consented.

Henry, Estelle and Margo were also leaving to shop for food for the coming days' activities. "I'll stay and get cleaned up for dinner and stand guard over the house," Thomas said to his departing friends. "Incidentally, I just received a call from a young woman that Matthew and I met a few weeks back." Looking at Matthew, Thomas said, "That was Robin. She wants to talk to me and will be here in about an hour." Thomas noticed the somewhat surprised look of his associates and said, "Matthew can tell you all about Robin. And no, I am not showering and shaving for her—I am doing it for all of you."

Thomas accepted their good-natured laughter and added: "Matthew, just tell the truth, please don't embellish it."

Thompson Manor

Jerry Fletcher had grown anxious. Concerned LaRouche might try another bumbling attempt to prove his worth, Jerry decided to go to Glastonbury himself and check out what was going on. He was staked out at Thompson Manor as its residents were vacating the house. He saw Henry, Estelle and Margo leave in one car and observed six others fill up a Range Rover and drive away. Jerry wasn't certain, but it appeared, at last, the Thompson Manor might be left unattended.

After the two carloads departed, Jerry approached the front door. It was unlocked. Not knowing what he might say if someone confronted him, Jerry ignored caution and let himself in. The house was quiet and seemed to be empty. As he entered the parlor, he heard running water upstairs and someone singing off-key. Jerry realized he only had a few moments and needed to move quickly.

His police training directed his focus to the only room that had a closed door—the study. Jerry tried the door. It was locked. Using a credit card, he slid the card down the doorjamb and within seconds Jerry gained entry. He decided to grab whatever he could and sort it out later. As he gathered several papers from the desk, he knocked a coffee cup and saucer to the floor. Jerry froze hoping the noise would not be heard above the running water in the upstairs shower. Jerry listened, but he heard nothing to indicate that his clumsy mistake had been noticed.

However, Thomas did hear the crash. Thinking that one of his friends returned for something they had forgotten, Thomas peeked out the window of his room and saw an unfamiliar VW parked in front. *It can't be Robin. I spoke to her no more than 30 minutes ago. Someone's in the house,* thought Thomas. Shirtless he exited his room, grabbing a heavy wooden walking stick from the umbrella stand in the hallway and quietly made his way down the stairs.

He learned much about physical force from Michael Moriarity and was prepared to use it. Back at Georgetown, he was regularly seen lifting weights and punching the speed bag in the athletic department weight room. After Michael's death, Thomas spent many evenings working out his anger by pounding the heavy bag with ever-greater intensity. He could never win against the bag, but he pounded away until he was exhausted. The exhaustion felt good. Finally, he would sit down, hang his head and watch as a pool of sweat formed on the floor below.

In the study, Jerry seized several papers from the desk. As he turned to leave, standing in the doorway was a wet and shirtless Thomas, his anger obvious. Thomas's muscles contracted showing the power of a man whose physical stature was normally hidden by priestly attire. He was in great physical shape and when he clenched his fists his forearms displayed the tight definition of a fighter. Thomas held the middle of the walking stick in his right hand, repeatedly striking the rounded top into his left palm.

Thomas was in control of the confrontation. Jerry was cornered still holding the papers he grabbed from the desk. He was no match for Thomas.

"You," said Thomas staring at Jerry. "Don't bother explaining or lying to me. I know you work for Fulgrum. You tell that weasel of a boss you have that he needs to show some courage and face me like a man." Thomas made Fletcher return the papers he was holding and then checked his desk to make sure nothing was missing. "If I see you around here again, I'll ignore my calling as a man of God and beat you to pulp. Now, get out of here while you still can."

Fletcher slid past Thomas and hastily went out the door and to his car. As Thomas followed Fletcher out the front door, another car arrived. It was Robin. Thomas was immediately self-conscious about his state of undress. He had done nothing improper, but nonetheless felt a twinge of guilt. As Fletcher drove off, Robin exited her car and proceeded up the walkway.

"Robin, I apologize. Please excuse me. I'll go back inside and finish getting dressed." He invited her in and asked her to be seated in the library. Thomas went back upstairs, finished drying himself off and put on socks, shoes and a clean shirt and combed his hair. Once he regained his composure, he joined Robin in the library.

"I am really sorry Robin. I can't imagine how that must have looked. I don't normally walk around half dressed in the middle of January, let alone wielding a club and chasing priests."

"Well, it's not what I would have expected," said Robin, "but I've seen stranger things. I'm sorry if I embarrassed you."

Thomas thought to himself, *she's right, I was embarrassed.*

Thomas regained his calmer demeanor. "Matthew and the rest of my associates will be back soon, and I am going to need to explain what just happened; but do not be concerned, I will not cut our conversation short, especially since you made a special trip. Robin, since we met, I felt that you wanted to tell me something. Please feel free to say whatever you wish. I promise to keep it in confidence."

"Father, I'm not Catholic, but I have Catholic friends and I think I understand what the confessional is all about. I'm really not much of anything when it comes to religion, so you don't need to hold anything I tell you in confidence. I trust you," responded Robin. "Especially if what I tell can be of help to you and others."

"Please go ahead," said Thomas.

"Well, Father, I guess I do have somewhat of a confession to make. When you and Rabbi Halprin were on my flight to London you were awake working for several hours while Rabbi Halprin slept. Finally you dozed off and in the process you dropped several files on the floor. I picked them up and took them to my station to straighten them up. I noticed one file folder was labeled 'The Doorway.'" Robin paused.

"Here is where my confession begins. I apologize, but while you slept I read what was in that folder. There wasn't much, but it caught my attention.

Thomas interjected, "I accept your apology and am grateful that you picked up my papers. I wondered how some items ended up in the wrong folders. Please go ahead, and don't worry, I am not upset."

Robin's demeanor changed. She pulled tight on her coat as if she felt a sudden chill. She lowered her head and spoke quietly, "Father The Doorway is evil."

Thomas waited and Robin slowly raised her head.

"Father, I just want you to know that The Doorway is an evil organization and I don't want you to get trapped by them."

"Robin, I've had my suspicions. Please tell me what you know."

"Father, I need to tell someone." Robin was now more composed.

"Father Ryan, you spoke to one of my roommates a week or so ago. Besides being flight attendants, we also do some acting, mostly in commercials. My roommates Walter and his partner Bryan both joined The Doorway last year. A couple of months ago, Bryan told me The Doorway wanted to do an infomercial and they wanted a woman as the spokesperson. I knew nothing about The Doorway, but Bryan was connected and he arranged for me to audition. To prepare, Bryan gave me a couple of issues of their monthly magazine, *The Portal.* I read a couple of articles and they seemed to be all about the end of the world and how The Doorway offers a way out.

"I went to Glastonbury for the audition, but it was the strangest audition I had ever been on. I was ushered in to meet Malcolm Collier and Niccolo. From the moment I sat down, I was uncomfortable. Malcolm was wearing a brown robe and sandals. He reminded me of Obi Wan Knobe from *Star Wars*."

Thomas covered his mouth to stifle a laugh. "Sorry Robin, my exact thoughts."

"Collier asked me many questions about my childhood, my parents and my friends growing up, and on and on. He never had me read anything, as you would do at a normal audition. He told me about the infomercial. He said it had two purposes. The first was to attract new members. The second was to explain how a member's identification code gets transferred from a membership card to somewhere on their left hand. Apparently the transfer of the bar code to the member's left hand will be done in batches beginning in early 2016.

"Finally, Collier got up and walked over to Niccolo, who was a well-dressed, tall, thin and mysterious looking gentleman. Wait, I want to take that back. He was not a gentleman." Robin paused to take a sip of water.

"I couldn't hear what they were saying to one another, but then Collier turned and said that Niccolo wanted to interview me in private. Collier left the room and I instantly got a chill, like someone just turned off the heat. I didn't even know him, but suddenly I wished Collier was back in the room. Father, I was afraid."

"Robin, it's okay. What happened next?"

"This is difficult," said Robin. "Father, Niccolo never said a word. He looked at me—slowly walked around me looking at me from all sides. He just stared at me and undressed me with his eyes. I could not get away. I felt tied to the chair. Then it felt like Niccolo was on top of me. I know what I am saying, I felt raped." Robin buried her head in her hands.

She looked up at Thomas. Robin was crying. "But Father, Niccolo never touched me. It was all in my mind. I felt so powerless, so violated. Father, I didn't do anything to cause this to happen. It felt so real and I felt so cheap, so dirty. Niccolo said nothing—he just grinned at me."

She continued. "After what seemed like an eternity, the feeling of being tied down began to go away. Niccolo turned away from me and went back to the window. I felt like I was untied from my chair. Collier came back in the room and simply told me that they would call me if I had gotten the part in the infomercial. I wanted to tell them I didn't want the job, but I couldn't speak. I just got up and left. I hurried home and showered for what seemed like hours. If I could have, I would have peeled off all my skin because I felt so filthy."

Robin looked at Thomas and said, "Please Father, tell me I didn't do anything wrong."

Thomas had heard and seen a lot in his twenty years as a priest. Yet Robert's confession and Robin's story had to be on the list of the most intense and personally painful experiences that had been shared with him, and both were caused by The Doorway.

"Robin," Thomas looked straight at her, held her hands and spoke softly. "Robin, what you experienced was all too real. I want you to take courage and faith in knowing you faced down evil and you survived. You are not alone. I have met Niccolo and I know what you have said is true. Be joyful in knowing Niccolo did not select you. He rejected you, not because you were bad for the part, but rather he rejected you because you are too good."

Thomas continued, "Robin don't blame yourself for what happened. You did nothing wrong and you did not cause or invite this to happen. The important point is that you did not give in to Niccolo. You have the power to erase the pain of this experience from your mind. Robin, what you fear most did not happen. You are absolved from any blame."

Robin was not Catholic and her time with Father Ryan was not in the confessional, but still she felt lifted up. She told her story and was not condemned or blamed in any way. She felt clean and light. She felt forgiven.

"Father Ryan, thank you for listening to me and for understanding. I can't begin to tell you how relieved I am. As much as I would love to see Rabbi Halprin again, I think it best I leave before they return. I don't want this feeling of being clean replaced by another—at least not for a while. Will you be here for a while? Will I be able to see you and Matthew again?"

"Robin, Matthew and I will be here quite a bit. I know there will be plenty more opportunities. You will learn more in a few days about what we are doing. And I will let Matthew know you send your best wishes."

Robin returned to Bath intending to find a new place to live and maybe new roommates, if any at all. The constant reminder of Niccolo brought on by The Doorway clock on her fireplace mantle, a conversation piece according to Bryan, was nothing but a dark memory for her.

Bath

As he drove back to Bath, Jerry called Fulgrum and sheepishly explained what he had done. Fulgrum was furious. "That was stupid, Jerry. Why did you pull such a boneheaded move? If I didn't need you right now, I would fire you. Lucky for you I can't tell Castillo or Alvarez or they would have both our heads. Keep this to yourself and get back to Bath. I'll tell the Cardinal I'm going back to Glastonbury. Did Ryan say anything of value?"

"I don't know the value, but he said he wanted to confront you face to face." Jerry continued, "Sir, before I got chased out empty-handed, I did sneak a peek at what Father Ryan was working on. It was a translation. There was a photocopy of a manuscript in what appeared to be Aramaic. Next to it was a manuscript of roughly the same length in English. And, sir, it appeared that it may be complete. As near as I could tell, it is three or four pages long."

Thompson Manor

When the others returned to the manor, Thomas told them about the confrontation with Fletcher, and the subsequent visit by Robin. The attempted break-in had a bigger immediate affect on the board members, but the session with Robin was of greater importance to Thomas, for what happened to Robin at The Doorway was similar to what happened to Robert.

Speaking of Fletcher's attempted break-in, Thomas noted he left empty-handed, but also emphasized that Freddy and his men were getting desperate. "We're going to have to be ever the more vigilant until we secure safer quarters for the artifacts. I don't think having just a person in the house is enough of a deterrent. What if Estelle had been the only one here and she had been overpowered?"

Helen was invited to join the board for dinner to discuss expectations and how best to prepare for the Monday morning press conference. The board also wanted her opinion on how to let the public know about the failed break-in. Her advice was to be cautious in what to say. Without irrefutable evidence of a link between Fletcher and the Vatican, accusing the Vatican might work against them. "It's a tough call. I am not saying you should remain silent, but don't bring it up. If the right opportunity presents itself, pounce on it, but wait for the right moment."

Helen also suggested beefing up security to protect the artifacts. She agreed just having one of the board members in the house was not enough. Again, Carol's familiarity with Glastonbury proved to be valuable. A retired American Marine Corps gunnery sergeant was one of her parishioners. Albert Teacher, who everyone called "Big A," had been stationed in England where he met and married an English nurse. He was now in his mid sixties, but remained in fantastic physical shape. At six feet three, 230 pounds, he was a formidable-looking man. There was something about him, and not just his size, which reminded Thomas of Michael Moriarity. Maybe it was his eyes. *Eyes tell a lot about a person,* thought Thomas. *Eyes can't lie.*

Carol also made a request to the Glastonbury chief constable to place a closer watch over the Thompson Manor, at least until after the press conference. With "Big A" in place, it was agreed the entire board would go to St. John's on Sunday afternoon for a walkthrough. Later Sunday evening, several Glastonbury business and community leaders would be invited to Thompson Manor for an overview of the Monday event. With Carol's help, Helen had done a great job rallying local support for the Glastonbury Codex. She positioned things so it wasn't Glastonbury versus the Vatican, but rather Glastonbury celebrating its part in revealing the word of Jesus Christ.

Preparations at the Vatican were also taking place; however the mood was much more guarded, primarily because of the uncertainty of what would take place on Monday. Cardinal Castillo and Alvarez did not like being on the defense, but they had little choice in the matter. They could speculate all they wanted on what might be in *The Letter* but, in the end, they had to wait like everyone else. About all they could do was to acquire press credentials for Peter Vacini as a Vatican reporter. Freddy originally intended to send Jerry Fletcher as the Vatican press photographer, but that changed because of the botched break-in. Freddy gave Vacini a set of prepared questions. The plan called for Vacini to present himself as a reporter as he would attempt to deflect attention away from his "official" Vatican status.

Sunday Early Morning, January 23 – Thompson Manor

It was dark and windy. The rattling of one of the shutters served as a reminder that winter was still in force. Thomas had risen early. It was barely 5 am, but he couldn't sleep. He quietly padded his way downstairs and clicked on the coffeemaker in the kitchen. He waited patiently for the coffee to brew. When it was done, he took a cup to the study and pulled out his translation one more time. He reviewed each hand stroke of the master writer and still marveled at the beauty and artistry of the ancient Aramaic. Thomas completed his translation the night before, but had not told anyone. Now for the first time, in the predawn quiet, Thomas would read *The Letter* from Jesus to his Uncle Joseph of Arimathea.

Thomas savored the moment. He looked around the room, Robert's study—Robert's most prized possessions everywhere. Thomas built a small fire in the fireplace and added two peat bricks. *Perfect*, he thought. The aroma of peat, the ticking of Robert's grandfather clock—Thomas existed in two places simultaneously. He was a boy sitting in his grandfather's lap and he was a man sitting in Robert's chair—the coexistence was seamless.

For Thomas, the sunrise had always been the fulfillment of a promise—a promise of a new day, and with it an opportunity to make all things right. He kept with him a small book he discovered while researching Native American religions, entitled *The Gospel of the Redman.* At times such as this, Thomas would open its well-worn pages to a passage, which held special meaning. "Silence is the absolute poise or balance of body, mind and spirit. The human who preserves his or her selfhood, ever calm and unshaken by the storms of existence—not a leaf, as it were, astir on a tree; not a ripple upon the surface of a shining pool, it is the ideal attitude and conduct of life." For Thomas, the time just before dawn presented an opportunity to achieve perfect equilibrium, for it was that moment when all living things were hushed awaiting first light.

Father Ryan sat in one of Robert's favorite leather easy chairs next to the fireplace. The early morning January air ushered in a chill. The peat fire gave off just enough heat and just enough aroma to set the mood. Thomas thought it uncanny he and Robert agreed on so much, even down to their choice in music. Thomas turned on Robert's CD player. Among the five CD's in the holder was one featuring the works of Vivaldi. Thomas thought, *how odd, just two months ago, I was sitting in my apartment listening to Vivaldi with the ticking of my grandfather clock in the background. But now, thousands of miles from home, I am doing the same all over again—the same music, the same ticking clock. What should be so very different is so very much the same.*

In the quiet morning hours before most people were awake, Thomas sat with the fruit of his efforts. Several long days and some sleepless nights produced a document, which Thomas hoped and prayed would be true. Even though he spent countless hours reviewing every character and every word, this time he would be reading it through for the first time.

He picked up his translation and heard a voice saying, "In the beginning was the Word. And the Word was made flesh and dwelt among us." Thomas's forehead was damp and his temples were throbbing. The time had come. Thomas closed his eyes and prayed, "Thy will be done." He gathered the three pages and read what Jesus had written 2,000 years before.

Uncle, peace be with you.

When my father died, you came to my mother's aid. As has been written, you raised me as your own son. I learned your trade as a son learns from his father. I traveled with you to many places and learned the ways of different people. The lessons I learned from you and from the Teacher helped shape who I would become.

I never owned a house, but was welcomed into many homes. I never worried about what I would eat or where I would sleep. Those who sought the Word fed and sheltered me. If I found no welcome, I would wipe the dust off my sandals and continue on. My cloak would keep me warm and would be my bed at night when I had none.

When I had endured the final sacrifice for which I had been sent by the Father, you were there at my side. When knowing me would put you in peril for your life and property, you claimed me and gave me your place to rest. Your reward was prison and then exile.

My purpose and my message may become lost with the passage of time. But know this, I did not come to start a religion. I came to start a revolution. I came to end slavery, inequality and war. I came to instill justice, mercy and freedom. My message was a threat to the established order. But silencing me did not put an end to the message.

Truth is the Way. For without Truth, there can be no integrity, and without integrity there can be no trust. And without trust, there can be no dreams, no hope and no change. Only Truth can set one free.

I taught all who would listen to hunger and thirst for righteousness, to temper justice with mercy, and to act with kindness; to be a seeker for justice, believing always the one who searches, finds; and the one who knocks, has the door opened. To know the right path is difficult and the right gate is narrow; but the wide road is easy and leads to destruction.

I know the future will always hold challenges. Rich men will build grand shrines of worship to honor me. Money will be required from the people and will be spent to adorn their houses of worship and pay the priests who serve them.

But the Truth does not require garish displays. How could a temple be grander than a mountain? How could a temple be grander than the cedars felled to build her? These monuments only serve to cloud the Truth. Those who are lost will worship the temples and not the Word. Truth is all around and free to everyone who would open their eyes, minds and hearts.

The evil one returned to me when I was raised from my lifeless sleep. He boasted how the rich will attempt to control the Truth and use it for their own advantage. He bragged that before the end-of-days, the rich would own me. He said they will put my image on every wall and use my name to increase their treasuries; and use the money to enlarge their places of worship and create even more images. In time, men will forget the Word and worship the image. He sneered when he said greed is the Devil's beast, and its excrement is weighed in gold.

He claimed credit for causing a mighty war, where awesome power not seen since creation would be harnessed and then unleashed. And once that power was out of the box, it could never be returned. He flashed an evil grin saying this great conflict will cause the near elimination of my chosen people. His agent on earth would torture millions of my people before putting them to death. However, the evil one chose to ignore that from the ashes a new nation called Israel will rise up.

He laughed saying more wars would be waged in my name; and all sides would claim Truth as their cause. People would be turned into slaves and the Devil would emerge victorious. But the Devil is wrong; for he does not understand peace is not the absence of war, but rather it is the presence of justice; and by seeking justice, we can someday put an end to war.

I sent him away and knelt down to pray. I prayed for the one who seeks justice to remain free, even if imprisoned or in shackles, for it is better to die free in bondage than to live as a slave surrounded by comfort. Uncle, if you begin to tire of the good fight and entertain thoughts of surrender, take heart and know I am with you always.

Many will deny the Word, or present false translations so as to confuse and then control. But worry not, for the unabridged Word survives. In the deserts of the Qumran, the Essenes have preserved the Word. In time, messages from the ancient ones will be recovered from the twelve caves, which will have protected the Word from those who sought to destroy it.

None of these messages is greater than the Letter from Elijah. No one was more loyal than Elijah. He bested Baal's Priests at Mount Carmel. He came before me to make straight the way. He was there with Moses on the mountain and he is whole in heaven with the

Father, for he was raised in a chariot of fire. Someday a seeker of the Truth will find his Letter.

Elijah's message is of the Father's love for all His people. The table has been set and the banquet has been prepared and all who accept the invitation are welcomed: sisters and brothers, rich and poor, whole and broken, Jew, Buddhist, Gentile, Pagan, and more. All people everywhere, seated as equals. All are invited to the feast. The price of admission is acceptance of the Word and acceptance of one another.

Elijah reminds us we must not abandon hope, despite what sufferings may be visited upon us. We must boast of our sufferings, knowing suffering produces endurance, and endurance produces character, and character produces hope and hope does not disappoint.

But in the end, it is about love. For without love we are nothing. Our tongues will cease and our bodies will return to dust, but love will remain. If we have love, we are rich beyond imagination. If we have love, we have been given much. And we who have been given much are duty-bound to give much in return.

The best gift to give is the gift of love. Give it freely and without expectation and you will receive love tenfold in return. Uncle, please care for and love my mother as you cared for and loved me. Help ease the pain she suffered as she watched the treatment of her son, a pain only a mother can feel.

Keep faith. And when things are darkest, look for me, for I will be there. Peace be with you always.

Three pages—a love letter from a grown man to his uncle who had done so very much for him. Thomas read it again and then again one more time. Religious bureaucracies, including the Vatican, but not just the Vatican, would not be pleased. There was too much in *The Letter* about the hoarding of riches by Church leaders—by a Church, which failed to reach out and use its largesse to help those in need. There was too much about truth and justice at a time when establishments everywhere were doing all they could to hide from the truth and avoid justice. There was too much about adorning churches with riches as though such adornment would serve as a replacement for adoring the Word.

No, the establishment will not be happy. Their excuse will be they need more time to right the wrongs. But the people will be happy, because *The Letter* strikes a blow for truth and justice. And all know the time is up. The wise but flawed leader, if such a leader exists, will step aside before being pushed aside. But if the flawed leader is truly wise, he will not need to step aside.

Thomas wondered how this would all play out. He knew how he wanted it to play out. He made nine photocopies of his translation to share with the rest of the team. His work was done, or was it? He felt safe and secure in Robert's study where the ticking clock and the smell of the peat fire made all those issues seem far away. But he could not stay. The time had come. He raised himself up and left the study.

Chapter XII

Split a piece of wood and I am there

SUNDAY MORNING, JANUARY 23 – THOMPSON MANOR

Estelle arrived at 6 am and was busy in the kitchen when Thomas walked past. "My, Father Thomas, you are quite the early riser this morning."

"'Tis going to be a busy day today Estelle and I need to get going." Thomas headed upstairs to shower, shave and get ready for the press conference dress rehearsal at St. John's. The press conference plan was straightforward. James and Thomas would present an honest report on what they discovered. There would be no sleight of hand, no diversion, no bait and switch. This was not the make-believe of theatre; this was real-life drama. The rehearsal was more about staging and presentation and not about image creation.

After the rehearsal, the team returned to Thompson Manor. James waited in the parlor with Carol, Helen, Toby, Benny and Margo, while Matthew and Thomas retrieved the pewter box from the wall safe in the library.

Once the box was removed and placed on the silk runner and the bookcase closed, James led the others, along with Estelle and Henry, into the library. Their show of reverence toward the artifacts as each item was presented had become ritual. Matthew presented the brilliant, uncirculated coin as coming from the time of Christ.

Next, James brought forth the cruets. He lingered as he had done previously and then told the story of St. Joseph of Arimathea and Nicodemus washing the body of Christ. Carol commented about how the cruets were identical to the ones depicted in the stained glass window at St. John the Baptist. James showed the faint stain lines on the cruets explaining his belief the cruets once held the sweat and blood of Jesus Christ.

Finally, Thomas carefully and reverently unwrapped the Glastonbury Codex. Each came forward to see the beautiful, flowing, powerful Aramaic script. Thomas handed out copies of his translation and all quietly read and reread the document.

Estelle cried softly as she read the translation, while the others stood in hushed reverence.

Helen gently interrupted the silence, "Father, you are not planning on handing out copies of your translation, are you?"

"No, these copies are for you and you alone to know and appreciate what we have here. However, please understand you cannot keep this copy. Please know that I trust each of you, but the risk of one copy being discovered accidentally is too great. Your copies must be returned to the safe until the message is revealed to all."

"Father Ryan, let's rehearse the press conference one more time, this time employing role-playing."

Helen continued in the character of a reporter asking a question. "Father Ryan, how can you be certain *The Letter* was really written by the hand of Jesus?"

Thomas paused a moment to study the question in his mind. "I cannot say with 100% certainty *The Letter* was written by the hand of Jesus Christ. However, there is considerable evidence to substantiate the likelihood it is authentic. There is the fact *The Letter,* kept with other artifacts, was dated to the time of Christ. A carbon-14 test was performed three times, dating the vellum parchment from 10 CE to 40 CE, and let me add, the tests have also shown the vellum is definitely Mediterranean.

"In addition, the context leaves little doubt that *The Letter's* recipient was Joseph of Arimathea. The author refers to Joseph as "uncle" and it has been established Joseph of Arimathea was Jesus' great uncle as he was an uncle of Jesus' mother, Mary.

"In another powerful statement He talks about Elijah." Thomas picked up his copy and read, *"'He came before me to make straight the way. He was there with Moses on the mountain and he is whole in heaven with the Father, for he was raised in a chariot of fire.'* This statement demonstrates the writer had intimate knowledge about Elijah, who by the way never died. Some have contended that John the Baptist is the reincarnated Elijah. Making straight the way is precisely what John the Baptist was called upon to do before Jesus arrived. When the writer states '*He was there with Moses on the mountain....*' He is referring to the Transfiguration, when Jesus appeared with Moses and Elijah.

"There are other less historical indicators, such as the confident and powerful handwriting, which demonstrates the author was certain of what he wanted to write. I really don't know anyone who can write a three-page letter without hesitation or pause. Then there's *The Letter's* pristine condition. *The Letter* is 2,000 years old, but shows no signs of age.

"However the most critical element is the fact *The Letter's* content is prophetic. Accurate prophesy is a form of proof that would make *The Letter* divine."

Continuing, Helen asked, "Father, can you give an example of what you mean by *The Letter* being prophetic?"

"It is easy to confuse the terms prediction and prophecy. A prediction is really a forecast of what is likely to occur in the future if human activity continues along its present course of action. However, prophecy is much more than prediction. A prophecy is more like a promise that an event will occur according to the master design of the sovereign. *The Letter* we have speaks of specific events, which are to take place in the future—the future from the perspective of *The Letter* writer of 2,000 years ago. Some of those prophesies have occurred and with a specificity unlike those of any other seer."

Thomas continued, "This is not at all like the predictions found in Nostradamus' quatrains. Whether those predictions have occurred is subject to the opinion of others. No, *The Letter* we have is objectively specific and not subject to interpretation."

"Can you give an example?" asked Helen continuing the mock interview.

"Yes, I can give you several. *The Letter* speaks of a great war where the awesome power of creation will be unleashed. This is a reference to World War II and the atomic bomb. *The Letter* also reveals other events in World War II such as Hitler's attempt to impose genocide on the Jews, the near elimination of God's chosen people, and then the subsequent establishment of the nation of Israel.

"There is also a prophecy about the discovery of the Dead Sea Scrolls in the Qumran Desert. The Dead Sea Scrolls were discovered in 1947. The author of *The Letter* stated the Scrolls would be found in Qumran, and that event has objectively occurred. That is why I believe *The Letter* is divine and from the hand of Our Lord.

"Remember that a prediction is really a forecast of what is likely to occur in the future based on existing human activity. Because the Dead Sea Scrolls were an unknown, their discovery cannot be predicted as a continuation of human activity. Their discovery was an accident, but the writer's knowledge of their existence demonstrates omniscience."

"Father Ryan, if you present like that tomorrow, you'll hit a home run. That was as close to perfect as anyone can get," reacted Helen.

"If I may ask a question?" begged Margo. Margo was part of the circle even though she felt her connection was tied to her relationship with James.

"Please do," answered Thomas. Thomas knew there would be millions, maybe hundreds of millions of Margo's who had questions and those questions needed to be answered.

Margo held her copy of *The Letter*. She felt inadequate in the company of the others, and feared she would ask a simpleminded question. "Father, in the beginning, the writer," Margo paused, "Jesus writes, '*The lessons I learned from you and from the Teacher helped shape who I would become.*' Who is the Teacher?"

The others looked down at their copies somewhat embarrassed for they failed to notice the "Teacher" reference.

"Margo, that's a good question. The short answer is, I really don't know. I have an assumption, but I am really not certain to whom He is referring.

The Letter is full of mysteries it may take a lifetime to discover and understand. The Letter is not the end, it's the beginning."

The scholars in the group, James, Matthew, Benny, Toby and Carol began talking amongst themselves with Margo, Henry and Helen looking on.

This was the first question put to Thomas for which he had no answer. Thomas began to feel a sense of foreboding—a feeling he felt many times before. He was about to be involved in a conflict he did not want—a conflict he hoped could be avoided. He knew what would happen next. He was about to be pushed and prodded and even punished for what he knew and what he would have to say. But what was to happen was out of his hands and Thomas felt his darker angels beginning to take control.

James spoke next. "Thomas, somehow we all missed the part about the Teacher, all except Margo, that is. You say you have an assumption about who the Teacher is. Do you want to share your assumption?"

"I'll tell you, but you must know this is just a guess—one which will take much study. It's a question of critical importance. Believers think of Jesus as the Teacher, but in the days ahead, the question will be, 'who taught the Teacher?' Thomas, head down, began speaking in a quiet voice as if he were talking to himself, "I have found a person—a Merlin type person, a Druid priest of the highest order. But I know so little about Druids. I found an old set of *The Commentaries of Caesar* in Robert's library. One book was sticking out slightly, like *The Cynic Epistles* were, remember? This was Book VI of *Commentarii de Bello Gallico*—Caesar's commentary on Gaul. I was about to push it back in place when I noticed a bookmark. I pulled it out. The bookmark was really a note with a name, Mac Giolla Chriost. I don't know if you remember, but the first meeting we had with Robert, here in the library, Robert introduced Mac Giolla Chriost. I asked him for some added clarification and he merely wrote down the name on a slip of paper and handed it to me."

"I remember," said Matthew. "Robert was not about to give you an answer. He wanted you to work for it.

Thomas quickly retrieved the book from the shelf. "I have not had time to fully research this, but Mac Giolla Chriost means 'servant of Christ' and it refers to a Scottish Druid order. When I looked at the page where the bookmark was placed, I found the following sentences about the Druids underlined.

> *They wish to inculcate this as one of their leading tenets, that souls do not become extinct, but pass after death from one body to another, and they think that men by this tenet are in a great degree excited to valour, the fear of death being disregarded. They likewise discuss and impart to the youth many things respecting the stars and their motion, respecting*

the extent of the world and of our earth, respecting the nature of things, respecting the power and the majesty of the immortal gods.

Thomas closed the book. "Let me tell you what I think this means. Throughout history men and women of daring acted boldly even in the face of death. Jesus Christ acted boldly in the face of death to show us the way of truth and hope. We know so little about the Druids. We do know they were teachers and they understood the awesome responsibility that comes with the nobility vested in the teacher—they knew that the teacher was, in fact, the servant.

"Margo, I'm afraid that not only did I not answer your question, I may have given you even more. There are going to be many questions like yours which will require much study and much faith."

Later that Sunday Evening – Thompson Manor

Helen's suggestion that Thompson Manor hold a Sunday reception was a stroke of genius. Several dignitaries were present, including the mayor, the district's MP (Member of Parliament), the chief constable and business leaders such as the regional Barclay Bank president. The opening of the Thompson Manor B&B and the launching of the Epistolic Institute were presented as The Institute's contribution to the revitalization effort of Glastonbury. James introduced each of The Institute's board members and the invited guests were thrilled to see Vicar Dunmore was on the board.

James also forewarned everyone that Monday's press conference could produce some controversy. The Mayor, especially, appreciated being informed as opposed to being caught off guard. The threat of controversy helped create a bond among the city leaders who appreciated the community ownership of the Glastonbury Codex.

Carol connected James with the Barclay Bank president and the two consummated an agreement for The Institute to buy the unused bank building.

Once the guests departed, James convened a brief meeting to review other business unrelated to the press conference. Helen excused herself while the board spent the next thirty minutes setting their agenda for the coming days. As each left the library, Matthew asked Benny and Carol to stay for a few moments.

"What's up?" asked Benny.

"Benny, Carol, you are both students of the Dead Sea Scrolls."

Both shook their heads in affirmation.

"There is something in *The Letter*'s translation which caught my attention. Because of Margo's question, I decided to read the manuscript with much more attention to detail." Matthew pulled out his copy of *The Letter*. "Listen to this. '*In time, messages from the ancient ones will be recovered from the twelve caves that will have protected them for nearly two thousand years from those dedicated to destroying the Word.*'

"Mathematics was never my strong suit, but the last time I checked, there were eleven caves in Qumran which contained scrolls or fragments, not twelve. That can mean only one of two things. Either *The Letter* is wrong, or there are twelve caves."

Benny closed his eyes and pinched the bridge of his nose where his glasses made a permanent indentation. Carol put her hand to her mouth covering a barely audible gasp.

Matthew continued, "My money is on cave number twelve."

"Do you know what this means?" Benny asked rhetorically.

"Yup, break out your old clothes," said Matthew.

Carol joined in. "And cave number twelve may hold a letter from Elijah. I have always wondered why a prophet as important as Elijah never left a paper trail. Maybe he did. It also makes sense from a numerological perspective. Twelve is a significant number, the twelve tribes of Israel, the twelve apostles, and now the twelve caves of Qumran."

Monday, January 24
Press Conference, St. John the Baptist Anglican Church

Considering the short lead time and some inconvenience in getting to Glastonbury, the response to the press conference invitation was better than expected. Fifty-four media representatives, all print reporters and their photographers, made the trip. BBC television, from their studios in Bath, provided video coverage for purchase by media who were unable to attend. Many news organizations, as well as the Vatican, bought the live feed. Cardinal Castillo and Cardinal Alvarez would be watching from Castillo's office.

Freddy managed to get in by using the press pass issued to Jerry Fletcher as the Vatican press photographer. He wore a baseball cap and glasses and hoped he could use the camera equipment to hide his identity.

Several in the media pooled their talents and resources and planned to share the coverage. The press release from The Institute talked of a significant archeological discovery. Randy Cross' article in the *Washington Post*, called it "quite possibly the greatest religious discovery of all time." Cross, who caused much of the uproar with his article, was there, as was Peter Vacini.

James opened the press conference stating it was important the conference be held in Glastonbury because that is where "The Glastonbury Codex" is and where it will remain. He introduced the Epistolic Institute board members taking a few minutes to present each member's credentials. As Helen distributed short bios, James noted, "While the Epistolic Institute is new, the collective experience of the board members gives The Institute credibility and standing in the archeological community.

"However, you are not here for the introduction of The Institute, but rather you are here because of a discovery that defies description. We are fortunate to have among us the world's foremost authority on the translation of Aramaic to English. I am pleased to introduce our lead investigator, Father Thomas Ryan."

"Good morning." Thomas began following a script he and Helen composed: "Occasionally a discovery of archeological significance, and in this case also of religious significance, is the result of an accident. Such is the case with what we present today. For most of his professional career, Dr. James Christopoulos has been in pursuit of what some have referred to as the Holy Grail. His pursuit brought him here to Glastonbury, England. However, the Holy Grail for Dr. Christopoulos is not a cup or a chalice of the kind portrayed countless times in movies as well as in works of art. No, for Dr. Christopoulos, the Holy Grail is actually a pair of cruets as depicted in the stained glass window behind me and on the screen before you. The window portrays St. Joseph of Arimathea cradling two cruets as he arrives here in Glastonbury, England around 30 CE.

"I will be telling you more about the cruets in a few moments. But before I do, let me first tell you about St. Joseph of Arimathea. Helen will be distributing an extensive background piece on him for your reference. Joseph of Arimathea was Jesus' uncle; actually he was Jesus' great uncle, who many believe helped raise Jesus from age 13 to 30. Jesus' earthly father, Joseph, is believed to have died when He was a boy of 12 or 13. According to the Talmud, if a boy's father died, an uncle would assume the role of father figure and mentor him to become a productive member of society."

Thomas continued, "We believe Uncle Joseph answered the call and raised Jesus as his own son and guided Him throughout His life. This would answer the question about where Jesus was for those nineteen unaccounted years of his life. Uncle Joseph showed great courage by never abandoning Jesus in His hour of greatest need, as so many of His followers did. He was with Jesus for most of His young adult life and was present at the Crucifixion. The picture on the screen is one of many artists' portrayals of Joseph of Arimathea catching the last drops of blood from the dying Christ. Joseph placed himself in harm's way by claiming the body of Jesus and burying Him in a tomb he acquired for himself. In the act of preparing Jesus' body for burial, Joseph and Nicodemus, another secret follower of Jesus, washed the blood and sweat from the body. Later, following Jesus' instructions, Joseph separated the blood and sweat into two cruets. The information Helen has provided gives considerable more detail."

Thomas paused. "Those two sacred cruets have now been recovered. Pictures of them are on the screen. The stains seen near the top of each cruet supports the belief they may have contained the sweat and blood of our Lord, Jesus Christ. However, to obtain a carbon-14 date or DNA sample of the stain, we would need to use all of it and we are not willing to do so. Some things need to be taken on faith.

"If the story ended there, it would indeed be one of the most significant finds of all time. Imagine being able to see and hold two vessels which once may have contained the blood and sweat of Jesus Christ. But the story does not end there. In fact, it begins there. Along with that incredible find were two other artifacts.

"The first is a coin, a Roman denarius in absolutely perfect uncirculated condition from the period around 30 CE. On one side is the likeness of Emperor Tiberius. Both sides can be seen on the screen. The "Tribute Penny," as it is known, played a significant part in the lesson Jesus taught: 'give to the emperor the things which are the emperor's, and to God the things which are God's.' In the case of this find, we believe the coin was placed along with the other two artifacts to establish a date. Over several years of archeological effort, many Tribute Pennies have been found, but none as beautiful as this brilliant coin.

"Found along with the cruets and the coin is an artifact unlike any I have ever seen in all my years of study. It is an artifact I am unworthy to describe much less to have touched. It is a codex, which we have named the "Glastonbury Codex." On the screen are several photos of the heavy leather cover. The writing on the cover says, '*Jesous Christos, Theou Uios, Soter*' or Jesus Christ, Son of God, Savior."

The reporters and photographers remained still. Thomas continued, "Protected within the hard cover of The Codex are fifteen sheets of writing. The first twelve pages are four separate translations. The source document, the remaining three pages, is on parchment vellum. The four translations were written over several hundred years by the family chosen to protect the artifacts. The Thompson family is well known and highly regarded in this part of Great Britain through the last member of the family, the late Robert Thompson. Mr. Thompson willed the three artifacts to The Epistolic Institute, along with a generous financial gift.

"The parchment letter, of which I will show just a portion, is a letter written in Aramaic, the language of our Lord, Jesus Christ. Dr. Tobias Merten,

Director of the Cambridge RadioCarbon Laboratory tested the parchment using the carbon-14 process. Three independent tests yielded the same dates, 10 CE to 40 CE, the period which corresponds with Jesus' adolescent and adult life."

Thomas struggled to maintain his persona as an unbiased scientist. He was starting to breathe a bit heavier and his temples were throbbing, both conditions not noticed by the audience. His planned remarks unintentionally changed as he spoke. Instead, Thomas began to *speak from the heart,* as Michael Moriarity would have advised.

"My background is translations, specifically Aramaic into English. Never before in all my years of translating ancient documents have I been presented with a manuscript such as this. I am not ashamed to say whenever I touch *The Letter* it feels alive. When I came upon a word that was difficult to translate, I heard a voice whispering in my ear guiding me to the correct word. When I lifted up *The Letter* I could feel how light it was, like angel's wings, while in my mouth was the taste of sweet honey and in my nostrils, the aroma of fresh flowers. When I gazed upon *The Letter* I could see more clearly than ever before. Not just the words, but also their meaning. Yes, I know what I am saying. The mere presence of *The Letter* arouses all my senses to a level I have never before experienced."

Thomas paused to collect his thoughts. Helen was one of the few who knew Thomas was not on script. His description was so pure, it alone had a texture those present could feel. She did not want him to stop painting the mental picture.

However, Thomas needed to return to the script. "I have completed my preliminary translation, but we are not yet ready to release it. Ladies and gentlemen, this is not a tease, but necessary to be absolutely certain what we have is authentic. With that said, I pledge on my professional reputation that I believe *The Letter* was written by Jesus Christ in his own hand. It is a letter from Jesus to His uncle, Joseph of Arimathea, and the contents are such we, at The Epistolic Institute, are confident of its authenticity.

I know I have not shared the contents of *The Letter,* but I believe this is a good time to pause and take questions."

Several reporters rose and shouted "Father Ryan." Thomas pointed to Cross.

"Randall Cross, *Washington Post*. Father Ryan, you just stated this is not a tease. So why are you holding this press conference if you are not prepared to release the contents of *The Letter*?"

Thomas remembered Helen's suggestion of revealing the break-in at "the right opportunity." Cross just threw a softball and Thomas knew it was time to take a swing at those who were attempting to stop him.

Ryan stood silent for a moment organizing his thoughts. "This is most difficult, especially for me, a Catholic and Jesuit priest." Ryan sighed. "We scheduled this press conference for today, despite knowing we would disappoint many by not sharing the contents of *The Letter*. We felt we had little choice. We recently learned that the Vatican planned to convene a press conference this Wednesday, where we understand they would deny the authenticity of our find. Had we waited until after their announcement, the truth would have been caught up in an unfortunate 'he said, he said' scenario. We simply could not let that happen. We could not let Jesus Christ become a pawn in a game … again."

Thomas continued, "Yesterday afternoon we had a break-in which I was able to foil. The thief entered the Thompson Manor presuming the home was empty and was caught with documents in hand. I made him drop the papers and leave. At this time we have decided to not press charges. We feel doing so would turn this important discovery into a sideshow and cause us to take our eyes off what is truly important.

"It is critically important we keep the discussion of this discovery on the facts. But what is so disappointing is I recognized the person who attempted to steal *The Letter*. He is a priest who works for another priest I know who tends to push the legal and ethical envelope. Both work for the Vatican, but I view them as renegades acting outside the boundaries of the Vatican's code of ethics. They are examples of what is wrong with the Church bureaucracy and their blind allegiance to maintaining the status quo. It is zeal run amuck. Let me be clear, I am not accusing the Vatican of theft, but rather I am accusing them of a lack of supervision over individual priests who are guilty of excess. Their attempt to steal *The Letter* makes me wonder what they are so afraid of, especially since they do not know what is in *The Letter*. It makes me wonder what they would do with *The Letter* if they were successful in acquiring it.

"Lastly, their demands to give them *The Letter,* while at the same time denying its authenticity, is in and of itself a contradiction. It's as though they are saying, we insist this letter belongs in the Vatican archives and we believe this letter is fraudulent. People, you can't have it both ways."

At the Vatican, Cardinal Castillo, was watching the press conference in his office with Cardinal Alvarez. When Thomas described the break-in, Castillo was furious, not only because Fletcher bungled the job and got caught, but because they had not told him what they had done. Cardinal Castillo, with Alvarez sitting by his side, was blindsided. The botched break-in was Watergate Vatican-style. Castillo often cut corners to get what he wanted, but he stopped short of breaking and entering, or condoning it. Alvarez' eyes were fixated on the screen. He reflexively patted the left side of his chest as if checking for his gun.

Purely by accident, Thomas pointed to Vacini for the next question. Fulgrum had given Father Vacini several questions from which he did not alter. His first question proved to be an amusing, if not embarrassing, segue.

"Father Peter Vacini, *L'Osservatore Romano*, Vatican News Service. Would it be accurate to say you are not cooperating with the Vatican in this matter?"

The question drew laughter, but Thomas ignored it wanting to give Vacini a straightforward answer. "It might be more accurate to say we have not communicated with the Vatican. I accept responsibility for that. It is not our intent to not cooperate with the Vatican. If anything, we do not see the necessity of involving the Vatican at the present time."

"If I may follow up?" asked Vacini.

Thomas nodded his head for Vacini to continue.

"Why have you not turned the artifacts over to the Vatican for safekeeping and investigation?"

"Father Vacini, I don't mean to answer your question with a question, but I am wondering why we would turn the artifacts over to the Vatican? The artifacts do not belong to the Vatican. They were the property of the Thompson family and we have no reason to believe anyone other than the Thompson family were the rightful owners. Robert Thompson, the last living member of the family, willed the artifacts to the Epistolic Institute.

"About the safekeeping of *The Letter*, I can assure you it is in pristine condition and has been well maintained for nearly 2,000 years. The fact it has remained in pristine condition in the rigorous England climate is yet one more reason why I believe *The Letter* to be divine. Because of yesterday's break-in and attempted theft, The Institute is making provisions for its protection and ultimate display to the public. In time, and I am not talking about a long time, all who are interested will be able to see *The Letter*. If, on the other hand, *The Letter* were to end up at the Vatican, I fear it would not see the light of day for a long time, if ever.

"Concerning the research and investigation of *The Letter*, I am afraid my answer may be immodest. Because of my considerable experience in Aramaic-English translation, I expect the Vatican would have asked for my translation assistance had *The Letter* been under their control.

"Lastly, after we have made *The Letter* available to the public, we will invite the scientific community to have unfettered access to the artifacts for legitimate scientific research."

Vacini attempted to ask another follow-up question.

"Excuse me, Father Vacini," inserted James, "let's go around the room and allow others to ask their questions."

Vacini was effectively boxed out.

James selected another questioner. "Daniel Hill, *Mendip Times*. Father, my publication is a local monthly magazine focusing on items of interest to people in the Glastonbury area. May I ask a question on a somewhat different topic?"

Thomas nodded.

"Father, as you know, Glastonbury is home to the organization known as The Doorway. I am wondering if you view The Doorway's mission as competition to Christianity and how you feel about sharing Glastonbury with The Doorway as home for The Codex?"

"Thank you Daniel, your question is not as far off the subject as some may think. First, please realize I am not trying to make a joke of the situation, but if The Doorway is correct in its prediction that the world will end in 2016, we will only share Glastonbury for a few years. And if the world does not end, then surely The Doorway will have to deal with many unhappy customers, which isn't good for business."

Intended or not, Thomas's answer produced polite laughter.

When the laughter stopped, Thomas continued. "Daniel, the real answer is at the core of why we are here today. I welcome The Codex sharing Glastonbury with The Doorway. There is no better teacher than a stark contrast. The Doorway offers the easy way out—pay your money and you get a ticket to the nearest Portal. Nothing more to it, just pay your dues and all's well.

"Christianity, on the other hand, is not easy. Christianity's path is truly the road less traveled, or as Jesus wrote in his letter: *To know the right path is difficult and the right gate is narrow; but the wide road is easy and leads to destruction.* There now, I have given you one piece of *The Letter.* However, there is more, so much more. To read His letter is to know there is a way—Jesus' Way. We live in a confusing world in the most difficult of times. We are pained all the more when we learn the people and institutions we trust have lied to us."

Thomas continued, "Let me give you another quotation from *The Letter*: *Truth is the Way. For without Truth, there can be no integrity, and without integrity there can be no trust. And without trust, there can be no dreams, no hope and no change. Only Truth can set one free.*"

This time there was no laughter.

There were several more questions which Thomas and James answered as truthfully as they could. Questions about where and how the artifacts were found, reactions by those who first saw the artifacts, plus several attempts to get Ryan to reveal more portions of what *The Letter* contained.

After forty-five minutes of Q & A, James suggested they wrap up the conference with one more question. James pointed to a reporter.

"Reggie Reynolds, *London Times*. You said the contents of *The Letter* would soon be released. When can the public expect to see *The Letter* and its translation?"

James responded. "Thank you, that's an appropriate question on which to end. We have every intention of making all the artifacts, including *The Letter* in its Aramaic form and its translation, available to the public. People will be able to visit Glastonbury to see *The Letter* at The Institute's headquarters. They will also be able to see *The Letter* and the translations online."

Before James could end the conference, Reggie Reynolds shouted out one more question. "Doctor, what date will *The Letter* be made available to the public?"

"It will be available beginning April twenty-fourth of this year."

The insistent Reggie countered, "Excuse me, but why April twenty-fourth?"

"Because that is Easter Sunday. We couldn't think of a more appropriate date for the Second Coming. Now, let me thank you all. I trust the trip was worth your time."

The reporters rose to their feet and applauded—all except one reporter and one faux-photographer.

As the audience gathered their belongings and prepared to leave, Thomas spotted Freddy. He beckoned to Freddy to follow him to the far end of the church where their conversation would be private.

"What is it with you, Fulgrum? You couldn't just stay away. Your mere presence here is an insult to all which is holy."

"Ryan, you're messing with a power you cannot understand, much less control. Look at you. You think your charm and wit will carry the day. You're nothing more than a speck. We can flick you off our shoulder like a fly. This is your last chance Ryan. I can give you the opportunity of a lifetime. Turn *The Letter* over to me and I will see to it that you have the privilege to see it side by side with its two complementary pieces. Any archeologist would give his soul for that opportunity and I can make it happen."

"What are you talking about Fulgrum? I have the complementary pieces." Thomas responded disdainfully.

Freddy was gambling with what he learned from Cardinal Alvarez to see if he could tempt Thomas. "Ah, but that is where you are wrong Thomas. There are treasures you know nothing about and will never see unless you start playing ball. I can make it happen. Wouldn't you like to see the other ancient artifacts holding the proof of your letter? Ironic isn't it, Father Frederick Francis Fulgrum, old 4-F, is now in a position to help you, if you just help yourself."

"Fulgrum, you are talking in circles. I have no idea what you mean and I doubt you have anything I would want."

"Is that so? Well, maybe, just maybe we have items in the archives you would find of interest. Who knows, maybe there is another letter to your

Joseph of Arimathea, or maybe, just maybe, there might be a lost source gospel everyone references with a single letter from the alphabet? I think you know what I mean—things Father Ryan might never see unless he remembers where his loyalties are."

"Fulgrum, I really do feel sorry for you. You never understood and you still don't. *The Letter* is not a prize or trinket you wear on a bracelet. It's not about power or position. You think nobility is a rank, a position of office. Don't you realize, what someone else gives you they can also take away? You're trying to tempt me into giving you *The Letter* so you can run to your bosses and show them what you got. And they will say 'good boy' and give you a treat like the lapdog you are. Go away Freddy. There is nothing you can do to make me join you."

"What have you got Ryan? Do you really think this phony document will attract a following? Go ahead and bury yourself in this backwater. You've had your fifteen minutes of fame."

"Father Fulgrum, I am afraid any honest answer I give you is one you will not understand. I see no reason to continue this conversation. I will pray for you."

"Oh, how clever, dismiss me with a prayer. By what power do you extend such a prayer?"

"Father Fulgrum, I have no such power. I merely pray to our Lord, Jesus Christ that He might open your eyes. Goodbye, Father Fulgrum." Thomas turned and walked away leaving Freddy standing alone.

Fulgrum stammered, "I am not done with you Ryan."

The Institute board members, accompanied by Helen Wickers, returned to Thompson Manor as the Glastonbury Business Association opened the George and Pilgrims Hotel for the post-conference reception.

"I need to get to the George and Pilgrims Hotel, but I just wanted to say, Father Ryan you were brilliant. You were spot on. And James, you successfully neutralized Vacini. It is a pleasure for me to work with pros like you. Thank you."

"Helen, you are more than welcome. And if you are interested in a new client, I think I speak for all here, The Institute sure could use your help. We have much to do between now and Easter."

"James, board members, I would be honored to serve."

As Helen departed for the reception, Toby said, "I told you she was good."

Tuesday, January 25 – The Vatican

Castillo and Alvarez scrambled to take the offensive. A press conference, even one well controlled by the Vatican, was dangerous. Instead, the Vatican decided to release a statement and not take questions. Vacini drafted the release, which went out with Cardinal Castillo's name:

The Vatican is greatly disappointed by the announcement made by The Epistolic Institute in Glastonbury, England on Monday, January 24. We are greatly concerned some potential religious artifacts may have fallen into the hands of people who may not be capable of ensuring their safety. This concerns us greatly. If the document in question is not protected from environmental degradation, it may become so compromised it will be of minimal value.

Additionally, the refusal by The Institute to safeguard the artifacts within the Vatican's resources makes us question whether The Institute is fostering an imitation in order to advance their organization. At this time, the Church cannot accept the artifacts as they have been presented.

Finally, we are concerned Father Thomas Ryan may have become an unwitting participant in a hoax that discredits his expertise. While we have greatly valued his translation expertise in the past, we recognize this translation is the product of one person and its accuracy relies solely on the integrity of the one translator. While we cast no aspersions on Father Ryan's past dedication to the truth, we are mindful how the influence of others can sometimes misdirect one, even someone with the highest standards.

We are hopeful, but not optimistic The Institute may accept our standing invitation for us to come together for the benefit of all who believe in Our Lord, Jesus Christ."

The *Washington Post* ran the release as a sidebar to an interpretive report by Randy Cross. Cross's damning headline: "Vatican Denies Jesus Letter Three Times."

No one was sadder than Thomas. He had done his best to study every pen stroke, to capture every nuance. He was never more confident he had gotten it right. He knew what he had done was true. How could those who never saw it deny his work?

The Rubicon had been crossed and there was no turning back. The events of the coming days would take on a life of their own. It was out of his hands. Easter was not that far away.

TUESDAY, FEBRUARY 1 – THOMPSON MANOR

The Institute opened a small office within the Barclays Bank building and the remodeling began, turning the building into The Institute's headquarters and future public viewing venue. Margo oversaw the remodeling process and did her best to answer questions about *The Letter.* The standard response was to ask questioners to be patient and wait for *The Letter* to be revealed on Easter Sunday. Having the bank building serve as The Institute headquarters was fortunate for it kept Thompson Manor reasonably sane and quiet.

Early Tuesday morning as Estelle was arriving at Thompson Manor, she found a shivering Robin Potter waiting on the front porch.

"You poor dear, you look frozen. How long have you been waiting here?"

"I don't know, at least an hour, maybe longer."

"Come in and warm yourself. I'll start some tea."

Estelle started heating the water and retrieved a comforter out of a linen closet and wrapped it around Robin.

"What brings you here so early, dear?

"I need to see Father Ryan. Please tell me he's here and not gone on a speaking engagement. I must talk to him."

"He's here, just calm yourself. He's normally down around seven. You are safe here."

Estelle poured a cup of tea for Robin and one for herself. She sat next to Robin and held her cold hands. "Is there anything I can do?" she asked.

Moments later, Father Ryan appeared in the kitchen an hour sooner than usual. "I couldn't sleep. Something has happened that made me get up."

He then noticed Robin sitting with Estelle, wrapped in a comforter. She was still shivering, but the comforter and hot tea had begun to work. "Robin? What are you doing here so early? It's only a quarter passed six."

"I need to speak to you. I'm in trouble and I'm afraid."

Thomas suggested they move to the library. Estelle promised to bring in pots of tea and coffee along with some freshly baked scones when they were out of the oven.

Robin was no longer cold, but she kept the comforter with her as they sat in the library. As promised Estelle brought in more tea, coffee and fresh warm scones.

"What is it Robin? What happened?"

"Well, Father, nothing has happened yet, but what may happen has me frightened. I got a call last night from Malcolm Collier. You know, that strange fellow at The Doorway, the one who looks like that *Star Wars* character."

"I know who you mean?"

"He told me Niccolo wants me for the infomercial and wants to see me immediately. Collier told me he would drive over to Bath this morning to pick me up. I told him I wasn't interested in doing the infomercial. His response is what has me so frightened."

"What did he say?"

"When I told him I wasn't interested, he simply said what I wanted didn't matter and he would pick me up at eight this morning and take me to Niccolo's place—not to The Doorway headquarters, but to Niccolo's place. I barely slept at all last night. I wanted to call you but it was late so I drove here this morning and was waiting out front when Estelle arrived. Father, what am I going to do?"

Before Thomas could even discuss a strategy, there was a knock at the front door. Estelle answered.

Thomas heard Estelle and a man's voice. He put his index finger to his lips signaling Robin to be silent and rose to see who was at the door. It was Collier.

Thomas arrived at Estelle's side. "Malcolm Collier, what can I do for you?"

"Might I come in? It is a bit chilly outside."

Thomas allowed Collier into the parlor and suggested that Estelle go to the library.

"Now, what can I do for you?"

"Niccolo asked that I go to Bath to pick up Robin Potter and bring her to him. This morning he said to stop at the Thompson house first to possibly save the drive to Bath in the event that Miss Potter was here. I see her car out front. May I assume she's here?"

"Who is in Thompson Manor is none of your business. I would like you to leave now."

"Interesting," responded Collier. "Niccolo suggested that might be the case and that might be your response. In that event, he instructed me to bring you instead."

"Malcolm, you cannot take me anywhere that I do not wish to go, but you may tell Niccolo that I will meet him at The Doorway headquarters at nine this morning. Now please leave the premises."

"Your suggestion is acceptable to Niccolo. He anticipated your response, which was only off by an hour. Niccolo assumed you would be at The Doorway at eight."

Collier departed and Thomas went to the library to let Robin and Estelle know what just took place. "I don't know what game Niccolo's playing, but it's not a friendly one, and Robin I think it best you stay here for now. Estelle, it might be safest if Robin were to stay here with us at the manor until this is resolved."

"Father, what does all this mean? What do they want of me?" pleaded a frightened Robin.

The activity woke James and Matthew. Bennu Hasani already returned to Egypt. Vicar Dunmore was at home, while Toby and Helen had gone back to Cambridge.

James and Matthew were surprised to see Robin. Thomas explained what had occurred.

"Thomas, you know who you'll be facing," said James.

Matthew concurred, "I assume you are prepared? He's a dangerous man, but he may have met his match in you."

Robin looked puzzled. "What are you men talking about? I don't understand."

"Robin," said Matthew, "Thomas knows what he's doing. He's familiar with the adversary and he won't take his eyes off him or take any real chances. Having said that, there is still an element of risk in what he must do."

"Please tell me what's going on. Father, what are you going to do? I don't want you in danger because of me. It's my problem. Maybe I should just go to Niccolo."

"Robin, you know who or what Niccolo is. Just search your mind. Niccolo is just the name he's using, but he has many names. He's not to be trifled with—he is powerful and dangerous. No human is more powerful. However while he may be more powerful than any human, Jesus Christ has authority over him. I will confront him and find out which demon he is. By the authority of Jesus Christ, I can compel him to give me his name and when I have his name, through Jesus I can compel him to leave you alone."

"Thomas, what are you saying? Who is this man? I'm scared. What are you doing on my account? Please don't do whatever you plan to do. I'm not worth it."

Matthew sat down next to Robin and held her hands. He looked into her eyes and said, "Robin, Thomas knows what he's doing. He's well trained and is one of the best at this. I assure you Thomas does not take this lightly. He might be a bit tired and worn out after, but he'll be okay. In fact, I think he thrives on these encounters. Now you stay here with Estelle and James. I'll take Thomas there and bring him home safely. Please don't be worried. Father Ryan knows what he's doing."

"Robin," said Thomas, "you stay here and be calm. I am going to go to my room to prepare and gather up what I need."

Thomas was gone approximately a half-hour. When he came back down, he didn't look any different and he didn't appear to be carrying anything. "I'm ready Matthew, thanks for driving me."

Before he left, he spoke to Robin. "Listen to James, he understands this stuff and don't worry, I know what I'm doing."

"Father Ryan, I'll pray for you."

Praying was new to Robin. She had little to no religious background. As a result her prayers would be original. Robin watched from the window as Matthew and Thomas departed. She closed her eyes and prayed.

"I sure hope you know what the hell your doing. Pun intended," said Matthew on the drive to The Doorway.

"I heard you tell Robin not to worry and that I know what I'm doing," answered Thomas.

"Tommie, that was meant to calm Robin. You and I know this is no game. Be careful. The beast is powerful."

"I'll be careful. This isn't my first rodeo. Just as soon as I know which one he is—just when he gives me his name, I will know what to do. However, a prayer from you won't hurt either."

Matthew pulled up in front of The Doorway. "Give him hell," said Matthew smiling.

"Thanks buddy." They clasped each other's hands. "See you soon." Thomas exited the car and entered the building.

In a car across the street sat Frederick Fulgrum and his streetwise cop/priest, Jerry Fletcher. They had been tipped off and were there to document the meeting.

The Doorway Headquarters

Thomas entered the lobby and was greeted by Malcolm Collier. "You are a punctual man. Please follow me."

Thomas looked down at his watch as it chimed nine times.

Collier led Thomas to his office where weeks before Thomas first met Niccolo. Niccolo was standing looking out the window at the Abbey grounds. He took no action to recognize that Thomas entered the room.

Thomas turned, looked at Collier and said: "I think it best you leave the two of us alone."

Niccolo looked at Collier and nodded. Collier gave a brief bow and left the room. As the door closed, the temperature in the room dropped such that Thomas could see his breath.

Niccolo turned and looked at Thomas straight on.

Thomas returned the stare, "I know what you are, but I don't yet know who you are." Thomas had a quiet calmness that Niccolo found unnerving.

Collier went down the hall to a conference room. Moments later, the receptionist escorted Frederick Fulgrum and Jerry Fletcher into the room. Collier arranged the meeting. Fulgrum and The Doorway had a common mission, to take down Father Thomas Ryan. Collier knew that Ryan was a danger to The Doorway since he demonstrated he could neutralize The Doorway's membership card with a simple drop of water, holy water. Fulgrum knew that Ryan was a danger to the status quo. All Fulgrum needed to do was plant a seed that Thomas Ryan was an ally of The Doorway, and Ryan's credibility would suffer among the many who trusted him.

Niccolo and Collier knew that a discredited Ryan would minimize his ability to harm The Doorway. An unholy alliance between Fulgrum and The Doorway was formed and Robin was the bait.

In the cold office stood two adversaries face to face.

"The young woman, Robin, is certainly a beautiful creature, wouldn't you agree?"

Thomas didn't answer.

"How sad it would be if she were to lose her beauty."

Thomas still stood silent.

"But if she is mine, she will never lose her beauty."

Thomas did not respond and could tell that Niccolo was becoming agitated.

"I intend to make her mine." Niccolo's voice was louder.

"That will never happen." Thomas said calmly.

"How will you stop me?" demanded Niccolo.

Thomas controlled his breathing and remained calm. "By the authority of my Lord Jesus Christ, I will stop you. Now tell me your name. You know that you must. By the authority of Lord Jesus Christ I command you, tell me your name."

Niccolo turned his back to Thomas and walked toward the window. Niccolo was powerful, but his power had limits. Regardless of his independence from God's grace, he was still under God's authority and when challenged had no choice but to submit.

Thomas calmly and firmly repeated his command. "By the authority of my Lord Jesus Christ, tell me your name."

Niccolo began to squirm as if he was experiencing pain. His face became red and covered with snakelike scales. His fingers transformed into claws.

"By the authority of my Lord Jesus Christ, tell me your name." Thomas's voice remained calm. He took the crucifix from around his neck and held it in front of Niccolo's face. Thomas's previously calm and quiet voice suddenly erupted into a yell, "By the authority of my Lord Jesus Christ, I command you to tell me your name!"

Niccolo's appearance had changed. His body was twisted, his face and hands were blood red, his breathing labored and emitted a foul stench. Ryan issued the command again and Niccolo could not resist. His twisted face looked upward. "ABADDON," he screamed loud enough to be heard down the hall in the conference room, into The Doorway lobby and out into the street where Matthew waited for Thomas.

Thomas closed his eyes as he processed the name. His next command was clear, forceful yet amazingly calm. He addressed the beast by its multiple identities. "Abaddon, Apollyon the Destroyer, King of the Locusts, Angel over the Bottomless Pit, by the authority of my Lord Jesus Christ, I compel you to renounce your claim on the woman, Robin Potter."

Thomas took out the vial of holy water—the same vial given to him by Michael Moriarity, the same holy water he used to render Robert's Doorway membership card worthless. He sprinkled a few drops on Abaddon. Abaddon resisted and tried to move away. Thomas pressed forward, being careful not to touch Abaddon, and sprinkled more holy water while repeating the command. Abaddon could no longer resist. He bowed, nodded his head, and agreed to release Robin.

Down the hall, Collier, Fulgrum and Fletcher were still somewhat startled by the booming voice of Abaddon. Only Fulgrum knew that Abaddon is one of the forms of the beast identified in the Book of Revelation. Fulgrum immediately began plotting how he could spin the news about Ryan meeting with and presumably striking a deal with the Devil.

Abaddon began his retreat inward changing back into Niccolo.

"My business here is done." Thomas turned to leave.

"You may have won round one, but this match is not over."

Thomas left The Doorway and climbed into the car.

"Tommie, are you okay? Who screamed Abbadon?" asked Matthew.

"That was our friend, Niccolo. Let's go home."

"Was Fulgrum part of your confrontation with Niccolo?"

Thomas surprised by Matthew's question asked, "No, why do ask?"

"Because I saw him go in there a little while ago."

Thomas had a confused look.

"Shortly after you went in, maybe five minutes or so, a guard came out and escorted Fulgrum and that Fletcher guy into the building. Didn't you see them?"

"No, I met only with Niccolo. Collier wasn't even in the room with us."

"How did it go with Niccolo?"

"He conceded round one, but I have a strange feeling. He gave in too easily. He'll leave Robin alone, but now I've got to figure out where Fulgrum fits into this drama. He must have struck some sort of deal with Collier or Niccolo. That's pretty low, even for Freddy."

ঌThompson Manorও

Estelle and James were relieved to see Thomas looking no worse for wear, but no one was more relieved than Robin. While Thomas and Matthew were gone, James explained to Robin what Thomas most likely was doing. Robin was well aware there was evil in the world, but without any religious upbringing she didn't understand the source of evil or the many faces that evil can assume.

"So, who was it?" asked James.

Matthew answered for Thomas, "Abaddon or Apollyon for you Greeks. By whatever name he chooses, he is still the Destroyer, the Angel over the Bottomless Pit."

"Please excuse me. I need to lie down for a little while. I'll be okay after I get some rest," said Thomas.

Robin was apologetic and ashamed that she caused so much trouble for Thomas. She really had no idea what Thomas was up against.

Sensing her angst, Thomas attempted to ease her mind. "Robin, please do not feel guilty. What I did had to be done. You're not at fault. Let me rest a bit and I'll be back down in a little while. Matthew can explain what happened."

Thomas went upstairs to his room.

James, Matthew and Robin continued talking after Thomas left.

Robin was still confused. "Rabbi Halprin, can you help me understand what is going on and what Thomas just did at The Doorway? Was he in any danger?"

"Was he in danger? Yes," replied Matthew. "But let me explain. James please feel free to jump in anywhere along the way. Robin, Father Ryan has a gift. That gift, coupled with years of training and practical experience, has made Thomas into one of the most effective combatants against Satan and his minions. Robin, our friend Thomas is one of about 3,000 priests who have received extensive education and training as exorcists. Evil exists in our world and the Devil is active. Even before the rigorous training he underwent, Thomas could quickly understand people for who they truly are."

Matthew continued. "I know you had little religious education growing up. And without some understanding of the forces of good and evil, doing battle with the Devil must seem like some strange fantasy. Robin, evil exists. I have seen estimates that claim 2 to 5% of the world's population is evil. Some people are evil and nothing accounts for their evilness. Whether it's Bernie Madoff who ruined many lives or Charles Manson who ruthlessly murdered several people, it doesn't matter. They don't show remorse because they just don't care about other people. And they are just two of most likely millions of people who are essentially the same, evil. Thomas's grandfather had a favorite quote that he passed on to Thomas: '*if you attempt to strike a balance between good and evil, you will have already sided with evil.*' That is especially true when you do battle with the Devil. You cannot negotiate a deal. That is a zero/sum game. A game with a winner and a loser."

"Rabbi Halprin, are you saying that Father Ryan was just now in the same room with the Devil, with Satan and they were fighting over me? And Father Ryan won? How can that be?"

"Robin, I believe in a merciful and just God. I also believe in a Devil or Satan or any number of names he uses to spread his message of darkness and despair. What Thomas did first was to force the demon to give up his name. In this case it was Abaddon or Apollyon the Destroyer. By knowing his name, Thomas would also know his powers. Abaddon is a fallen angel who is the lord over the bottomless pit and his minions in the pit have limited powers, as does Abaddon and Niccolo. Evil exists and demons are very real. Yes, Thomas was in the same room with the Devil who meant him real harm. Yet he was successful because truth was on his side. Unfortunately, it was just one round in a battle that knows no end."

"What happens next?"

"Robin, Thomas won the battle over you. Niccolo has given up his claim on you. Unless the battlefield changes, you can be worry-free about Niccolo's plans for you."

"But is Father Ryan all right? Did the Devil hurt him?" asked Robin.

James responded, "What Father Ryan did required a tremendous amount of energy and a confrontation like that will sap his strength, but he'll be fine. Rabbi Halprin is right when he says that Thomas rather enjoys his confrontations with evil. Thank God that he has been successful in every one of the battles to the present."

The Doorway Headquarters

Collier led Freddy and Jerry into the office with Niccolo. Again, Niccolo stood next to the window and communicated through Collier. Freddy and Jerry took a seat as Collier went to Niccolo to get his instructions. Their conversation lasted close to ten minutes—a very unnerving ten minutes for Freddy and Jerry.

Finally Collier returned to his desk, sat down, stretched out his arms. "Well, Niccolo is pleased with the result. He believes that he convinced Father Ryan that the battle was over Robin Potter when, in fact, it was over Ryan himself. Niccolo has no interest in the woman. He deceived Ryan into believing that Ryan won the contest. Niccolo played him along just enough."

Collier continued, "One more thing: Niccolo is not at all pleased with the way you portray The Doorway, and finds it unacceptable for you to disparage us while you slander Ryan. Our goal is to minimize Ryan's ability to influence our members to leave the fold."

Freddy responded, "My goal is to create the impression that Father Ryan and The Doorway have formed an alliance and that Ryan is relying on the dark arts to assist him in his translation of *The Letter*."

Niccolo signaled Collier to come to his side for more instructions.

Collier returned to his desk. "Niccolo wants you to portray The Doorway in a more positive light. He suggests that you plant the story that Ryan came to The Doorway wanting us to join him in the pursuit of the dark arts, but that we not only refused to join him, we contacted you for assistance."

"I like that. Agreed," responded Freddy.

Late February

Two months before the release of the translation all was falling into place. The Epistolic Institute had a new home. The Barclays Bank building was being remodeled with an accessible and secure viewing area for all visitors. The plan for the display was beautiful. There would be large photographic representations of *The Letter* along with the translation on one wall. The cruets and Tribute Penny would be encased beneath a replica of the stained glass window at St. John's. Helen and her Trinity Media staff were doing a magnificent job on the representation of the artifacts. Citizens of Glastonbury were kept informed on the progress and were given opportunities to participate. The "Glastonbury Codex" belonged to the community and the community wrapped its arms around and celebrated it. The Codex had found a home.

The Epistolic Institute expended nearly all of Robert's gift to acquire the Barclays' Bank building and ready the Codex for public access. James brought up the problem at a meeting of The Institute board saying he felt a subtle, non-aggressive fund-raising appeal did not violate The Institute's charter. Thomas disagreed, saying the Vatican would pounce on such a move as proof The Institute existed for selfish reasons. James, without the knowledge of any board member already contributed $100,000 from his inheritance to The Institute. When discovered, the Board members collectively added another $100,000 to the cause. Helen pledged the assistance of Trinity without further charge. The Epistolic Institute had enough money to complete the preparations.

As it often happens, word got out about the financial issues facing The Institute and without anything being said, without even the hint of a plea, it began to happen—letters arrived in volumes never before seen in Glastonbury. Small checks, large checks, cash, and cards with pennies and nickels from children. Glastonbury craftsmen and laborers showed up at The Institute's door with tools in hand ready to help with the remodeling. People voted with their wallets and their work, a message not lost on the religious bureaucracy.

There was no time to waste. Easter was only eight weeks away and there was still much to do. Media requests for interviews and background information became a daily occurrence. Everyone wanted a piece of Father Ryan. Helen handled all media requests promptly and politely. Not that she would have otherwise been rude, but there was something about this client and its message that caused a change in Helen. Despite the frenzy surrounding the preparations, she found herself uncommonly serene. Helen familiarized herself with *The Letter's* message and was able to respond knowledgeably to many questions from the media.

Father Ryan resigned his position at Georgetown even though Dean Carroll told him he could stay on. Thomas decided it was better to leave than to be shown the door.

There wasn't enough of Thomas or James to satisfy the interview requests. The media relentlessly pursued anyone connected with the project, and became as annoying as paparazzi.

Bennu Hasani managed to stay in the background, away from the media circus. Since he had the most computer knowledge, he agreed to oversee the development of The Institute's website, www.epistolicinstitute.org, which would include an easy-to-use protocol for responding to the myriad requests for information. Lauren Systems, one of the largest and most experienced web masters in England, offered to design and host The Institute's website pro bono. Williams Lauren, the company president, and a devout Christian, volunteered to be personally involved in the project.

Hasani and Lauren worked well together, but the complexity of the project was beyond Hasani's skill level. It was becoming apparent that Williams Lauren, while an excellent businessman, also lacked the requisite skills needed to do the detail work required. Williams was not as current as many of his employees. Fortunately, Hasani and Lauren were not too proud to admit they needed help. Also fortunately, Williams was able to call in one of his able technicians, Trevor, to complete the work.

With less than four weeks before the Easter unveiling, Trevor wrapped himself around the project. Without complaining or pointing out mistakes, he went about the task of repairing or scrapping much of the work done by Hasani and Lauren. Time was of the essence and when Trevor finally completed the work, there was barely enough time for a full test-run.

ೋFriday, March 11ೋ

It was 5 am and Thomas awoke to his cell phone ringing. This was a new phone and few people knew the number. His previous phone was rendered useless by nonstop calls. Thomas squinted at the clock and struggled to wake up. He lifted the phone to his ear and managed a groggy "Hello, who is this?"

"Randy Cross. Good morning partner, did I wake you?"

"No Cross, I had to get up to answer the phone anyway. What do you want that can't wait a few more hours?"

"In a few more hours, I will be sound asleep," responded Cross.

"Funny. What do you want?

"You are not going to believe who just called me. This is weird."

"Randy, I can't play guessing games this early. Just tell me who called and what it's about."

"About a half hour ago, Peter Vacini called me. You know him. He's the priest who played reporter at the press conference. He used to work for Freddy. Now he reports directly to Cardinal Castillo. He was in New York and was instructed to call me."

"Okay, I'm awake. Why did he call you? What does he want?"

"Actually Thomas, he wants you, or more to the point Cardinal Alvarez wants you. He called me because he couldn't get through to you and thought I could."

What does Alvarez want with me?" asked Thomas

"Well, I can think of a couple of things; but according to Vacini, Alvarez wants a meeting with you and he intends to come to Glastonbury to meet you. They want me to set it up because you trust me. Is that true Ryan, do you trust me?"

"Do I have a choice?"

"Touché"

"All right, Cross, what's the next step?"

"Alvarez wants a private meeting with you at the Thompson Manor. No fanfare, no bells and whistles, no press. Alvarez wants to fly in under the radar. Maintain plausible deniability, if you get my meaning. He's left it up to you, well sort of. He'd like to meet you on either Monday or Tuesday of next week. What say you Ryan?"

"What do you make of it Randy?"

"Frankly I don't know. I don't know if he's going to try to bribe you or try to scare you."

"Or both," responded Ryan.

Ryan continued, "I guess there's only one way to find out. Pass the word back through the pipeline. Tell them Tuesday afternoon would be best for me."

"Will do. And Ryan, I think you owe me another scoop."

"And you owe me a few hours of sleep. Let me know when you get a confirmation. I'll most likely be awake. Bye, Randy."

Thomas was now wide awake. With no reason to go back to bed, Thomas dressed, went downstairs and started the coffee pot. Now that he had some unplanned time, Thomas decided to take his coffee to the library and peruse the bookcase. He was drawn to Robert's book containing a collection of writings—mostly Robert's own unpublished works, but also a few others, such as the Tennyson draft. The book was quite orderly; Robert's short stories followed by some poems, the Tennyson's draft, and finally several essays written by Robert. Some of the essays were Robert's perspective on critical issues facing Great Britain, plus a few were focused on religious controversies.

The last essay looked fairly new. The paper on which it was written seemed crisper, fresher. The handwriting was a bit jerky, possibly from a hand that was unsteady. Thomas did not recall seeing it the first time he reviewed Robert's book, so Robert had to have put it there shortly before he died. The essay was twelve handwritten pages with the title, *A Defense of the Royal Druid Order.* Clearly not a light or even interesting read for most of the population. But it was most likely Robert's last work and Thomas would have to read it.

Matthew wandered into the library and Thomas put the book and essay back on the shelf.

"I couldn't sleep," said Matthew. "I thought I heard a phone ring at some outrageous hour and I couldn't get back to sleep."

"That was my phone and it was five o'clock."

"Who called at that hour?"

"Matt let's get a cup of coffee and I'll explain."

Estelle was in the kitchen and she greeted Thomas and Matthew as they entered. "My, my, another early day. If you go to the library, I will bring more coffee and scones in a few minutes."

The activity in the kitchen managed to wake the Lord of the Manor, who now occupied the downstairs master suite.

James shuffled into the kitchen. It was now 6:15. "Good morning Estelle. Why are you two up so early?"

"Thomas had a mysterious call at 5 am and was just about to tell me about it. Care to join us in the library?" answered Matthew.

"Give me five minutes and I'll be right there."

Five minutes later, the three friends were sitting in the library as Estelle wheeled in coffee and fresh scones.

"I swear I've put on ten pounds since I've been here," said Matthew. "So Thomas, what was the call about?"

"This a bit out of the ordinary, but then again what hasn't been in the last three months? It was Randy Cross and he had a strange request. He told me he just had a conversation with Peter Vacini who called him from New York. Vacini now works for Cardinal Castillo. So Vacini called Cross because he didn't have my phone number and he figured Cross could contact me. Bottom line is this: Cardinal Alvarez wants to talk with me and he's coming to Glastonbury next Tuesday for a meeting here at the manor. That's pretty much it. He doesn't know what Alvarez wants, and I don't know either."

"Curiouser and curiouser," offered James.

"Is this a one-on-one meeting, or are we supposed to join you?" asked Matthew.

"I'm guessing it's just him and me. A Cardinal talking to a priest—maybe a dressing down, maybe a trade, maybe a request for help. I haven't a clue what he wants," answered Thomas.

"We'll let the two of you meet in the library and stay out of your way. I'm going to spend that day over at the Institute office," said James.

"I'll join you," answered Matthew. "Luckily, I'll still be around for an instant replay. I'm going home next Wednesday and probably won't be back until Easter week."

Tuesday, March 15

Cardinal Alvarez flew into Bristol International Airport in Bath and had a black stretch limo waiting for him. He spent the drive from Bath to Glastonbury on his cell phone and was still talking when the limo pulled up in front of Thompson Manor. Although he intended to arrive without attracting attention, a black stretch limo in Glastonbury is a signal that someone of stature has arrived. Ever since the announcement of the discovery of The Letter, the paparazzi was never far away. Cardinal Alvarez exited the limo wearing a black cassock with red trim, a broad red sash around his waist and a scarlet zucchetto (skullcap). He was an easy target for photographers lurking in the shadows.

Estelle opened the front door as he approached and he walked straight into the house without waiting for an invitation. Thomas greeted him with the honor a Cardinal deserves, bending at the waist to kiss the Cardinal's ring. Thomas introduced him to James and Matthew.

"Welcome to Thompson Manor, Cardinal Alvarez," said James. "Rabbi Halprin and I will be spending the afternoon at The Institute's new building leaving you and Father Ryan some privacy. Is there anything that you need from Rabbi Halprin or myself before we leave?"

"I think not, but I do appreciate your offer."

James and Matthew took their leave as Thomas escorted the Cardinal into the library. Estelle arrived on cue with tea, coffee and her homemade scones. Alvarez accepted a cup of tea and a plated scone while Thomas had a cup of coffee. Estelle bowed and excused herself.

Alvarez spoke first, "This a charming house and a fine room to sit and chat." His comment was sincere, not gratuitous.

"Thank you, but I claim no credit whatsoever for the surroundings."

"Let me get right to the point Father Ryan. We seem to have an impasse and I want to explore firsthand what can be done to solve the problem. My coming to you is more than just a gesture. We could have summoned you to Rome, but I didn't want to start our relationship in a heavy-handed way."

"You are most considerate," replied Thomas.

"Father Ryan, we have a problem, or maybe I should say you have a problem, and maybe we can resolve it here and now. You recently visited The Doorway, a nefarious anti-Christian organization in the same city where the Glastonbury Codex resides. We have video of you entering The Doorway offices. This I am told was not your first visit. We know of at least two visits. This does not look good. Would you like to explain what you were doing there on both occasions?"

"I'm sorry your Eminence, I'm bound by the Seal of the Confessional and it is my absolute duty not to disclose anything I learn from the penitents."

"Ryan, first drop the Eminence crap, it's annoying when one is having a conversation. Could it be that you are interpreting the Seal too literally?"

"Your E….," Thomas paused "Excuse me, but whose responsibility is it to interpret the Seal?"

"It is your responsibility Ryan, but I was merely opining on whether or not one is too narrow in their interpretation of the Seal."

"I am afraid sir I cannot answer your question."

Alvarez could tell that ploy was not going to work. Besides, it was based on information he received from Fulgrum, and Fulgrum had fallen completely out of favor. Alvarez decided to try the good cop approach.

"Father Ryan, I don't want you to think that none of us believe you. However, without being able to study the letter you claim was written by Jesus himself, I'm sure you can see why we might have questions. Father, you are aware I am responsible for the Vatican Archives and as such, I am aware of some wonderful works that have never been made public. It could be that those works might substantiate your claim."

"I don't mean to challenge your authority," Thomas countered, "but why haven't these 'wonderful works', as you call them, been made public or at least shared with the scientific community?"

Alvarez clenched his jaws shut and inhaled deeply. Thomas was being impertinent and Alvarez was not one to be challenged; but his mission was not accomplished so he held his anger in check.

"It is not for you to decide when certain records are made public. We have deemed that it is not yet the right time to release those records."

Thomas wasn't going to start an argument and decided not to retort with "why not?"

The two men stared at each other waiting to see who would speak next. Thomas took the initiative. "Cardinal Alvarez, I am aware that a letter from Pope St. Peter, called the Petrus Letter, may exist, along with a lost gospel from St Matthias. It is my understanding that these records may substantiate our claim for the legitimacy of the Glastonbury Codex. Are these the works you speak of?"

Alvarez looked away. Strike two. He had been checked and was not going to be dragged into a discussion about the Petrus Letter and the "Q" Gospel. Alvarez got up from his chair and turned his back to Thomas to indicate that line of conversation was over. He moved on to his third and final gambit—the one he believed would produce the desired result.

As he slowly turned around, Alvarez addressed Thomas as though his next thoughts were being held back out of compassion.

"Father Ryan, I have some news that I believe you will find most disturbing. Ironically it's an issue over which you continue to be most critical of Church policy and procedure. But the sad truth is, I am faced with a dilemma. I have to decide if we are going to open an investigation on the charge of pedophilia against your late friend, Father Michael Moriarity. You have rightly chastised us for inaction against pedophiles and we have begun a campaign to right certain wrongs. This potential case against Father Moriarity is complicated because he is dead and can no longer defend himself. But, I am sure the heinous nature of this evil act against innocent young boys knows no statute of limitations in the eyes of the Lord."

Thomas was furious. How could Alvarez destroy the reputation of a fine man when he had no such evidence? "That's a lie and you know it." Thomas stepped over the line of protocol and respect that is afforded someone of Alvarez's office. There was no point in maintaining the false veil of a dignified conversation.

Alvarez regained the upper hand. "Settle down, Father. Remember your place. I have not yet decided if I will order the investigation. Then again, that might not matter. After all, in today's world once the word leaks out, and it always does, people will jump to conclusions. Perception is reality. Wouldn't you agree? Frankly, a lot depends on you and how much you cooperate.

I do believe you were his best friend and your testimony could prove very important."

Thomas could hear Michael Moriarity's voice; listen to your heart, for that is where the soul resides.

His response was calm and clear. "Cardinal Alvarez, have you no decency? Are you willing to destroy a man's reputation, a good and decent man who cannot defend himself? I underestimated you. I always thought you were tough, maybe even rough, but in the end, fair. I never thought of you as one to practice deceit, for that would surely undercut your authority. You're offering a trade that is beneath the dignity of a response. In return for my cooperation regarding Jesus' Letter, you will leave the memory of Father Moriarity unsullied? I pity you sir. It is beyond my limited priestly powers to beg for your forgiveness. I will pray for you."

"My, my, Father Ryan certainly has a lofty opinion of himself. You are going to pray for me? I don't know if that is a joke or a bloated ego run amuck."

Thomas did not respond. There really was nothing more to say.

"Well then, I think this conversation is over. I have tried to find some balance and have been rebuked each time by your unwillingness to strike a balance."

Thomas did not speak, but the memory of his grandfather's warning was at the forefront of his mind. Thomas, always be on guard, and remember, if you strike a balance between good and evil, you will have sided with evil.

Alvarez moved toward the front door and Thomas followed.

"Good bye Father Ryan."

"Good bye Cardinal Alvarez." Thomas bent forward to kiss the cardinal's ring, but Alvarez pulled his hand back.

Alvarez was out the door and into the limo and on his way back to Bath. His three attempts to bring Father Ryan back in line with the official position failed.

April 24 – Easter Sunday

Hasani and Lauren were cautiously optimistic they were prepared for the web launch, but on the big day, the response was overwhelming and the website crashed. The number of visits to the website was more than the multiple servers could handle. By the end of the first day, more than 22 million people registered as users, and an even larger number attempted to gain access, but could not get in. The site was "comment enabled" and while *The Letter* itself ran just three pages, there were more than 600 pages of comments from tens of thousands of individuals. The comments were heavily supportive. Eighty-nine percent of the first two day's respondents gushed with praise over the release of *The Letter* and for the courage it took to stand up to the religious establishment.

The reactions from several Christian denominations were mixed. Some were cautiously supportive, claiming this to be an opportunity to create a new dialog on what it means to be Christian, and on what Jesus' plan was when He began His public ministry. Some religions announced they would conduct further studies, while at the same time take the pulse of their members.

The Vatican's official position was *The Letter* and the other artifacts were most likely well done forgeries. At the same time, the Vatican continued to insist *The Letter*, the coin and cruets be sent to the Vatican for safekeeping and further study. They continued to attempt to create the impression the artifacts should be considered property of the Church and should be "returned" immediately. If The Institute refused to comply, then the Vatican would have no choice but to take the position the artifacts, and especially *The Letter*, were forgeries and Catholics everywhere should ignore or reject their message.

The Vatican found the large and overwhelmingly positive response by the public to be troubling. Avoiding a schism among the faithful was essential, as was maintaining the Vatican's status as the authority in all matters of Catholic doctrine.

The Letter's translation was viewed by many Church bureaucrats as a harsh and unjustified critique. They felt that *The Letter* implied that churches were businesses, where money was collected with the hinted promise of salvation. *The Letter* did not criticize people coming together, praying together and forming congregations to better know and serve God. But *The Letter* did strongly reject the need for lavish worship centers where money is often spent to create idols, which are then worshipped in place of the Word.

The message in *The Letter* was clear. One does not need a church or an idol to be able to talk to God. The Truth is all around and free to anyone who would open their eyes, their minds and their hearts. If there was one passage in *The Letter* especially frightening to the religious establishment, it was, "I did not come to start a religion; I came to start a revolution." It was the kind of message that would be most appealing to those on the bottom rung of society, to those on the outside looking in.

Cardinal Castillo and Father Peter Vacini met several times to develop a strategy for denying the authenticity of *The Letter* without appearing to deny Jesus. Vacini suggested the Vatican issue a statement declaring the message in *The Letter* was inconsistent with the teachings of Jesus as revealed in the Gospels and the Letters from St. Paul, and must therefore be considered fraudulent. Vacini suggested the Vatican challenge the Epistolic Institute to prove why they believe the message in *The Letter* is consistent with what is known about Jesus Christ.

Cardinal Castillo's approval of Vacini's suggestion was also a less than subtle criticism of Freddy's efforts. As a result of the bungled break-in, Cardinal

Castillo relieved Father Fletcher of his duties with the Vatican, and sent him back to New York to work in an inner city parish. Freddy was also demoted, but to some lesser position within the Vatican. As Freddy's star began to fall, Vacini's was on the rise. The Cardinal was beginning to rely more on Vacini and asked him to develop a position statement. With the approval of Cardinal Castillo and Cardinal Alvarez, the statement was released to the press as well as to the dioceses and parishes around the world.

> Holy See Challenges the Authenticity of *The Letter*
> Dateline: The Vatican
>
> The Holy See understands the frenzied public reaction resulting from the release of a document known as *The Letter* and the desire and hope for such a letter to be real. The See urges all Catholic faithful to use extreme caution in accepting the validity and authenticity of this document. The Epistolic Institute acquired this letter from a source whose credibility and veracity can no longer be determined. It is important for all to realize the Epistolic Institute is a new organization, which as yet has not been thoroughly vetted. While the institute has attracted some experienced scientists to serve on its board of directors, the institute's unknown level of stability in protecting the artifacts is of great concern to the Vatican as well as for all Catholics around the world.
>
> The Vatican has long served as the world's most secure repository of ancient religious artifacts. We have on several occasions invited the institute to transfer the recently acquired artifacts to the Vatican Archive and Resource Center where appropriate research can be done to ascertain their legitimacy, while protection from environmental degradation can be assured.
>
> We are also troubled by the lack of access to the artifacts despite our many requests. This restricted access affects all religious archeological investigators, not just those at the Vatican. Without the ability to study the original letter, we cannot attest to its authenticity. Let us be clear. The Holy See is not denying Jesus, as has previously and maliciously been reported. However, without the access needed to thoroughly evaluate the document, we do not accept this letter as being written by Our Lord, Jesus Christ.

Since requests for access by the See have been rejected or ignored, we now call upon the Epistolic Institute to reveal the proof, which documents their claim this letter is authentic. Further, the Holy See calls upon The Institute to demonstrate how their translation is consistent with the known traditions and teachings of Jesus as found in the sacred Gospels and Letters from St. Paul and others.

This request is being made on behalf of the billions of Catholics and fellow Christians around the world who have faith in those institutions that have long served to deliver the holy word of Jesus Christ. The Epistolic Institute must recognize it has a duty to insure that the beliefs of Christians are not compromised. The See is prepared to offer its expertise to assist the institute in this most important task. If the institute does not accept this final offer to assist, it will only substantiate our belief this purported letter from Jesus Christ is nothing more than a clever forgery.

Finally, the See cautions Catholics everywhere not to associate with this letter or with the Epistolic Institute. Catholics should not contribute money to the institute nor should they be involved in the activities sponsored by the Epistolic Institute. Normal curiosity is certainly expected and is not considered harmful. However, monetary investments for travel to view the letter are deemed excessive and beyond normal curiosity. Local parishes need to educate the faithful about falling victim to such exploitation. Educational materials from The See will be distributed soon.

The faithful are reminded to maintain their loyalty and support of the One True Holy and Apostolic Church. Faithful with questions should seek answers from parish clergy and lay ministers who have received the educational materials mentioned above.

Reaction to the press release had the impact the Cardinals hoped for. The goal was to put The Institute on the defensive. The Vatican said prove it—prove your message from Jesus is consistent with what we know about Him. The statement hit its mark. A seed of doubt was planted and there was an immediate drop in hits to the website. The Institute felt the sting from the Vatican's arrow.

Thomas felt betrayed by the organization he loyally served for over 20 years. What irony. Had Vatican archeologists discovered *The Letter*, it would have been he they would have called upon to do the translation. Now the lines were drawn and Thomas was on the outside looking in. It was a fight he did not want. He felt as though his years of service had been pushed aside. From the Vatican's perspective, it was "them" versus "us," and now Thomas was one of "them."

The Vatican laid down the challenge—Father Ryan, prove your translation of *The Letter* is accurate. Sadly, Thomas realized for him the challenge was not a simple either/or proposition. He realized even if he proved *The Letter* to be accurate, he would still have to leave the Church. He knew if he were to prove the accuracy of his translation, it would create a gap too wide to bridge. Once he accepted the Vatican's challenge, there would be no going back.

But what choice did he have? How could Thomas deny what He had written? How could he turn his back on his colleagues and how could he reject the countless millions who had their faith renewed by a letter? *How painfully poetic,* thought Thomas, *all I need to do is deny Jesus, deny myself, and deny the millions of fellow believers, and I can return home and all will be forgiven. All it takes are three small denials.*

The Tor

It was a warm, windless and sunny day when Thomas took a stroll along the Tor. He sought out the one whose advice mattered most. Upon reaching the spot where only a few months before he spread the ashes of Robert Thompson, Thomas stood and spoke quietly. "Excuse me Robert and Shamus, I have come for some advice. I have a difficult decision to make and I was wondering if you would listen to what I have to say."

It was as though the ground said "be seated" and Thomas sat down on the soft grass. Somewhat jokingly Thomas said, "Robert, you will be pleased to know the ground where your ashes are spread is the greenest and most lush of all the Tor."

For a while, Thomas just sat listening to the sounds of nature. Chirping birds, some rustling of tree branches caused by a gentle gust of wind, the happy sounds of a family with two small boys out for a walk.

He began the great debate in his own mind. He was confident his translation was accurate, but he wondered, was it true? *Am I prepared to walk away from an institution that's been my home for over 20 years? What if the Vatican's right?* Thomas did not approve of the actions of Freddy and his band of investigators, but Freddy was not the Church. Thomas was even more troubled by Cardinal Alvarez's attempt to gain his cooperation. Alvarez resorted to intimidation, bribery and even false witness to stop Thomas.

It was absolutely necessary for Thomas to examine his own motivation. He asked himself several questions. *What if I want too badly for The Letter to be true? Did I put too much of myself in the translation?* He warned others about trusting the word of Josephus, just because Josephus was one of the few early Christian writers. He also questioned the accuracy of the Dead Sea Scrolls. He recalled an answer he gave at the Georgetown lecture: "Are we to accept the scrolls are truthful just because the manuscripts are old? We stand in awe of that find. But what if the author of the scrolls was wrong—or worse yet, writing with an evil intent?"

The Catholic Church had undergone some rough times. True, it was their fault for not being more forthcoming and vigilant in removing pedophile priests. However, even that most egregious error had nothing to do with *The Letter*. Thomas continued his internal debate. *Was the* Church *being honest in their claim of wanting to safeguard The Letter? Wasn't their request to see the original Letter a reasonable request any scientist would make? After all, The Letter was a challenge to the very core of the Catholic Church establishment.*

Thomas knew many honest and devoted priests. He could feel the conflict they surely must be feeling, and Thomas wondered if he was letting them all down. He had doubts about the existence of God throughout his priestly career. However, this time, this hour, he felt more torn than ever before.

Thomas knelt on the ground and prayed for the faith and wisdom to make the right decision. The sun moved behind the Tor bringing a chill to where Thomas was on his knees. Finally, he stood up feeling a bit stiff. He thought about Jesus Christ spending the night on His knees in the Garden of Gethsemane before His betrayal and ultimate crucifixion. *What a minor inconvenience I've endured compared to what our Lord suffered when He was nailed to a cross. It might be good for us all to spend a little more time on our knees.*

As Thomas prepared for the days ahead, one phrase seemed to reverberate in his mind—*only the truth will set you free*. He wondered, was something true because it was accurate? Was something true because it "felt" right or true? He remembered before he went into the seminary, he worked as a reporter for a small city paper. His editor drilled one word into his head–accuracy, accuracy, accuracy. Thomas was certain his translation was accurate, but was it true?

Thomas's prayers were answered when he finally realized it didn't matter what would become of him. *Thomas, not everything is about you,* he said to himself. If his evidence was insufficient or wrong and *The Letter* was false, what did it matter what became of Father Thomas Ryan? If *The Letter* was true, then let the chips fall where they may. He listened to his heart and realized he had a higher allegiance to the truth.

The Vatican's challenge was for The Institute to show the translation of *The Letter* as a truthful portrayal of Jesus. Was the translation an accurate description of the life and times of Jesus? Were the words used in the translation consistent with words Jesus Christ would have used in conversation and writing? Thomas knew he could not say with 100% certainty Jesus wrote *The Letter*—no one could.

Aided by Matthew and James, Thomas decided a commentary on the translation would be the best way to demonstrate the words in the translation are accurate. The commentary approach was frequently used to explain and annotate religious writings. Robert had three Bible commentaries in his library, the Barclays, the Wycliffe and the Matthew Henry Commentary. In addition, the Internet had several other commentaries to choose from. Before they began, Thomas reminded his two friends that commentaries too often become academic, dry and unemotional. "We need to be sure we do not let the process overwhelm the beautiful humanity in Jesus' message."

Time was a factor. To blunt the challenge by the Vatican, the three men needed to work quickly. Thomas, Matthew and James cloistered themselves at Thompson Manor for three days and nights of research and writing to produce their response to the Vatican challenge.

The commentary was posted on The Institute's website as well as covered by news outlets, and the worldwide reaction was immediate and explosive. The Vatican denounced the commentary as defensive and self-serving. Welcoming women into the priesthood as *The Letter* suggested would have a devastating effect on the Catholic Church bureaucracy. Lay and religious Catholics (priests and nuns) were instructed to ignore, or if the opportunity existed, protest *The Letter*.

Despite the condemnation by the Vatican and by other entrenched religious bureaucracies, interest in the Glastonbury Codex, the cruets and the coin returned to an even higher level than before. People from all over the world came to view the artifacts. Millions more logged onto the website to see and read the translation of *The Letter* from Jesus Christ.

The Epistolic Institute selflessly insisted there would be no admission fee charged to visit the exhibit or to access the website. People could download and print *The Letter* free of charge. This was a conscious act written into the bylaws of The Institute and prominently displayed on all of their materials. Visitors to the exhibit in Glastonbury received an attractive reproduction of *The Letter* at no cost. School groups were welcomed to visit, and if that was not possible, free DVDs with copies of *The Letter* were sent to any school requesting materials from The Institute.

The decision to not charge admission ran counter to most similar exhibitions. Then again, there was no similar exhibition. Jesus was a man of the people. He never begged or asked for money, nor charged for lectures, miracles, or for the wisdom of his ways. Yet He never wanted for any material thing; for those who loved Him, invited Him into their homes and to their dinner tables. As He wrote in *The Letter*, "*I have never owned a house, but was welcomed into many homes. I never worried about where I would sleep or what I would eat. Those who sought the Word would feed and shelter me.*"

The Institute never found itself in need; people gave of their own free will. It was a message not lost on the Vatican. What the people gave was put to good use by giving back. The gifts were used to maintain the exhibition and to provide materials for whoever requested them.

Attempts to discredit the efforts of The Institute failed. Visits to the exhibit and the website, as well as spontaneous, unsolicited contributions were all on the rise. For Thomas, James and Matthew, truth carried the day.

Epilogue

I am the dance and I still go on

PALM SUNDAY, ONE YEAR LATER
ST. STANISLAUS PARISH, WASHINGTON, DC

Thomas sat in the last pew of St. Stanislaus Church, a small, poor parish in inner city Washington, DC. It was Palm Sunday, the beginning of Easter week. Thomas was not paying full attention to the service. Rather he sat there with his eyes closed, reflecting on all that transpired in the past year.

His friend, James, was now a permanent resident of Glastonbury. He and Margo married shortly after *The Letter* was released. It was a beautiful ecumenical ceremony celebrated at St. John the Baptist Church by an Anglican vicar, a Jewish rabbi and a Catholic priest.

Soon after, Margo learned she was pregnant. Although both James and Margo were in their 40's, they were rewarded with a beautiful, healthy baby boy, whom they named Robert Thompson Christopoulos. The baby's baptism was also celebrated by the same three doctors of the Church. That baptism was Thomas's last official act as a priest.

James's time was consumed with running the Epistolic Institute, giving lectures and responding to the unrelenting requests for media interviews. Margo, with the able assistance of Estelle and Henry, ran the Thompson Manor Conference Center/B&B. The local presence of the Glastonbury Codex guaranteed a full house. Robert's study became Margo's office where she carried on the business of the Manor with the young Robert by her side.

The Institute's board members met often that first year, and frequently chose to meet in the manor library, as opposed to meeting at The Institute.

Thomas's other childhood friend, Matthew, saw his standing in the Gold family greatly elevated. The Golds were somewhat boastful about their son-in-law. Matthew, on the other hand, preferred his privacy and didn't revel in his newfound fame. Matthew's father, the senior Rabbi Halprin, was proud of his son, not just for what Matthew helped accomplish, but for the way he handled the notoriety with dignity and grace. It could have become a sideshow: "Jewish Rabbi Defends Jesus Against the Vatican." But Matthew would have none of it.

Sara was also proud of her husband and understanding of the demands on his time. At one point, the Towson University faculty wives prevailed on Sara to persuade Matthew to give a special private luncheon talk, a sort of behind-the-scenes look at what happened during the discovery of the Glastonbury

Codex. When Matthew arrived at the University Club, he was astonished to see not just the faculty wives, but their husbands also. It was not the traditional PowerPoint lecture. Rather, 80 or so people sat around tables and enjoyed a light lunch, as Matthew, wearing a wireless microphone, walked among the attendees, speaking informally and answering questions. Sara thought he might be annoyed, but she was relieved when, on the drive home, Matthew said he enjoyed the event and the opportunity to meet faculty members from other departments.

Matthew's status at Towson grew and requests for his time had to be carefully managed. He still taught undergraduate students and loved teaching, but now requests for lectures, interviews and consultancies were becoming a regular occurrence. Beyond his normal duties, he had a burning desire to get back in the field and team up with Benny Hasani and Carol Dunmore in the search for the twelfth Qumran cave.

Carol's role as Vicar of St. John the Baptist remained her principle assignment, but now she was awarded an assistant to help shoulder some of her parish responsibilities. The Institute board allocated an annual payment of £25,000 to St. John's to help defray the costs of the assistant vicar. James asked Carol to serve as the liaison between The Institute and the Glastonbury Business Association, as well as Glastonbury political leaders. In addition to serving as the liaison, Carol was often seen greeting visitors and giving short talks at The Institute especially to school groups. She always enjoyed meeting students who were less reserved in their expression of wonder.

St. John's also benefitted from a significant increase in Sunday service attendance. "Nearer my God to Thee" became the unofficial anthem of the church, as new parishioners and visitors to the exhibit came to view the stained glass window of Joseph of Arimathea holding the sacred cruets. Carol insisted St. John's remain available to all without charging fees for tours or otherwise attempting to capitalize on the Glastonbury Codex.

She was also eager to team up with Benny and Matthew in a search for Qumran cave number 12. The Institute board voted to fully fund an expedition to be led by the three board members.

This was an expensive endeavor and The Institute, true to its belief system, undertook a novel approach in its decision-making. The Institute asked visitors to both the website and the exhibit for their opinion on funding such an expedition.

Ninety-two percent of the over one million respondents, enthusiastically endorsed The Institute funding the expedition. The vote wasn't necessary, but it was further example of The Institute's promise to listen to comments from supporters. This would be Carol's first such expedition and her excitement built as she prepared for the adventure. Benny cautioned her the trip would not only be physically strenuous, but often such attempts did not yield the hoped for outcome. Carol was just happy to be included and took her preparations seriously.

Thomas remained seated in the last row pew of St. Stanislaus as he recalled the others who played a role in the adventure. Toby Merten's carbon-14 tests, authenticated by his Cambridge laboratory, had been essential in helping establish the scientific credibility of *The Letter.* Thomas remembered how completely captivated Toby was upon seeing *The Letter* and then immediately joined forces with The Institute.

Toby's introduction of Helen to the team was pivotal. Without her able work under a nearly impossible schedule, all could have been lost. The word might never have gotten out had she not orchestrated a picture-perfect press conference. But then her efforts would never have been engaged if it hadn't been for Randy Cross, who first unearthed the Vatican strategy and then buried the same with well-placed, accurate "bombshell" articles in the *Washington Post*. Randy's efforts gave the Epistolic Institute just the help it needed to let the truth shine through.

The Doorway continued to grow, and the time for the activation of the Portals grew shorter. Their Armageddon was still years away. They would be yet another challenge for Thomas. He knew their dirty little secret and he knew how to stop them. He also knew there was time before they would implement the transfer of barcodes from membership cards to the owner's left hand. However, Thomas could not fight them by himself. He needed a platform that would give him the credibility as well as the opportunity to reach out to the many that already joined.

The Institute would be his platform, but the time was not yet right. He knew that defeating The Doorway would require a quick and decisive move—a move so rapid the organization would not be able to respond in time to counter his efforts.

Then there was Frederick Fulgrum. Thomas had to stifle a laugh as he pictured Freddy chasing about any and all leads, such as Malcolm Collier at The Doorway, who was at best an empty suit imitation of Obi-Wan-Kenobi. What a mental picture—Ichabod Fulgrum chasing after Obi-Wan-Collier.

Fulgrum was a sad case, thought Thomas. His memory of the brief confrontation he had with Freddy at Robert's memorial was a reminder he promised to pray for him. *He needs prayer more than most,* thought Thomas. *Freddy is so filled with envy, he not only lost his way, he has no sense of direction. Such a waste of a life,* thought Thomas. *Sad to say each of us, even Freddy, only gets but one.*

Thomas thought about the clumsy attempts by Freddy to portray himself as Thomas's friend, something no one took seriously. *Old 4-F*, he said to himself, as he thought about how Freddy would introduce himself in that knife sharp staccato fashion, "I am Father Frederick Francis Fulgrum." He later learned how Freddy bribed Father LaRouche by dangling a transfer to Perpignan, France. Thomas recalled the line from the movie, *A Man for All Seasons,* wherein Thomas Moore said to Richard Rich: "Why Richard, it profits a man little to trade his soul for the whole world, but for Wales." There was LaRouche selling whatever information he could peddle and all he got was Perpignan. Rumor had it that LaRouche was placed on administrative leave for substance abuse.

Thomas learned from Randy Cross that Freddy had been demoted. It would seem that Freddy's expense account purchases of costly meals and alcohol did not square with an internal Vatican audit. With so little to show for his expenses, Cardinal Castillo was not about to come to Freddy's aid. Freddy was reassigned somewhere within the vast confines of the Vatican. Peter Vacini was elevated to Freddy's old position.

Thomas recalled the two bumbling break-in attempts by ex-cop-turned-priest, Jerry Fletcher and how Sean Boyle and his men bested him the first time. He felt a tweak of pride when he thought about his own confrontation with Fletcher. Wet and shirtless, he protected the artifacts. He was grateful for what he learned from Michael Moriarity—when and how to fight, and how not to. He smiled thinking about Sean Boyle and their late night stroll on the Tor reuniting two old friends, Sean's father, Shamus Boyle, and Robert Thompson.

Then there was the beautiful young woman Robin. She was still a flight attendant, but now she lived alone in a nice flat in Bath managed by Sean Boyle's company. She would stop by The Institute headquarters often, especially when she had long layovers, and would volunteer her time however she could. Starting out in the gift shop, she ultimately became a part-time guide under Carol's tutoring. She studied everything she could lay her hands on. She was happy and Thomas thought she was the perfect lesson in life. She acted bravely to help others and in the process she saved herself.

But mostly, Thomas thought about Robert, the old Scot with a twinkle in his eye. A man so much like his Irish grandfather, at times they were hard to separate in his mind. There was Robert the humorist, spinning tales, telling jokes, laughing hardest when the joke was on him. There was Robert the philanthropist, making The Institute a reality and sharing what was his with those who cared for him. There was Robert the artist/poet, the unpublished author, the student always in pursuit of learning, even if it meant putting a book back on the bookshelf anywhere other than where he removed it.

There was Robert the sage, the man who always seemed to know what you were thinking, always one step ahead, always anticipating. Lastly, there was Robert the man who lived a life of devotion to God and his fellow man. His was a devotion which earned him medals on earth and which surely earned him a place of honor in Heaven. He was a wise man who achieved a level of immortality by refusing to be mortal. He left behind some of his work—work, which remains unfinished, and since only Robert could complete the work, neither the work, nor therefore Robert, could ever be finished. Robert knew the only way to achieve immortality was to be remembered. Not only would Robert be remembered, he would never be forgotten.

If anyone embodied one of Thomas's favorite sayings, it was Robert: "Every saint has a past and every sinner has a future." Thomas would never forget Robert's courage to admit that he grievously erred and how he then showed the strength to stand firm in the winds that would blow against him.

The priest celebrating the Mass began to deliver his sermon and Thomas looked up, shaking off the memory session so that he could give the celebrant his full attention. The priest's name was Father Aaron Romanski; he was a big man, six feet two or three. His chiseled physique was hidden behind his robe, but Thomas sensed the priest was a powerful man. He had a kindly countenance with a baritone voice that didn't require amplification and a presence that made people feel comfortable and safe.

The sermon was taken from the song, Lord of the Dance. Father Romanski reminded all that this was Palm Sunday, the day that 2,000 years before saw Jesus riding triumphantly into Jerusalem on a donkey while followers placed palm branches along his path. But by the end of that week, Jesus had been crucified on a cross. Father Romanski had a beautiful voice and he finished his sermon singing the fourth and fifth stanzas:

I danced on a Friday and the sky turned black;
It's hard to dance with the devil on your back.
They buried my body and they thought I'd gone,
But I am the dance and I still go on.

They cut me down and I leapt up high,
I am the life that'll never, never die;
I'll live in you if you'll live in me;
I am the Lord of the Dance said He.

Thomas was impressed. He had given many sermons, but he never sung one. A few minutes later came the moment in the Mass, which matters most:

the Consecration of the Host. In fact, it is the Consecration that transforms a Sunday service into a Mass. It was a ritual Thomas performed thousands of times—replicating the tradition started by Jesus Christ. He heard the words, "This is My Body, This is My Blood," and began his walk down the aisle. The young priest put the host on his tongue and Thomas whispered, "Thanks be to God."

He returned to his pew, remembering those fateful days last January—a memory as vivid as if it was yesterday. Once again, he could feel the beads of sweat forming, his temples throbbing, his hands thickening, his throat sealing and his heart burning. He was once again unwrapping The Codex, genuflecting and saying, "Thy will be done." How could one as unworthy as he have been granted the privilege to touch that sacred parchment? *Jesus Christ held The Letter, just as He held the consecrated bread.* This was His body, this was His blood.

Thomas's life would never be the same. He left Georgetown, but not the priesthood. He would lecture, always carefully choosing the right venue. He would receive an honorarium—making a living was still a necessity. But the honorarium was never a factor in deciding where to speak. Several booking agents approached him with outrageous offers and he turned them all down. Margo Christopoulos agreed to be his booking agent and she seemed to know where Thomas would feel most comfortable speaking.

He received a modest stipend and expenses from The Institute to serve on the board and help set its direction. He continued to write, mostly for religious and archeological publications. He even wrote some poetry and fiction. But there was one piece, which he never expected to finish, one piece, which he was certain he would never have published. He would never finish it, because it could never be finished. He learned that from a wise man.

The piece he would never complete was, in some ways, the beginning of this remarkable journey. *The Lost Years of Jesus Christ* could never be written, that is, if the author had any respect for the Truth. Why? In part, because Jesus was, and continues to be, everywhere, "if one but opens his eyes." Was He in Glastonbury, England? Yes. Was He in Egypt? Yes. Was He in the desert at Qumran? Yes. And in Tibet, China, Mexico, South America, Easter Island? Yes.

He was and is everywhere and He was never lost.

The book could never be finished. Oh, it would be good to write drafts or editions, to tell the tales from Jesus' young boyhood on. To tell the tales which may or may not be completely accurate. But, if those tales and myths would help us to better understand Jesus, as long as it serves the truth, then it isn't necessary to wait for the imprimatur from the Pope. In a rare private moment, Robert explained to Thomas that truth and reality are not the same. All the facts may be correct, but the story may still not be true. And, it is also the same in reverse. It is not necessary for something to have occurred in order for it to be true.

Thomas raised his head and heard the priest say. "The Mass has ended. Go in peace and may the grace of Our Lord, Jesus Christ be with you always." Thomas remained in his pew as the parishioners filed past, shaking hands with one another as a sign of peace. An elderly man stopped where Thomas was sitting. Thomas stood up; the old man smiled and extended his hand saying, "Peace be with you always." Thomas shook his hand and returned the message, "And also with you." Thomas sat back down. He wasn't ready to leave yet.

Acolytes were scurrying about cleaning up the sanctuary, eager to get outside and play. Several of the lights had been turned low. Moments later, the young priest who just celebrated the Mass was standing before Thomas.

Thomas rose.

The young priest extended his hand. "Hello, I am Father Aaron Romanski, but please call me Aaron. Thomas nodded and was about to speak when the priest said, "And you are Father Thomas Ryan."

Thomas nodded again.

"Please sit down. Now what can I do for you, Father Ryan?" asked Aaron.

"First, please call me Thomas."

"Agreed," said Aaron.

"Aaron, the priest who ran this parish before you was a dear friend of mine."

"Ah yes, Father Michael Moriarity. I am sorry to say I never met him, but I have heard nothing but wonderful things about him. I am sorry for your loss."

"Thank you, Aaron. When Michael was here, he ran an active boxing program which was successful in getting several young men off the streets and ultimately into jobs," continued Thomas.

"Yes, I have heard a great deal about the program," said Aaron.

"Father, I used to help Father Moriarity, and with your permission, I would like to volunteer to start the program back up."

Father Romanski was taken aback by Thomas's offer.

"That is most generous, Thomas. Of all the things we would like to do here, none has been requested more by our parishioners than that program. I have heard from many of our parents and even the police in the area about how it taught young boys discipline and helped them develop a perspective about life beyond the street. I did some boxing in college myself and I know firsthand about the discipline. I would love to restart the program, but I'm alone here and the demands on my time really don't afford me the opportunity. If you are serious, you are an angel," said Aaron.

"Father, I need to warn you, I come with some baggage. I am hardly the darling of the church anymore. I hesitated to offer to help earlier because I didn't want to make things any more difficult for whoever ran this place," responded Thomas.

"Thomas, don't worry about the reaction. Look around here. We are hardly the centerpiece of the diocese. Sometimes I wonder if they even know St. Stanislaus exists. In many ways, I like it like that. If they don't know we exist, it gives me a lot more freedom to do what my heart tells me. The only problem I see is that our equipment and locker room are in pretty bad shape. I'm afraid the shower quit working about six months ago."

"Aaron, I work with a nonprofit and I think we could find some money to fix things up and make it work. These are boxers, not bankers; it doesn't need to be plush."

"My God, you are an angel," repeated Aaron.

"So, Aaron, is it a deal?"

"You're on, Thomas."

The two men stood and shook hands to seal the deal. Thomas sensed that a new friendship was about to begin.

"Then, I will get started." Thomas turned and walked toward the church exit.

Aaron called out, "Father Ryan?"

Ryan stopped and looked back.

"Thomas, if you need a sparring partner, I'm available."

Appendix

Commentary on *The Letter* from Jesus Christ to Joseph of Arimathea

The Epistolic Institute Contributing Editors:
James Christopoulos, Ph.D.; Matthew Halprin, Ph.D.; Thomas Ryan, S.J., Ph.D.

Introduction

The Epistolic Institute has been challenged to prove its claim that the document known as *The Letter* was written by the hand of Jesus Christ. With full reliance upon faith, we welcome the challenge, for it affords one more opportunity to win over the hearts and minds of those whose faith is not sufficient to accept *The Letter* as the written word of Our Lord, Jesus Christ.

We recognize it may never be possible to prove our assertion with 100% certainty. Nevertheless, we believe the overwhelming body of evidence detailed here supports the belief *The Letter* was written by Jesus Christ. Since *The Letter* is not signed, we cannot know with 100% certainty Jesus is the author. However, even had *The Letter* been signed by Jesus, that alone would not be proof, for no one can attest to Jesus' signature.

We will present evidence based on the physical composition of *The Letter*, as well as the content and word selection. We will also comment on the other artifacts discovered with *The Letter*.

It is somewhat ironic that the prime focus of attention is on *The Letter*, for its find was accidental. Had *The Letter* not been discovered, the recovery of the two cruets, said to have once contained the blood and sweat of Jesus Christ, would have been a significant find on its own.

Physical composition of The Letter and artifacts discovered with The Letter

- Three artifacts were discovered in a pewter box hidden in wall safe in the home of Robert Thompson of Glastonbury, England. According to the Thompson family records, the pewter box is believed to have been constructed by St. Joseph of Arimathea around 50 CE. Since Glastonbury is home to many tin mines and since pewter is more than 90% tin, it is logical to assume local resources were available to construct the box. The fact the box may have been constructed by one of our earliest saints is significant by itself and should be celebrated. The symbol on the lid of the box is a fish, not a cross. The ichthys, or fish symbol, was used by early Christians to represent Jesus Christ. The cross symbol was introduced around 300 CE.

- *The Letter* was discovered along with two other artifacts. One of the artifacts is a denarius with the likeness of Emperor Tiberius, from around 30 CE. This coin has often been described as a "Tribute Penny." The coin is an authentic denarius in brilliant uncirculated condition. We believe the coin was placed in the box to serve as a marker to help in establishing a date for the placement of the artifacts.

- Also found in the box were two perfectly matched amber cruets we believe once contained the blood and sweat of Jesus Christ. There is a stain line near the top of both cruets and on one of the cruets the stain line is slightly more pronounced than the other. It is a color similar to rust and it is our conviction the rust-colored stain may be the remnant of blood. Tobias Merten of the Cambridge RadioCarbon Laboratory supports our belief. It may be possible to establish a date for the stain through a carbon-14 test, however to do so would most likely require scraping all the remnant stain off of each cruet, and that is something we are not prepared to do. Some things must be taken on faith.

  We also believe these cruets were brought to England by St. Joseph of Arimathea around 34 CE. There exists a stained glass window in St. John the Baptist Anglican Church in Glastonbury, England that depicts St. Joseph carrying the two cruets. To view a picture of the stained glass window, one only needs to log on to the St. John the Baptist Church website at www.stjohns-glastonbury.org.uk.

- *The Letter* from Jesus Christ to St. Joseph of Arimathea was found in the pewter box along with the coin and cruets. It is protected within a heavy leather book cover similar in appearance to the Nag Hammadi Codex. The leather front and back covers are each approximately three-quarters of an inch thick and were meant to protect its contents. We have named the book the "Glastonbury Codex."

  The Codex has a beautiful hand tooled dark leather cover. On the cover are the ancient Greek letters ΙΧΘΥΣ and the early Christian symbol of a fish. The letters Iota, Chi, Theta, Upsilon, Sigma are a

Greek abbreviation meaning "Jesous Christos, Theou Uios, Soter," or in English, "Jesus Christ, Son of God, Savior." Thompson family records also indicate that the leather-tooled codex was constructed by St. Joseph of Arimathea.

The Codex contains fifteen sheets of writing. Twelve of the sheets consist of four separate translations, each three pages long. The remaining three sheets on parchment vellum contain early Aramaic writing in a script commonly used around 0 to 50 CE. While the twelve pages of translation do have minor historical significance, the three-page parchment document is "*The Letter*" from Jesus Christ to his Uncle Joseph.

Using the carbon-14 test, we were able to date the vellum parchment. Three separate carbon-14 tests were completed by Tobias Merten, Director of the Cambridge RadioCarbon Laboratory. All three tests yielded the same result and show the parchment dating from the period of 10 CE to 40 CE.

- The carbon-14 test also validated that the vellum upon which *The Letter* is written is from the Mediterranean area. This is consistent with where Jesus would have been when He wrote *The Letter*, shortly after His Crucifixion and Resurrection.

- *The Letter*'s recipient is believed to be Joseph of Arimathea. The author of *The Letter* refers to the recipient as "uncle." It is widely accepted Joseph of Arimathea was Jesus' great uncle, as he was an uncle of Jesus' mother, Mary.

- *The Letter* is written in Aramaic, the language used by Jesus. Father Thomas Ryan, regarded by many, including the Catholic Church, as an expert in the translation of documents from Aramaic to English, notes the writing style is confident, powerful and graceful. One cannot detect any hesitation by the author. There are no correction marks and it appears the writer knew exactly what message He wished to send. It is the handwriting style exhibited by the most influential writers of the day and is certainly consistent with a writing style that one would expect from Jesus Christ.

- *The Letter* is in pristine condition despite the fact it is 2,000 years old. It seemingly refuses to age even in the somewhat inhospitable climate of England. We believe divine intervention has played a role in the preservation of *The Letter*.

- Portions of *The Letter* are prophetic. It speaks specifically of events, which have already or may still take place in the future from the date when *The Letter* was written. It speaks about a war where millions of Jews are tortured and put to death, and predicts the detonation of the atomic bomb. It also reveals the discovery of the Dead Sea Scrolls in the caves of the Qumran desert. The level of specificity in the prediction adds credibility to the belief *The Letter* is divinely inspired. Unlike the vague predictions from Nostradamus, these prophetic statements are specific, measurable, and in several cases, have already occurred and have had their occurrence independently verified.

Analysis of the Content and Word Selection in *The Letter*

The Epistolic Institute has been challenged by the Vatican to demonstrate the words in the translation of *The Letter* are consistent with the known traditions, as well as the life and teaching of Jesus Christ as found in the gospels and letters from St. Paul and others. In the following analysis, we have divided the translation of *The Letter* into 12 distinct word or message groupings. Each individual grouping has been analyzed and a search for similar language in other documents contemporaneous to the time of Jesus has been accomplished.

An analysis of the message in *The Letter* found similarities with the New Testament gospels and the letters from Paul, James and Peter. There are two word groupings that can be traced to the Old Testament in 1st and 2nd Kings. Lastly, some of the corresponding content can be found in non-canonical gospels and other sources from the time when *The Letter* was written.

The following analysis demonstrates how closely the messages correspond to what is known about the life and language of Jesus Christ. It is critical to note we also believe the "teaching" messages in *The Letter* were first uttered by the Christ and only then incorporated into the writings of others. Jesus is not parroting the words of others, rather He was first to speak them. As they later appear in the writings of others demonstrates Jesus is the teacher and not the other way around.

ANALYSIS OF THE 12 MESSAGE GROUPINGS FOUND IN *THE LETTER*

1. *The Letter* begins and ends with the words, *Peace be with you.* This is a phrase often used by Jesus Christ and others as a greeting or farewell. While today it is used in many denominational liturgies as a non-threatening greeting, it had to have been a greeting that was bold for use by common people who were thought to lack the power to bring about peace.

2. The writer of *The Letter* next speaks about the recipient as one who raised him as his own. Note the following: *When my father died, you came to my mother's aid. As it has been written, you raised me as your own son. I learned your trade as a son learns from his father. I traveled with you to many places and learned the ways of different people. The lessons I learned from you and from the Teacher helped shape who I would become.* We believe Jesus' earthly father (also named Joseph) died when Jesus was 12 or 13 years old. According to the Jewish Talmud, when a boy's father died, an uncle would assume the role of father. Since Joseph of Arimathea was an uncle of Mary, Jesus' mother, he was also Jesus' great uncle. He was a secret follower of Jesus and was present at the crucifixion and claimed Jesus' body, as was the right of a member of the family.

   It was common in that period for a boy to learn the trade of his father by serving as an apprentice. Jesus' earthly father is often misidentified as a carpenter. However, he was a tecton, that is, one who was a builder and who used tools while working with wood or stone or metal. Later in life, Jesus did not demonstrate the skills of a tecton, his earthly father's trade. Rather He demonstrated considerable knowledge about fishing and seafaring. Joseph of Arimathea was a merchant and, while under his care, Jesus would have traveled with him, which could explain Jesus' statement that He "traveled." It would also explain His absence from the Palestine area for 19 years. We must offer a caveat, which will require more investigation. We admit we are not able to identify the person Jesus refers to as the "Teacher."

3. The author next notes that He was a wanderer. He writes: *I never owned a house, but was welcomed into many homes. I never worried about what I would eat or where I would sleep. Those who sought*

the Word fed and sheltered me. If I found no welcome, I would wipe the dust off my sandals and continue on. My cloak would keep me warm and would be my bed at night when I had none. We know Jesus visited many places as He gathered His followers. This message is similar in content to the gospel of Luke 10:4-12, where Luke recommends staying with those who welcome you. Luke writes, "And if you find that you are not welcomed, then wipe the dust off your sandals and move on."

4. The author next states: *When I had endured the final sacrifice for which I had been sent by the Father, you were there at my side. When knowing me would put you in peril for your life and property, you claimed me and gave me your place to rest. Your reward was prison and then exile.* This may be one of the most powerful validations that this is a letter from Jesus Christ. This is a clear reference to the crucifixion, "final sacrifice for which I had been sent by the Father." That Joseph of Arimathea was at Jesus' side at the crucifixion is well documented. He was there when the Roman centurion pierced Jesus' side and he caught the last drops of Jesus' blood. Later, risking life and property, Joseph claimed Jesus' body from Pontius Pilate. He acknowledged as a relative of Jesus, it was his right to claim the body.

   Joseph of Arimathea, along with another secret follower, Nicodemus, washed the sweat and blood from the body, wrapped the body in fine linen, and placed Jesus in the tomb Joseph prepared for himself. Within days, Joseph of Arimathea was arrested, briefly imprisoned and then exiled. This fact is well documented in the four Gospels, Matthew 27:57-61, Mark 15:42-47, Luke 23:50-56, and John 19:38-42. A version of the story also exists in the non-canonical gospel of Nicodemus and the Acts of Pilate.

5. *The Letter* is filled with important messages. Virtually every line reveals something about the author and His vision for the future. One of the most important messages is the following: *My purpose and my message may become lost with the passage of time. But know this; I did not come to start a religion. I came to start a revolution. I came to end slavery, inequality and war. I came to instill justice, mercy and freedom. My message was a threat to established order. But silencing me did not put an end to the message.*

   This may be the most dangerous statement aimed at yesterday's as well as today's religious denominations. Throughout His public life,

Jesus' teachings were a constant challenge to the Romans, as well as the Jewish Sanhedrin. His final week began with Jesus overturning the tables of the moneychangers and ended with His crucifixion. The message in the Gospels of Matthew and Luke, speak of the revolution to come. In Matthew 10:34-39 it is written, "Do not think that I have come to bring peace to the earth; I have not come to bring peace, but a sword." The revolution Jesus envisioned called for all of us to boldly challenge those elements of life that do not adhere to the truth.

6. Another powerful piece of evidence that Jesus is the author of *The Letter* is the message about "The Way." Christians believe the path one needs to follow to gain salvation is embodied in Jesus' teaching about The Way—but just what is The Way? Here is what *The Letter* states. *Truth is the Way. For without Truth, there can be no integrity, and without integrity there can be no trust. And without trust, there can be no dreams, no hope and no change. Only Truth can set one free.*

   The apostle James is thought by many to be the brother of Jesus. In chapter 14 of the brief New Testament Letter from James, James identifies Truth as the Way. One constant in Jesus' teachings is the concept of "Truth." Jesus' Way of Truth was not merely a matter of speaking the Truth—it was a concept of living the Truth.

   In the Gospel of John 8:32, John writes, "and you will know the truth and the truth will make you free." John, the Gospel writer is reporting what he has learned in song and story. He was not there with the Lord. His Gospel was written approximately 60 years after the crucifixion. Examples of living The Way by focusing on social justice for all can be found throughout the Acts of the Apostles believed to be the second book of Luke.

7. Again the author of *The Letter* is preaching "The Way" as only Jesus could. We will compare these words from the author with what is written about Jesus" teachings. The author of *The Letter* writes: *I taught all who would listen to hunger and thirst for righteousness, to temper justice with mercy, and to act with kindness. To be a seeker for justice, believing always the one who searches, finds; and the one who knocks, has the door opened. To know the right path is difficult and the right gate is narrow; and the wide road is easy and leads to destruction.* This message is found throughout the New Testament.

The Beatitudes in the Gospel of Matthew address righteousness, while the Letter from James and the Gospel of Matthew also address justice, mercy and kindness.

In the Gospel of Luke 11:9-10, Luke writes, "Ask and it will be given you; search and you will find; knock and the door will be opened for you. For everyone who asks receives, and everyone who searches finds, and for everyone who knocks the door will be opened."

The Gospel of Matthew 7:13-14 states, "For the gate is narrow and the road is hard that leads to life..." Matthew's message is that the difficult road is the one we must follow for it is the one that leads to salvation. This is what Jesus meant when He taught it is easier for a camel to go through the eye of a needle than for a rich man to enter heaven. Following the Way is not easy, nor was it meant to be easy.

8. The author continues to predict what the future holds in store when He writes: *I know the future will always hold challenges. Rich men will build grand shrines of worship to honor me. Money will be required from the people and will be spent to adorn their houses of worship and pay the priests who serve them. The Truth does not require garish displays. How could a temple be grander than a mountain? How could a temple be grander than the cedars felled to build her? These monuments only serve to cloud the Truth. Those who are lost will worship the temples and not the Word. Truth is all around and free to everyone who would open their eyes, minds and hearts.* The Letter from James 2:6-7 and the Gospel of Luke 21:1 both discuss how the rich will attempt to use their wealth to gain salvation believing erroneously they can buy their way into heaven. The author predicts the rich will continue to use the poor to build their institutions and then exclude the poor from them. History is littered with the record of dispensations purchased by wrongdoers using bribes rather than penance.

While the Gospel of Luke 17:20-21 teaches the Kingdom of God is all around, much more is found in non-canonical sources such as the Gospel of Thomas discovered in the Nag Hammadi Codices. The Gospel of Thomas is sometimes referred to as the Sayings Gospel for it merely lists "sayings" attributed to Jesus Christ without story or embellishment. It is controversial and not well regarded by the Church bureaucracy. Many of the "sayings" in the Gospel of Thomas run counter to the way things are today and its message would be a difficult one for the Church to embrace. However, since Thomas, the apostle, may have written the Gospel of Thomas, it may have been written much closer to the lifetime of Jesus. These words are not found in other writings, but they are consistent with the Lord's message and eloquently stated. In the Gospel of Thomas we learn the Truth is free to all who would draw near and listen. And Jesus said, "split a piece of wood and I am there."

9. Jesus was tempted by the Devil on more than one occasion. If the Devil could win Jesus over, it would be a monumental victory for the forces of evil. The Evil One or the Devil is found in the Temptation of Jesus in the Gospels of Matthew 4:1-11, Mark 1:12-13 and Luke 4:1-13. That Temptation occurred after Jesus' baptism by St. John the Baptist and His return from forty days in the wilderness. The return of the Devil is also found earlier in Jesus' ministry in the Gospels of Matthew 13:43-45 and Luke 11:14-26. The reference in *The Letter* is to a still later unrecorded visit by the Devil after Jesus' resurrection, i.e., His "lifeless sleep." While we can find no reference to this visit, clearly the Devil was never far away. Many have suggested the Devil was present in Judas Iscariot as he led Jesus into the hands of the soldiers who arrested Him.

   Listen to the author in this message on the Devil: *The evil one returned to me when I was raised from my lifeless sleep. He boasted how the rich will attempt to control the Truth and use it for their own advantage. He bragged before the end-of-days, the rich will own me. He said they will put my image on every wall and use my name to increase their treasuries and use the money to enlarge their places of worship and create even more images. In time men will forget the Word and worship the image. He sneered when he said greed is the Devil's beast and its excrement is weighed in gold.*

   While some of Jesus' encounters with the Devil are found in the Gospels, this is a new reference, which has not been seen before. However, one can see the prophetic nature of His writing. With the rise in popularity of television evangelists and with their emphasis on building grander and grander cathedrals, this message should be a caution to all to be wise enough to distinguish the difference between a church and the Word, and to remember, a church, regardless of how ornately decorated it is, is still only a building. Great care must be taken not to confuse the image of Jesus with the message of Jesus.

Early popes sought power and money. They bought works of art so they might live luxuriously. While their intent at the time was purely selfish, it is ironic that all people today can enjoy the beauty of the paintings and sculptures they commissioned.

The author continues to discuss more of the Devil's message in this next passage, which also reveals a prophetic side to *The Letter: He claimed credit for causing a mighty war, where awesome power not seen since creation would be harnessed and turned into a weapon. And once that power was out of the box, it could never be returned. He flashed an evil grin saying this great conflict will cause the near elimination of my chosen people. His agent on earth would torture millions of my people before putting them to death. However, the Evil One chose to ignore that from the ashes, a new nation called Israel will rise up.*

This example of prophecy helps validate the divinity of *The Letter*. Although many wars have been waged since Jesus walked on earth, this is a clear reference to World War II. The awesome power, which we cannot put back in the box, must be the atomic bombs dropped on Hiroshima and Nagasaki. The Evil One's agent on earth who tortured millions of Jews before putting them to death must be a reference to Adolf Hitler. And the new nation, which rose from the ashes, is the state of Israel.

The Letter has one more passage involving the Devil: *He laughed saying more wars would be waged in my name, and all sides would claim Truth as their cause. People would be turned into slaves and the Devil would emerge victorious. But the Devil is wrong, for he does not understand peace is not the absence of war, but rather it is the presence of justice; and by seeking justice, we can someday put an end to war. I sent him away and knelt down to pray. I prayed for the one who seeks justice to remain free, even if imprisoned or in shackles, for it is better to die free in bondage than to live as a slave surrounded by comfort.*

This saying has not been seen before, however similar messages may be found in biblical apocrypha such as the non-canonical Gospel of

Nicodemus or the Gospel of Mary Magdalene. This saying demonstrates Jesus' repudiation of war was absolute. Jesus did more than talk about peace and justice. His life on earth is the model for those who hunger and thirst for righteousness and temper justice with mercy.

Jesus' encounter with the Devil ended when Jesus told the Devil to leave Him. When the Devil left, Jesus knelt down and prayed. He accepted His own imprisonment and finally, death on the cross. The teaching moment came when Jesus allowed Himself to be imprisoned knowing He had the power to set Himself free. This allowed Him to demonstrate, despite His imprisonment, that He remained a free man. Jesus' crucifixion and resurrection is a seminal moment in human history. If Jesus had given in, He could have lived, possibly in comfort, but then His life may have been unremarkable and the world unchanged by his presence. By dying, He made it possible for all to be free.

10. The author next speaks of more letters yet to be found in the area where the Dead Sea Scrolls have been recovered. This is most interesting for it introduces yet another prophetic message. Here again is *The Letter: Many will deny the Word, or present false translations so as to confuse and then control. But worry not, for the unabridged Word survives. In the deserts of the Qumran, the Essenes have preserved the Word. In time, messages from the ancient ones will be recovered from the twelve caves, which have protected the Word from those who have sought to destroy it.*

    This is a second example of a prophecy, which as with the first helps validate the divinity of *The Letter*. Jesus wrote about the discovery of the Dead Sea Scrolls, which happened approximately 1,900 years later. It is the specificity in Jesus' prophecy, which differentiates Him from prognosticators, such as Nostradamus, whose vague predictions are open to interpretation.

    The author of *The Letter* writes about one of the Lord God's most beloved servants, Elijah, and makes a further prediction that a letter from Elijah will someday be found most likely in the twelfth cave of the Qumran. Here then is the message followed by our analysis: *None of these messages is greater than the Letter from Elijah. No one was more loyal than Elijah. He bested Baal's Priests at Mount*

Carmel. He came before me to make straight the way. He was there with Moses on the mountain. And he is whole in heaven with the Father, for he was raised in a chariot of fire. Someday a seeker of the Truth will find his Letter.

The message about the twelfth cave in the Qumran and a letter from Elijah appears only here in *The Letter*. This statement is not only prophetic, but it also lays down a challenge, for to date only 11 caves of the Qumran have revealed scrolls. Discovery of the letter from Elijah is a prophecy that has not yet come to pass.

The story about Elijah besting Baal's Priest is found in the Old Testament in 1st Kings 18:20-40. The Old Testament has several references about Elijah's faithfulness, even when faithfulness would put him in great peril. The words "there with Moses on the mountain" are a reference to the Transfiguration, which took place on a mountain. The Transfiguration can be found in four Gospels: Matthew 17:1-13, Mark 9:2-13, Luke 9:28-36, John 1:14, and the 2nd Letter from Peter 1:16-18. In the story, Jesus is seen on a mountaintop with Moses on one side and Elijah on His other. The reference to "making straight the way" is the belief by many that John the Baptist was the reincarnation of Elijah.

The story about Elijah being raised up to heaven in a chariot surrounded by fire is found in the Old Testament in 2nd Kings 2:11-12. The reference to Elijah as being "whole" means Elijah was raised up to heaven while alive. This is one of many word groupings, which closely parallel scripture.

The Letter continues with more about what is to be found in the letter from Elijah: *Elijah's message is of the Father's love for all His people. The table has been set and the banquet has been prepared and all who accept the invitation are welcomed: sisters and brothers, rich and poor, whole and broken, Jew, Buddhist, Gentile, Pagan, and more. All people everywhere, seated as equals. The price of admission is acceptance of the Word and acceptance of one another.*

Elijah's letter has not yet been discovered, but similar wording to this passage in *The Letter* can be found in the Gospel of Mark 12:14, the Gospel of Luke 20:20-21 and the Letter from James 2:1-6; the invitation to all is another example of Jesus' openness. While this may be difficult for established bureaucracies to accept, the point is, we are all God's children and we all share in the banquet. This message calls for an end to all forms of discrimination, regardless of how subtle they may be. For example, while the Catholic Church has done much good around the world for people in need, it has not been open to women participating in the pathway to the priesthood.

The author of *The Letter* reveals an intimate knowledge as He continues to reference the letter from Elijah: *Elijah reminds us that we must not abandon hope, despite what sufferings may be visited upon us. We must boast of our sufferings, knowing suffering produces endurance, and endurance produces character, and character produces hope and hope does not disappoint.*

This is virtually identical with Paul's Letter to the Romans 5:3-5 and further supported by the Letter from James 1:4. Since Elijah's message about the courage needed to endure suffering would certainly predate Paul's Letter to the Romans, Elijah's message may have been an inspiration to Paul had Paul access to it.

11. The author of *The Letter* again identifies the recipient as Uncle, which further supports our contention the author is Jesus. Here is what He writes: *Uncle, if you begin to tire of the good fight and entertain thoughts of surrender, take heart and know I am with you always.* Even the idea of the good fight can be found in subsequent writings. For example in Paul's 1st Letter to Timothy 6:11-12, Paul introduces the "good fight of the faith." Jesus is not encouraging fighting; rather, He explains sometimes "standing fast" in the face of evil is fighting the good fight.

12. *The Letter* concludes with a message that has always been central to the teachings of Jesus. The author writes: *But in the end, it is about love. For without love we are nothing. Our tongues will cease and our bodies will return to dust, but love will remain. If we have love, we are rich beyond imagination. If we have love, we have been given much. And we who have been given much are duty bound to give much in return.* This philosophy was later expressed in Paul's 1st letter to the Corinthians chapter 13. That message may be one of the clearest messages about love. It is a message, which seems to find its

way into most modern-day Christian wedding ceremonies. But Jesus goes beyond by saying, if we have love we must pass it on, for it is the greatest gift which must be shared.

The best gift to give is the gift of love. Give it freely and without expectation and you will receive love tenfold in return. Uncle, please care for and love my mother as you cared for and loved me. Help ease the pain she suffered as she watched the treatment of her son, a pain that only a mother can feel.

As He talks about love, Jesus asks Joseph of Arimathea to care for His mother, i.e., Mary. He reveals He was aware of how she must have suffered to see her Son upon the cross. Although He doesn't say so, one can only assume His pain was magnified by the knowledge His mother was looking on.

Keep faith. And when things are darkest, look for me, for I will be there. Peace be with you always.

It's all there in one short saying—faith, hope and love. Faith that He will be there; hope that allows one to endure; love that He suffered for us and He will be there, in the end, for us. This is Jesus' message throughout His public ministry, and the "Way" for all to follow.

Commentary Conclusion

This amazing discovery has opened our hearts and minds and has allowed us to seek answers to millennia-old questions. What did Jesus mean when He said: "I did not come to start a religion. I came to start a revolution. I came to end slavery, inequality and war. I came to instill justice, mercy and freedom."

This question may be at the heart of the discord over *The Letter*. It may be that those who refuse to accept the idea are fearful that all they built up may be for naught. It need not be that way, for Jesus had 12 disciples and thousands of followers during His ministry on earth. He taught His followers to follow the Way by being true. His mission was to change the existing order, and to do so would require believers and truthful followers.

The thousands of beautiful churches adorned with magnificent works of art are not evil, but neither are they salvation. It is not necessary to tear down all that has been built up; it is only necessary to invite all to enter and share in the majestic beauty.

Jesus calls us to dedicate ourselves to alleviating the problems that have been with us always: poverty, illiteracy, hunger, slavery and war. We believe Jesus was calling for the end of prejudice and discrimination. We believe Jesus would have wanted the poor and illiterate to be welcomed into the beautiful churches so they could view and be inspired by the magnificent art. We believe Jesus would have welcomed women as full partners in the priestly fraternity. We believe He would have ended slavery by changing the hearts of slave owners. We believe He would have taught all people an appreciation for the value of every human being. And we believe Jesus would have ended war by instilling justice in the hearts and minds of all people.

With prayerful hope, we trust we have openly and honestly answered the challenge put to the Epistolic Institute. We have responded to the best of our ability and readily admit there are portions of *The Letter,* which cannot be referenced to some earlier work, for there is no earlier work. But we have faith these are the words and the message of Our Lord. To those who still harbor doubts, we humbly urge you to look inward and seek the faith, which first allowed you to believe in Jesus Christ. With faith, all things are possible.

In Christ Our Lord we pray, may peace be with you.
The Epistolic Institute

Although somewhat new to writing, **Thomas Miller's** approach to fiction is ingeniously unique. He creates intriguing characters, breathes life into their literary bodies and gets out of their way so they can write their own story. He practices his craft in Madison, Wisconsin where he lives with his wife, Nicki, one precious puppy dog and two fiercely independent cats. (Is there any other kind?)